Darcy and Elizabeth: A Peculiar Courtship

***

A Pride and Prejudice Variation

By Alice Morgan

Chapter 1

"Pride and Prejudice", Chapter 35:

> *Elizabeth awoke the next morning to the same thoughts and meditations which had at length closed her eyes. She could not yet recover from the surprise of what had happened; it was impossible to think of anything else; and, totally indisposed for employment, she resolved, soon after breakfast, to indulge herself in air and exercise. She was proceeding directly to her favourite walk when the recollection of Mr Darcy 's sometimes coming there stopped her, and instead of entering the park, she turned up the lane, which led farther from the turnpike-road. The park paling was still the boundary on one side, and she soon passed one of the gates into the ground.*
>
> *After walking two or three times along that part of the lane, she was tempted, by the pleasantness of the morning, to stop at the gates and look into the park. The five weeks which she had now passed in Kent had made a great difference in the country, and every day was adding to the verdure of the early*

trees. She was on the point of continuing her walk when she caught a glimpse of a gentleman within the sort of grove which edged the park; he was moving that way; and, fearful of its being Mr Darcy, she was directly retreating. But the person who advanced was now near enough to see her and stepping forward with eagerness, pronounced her name. She had turned away; but on hearing herself called, though, in a voice which proved it to be Mr Darcy, she moved again towards the gate. He had by that time reached it also, and, holding out a letter, which she instinctively took, said, with a look of haughty composure, "I have been walking in the grove some time in the hope of meeting you. Will you do me the honour of reading that letter?"

If Elizabeth did not expect the letter to contain a renewal of Mr Darcy's offers, she had formed no expectations at all of its contents. She watched him turn from her and walk with his usual prideful stride down the lane. He slowed once, turned his head, and returned the stare she focused intently on his back. Just before he fully turned his entire body, he resumed his original purpose and lengthened his stride with the seeming intent to put as much distance as possible between himself and her.

Elizabeth tucked her bottom lip between her teeth and remained steadfast where he left her, trying desperately to decide whether to burn the letter before reading it or chase after him to return it. She finally decided to run after him but looked down the road and realised she could no longer make out his form in the distance.

Finding no other alternative, the lady decided to do what she did best when distressed; she went for a walk. Rambling in no particular direction while holding the thick letter between both hands, she allowed her feet to take her in any direction they willed. The breeze brushed next to her, but she didn't feel its touch. The birds chirped in a nearby tree, but the thoughts in her head proved much too loud to pay attention to anything else. She did notice the squirrels chasing after one another along the side of the path, but only after she narrowly missed stepping on one.

She remained acutely aware of the stiffness of the paper under her fingertips, but could not decide on the letter's fate. After walking along the lane by the parsonage and still coming to no conclusion regarding Mr Darcy's letter, she ventured into the wooded park which separated the parsonage from Rosings. With considerable determination, she finally forced all the thoughts in her head to flow in a single direction. Her curiosity defeated! Her determination to dismiss him without further notice was done for. She wanted to know what the letter contained.

Elizabeth surveyed the area to find a place to rest where she might comfortably read her letter. Eventually finding a soft piece of moss upon which to sit where she hoped no passers-by might observe her, she carefully sat down to avoid any mud or dirt stains on the light print blue muslin dress. She took a deep breath, broke the wax seal and satisfied her curiosity.

After her first perusal of the letter, she cared not who saw or heard her; Elizabeth could not keep the thoughts spinning in her head silent any longer. "It cannot be true! None of it! How dare he attempt to legitimise his dastardly behaviour toward Mr Wickham and my sister? He is a worse villain than I originally believed. Now he is also a liar of the worst kind!"

She leaned her head against the stiff bark on the tree where she sat and closed her eyes. Her every thought refused to believe Mr Wickham could behave as infamously as accused by Mr Darcy. His every look at her appeared so truthful and sincere. How many times did she blush from his attention? How many laughs did they share in private? She found him to be one of the most amiable men of her acquaintance. The charges laid against him by Mr Darcy went so far beyond anything she imagined that she refused to accept any evidence of their validity.

Her mind meticulously flowed through each of her interactions with Mr Wickham to defend his behaviour against Mr Darcy's accusations. Her eyes closed again after she placed her fingers to her temples, and in a voice much softer than her previous outbursts, she quietly said to herself, "Remember, I must remember everything. I must have seen or heard something to provide my own proof to contradict Mr Darcy's claims." She had to protect the veracity of her beliefs of the two men in question. She didn't want to face the ugly truth about herself if proven wrong.

While sitting under the shade of the ancient oak, her first memory jumped to the initial interaction she observed between the two men. Mr Darcy's face turned several rather unattractive shades of red while Mr Wickham immediately paled upon recognition. Even when in uncomfortable situations, she never saw Mr Darcy allow his emotions to show so obviously on his countenance. Something about Mr Wickham made him emotionally react before he could temper his response. After seeing his face, no one could doubt the gentleman's obvious anger at the mere sight of the other man. The immediate manner which Mr Wickham's face drained of colour suggested he panicked upon recognising the gentleman on the horse. If Mr Darcy's letter rang true, both gentlemen behaved exactly as they ought to have.

"It cannot be true; there must be another more plausible explanation than the obvious," she told herself again. "There must be another explanation."

Elizabeth allowed her imagination to roam wild hoping to find some alternative. Possibly he believed that Mr Wickham came to Meryton to besmirch his good name? How would he know he already performed that service quite well on his own, without the added help of Mr Wickham's background history of the gentleman? That didn't explain why Mr Wickham would be frightened of Mr Darcy for spreading the truth about his character. Perhaps he feared that the gentleman from Derbyshire could end his newly acquired career in the militia. Mr Wickham feared Mr Darcy would use his influence to require him to leave Meryton without a recommendation from Colonel Forster. Once again, Mr Darcy had it within his power to ruin Mr Wickham's career. Would that man stop at nothing to ruin his childhood friend?

She tried to convince herself she discovered the proof she needed, but even in her distressed state, she realised the flimsiness of her mental argument. Elizabeth brought her knees to her chest and allowed her chin to rest on her arms. She strained to remember every detail of her second conversation with Mr Wickham during which he relayed his grievances toward Mr Darcy. Elizabeth looked at a small squirrel with a particularly fluffy brown tail and light brown stripe running down his back. The squirrel nearby seemed more intent upon the nut than answering her question, but with nothing else with which to converse, Lizzy laid her next question at the foot of the small rodent. "Did I first mention Mr Darcy during our discussion or did he?" Perhaps Mr Wickham only responded to her initial statement of dislike of the gentleman in question. She glared at the squirrel that had no intent to answer her question.

Elizabeth was left with no choice but to provide the answer.

Within two minutes of the beginning of their conversation, Mr Wickham detailed their history together. She scarcely allowed herself to admit it was most unbecoming of him to speak ill of Mr Darcy and relate intimate details of their lives to a relative stranger.

She lifted her head searching for the small squirrel to continue their rather one-sided tête-à-tête. Desperation tinged her tone, “But if Mr Wickham lied, why would Mr Darcy simply not expose him?” But if she believed his letter, in her heart she knew the reason. The man held the information to damage his sister’s reputation. Even she hold him in enough esteem as to understand he would not risk the exposure of his young sister. But still, the charges against Mr Wickham were too ghastly to be true. What kind of man could do that to a young girl? What kind of man could create such a fabrication of lies? One had to be wrong; there was only enough goodness for one man. She directed her anger and the rise in her voice at the undeserving squirrel, “Why can’t you just concede that Mr Darcy is the undoubted villain?” Hearing the sudden change in her voice, her company scampered off, not bothering to take the prized nut with him.

Finally, she remembered the Netherfield ball. Mr Wickham told her that Mr Darcy had wronged him so he had no reason to avoid Mr Darcy; however, Mr

Wickham was absent that night. Trying one more time to defend Mr Wickham, Elizabeth's mind agreed with the reason Mr Wickham offered after she spoke with him regarding his absence; he simply did not want to ruin Mr Bingley's ball by making his houseguest and close friend uncomfortable. "A perfectly logical explanation and one which I will relate to Mr Darcy if ever unfortunate enough to be in his company again."

When she saw the squirrel tentatively making his way back to his forgotten prize, she could not help but ask him in a voice much calmer than the ones which made her friend scurry away, "If Mr Darcy is so obviously the villain, why must you remain so determined to give credence to his claims?"

She looked into the large black eyes of her small companion as Mr Darcy's words regarding Mr Wickham flowed in her head. "Mr Wickham is blessed with such happy manners as may ensure his making friends – whether he may be equally capable of retaining them, is less certain."

The squirrel grabbed the nut climbed up the tree. Apparently, Mr Darcy's rather unusual choice of emissary refused to say any more on the subject. Elizabeth stared at the tree which housed the squirrel and wondered what else Mr Darcy might say to defend his actions. While one gentleman disparaged the other to anyone that might listen, the other refused to slander his nemesis beyond vague and infrequent statements. Why would Mr Darcy remain silent when fully aware of the defamatory remarks against him?

Her squirrel returned, this time with a friend following close behind. She sighed in resignation, "I know, his sister." If his sister did not need protection from slander caused by Mr Wickham, surely he would tell the people of Meryton the truth. In addition, he offered the testimony of Colonel Fitzwilliam to verify the veracity of his letter. What did Wickham offer her? She had no reason to doubt Colonel Fitzwilliam although until today she had no reason to doubt her notions of Mr Darcy or Mr Wickham either.

Elizabeth looked at the two adorable squirrels who seemed more interested in playing with each other's furry tails than her plight. The woman felt the tears begin to form in her eyes. They seemed so happy, so carefree; just as she felt a few weeks ago. She allowed the words hanging on her heart to finally be said aloud, giving them immediate credence. "What if I was wrong? But how could I be so mistaken when Wickham seemed to enjoy my company so much?"

The shame flowed over her. Mr Wickham flattered her pride, and she rewarded him with her unequivocal trust. She never thought of herself as prideful; she kept that character flaw reserved for a certain gentleman from Derbyshire. As much as she tried to make a joke of his dismissal of her at their first meeting, it still wounded her. More than she wanted to admit. She allowed her pride to colour every one of their subsequent interactions. She believed one man because of the affability of his nature and condemned the other for his aloofness.

The pulsations in her temples intensified. Words continued to swim inside her head in a whirlpool. She couldn't control their destination or their conclusions. While she might still doubt the testimony of Mr Darcy or his cousin, how could she still discount the warnings of her beloved sister and aunt whom she trusted the most? Both warned her that she should not allow her prejudice of Mr Darcy to inhibit her ability discern the character of his enemy. Neither one believed the tales of Mr Wickham's woo, while she swallowed them whole. She remembered relating the tale of Mary King to her aunt. She vainly believed herself to be a favourite of Mr Wickham's before Mary King inherited a small fortune. A woman that he scarcely acknowledged before suddenly became the only recipient of his affections. If Mr Wickham proved mercenary enough to switch allegiances so suddenly in Meryton, might he be willing to seduce a fifteen-year-old Georgiana Darcy for her much larger fortune?

Using her sleeve, Elizabeth wiped the tears running quietly down her cheeks. Looking back to the squirrel that had since lost his companion but remained firmly fixed to his favourite tree across from her, she finally allowed herself to say aloud the question that swarmed in her head, “What if Mr Darcy told the truth in his letter?”

She watched as the squirrel stopped its search and stared intently back at her. Her head dropped back into her arms as the uncomfortable feeling in the pit of her stomach that plagued her since seeing Mr Darcy approach her reached its most painful point. “How could I have grossly misjudged them both?”

Frustration boiled inside of her; she needed to release it. She did not have the time to walk for several miles to adequately tire herself, so she chose the next best method to relieve her growing tension. She stood, faced the same tree that offered her its support only a few moments before and raised the hem of her skirt up to her knees with one hand. With the other hand, she steadied herself a few feet from the trunk of the tree and moved her foot back. She took a deep breath and with all the force she could muster, she crashed her heel into the trunk. After three heartfelt kicks, she switched to stomping both feet on the ground for fear she might break her foot in her attempt to release her anger.

She finally sat back down, her rib cage expanding with each laboured breath. She looked back at her squirrel friend staring curiously at her and partially hidden by his tree, “Don’t look at me like that. Women aren't allowed to box or fence in order to relieve stress.” The squirrel didn’t look convinced, “Don’t worry, I would never kick a squirrel.” She watched the red animal scamper to the other side of the tree, seemingly unsure of her promise. Despite herself and her distress, she allowed the small laugh that surfaced from inside.

Feeling significantly calmer, she moved on to the other matter discussed in his letter. She arched her eyebrow, voice full of conviction, she addressed her furry confidant, now poking his head around the tree once more to return her gaze. “At least I know that my sister is blameless in the matter.” After all, the same man who showed her so little affection that she had no knowledge of his feelings had no right to question the reserve of another showing her affection to the man she loved. Surely Mr Darcy should be the greatest advocate for anyone who appreciated the value of being reserved when in the company of their beloved. Jane could not win. No matter how she acted, Mr Darcy would have found fault and removed his friend. If Jane had made her feelings clear to Mr Bingley, so he was in no doubt of her affection from the beginning of their acquaintance, Mr Darcy would surely equally criticise Jane for showing too much affection. Even worse, if Jane behaved as Charlotte suggested and presented even more affection than she felt, Mr Darcy would have encouraged his friend to depart Netherfield even earlier than the Netherfield ball. Regardless, even if he believed her affection to be less than his friend's, he should have allowed Mr Bingley to determine if Jane’s affections were sufficient to continue their relationship.

She looked up the tree to the branch, barely able to make out the rodent who no longer seemed interested in her open-ended questions, "Why can't you do what others want instead of following your own needs, Mr Darcy?" The gentleman insisted on arranging people and events to suit his needs without regard to the resulting circumstances for others. He refused to take those outside his inner circle into account when making decisions. Still looking up at the branch holding her confidant, "Even you refuse to remain here where I need your assistance. Whose testimony can you provide to further your cause? I don't see your friend anywhere to defend you."

It was during this censure that she remembered the words spoken by Colonel Fitzwilliam during one of their many conversations in the parlour. The gentleman impressed upon her the responsibilities thrust upon his cousin at a young age. He envied his cousin's ability to arrange his life as he chose but did not resent the magnitude of duties entrusted to his slightly younger cousin. Even in a community as small as Hertfordshire, she knew what often occurred when young men found themselves with too much responsibility and too much money. Instead, Mr Darcy increased his property, took prodigious care of his remaining family, and refused to gallivant around town with the other young men of considerable means.

"Is it possible you acted in what you thought of as the best interest of your friend?" If he did act in the defence of his friend, could she fault him irreparably for his actions? "How would I encourage Jane to behave if the situation were reversed? What if I thought Mr Bingley to be mercenary in his motives?" Elizabeth put her head back on her arms; she would protect her sister through anything.

She narrowed her eyebrows allowing her mind to come to a conclusion previously unknown. What about Mr Bingley? He did not trust the strength of his own feelings or the private signs her sister gave and allowed himself to be persuaded by his sisters and his friend. She trusted the opinions of her close confidants, but she placed the blame for her resulting decision on herself. Did she not refuse to hide behind her father's opinion when he supported her decision to refuse Mr Collins? Even if he did not support her, her refusal to marry Mr Collins would remain. Mr Bingley was responsible for the heartache of her sister and must accept the consequences of his actions, just as she accepted responsibility for her actions.

Elizabeth unknowingly pursed her lips in a rather unattractive manner. Searching for her red friend but not seeing him, she settled once again for the empty branch. "Can I blame Mr Darcy? His friend is a gentleman of sense, education and considerable means. Mr Bingley should not rely on his friends to make the most important decisions of his life. What kind of husband would he be?" She left the rest of the questions swirl in her head. Whose opinion would he value most when making a decision that affected her sister? Would he simply avoid making any decision at all if Jane and Mr Darcy differed in their estimations of a circumstance? Where would Mr Bingley's loyalties ultimately lie if married to Jane? Perhaps Mr Bingley would not be the husband she believed her sister deserved. Mr Darcy's actions seemed so different when casting in the light projected from his letter.

Did she misjudge the man so terribly? Not only did she miscalculate the reason behind his actions separating his friend from her sister, she grossly misjudged his relationship with Mr Wickham. She closed her eyes and placed her fingertips back to her temples; her head felt like it might split open. The words of his letter swarmed in her head as she seemed to hear his voice repeating each important passage. Why can she not clear that man from her mind? The confusion overwhelmed her; how did she misjudge the gentleman so horribly?

She read the letter to confirm her opinion of the gentleman and now she sat completely confused about all the important matters in her life. Before she opened the letter, she did not doubt the validity of her opinions of Mr Darcy or Mr Wickham or anyone else in her life. Now, she forced herself to re-evaluate each of her opinions. If she proved so completely wrong about something she was absolutely sure of, what about everything else she believed?

Realising she spent more than an hour in the wood, Elizabeth decided that she must return to the parsonage. She stood, brushed off the bottom of her dress, and found her way back to the lane. She must find a way to speak to Mr Darcy again.

Chapter 2

Several hours after leaving for her walk, Elizabeth finally returned and entered the freshly painted parsonage. She silently handed her bonnet and spencer to the maid and walked towards the noises originating from the parlour. She heard Charlotte's soft voice answering Colonel Fitzwilliam's inquiry as to her plans for returning to Hertfordshire. Elizabeth entered the room and sat down next to her friend, trying not to interrupt their discussion.

"I have no immediate plans to travel to Lucas Lodge. As you may guess, the visits by my father, sister, and dearest friend alleviated much of my longing for home. I fear that as soon as Elizabeth and Maria leave, my plans to return home may change. Of course, those plans will be dependent upon Lady Catherine granting my husband time to accompany me on the journey. She has already proven very generous this year in allowing Mr Collins time to visit Hertfordshire twice."

"My dear Charlotte, it is so good of you to remember how charitable Lady Catherine was to allow me additional time away from our parishioners for our wedding," Mr Collins interrupted without any regard to whether his wife concluded her answer. "Cousin Elizabeth, have you not been astounded by Lady Catherine's constant attention to our well-being during your visit? You have been privileged to so many examples of her kindness. I am sure that you find yourself wishing you could constantly be the recipient of her generosity and are even envious of those who are able to receive it on a regular basis. Is Rosings not the grandest home in England?"

Charlotte blushed slightly at her husband's innuendo. Feeling embarrassed for her friend's ill-mannered husband, Elizabeth explained to the group that her friend was indeed fortunate for the concern that her husband's patroness bestowed upon them. She finished by stating that Lady Catherine's attention showed her the qualities which are most important to establishing peace and happiness on an estate. Charlotte looked appreciatively at her while undoubtedly Mr Collins took her words as proof of her own unhappiness at her refusal of his marriage proposal.

Colonel Fitzwilliam cleared his throat and looked expectantly Elizabeth, "Did you enjoy your walk, Miss Bennet? The weather is beautiful this time of year."

Thankful of the Colonel's good manners, but not yet ready to be the subject of conversation, she took a deep breath before answering. She hoped it might calm her voice; its shakiness would certainly reveal her anxiety.

"It was a beautiful day, and I simply wandered until I lost all sense of time. I must confess that I will miss the scenery when I depart for London next week." She couldn't help but add, "I am surprised that you and Mr Darcy did not take advantage of the weather for a long ride today."

The man eyed the woman sitting to his left. From the way he studied her face, Elizabeth ascertained the anxiety still existed in her voice, particularly when she mentioned Mr Darcy's name.

"I did not see Darcy until just before we left Rosings to call upon you. He said that business detained him all morning, and he left soon after arriving here to begin preparations for our departure tomorrow. Darcy is always very conscientious when making travel arrangements for those he is responsible for."

At the mention of Mr Darcy's sense of responsibility, Elizabeth's thoughts returned to the gentleman's determination to control the lives of those he cared for. When Colonel Fitzwilliam related his actions, the consequences seemed so benign and even thoughtful. His cousin even seemed relieved and thankful for his cousin's attention. Did the man realise how difficult his actions made it discover the truth of his character? Depending on whose perspective she listened to, Mr Darcy either seemed a saint or a devil. She must find a way to speak to Mr Darcy again. She needed to know how much she misjudged him. If she didn't find a way, she would spend her entire life wondering about each decision and assessment. Could she ever trust herself again?

Elizabeth felt her cheeks flush and looked at her friend, hoping to silently communicate her desire to remain quiet. When Charlotte answered for her, she knew her silent message was successful. "We will be quite disappointed when you and Mr Darcy leave tomorrow. I am sure we all will miss your company and conversation. We became quite accustomed to your presence at Rosings. Without you, Mr Darcy, Maria, and Elizabeth, our parties will seem quiet. Will you be returning to Rosings next Easter?"

"We have ventured here every year for the past seven years and I know of no reason why we should not return next year as well."

Mr Collins interrupted the Colonel, "Unless of course there is another happy event that draws your cousin to Rosings sooner than next Easter. Of course, you would be accompanying him to stand beside him at such a happy event. I hope to find myself in the unique position to have a particularly impressive vantage point to view the happy occasion of which I believe we both will be playing a part in." Mr Collins finished with a smug and knowing look directed at Colonel Fitzwilliam.

Elizabeth watched the exchange as the Colonel looked back at the parson with an uncomfortable expression on his face. Finally gaining his voice, he bluntly retorted, "Mr Collins, I can think of no forthcoming events which will require our presence at Rosings any sooner than next Easter. I am sure that my cousin would agree with my statement. Unfortunately, I have stayed past the time I planned and need to return to Rosings to make preparations for my departure."

Elizabeth realised she was about to lose her last opportunity to clarify her misunderstandings with Mr Darcy. Thinking of no other way to communicate her desire to speak with him one last time, she turned to Colonel Fitzwilliam and asked, "Sir, might I ask a favour of you since you will be returning to Rosings?" After the gentleman agreed, she continued, "Mr Darcy lent me a book upon his arrival and I wish to return it to him. If you could please wait a few moments for me to retrieve it from upstairs, I would be very grateful."

"Of course Miss Bennet, I would be honoured to be of assistance."

Elizabeth quickly stood and raced up the stairs to her small bedroom. She reviewed the small selection of books she brought with her from Longbourn. Realising there was a chance she might never see the book again, she took the risk and selected one of her favourites. Looking at the writing desk in her room, she quickly formulated a letter and slipped it inside the book and hastened to the door. Just before she left her bedroom, she looked down to the slight bulge in the book. She did not want to risk the Colonel accidentally dropping or opening the book, revealing the letter's presence. Looking around the room, she eyed a small piece of brown paper she meant to use to protect a small trinket she bought for Jane. Deciding on a better use for the paper and string, she quickly wrapped the book and tied the string. She finally picked up her precious package, held it tightly to her chest, said a silent prayer for the success of her plan, and returned to the parlour before the Colonel left.

"Colonel Fitzwilliam, thank you so much for your help. If there is any way that I can return the favour, please let me know," Elizabeth said as she handed him the small package.

"Miss Bennet, this is no imposition, and it is a pleasure to be of assistance."

The gentleman said a final farewell to Mr and Mrs Collins and promised to call upon the parsonage next Easter when he arrived for his annual trip. Elizabeth stood with the others and tried to delicately push past Mr Collins to walk the Colonel to the door. She once again sent a silent message to her friend, hoping to convince her to allow her to escort their guest to his horse privately. She allowed her eyes to thank her friend when

Charlotte asked for her husband's immediate assistance with a matter on the other side of the parsonage.

Before Elizabeth made her final goodbye to Colonel Fitzwilliam at the parsonage gate, she asked him to ensure that Mr Darcy received the book as soon as possible. The man placed the book in his saddlebag, looked at her questioningly, and asked if she needed to discuss anything else with him before his final goodbye. She only told him she hoped the fate might cause Mr Darcy and him to cross paths with her again in the near future, but until that time she wished him a pleasant journey. The Colonel expressed a similar sentiment, bowed and took his leave. Elizabeth could do nothing but watch him ride down the lane to Rosings with her future tucked safely away in his saddle bag.

Chapter 3

Darcy watched from his bedroom window as his cousin rode through the gates of Rosings. Did Richard talk to Elizabeth? Did he clarify what happened with Georgiana? Darcy couldn't leave this place without knowing if she believed him. He poured out his heart to her. But did it change anything? Now his cousin held the information which would largely determine how many bottles of scotch he would consume to quiet his thoughts.

Finally, he heard Richard's loud knock on his door. His cousin stepped in and closed the door behind him.

"Were you able to see Miss Elizabeth when she returned from her walk?"

"I did. She did not return for almost an hour after you left the parsonage and I was preparing to leave myself when she finally arrived. I never had a good opportunity to tell her about Georgiana. When I told her we planned to depart tomorrow, she asked me to return a book to you that she borrowed."

Richard held up the brown package in view of the corner of Darcy's eye. In an impulsive moment and with no attempt at civility, he grabbed the package out of his cousin's hand.

In a much louder and more forceful voice which he knew betrayed his emotions, he asked, "She gave this to you? What exactly did she say?"

"She asked that you receive the book as soon as I returned to Rosings. She also said she hoped that her path might cross with ours again in the future."

Darcy's face relaxed momentarily, but he soon replaced the ease with confusion. "She said she hoped her path might cross with both of ours again?"

"Yes, she quite clearly included both of our names in the sentiment."

Darcy closed his eyes for several seconds, and then took a deep breath trying to steady his hands and the beating of his heart. "Thank you for the book, Fitzwilliam. If you don't mind, I would appreciate some privacy before dinner."

To his surprise, the Colonel didn't grant his request. "Before I go Darcy, we need to talk. As Georgiana's guardian, I deserve to know why you chose to relate the details of her failed elopement with a stranger."

"Miss Elizabeth is not a stranger."

"You've changed since you returned from Hertfordshire. You proved even more withdrawn from society and your friends than in the past. And you seemed even more miserable while in company than normal. Eventually I became convinced you finally decided to marry. After all, what else could cause such devastation to a man's humour?"

Darcy squared his shoulders in response to the cousin's question. As he could not make any other response, he continued to stare out the window.

When he gave him no verbal answer, Richard put the hand to Darcy's shoulder and continued his inquiry with more than a touch of sympathy in his voice.

"You need to decide what will make you happy, Darcy. For once, do not let family obligations determine your future. Georgiana and I love you and only want what is best for you."

As he definitely was not ready for that conversation, Darcy moved the discussion to a more acceptable topic.

"Please let Lady Catherine know that I will be down in an hour."

"And what shall I tell our dear aunt when I see her and she demands your presence immediately?" The

Colonel responded in a tone that bordered between a teasing and serious manner.

"I don't care right now. Please Fitzwilliam, just give me an hour."

"Alright, but remember that I am here whenever you need to talk."

Darcy watched as his cousin made a reluctant exit from the room. As he stood alone in his sitting room, he moved to staring at the parcel in his hands. The book wasn't particularly thick or thin. How could such a small package contain his future? The decision of whether to leave it open or closed eluded him. As long as he left it closed, Elizabeth might one day wish to see him. As soon as he opened it, he would learn his fate. He would know whether he might one day look into the eyes of the woman he loved as he tenderly woke her from her nightly slumber...

Chapter 4

When the clock chimed the hour, Darcy realised he already stood at the window for well over an hour trying to decide whether to face his fate. He dreaded the lecture he would undoubtedly receive when he finally arrived for the dinner that Lady Catherine arranged as a farewell to her nephews. He rang for his valet to change clothes, knowing that arriving for dinner in trousers fifteen minutes earlier would prove much worse than arriving a little later in proper attire. Marcus must have anticipated the short timeline available to dress him for the meal because he arrived in the dressing room with a clean black coat and breeches to immediately begin his master's dinner preparations.

After Marcus had finished his ministrations, Darcy heard a slight knock on the door and saw Richard tentatively peak his head in the room. The man stepped in and closed the door behind him.

"Darcy, are you coming downstairs for dinner? I couldn't decide what to tell Lady Catherine regarding your absence from the parlour. I decided that if we confronted the old bird together, I wouldn't have to answer her inquiries as to your whereabouts. This way, we can redirect any uncomfortable questions toward the other in hopes that she will simply forget about her previous tirade." Richard paused for a moment, leaving Darcy to decide what the slight spark in his eye would lead to. His next statement satisfied his curiosity. "If only there were other diversions which might direct her attention from us. I don't suppose you suddenly learned to play the piano, or she invited unexpected guests? Alas, I believe the only conversation that Lady Catherine would rather have tonight than condemning our tardiness is your engagement to Anne and we both know how you feel about that. I feel fairly certain I can redirect any questions dealing with that particular matter to assist you if you will do the same for me when she mentions my need to marry or resign my commission."

Darcy eyed his cousin. "Fitzwilliam, I can honestly say I don't think that anything will dissuade Lady Catherine from whatever topic she chooses to discuss this evening. I still have some preparations I need to make before our departure in the morning and cannot stay for conversation after dinner."

"I see your plan is to simply leave me to my own devices and hasten your own escape to leave unscathed from her wrath. Well, I do think we should at least have some reason to explain our late arrival. I am anxious for your idea since you don't seem to want to follow mine."

"We will simply apologise for our tardiness and proceed with whatever conversation she begins."

The Colonel rolled his eyes before responding, "What a brilliant plan Darcy. I cannot wait to see how well this well-thought strategy fares in battle. But since we have a plan, we better begin. Are you ready to face the enemy?" He bowed gallantly in a display worthy of Mr Collins and waited for his cousin to quit the room before he himself ventured into the dragon's rather hideously decorated lair.

"Darcy! Fitzwilliam! What explanation do you have to explain your tardiness? I am sure you were told that I expected you both over an hour ago." Richard raised an eyebrow and looked at his cousin.

Darcy spoke quickly and with a sense of finality, "We apologise for our delay, Aunt. We were unavoidably detained by a matter of business." His countenance told even Lady Catherine that he did not intend to answer any further inquiries regarding the subject. The other two members of the parlour shared the same look when the great lady quickly changed the subject to something everyone knew would occur sooner or later during the night. Darcy almost preferred to finish the topic he knew he must discuss as soon as possible instead of delaying the inevitable. How strange it was that in every other aspect of his life he preferred to meet his obligations directly, but with the book upstairs containing his future, he wanted to make time stand still, letting him hold on to his hope forever.

Lady Catherine's loud voice interrupted his reverie. "Anne and I will certainly miss you when you depart. It seems as though your attachment to Rosings grows greater each year. I trust you will not wait until next Easter to visit your Aunt and dearest cousin again." She looked at him with a satisfied grin; she almost seemed to challenge him to disagree with her, knowing full well that his familial obligations forbade it.

"Darcy and I both anticipate very busy schedules over the next year, Aunt. Unfortunately, that will likely deny us the opportunity to visit with you until our regularly scheduled visit next spring." After rescuing them both, the Colonel proceeded to entertain Lady Catherine and Anne with his expected exploits for the next year until the butler finally announced that dinner was ready. Occasionally Darcy interjected a comment or two into the conversation but allowed Richard to take the lead as was their norm in a company.

Lady Catherine demanded Richard's arm when walking into dinner to pair her daughter with other nephew. Darcy bowed slightly to his female cousin and offered her his arm. He escorted the lady to her designated place without uttering a word. He then took his own set place between the two women while Richard sat on aunt's left side.

Wasting no time, as Lady Catherine already seemed rather upset at Darcy's thorough examinations of her windows in the parlour, she began her inquisition as to the affairs that made him decide his sudden departure date.

He kept his answer rather cryptic. "My business deals with a problem of an unexpected acquisition. Originally, I believed the change in ownership to be a relatively simple affair. However, the transfer proved significantly more complex. I hope it will be remedied soon enough, but it will take my personal attention to conclude the transaction." At the end of his speech, he narrowed his attention to his rather confused looking aunt; she must want more details than his obscure answer provided.

Not disappointing him, Lady Catherine immediately probed him for specific details. "I hope this purchase is worth shortening your visit to Rosings. Nothing should trump the importance of family and ensure their happiness."

"Lady Catherine, I am in complete agreement. The happiness of one's family should be the paramount concern of any gentleman. He should do whatever is necessary to ensure the fulfilment of his heart." Darcy surprised even himself with his last statement. He was unused to divulging such a private thought to his Aunt. When he saw the satisfied smile light his aunt's face, he knew she misunderstood his intentions. But he also had no intention of clarifying them. Little did she know that his last statement ended any hope she might possess regarding the union of Pemberley and Rosings.

Dinner course followed dinner course, each more elaborate and heavy than the previous. By the end of the meal, Richard remarked that he should ask for his Aunt's assistance during his next battle. If he filled his opponents with the same food which she fed to her nephews, they would feel so full and content afterwards they might sleep through the battle. Sensing the opportunity finally presented itself for Darcy to make an early departure, he thanked his Aunt for a wonderful meal. As he had a few more preparations to make before his departure and was sure his business would be difficult to finish following such an exquisite meal, he needed to begin immediately.

Lady Catherine's eyes narrowed, but her nephew refused to give any more details. "Darcy, I will excuse your early departure tonight if you promise to join Anne and me for breakfast in the morning." The strident tone of her voice made it perfectly clear that he had little choice. The gentleman nodded his head, as much as it pained him, and agreed with his Aunt's arrangement. He bid goodnight to Richard and told him he would see him at breakfast. Finally, he bowed to the ladies and bid a final goodnight to the entire party.

Soundly shut the door to his sitting room, Darcy leaned against it, closed his eyes and let out a deep breath. After several minutes of relishing the solitude of his room, he walked into his bedroom and carefully opened the drawer of his bedside table. He stared at the innocent-looking parcel that lay exactly where he left it and picked it up as though it might shatter if he handled it carelessly. He placed it on the table, still not ready to face his fate. Not wanting his solitude interrupted by Marcus' presence, he chose to slowly undress himself until he remained clad only in his shirt and breeches.

He could not think of anything else to delay opening the package which seemed to stare back at him whenever he glanced at it on the table, an act which occurred every ten to fifteen seconds. Finally, he picked it up and sat on the small sofa situated in front of the fireplace in his bedroom. He fiddled with the string before finally pulling the end of the bow knot. Once he removed the string, a surge of impatience persuaded him to rip off the paper. In his hands, he found a well-worn copy of Romeo and Juliet.

He looked questioningly at the book when he felt a slight bulge situated between the pages. As he opened it to the offending section, he found a carefully folded letter. He gently fingered the single page letter with his name prominently displayed on the front.

Taking a deep breath he leaned forward in anticipation as he unfolded the letter.

Mr Darcy,

Please forgive my presumption in responding to your letter with one of my own. Unfortunately, because your cousin is waiting downstairs for me to finish this one, mine cannot give the same commitment to clarifying the roots of our many misunderstandings as the one I received. You once told me that my greatest fault is to willfully misunderstand others. In hopes of remedying this particular failing, I hope you are willing to meet me during my favourite walk towards the pond in the wood behind Rosings tomorrow.

I will refrain from bidding you adieu, for I hope to be able to greet you good morning in so few hours that a goodbye hardly seems appropriate. As such, I will simply say I eagerly await my morning walk and hope you look forward to seeing the sunrise over the pond as much as I do.

E.B.

Darcy sat without blinking, staring at the letter in disbelief. Her letter completely changed his fortune. She wanted to see him! She teased him. She believed his letter. She didn't despise him. He had a justifiable hope.

Hope.

He read the word four times in her own letter to him. This must mean she forgave him for interfering with Bingley and her sister. Her anger must have coloured her response and when she learned of his actual motives behind interfering in his friend's life she realised she responded too hastily to his proposal. He never felt more certain he would leave Rosings engaged to Miss Elizabeth Bennet. He only had to ask her for her hand again when he saw her next. He couldn't resist bringing the letter to his lips; after all, it was the first of many love letters he hoped to receive from his beloved Elizabeth.

He couldn't possibly leave Rosings in the morning as planned. He had an appointment to keep at sunrise and nothing would keep him from his purpose. Darcy rang for his valet and paced impatiently around the room until his trusted servant appeared.

"Marcus, I must reschedule our departure from Rosings. I received word that my business problem has been resolved without my immediate presence in town. Colonel Fitzwilliam and I will remain at Rosings for another several days. I will inform you later of the exact date we intend to depart." He couldn't suppress the smile forming on his lips. When he finally would leave depended entirely on his fiancée. Certainly, she didn't expect him to allow her to take the post to London when he could escort her personally. No, of course, she expected to immediately be placed under his protection and care. She expected nothing less from him. He only needed to convince her father of the necessity of a quick engagement. His smile grew from the slight upturn of his lips to one of a full-fledged happiness.

"Yes sir. Would you like me to wait to inform Lady Catherine's servants of this change until the morning or would you like me to inform them now?"

"Please wait until the morning. I am sure nothing will happen to change my plans again, but just in case…" Darcy's voice and smile trailed off. But just as quickly as the doubt surfaced, he suppressed it back to where it originated. "That will be all for tonight. And Marcus, I will be taking an early morning walk tomorrow, so wake me an hour before sunrise. I absolutely cannot be late." Marcus nodded his head, collected Darcy's discarded clothing scattered around the room, and left quietly. The sleep that Darcy found that night was void of the day's longing and distress; instead, he dreamed of a bright future that seemed unattainable only a few hours before.

Chapter 5

Elizabeth shifted on the lumpy mattress, trying to find sleep that remained elusive no matter how many times she changed her body position. Mr Darcy's words still flowed through her mind. She wondered if the man who held her thoughts for the past two days would agree with her idea. If only she didn't have to wait several hours to find out.

She heard the clock in the hallway chime eleven o'clock and became increasingly annoyed that she laid there for over two hours with no rest. Finally, she got out of bed and lit one candle in her room, attempting to read from one book she brought with her. Instead, she thought only of the book now in the hands of Mr Darcy. After staring at the same page for what seemed like an eternity, she felt the futility of her quest and rose from her bed.

She walked around the room and finally sat at the vanity where she picked up the brush to carefully untangle her curly chestnut coloured hair while staring silently at her reflection in the mirror. Instead of analysing the slight freckles on her face or the colour in her cheeks which appeared whenever she thought of Mr Darcy, Elizabeth stared back at her own green eyes that Jane once told her betrayed her soul. She always thought of herself as intelligent and witty, but the eyes that looked back at her held no self-assurance or wisdom. They were confused and void of humour or laughter.

She wondered if Mr Darcy received her letter and if he did, whether he loathed her to the extent that he could not weather meeting with her. The painful longing in her heart betrayed just how much she wanted to see him again. She knew being left to wonder how she misjudged him would be far worse than facing his reproofs of her own character. She remembered her feelings while she wrote him the letter. She did not know exactly what they needed to discuss, only that they needed to discuss something. To part on such terms as they currently held would be unpardonable. Neither one could move on and live a fulfilling or content life without first closing this chapter.

By the time the moon began its retreat from the sky, she had slept precious few hours but did have a carefully devised plan she hoped would provide them with each with the answers they deserved. She rose from her bed and changed from her nightgown into a simple emerald green dress that accentuated the colour of her eyes. Elizabeth silently thanked her mother's inattention to her which forced her to learn to dress herself without the help of a maid.

She looked in the mirror and frowned upon seeing her hair's refusal to stay in a presentable style. Whenever she managed to capture one lock with a hairpin, two seemed to fall out in its place. Oh well, hopefully, Mr Darcy would excuse her untamed look. With everything in their past, a few misplaced curls could not possibly be the worst offence he held against her. She took a final look in the mirror before she left. When she remembered her planned course of action, she saw some semblance of self-confidence in her countenance, but she knew it could vanish as quickly as it arrived if forced to walk back in solitary to the parsonage.

***

Although the sun had not yet risen, plenty of light existed for her to find her way along the well-worn path through the woods. Over the past several weeks, she found the woods to become an almost familiar friend. She knew its turns, its hills, its pits, and its difficult trenches. She usually enjoyed the sights and sounds of the forest waking up to a new day but its beauties could not hold her attention as her mind was preoccupied with much more important matters. She hurried along the path, not wanting to miss the sunrise over the pond. The guilt of arriving there after Mr Darcy already left without seeing her momentarily overwhelmed her. She stopped to put a hand on the solid tree next to her, waiting to calm her heart before continuing. She looked at the horizon in the east to see if the sun began its ascent. She found a comfortable spot next to a large tree and waited for the sun to rise, lost in the many thoughts circulating in her head.

***

As Elizabeth stood by the pond watching the sunrise, Darcy thought he never saw her look more beautiful than at that moment. If she only asked, he would find a way to move even the heavens for her.

He did not know how long after he arrived at the pond, but when he did, he could not bring himself to venture any closer than several hundred feet from his beloved. Instead of walking to her, he silently stood behind, watching. She seemed to melt seamlessly into the landscape. He focused intently on the unruly curls falling down her neck that refused to stay in her hair arrangement. He knew he shouldn't appreciate the haphazard arrangement, but it gave their covert meeting an even more intense feeling of intimacy. Did she know how her figure seemed even more feminine when examined from behind?

At last, he determined the only thing more perfect than watching Elizabeth at this moment was to stand beside her, envelop her in his arms, and join the perfect picture. And what an image they would make! He smiled to himself as he realised that his dark green jacket matched her dress perfectly. As he closed the distance between them, Elizabeth turned to walk toward him.

"Mr Darcy!" She exclaimed, obviously shocked at his presence.

"Miss Elizabeth, you look surprised to see me. I thought you heard me walking towards you. I was standing over there watching the sunrise," he stated while pointing to a tree a fair distance from the point they now stood at. He paused for a moment before continuing, "You seemed so peaceful that I did not want to disturb you yet."

He watched as she took a deep breath before speaking. "It seems I was lost in my own thoughts and didn't hear your arrival."

He had to strain to hear her last words as her voice trailed off in a much softer volume.

"The Colonel Fitzwilliam often accuses me of creeping towards him without his notice and then startling him. It seems I have a talent for staying in the background. I apologise for frightening you as it was not my intention."

Not knowing what else to do or say, Darcy stared at her in silence, hoping to eventually break their unease. He searched her face for a sign, any sign that might lead him to renew his addresses. Unfortunately, the longer he examined her face, the greater the distress in his stomach grew. Reflected in her gaze was not love or uncertainty of his continued affection for her. Somehow he knew that if asked for her hand, he would be rejected again.

What did she mean to gain from the meeting if not to apologise for her behaviour and accept his proposal? He was the one who had been wronged in their previous interaction! She accused him of horrendous actions toward a man who tried to destroy his family. Now that she knew the truth she still refused to let go of her wounded pride stemming from his botched proposal.

Suddenly he felt a need to get away; he could not remain in her presence any longer. He needed to immediately return to Rosings and keep his original plan to return to the town that very morning.

He turned to leave, abandoning the woman in front of him. He could not even manage to bid her a verbal goodbye; he only bowed his head in farewell. He wanted to leave her in the same state he felt. Before he could make his hasty retreat, he felt a small hand grab his arm and hold tightly.

"Mr Darcy, please!" Darcy spun around and looked deeply into the eyes that held his heart. At that moment, he could no more deny her request than deny a plea by her to capture the moon. "Please don't leave yet." She bit her bottom lip for a moment before continuing.

"How am I ever to remedy my propensity to misunderstand those around me, if I have no one to teach me?"

He continued to hold her gaze, unsure of where she found the strength to tease him. The lightness of her words did not seem to match the troubled look in her eyes. Upon hearing her tone, nausea in his stomach settled slightly. At least he knew she no longer hated him, but she still didn't love him. Would her hatred be easier to bear?

"I know that we misunderstood each other so poorly in the past and I would like to try to avoid those misunderstandings in the future. I fear this meeting is another perfect example of our problem."

His curiosity was momentarily piqued. Why would she want to see him if not to accept his marriage proposal? She didn't seem angry with him anymore. Now she really did seem distressed. But certainly, she didn't believe they could simply be friends.

Darcy nodded at her to continue, but strained to hear her for the voice she used did not hold the same confidence as the one she used to tease him only a minute before. "I find myself extremely embarrassed at how easily I believed the lies of Mr Wickham. I always prided myself on my ability to discern the character of others. Now I find that I am questioning all those beliefs which I held most dear. If I could be so mistaken in one respect, does it not follow that I could be equally mistaken in others?"

Darcy took pity on the woman standing in front of him. It was not her fault she believed Wickham; everyone believed Wickham, it was the man's talent in life.

"Miss Bennet, please do not blame yourself. Mr Wickham even persuaded my own dear father to believe his lies. He was even a dear friend of mine once."

Elizabeth turned her head away from her companion as she replied in an even much quieter tone than she previously used, "Sir, I appreciate you trying to shield me from reproof, but we both know that is not the only respect I proved lacking in my ability to properly understand the attitudes and attention of those around me."

Maybe he didn't need to leave. Maybe he could still change her mind. Unsure of how to respond but sure he did not want to leave her side, Darcy simply offered her his arm and asked if she would like to accompany him on a walk around the pond. Elizabeth nodded slightly and thrilled him as the warmth of her fingers surrounded his arm.

As Darcy had no idea what to say, he planned to leave the direction of the conversation to his partner. At least Elizabeth looked to be contemplating her next speech. Whenever she decided to talk again, he would answer, but he refused to direct their discussion. There was only one thing he wanted to discuss, and he knew that the topic would not be well received.

"Are you leaving for town today or will you be able to extend your visit by a few days?" Elizabeth looked at him with anticipation. It seemed an idle question, but her expression made it clear that it held much more significance.

"My plans are not fixed at this moment. I had planned to leave this morning, but I received information last night that persuaded me it might be beneficial to remain at Rosings for a few more days. As of right now, I am unsure what I plan to do," he said apprehensively and waited for any response from Elizabeth. He was rewarded with a small smile and her decision to continue the conversation.

When Elizabeth stopped walking, he did the same. She turned to face him and looked intently into his eyes as if trying to prove the sincerity of her words. "If you are willing, I would like to use the next several days to, shall we say, improve my mind."

Darcy suppressed the shiver of desire that he always felt when he thought of his past interactions with Elizabeth. His thoughts flashed back to the parlour at Netherfield when she told him she "had never seen such a woman. She would be a fearsome thing to behold." If only she realised that the most fearsome woman he knew currently held his gaze.

If she could pretend ease, so could he. Besides, this conversation had certainly taken a turn for the better.

"And how do you propose that we improve your mind?"

"I was hoping that you might ask that question. I have a proposition for you." She took a deep breath before continuing. "Over the next several days, we each shall meet along this path and ask each other five questions. These questions must be answered with complete honesty and in their entirety. If either one of us breaks these rules at any time, neither one will benefit from the endeavour and it must be ended immediately. We must be able to trust the information that the other relays to us. If we cannot place faith in the confidences of the other, we may actually be in a worse position than we currently find ourselves."

That certainly wasn't what he thought she would say when he read her letter last night. He needed time to think. Unsure of how to respond, Darcy indicated that he would like to continue their walk around the pond by once again offering her his arm.

"Miss Elizabeth, what is it you hope to gain from this?"

"I hope that at the end of your visit, I learn how and why I misjudged both you and Mr Wickham. I hope to either regain faith in my earlier estimations of others or have the foundation which to review my opinions in order to form a more accurate picture of the world." Finally, at the end of her short speech, she looked up to her partner and said in a stronger voice, "In short, I hope to improve my mind and my opinion of you."

They continued their walk as he gained the courage to ask the only thing he really wanted to know. "And what do you hope that I will gain from this?"

Elizabeth blushed and laughed slightly, "Mr Darcy, at least I need not fear you will be too timid to answer any questions I have." She took a deep breath, stopped walking, and matched his forthrightness with her own answer. "I fear I am not the only one who needs to occasionally re-evaluate my first impression of others."

Darcy gazed intently at the face of the woman he loved before indicating he wanted to continue their walk; he was not yet prepared to respond to her statement. As they walked, he changed his focus from watching her through the corners of his eyes to the path in front of them. Only then did he allow his mind to ponder the possibilities of this arrangement. Perhaps this could be the opportunity he needed to change her opinion of him. Although he believed his impressions of others proved accurate, for he rarely changed his opinion of others once formed, he might be willing to review his opinion of Elizabeth's elder sister. Surely she knew the nature of Miss Bennet's heart better than he. However, if they behaved and spoke with complete honesty with one another to form an accurate picture, she must be willing to make a concession of her own. He believed it was his best, and only option to gain her acceptance of his love and more importantly, to earn hers in return.

Looking at her would prove too difficult, so without pausing on their walk, Darcy began with the same voice he generally reserved for dictating his directions for Pemberley. "Miss Elizabeth, you ask me for complete honesty. I fear you may not appreciate the honesty of my answers or my actions. I am still in love with you and a mere two days could not possibly change that." He heard the frustration begin to plague his voice. He took a deep breath to try to calm himself before continuing. "I understand you do not feel the same. If I could not fall out of love with you in two days, I suppose I could not reasonably expect you to fall in love with me in those same two days, even with several new pieces of information regarding my character. To change an opinion so suddenly would not be a compliment to either of us."

He took a chance and looked over quickly and remarked that she looked as apprehensive as he felt. "I will agree to this arrangement if you agree to not stop me from trying to earn your affections or display my love for you. I promise I will still answer each question with complete honesty and not stifle a response for fear of your reaction or how it might impact our future." He cleared his throat, trying to hide his aggravation as much as possible, "But you cannot expect me to spend several hours a day in relative privacy with you, imparting some of my most personal experiences and feelings, and not betray any of my feelings toward you. That is something I know I cannot do." At the end of his speech, he finally stopped walking. Not knowing what else to do, he took her hands in his and waited impatiently for her response.

***

Mr Darcy had no idea how long it might take for that response to come, for Elizabeth had no idea of it herself. The only thought circulating in her mind was whether her heart might explode. When they began their discourse, she thought her heart never palpitated as quickly in her life, but that speed paled in comparison to its current throbbing. Trying to ease its pace, she finally lowered her gaze away from the dark eyes fixated on her to their interlocked hands. If possible, the change in her focus only caused her heart to beat faster. She became suddenly aware of the thumb stroking her gloved knuckles. She needed to focus on something else; anything else that might clear her mind. After all, he deserved the same honesty which she asked of him.

So she closed her eyes to allow the questions to circulate uninhibited in her head. What answer could she possibly give to such an honest and feeling response? To deny him outright and bear the pained look on his face was unfathomable. To accept his condition in its entirety might be construed as an implicit acceptance if he offered her his hand again, and she could not agree to that either. She never intended for him to renew his addresses when she sent the letter; it never occurred to her he might even desire to do so after how abominably she treated him. She hoped to both alleviate any discomfort if they met again and to help her understand how she made such a grievous mistake to avoid the same problem in the future. She did not expect it to lead to a future understanding. Elizabeth knew that if Mr Darcy were to propose again, he would receive the same answer, even if she would not deliver it in the same manner as she previously presented it.

He spoke of their shared future. Could she imagine a future with Mr Darcy? Two days ago it seemed impossible. Nothing could persuade her to become his wife. Marrying Mr Darcy was not the goal of her proposition. She only wanted to look at her past without regret and view her future without fear of repeating past mistakes. Unsure of how her favourite philosophy invaded her mind at that most inopportune time, she remembered to think only of the past as its remembrances gave her pleasure. According to her own philosophy, she should not let past disappointments dictate her future happiness. Only a fool though would discount lessons learned when making decisions for the future.

She strained to think of more than a handful of interactions with the gentleman before her that gave her pleasure, but she could not. Their interactions always left her far from peaceful. Even his presence affected her as no man ever had. But no matter how much he wanted it, she could not agree to the future he proposed.

Once answered him, she knew it needed to be worded very carefully if he would agree to continue with her plan.

"Mr Darcy, I can make no promises regarding our future. Although I hope this time together will help us correct misperceptions and improve our characters, I cannot offer a guarantee it will affect our future to the degree that your wishes are realised." She took a deep breath before continuing, with the uncomfortable realisation that her next sentences might dictate more than the next few days of her life. "I have asked you for complete honesty in a very uncomfortable situation. It would be unfair for me to ask you to follow my request only when it suits my purpose. I realise that complete honesty will dictate not only our words but our actions and I am willing to accept that." She contemplated stating that she expected him to still conduct himself as a gentleman, but she knew that would not only insult him, it did not need to be said aloud.

***

Darcy studied her impertinent demeanour and reviewed his options. If he left Rosings now without trying one last time to earn her love, he would never forgive himself. But at least he would not add to the already considerable pain in his heart by tempting fate one more time. To stay and follow through with the plan meant opening his heart and soul, something he never did before. To compound the dilemma, he must expose himself with no guarantee he might reap the rewards of his efforts. He would come so close to knowing what sharing a life with her would be like, but not knowing if he could hold on to that experience forever.

Both situations presented him with the chance for a future alone and desolate without Elizabeth. Only one offered him a chance for happiness even if it did offer greater pain if he failed. He remembered his resolution made the previous night at dinner; he would not fail in his attempt. He nodded with a confidence that only suddenly came upon him. He was a Darcy and Darcys do not fail or retreat. They fight!

Chapter 6

They continued to ramble slowly through the forest in no particular direction until Elizabeth, finally tiring of the silence, asked, "Mr Darcy, would you prefer to ask or answer the first question? As this plan was my idea, I feel I should give you the option of what position you prefer. I suppose I should also let you know some other rules for our plan that I thought of during our walk." She quickly blushed and followed her statement with an apology of sorts for demanding his acceptance to her rules, "If you agree to them of course. If you choose to ask me a follow-up question or have a comment to make during my answer, I hope you will feel free to do so and I shall do the same. It is my wish that by the end of the week we will have had had ten full conversations. This will be, of course, completely by accident rather than design, but at least it might prove that we no longer need to spend an hour in a room alone in complete silence." She gave him a mischievous grin and waited for his answer.

Darcy nodded his head in agreement. "Would you tell me more about your family?"

Unsure that she heard him correctly, Elizabeth looked at the gentleman rather questioningly. "You have already met most of the members of my family. I thought you would rather learn something completely unknown."

"Yes, I have met them, but I would like to know them through your eyes. As you said, we both have a problem with misperceptions."

Elizabeth nodded in understanding and thought about how to begin. She needed to be honest, but that also meant she could explain her relatives' good qualities in addition to the ones she knew Mr Darcy already detested.

"You know the immediate members of my family, of course, but I shall try to renew your understanding of each one. I suppose I should begin with my parents, my father in particular." Her hand tense on his arm. She was about to discuss the most important people in her life; what if she couldn't make Mr Darcy understand?

"My father loves quiet and solitude, as that closely reflected the manner of his own upbringing. His own parents passed away five years before he met my mother. During that time, his manners and temperament became fixed, much as I am guessing that yours did when placed in a similar situation." Elizabeth paused in her story and looked at her walking partner for confirmation of her guess. If he wanted to spend time with her, he was going to have to learn to carry on a conversation. And that meant he needed to contribute at least a word or two.

"How a man chooses to spend his first years in control of his own destiny greatly impacts how he spends the remainder of his life. He has the opportunity to learn what things he values for their own merit and what previous actions he took merely because his parents demanded it of him. His habits become formed and with time it is more difficult for him to alter those behaviours. However, I do not believe it is impossible if he has the proper incentive."

Elizabeth's cheeks crimsoned due to the understanding of his implied meaning. She quickly glanced at her walking companion; he seemed more at ease than she would have believed. His face didn't appear to tense at her question; he seemed almost happy just to be next to her. Perhaps honestly displaying her feelings would prove more difficult for her than for him. She never even considered that possibility. He already knew what he wanted while she feared her own indecisiveness would become a permanent part of her character.

Instead of responding to his comment, she chose to continue with the story about her parents. "My father neither neglected nor increased his estate, unsure whether he would ever have an heir to pass it on to. He preferred to allow things to go on as they always had.

Because his own father and mother led relatively quiet lives, he chose not to attend assemblies or large parties, as his parents enjoyed the solitude of Longbourn when they lived. He enjoyed spending time reading and visiting with close friends, most of whom he knew his entire life. He enjoys a meal with one or two close friends and retires with them to his library to play chess, drink brandy, and discuss the current state of affairs in England. One evening, his childhood friend Mr Phillips invited him to dinner. What my father did not know when he accepted the invitation was that the sister of Mr Phillips' new wife would also be joining them. My father soon found himself in the midst of a matchmaking scheme designed by my Aunt Phillips. He sat next to the very lovely Miss Frances Gardiner throughout the dinner. By the end of the night, my father made his first and only rash decision of his life. He decided to ask my mother to marry him the next day. She was everything he was looking for in a wife; she was quiet, beautiful, and professed a deep love for living in the country."

"Within a few days of their engagement, he discovered that she loved to attend assemblies and parties and pleaded with my father to accompany her. I think he realised the unhappy path their marriage would likely venture down before she even walked down the aisle. He resigned himself to finding whatever unexpected joy might present itself in his life, for he became increasingly positive that his wife would not be the source of his happiness. I often believe that the constant source of noise in our household is more a vexation to my father's nerves than to my mother's." She couldn't help but laugh at her own little joke. She looked up to Darcy and saw him display a small half-smile. At least she could gain some comfort by the fact that he listened to her still. "Instead of trying to maintain quiet in a household filled with six women, he simply chose to retreat to the solitude of his study."

Elizabeth looked at the ground and stopped walking before deciding whether to continue with her next thought. She remembered her own promise of complete honesty. Somehow the requirement seemed much easier earlier than it did now. But if she could not offer what she required of him, she would never learn how to prevent future misjudgements of her acquaintances. She tilted her head and glanced up into his deep dark eyes. He did not try to force her to continue; he seemed to realise she would continue in her own time. Perhaps there would be a benefit to spending time with a man who did not expect her to entertain him and understood the need for silence to collect one's thoughts prior to speaking. With four sisters, if she did not immediately insert herself into the conversation, it would leave without her being able to take part in it. Elizabeth took a deep breath, began walking, and decided to continue.

"Through watching our parents, Jane and I vowed to only marry for the deepest love. We observed what a marriage without affection at its base develops into. Neither one of us could accept that fate as our own. We decided we would become governesses or companions before accepting a proposal based solely on security." Elizabeth allowed her last sentence to trail off into silence. She guessed the thoughts flowing through his mind at her last statement. He proposed to one of the only two women in England who vowed to marry for the deepest love and without consideration for the man's wealth. If only he knew that piece of information three days ago, they might not find themselves in the position they currently did. But she refused to lament on what might have been if only one thing changed.

Eventually, Elizabeth realised his discomfort must far exceed hers and decided to move on with the tale. "My mother's lively disposition suffered under the constant quiet companionship of my father. With each daughter born, her character strayed from spirited to desperate. She now lived with a man who did not love her, did not want to spend time with her, and bore no son to ensure her security. So she attached herself to Jane, her most beautiful daughter and Lydia, the daughter with the character most similar to her own."

At that point, Elizabeth decided she might as well tell Mr Darcy everything. She had little to lose through honesty on a subject he likely already realised the truth of. "After Lydia was born, my mother's attitude began to centre on finding security for herself and her daughters. She devoted her time to teaching us the values which allowed her to find a suitable husband. She wanted us to behave without regard to the dictates of our hearts. She encouraged my father to propose by behaving in a manner pleasing to him and through her beauty, not through her own accomplishments or character. Because he proposed only one day after meeting her, why should she question the methods she used to secure him? They seemed to work impressively well."

Elizabeth continued, still refusing to look at Mr Darcy and instead focused her gaze on several squirrels playing in a hollow log. She already knew his likely reaction to her words. Realising he had no intention of commenting further, she continued. "I am unsure whether to be thankful or not that her daughters did not seem inclined to follow her instruction. If one of us had followed her advice, she would likely be assured of some form of security once my father passes away. I feel sorry for her situation; she is merely doing what she thinks is best to create a better life for herself and her children. Many people have far worse motives for their behaviour. And although I do not agree with her methods, I can sympathise with them."

Having come to a natural point in her story to pause, Elizabeth indicated she wished to sit on a fallen tree to enjoy the stillness of the morning. She could not feel surprised when Darcy chose to sit down next to her, refusing to relinquish her hand from his arm.

"Jane was always too kind and good to give up on love and the achievement of complete happiness. I was too rebellious and influenced by my father to follow anything my mother taught. Mary preferred Fordyce's sermons to the lectures of our mother. Kitty followed Lydia's lead whenever given the opportunity. And Lydia only wanted to enjoy life and refused to look beyond the next assembly or redcoat for entertainment." Finally looking up and seeing that Mr Darcy could not disguise the disgusted look on his face, she momentarily stopped talking and looked questioningly at him, silently asking whether to continue.

He soon seemed to recognise the disgust plainly evident on his face and let the mask of indifference that she knew so well fall on his countenance. She waited for him to say something before she continued.

With an uncomfortable look, he finally responded, "I should be thankful that neither you nor your sisters followed your mother's advice. In a way, your mother's example led to my own hope for happiness. If she had continued to act in a manner pleasing to your father, and against her own nature, you might have felt that a marriage of convenience could turn into an acceptable prospect for your own future."

Elizabeth narrowed her eyes and looked at the gentleman before her as though she never saw him before. This could not be the same Mr Darcy who only a few days ago so abominably criticised almost every aspect of her family.

"Sir, I am surprised that you would feel that way. Perhaps you would prefer an unhappy marriage of your own to be an example to your children?"

"No, I believe that a joyful marriage between a husband and wife that love each other deeply will provide the best example for our children." Elizabeth couldn't stop her cheeks from colouring upon the words 'our children,' but did not prevent him from continuing. "You said yourself that only you and your elder sister chose to use your parents' example to settle for nothing less than the deepest love. What of your other three sisters? Perhaps if all five Miss Bennets matured in a loving home, you might each settle for nothing less than love. Instead, your younger sisters learned the opposite lesson as you and Miss Bennet. And as for my last statement, I decided to take a lesson from my friend who always says the correct statement in awkward situations. I only hope I proved half as eloquent as Mr Bingley."

"Mr Darcy, I will willingly provide the praise that should rightly be given by Mr Bingley. He could not be prouder of your speech; to have influenced his friend toward better humour must be the greatest compliment he could receive. It seems we both are taking this time to learn from others." Realising the irony of her speech only after she finished it, she understood that from the look on his face it remained too soon to begin that conversation strain. Mr Darcy remained to look forward without moving to meet her eyes after her mention of influencing one's friends.

Elizabeth decided to leave a discussion about influencing one's friends to another day. She wished she hadn't said that, but she could not take it back now. She might as well continue with the story of her family and distract Mr Darcy from her words.

"I wonder if Jane and I learned different lessons than our sisters because we each received the undivided love of a parent. Our younger sisters were largely ignored by our parents. My mother spent time with Lydia only to be entertained by her antics; in a way, she lived vicariously through Lydia and therefore granted her anything Lydia desired. Jane had the unquestioned love of our mother and my father granted me the same devotion. He found that even if he could not have a son, he could at least educate me in the same pursuits he planned to teach his male offspring. I learned to love reading, debating, playing chess, fishing, and roaming around the countryside. The only thing he tried to teach me which I did not develop a love for was riding. My character and interests are largely a reflection of him."

"Did he teach you to fight as well? That seems to be the only aspect you are missing to complete your gentleman's education," Mr Darcy teased to Elizabeth's utter surprise.

"As you said yourself, a lady must have a well-rounded education to be accomplished. But alas, he wouldn't teach me to fight," she paused and smiled before continuing, "The Lucas boys had already taught me that by the time he thought to do so."

Darcy let out a deep and hearty laugh after Elizabeth's declaration. "I suppose when you are at Pemberley, I must check all the gardeners to see which has the black eye in order to find my wife. I can't see you hiding away in the music room with Georgiana when you are trying to avoid me. I should warn you now I am quite an accomplished boxer."

At least he wouldn't be afraid of her temper; then again, he claimed at Netherfield that he could not vouch for his own either. What an interesting pair they would make settling their problems in the boxing ring, she thought.

"Well, I heard you are a fearsome thing to behold on a Sunday when you are kept inside. After a rainy afternoon, I may need to check your friends for black eyes in order to find you amongst Pemberley's massive hallways." That was not what she meant to say! She didn't need to raise his hopes just to dash them. Deciding it was best to move on to something more serious, she continued with her story.

"The person with the second greatest influence on me was Jane." Mr Darcy winced at the mention of her elder sister's name and Elizabeth knew exactly why. He likely wanted to avoid it but knew if he tried to stifle her comments or defend his observations of her, she would declare an end to their agreement. If he hadn't scared away from her yet, it was unlikely that he planned to. Just in case, Elizabeth decided they likely needed to continue their walk in hopes of distracting his mind with something other than leaving her side. She stood up making no attempt to retrieve her hand from his arm.

"From my earliest memories, Jane was the perfect daughter and elder sister. She willingly and happily obeyed our parents. She receives her greatest joys in life from helping those she loves; I have never seen her display a selfish inclination in her life. Jane never met someone she disliked and if she found it difficult to love the person, she simply focused her positive energy on the person's redeeming qualities, whether those qualities actually exist. In short, she is the daughter to make every parent proud. She is also my closest friend and confidant and I could not love her more dearly. My another sister, Mary, received the unfortunate birth position of being the middle child. Jane and I were close friends from birth. Kitty and Lydia grew up more as twins than as mere sisters. That left Mary without the constant companionship and guidance that the rest of her sisters had. Surrounded by equal competition with each of her younger and older sisters, she constantly tries to differentiate herself from her sisters which proved a rather unenviable task. Her four sisters each quickly claimed their own dominate personality trait. Jane took the goodness trait, I grabbed the rebellious streak, Kitty settled on indecisiveness, and Lydia decided to focus her energy on excessiveness. Mary took her time deciding which sister she wanted to be and by the time she finally decided, all the usual defining characteristics were taken."

"Eventually, she found her own niche and decided she would be the moral compass and example for her sisters. That included a deep study of religion and all things she believed a young lady should strive to achieve. Instead of reading texts that challenged typical religious teachings and would force her to re-evaluate her own beliefs, she settled on the more strict texts which did not allow for deviation of opinions. Our parson's wife, who strongly influenced Mary in her choice of texts, also told her that a young lady should devote herself to the practice of a musical instrument. As none of her sisters showed a strong interest in the piano, she found another source to differentiate herself from us." Elizabeth sighed after a making a mental revelation that she never put into words before. "Mary is constantly overlooked by both my mother and father. She is still trying to find where she belongs, both in our family and in the world. When she craves attention from outside our home, I am ashamed to think that it is because her family has not done more to watch over her."

Without knowing where her next revelation might lead, she continued her disclosure, almost curious at its outcome. "If I have more than two children, I will make sure treat each child with equal love and affection. I would not want them to have to look for it outside the home as Mary has to do. It also made me look at my own shortcomings for not spending more time with her. Perhaps it is not too late..." Elizabeth allowed her voice to drift off and think about what she could do to help Mary when she returned to Longbourn. Then again, her own character flaws presented a unique set of challenges that Mary likely did not want to contend with. On second thought, Jane might be a better source of guidance than she could offer their middle sister.

Darcy took the opportunity to speak once again. "I have no doubt that we will ensure that each of our children is loved and taught what behaviour is acceptable and unacceptable. We shall encourage their education and impart them with guidance to help them mature into adults we shall be proud of." He proved nothing if not determined. Elizabeth wanted to say something to contradict his last statement, but Darcy proved too quick. "If you would like to spend more time with Miss Mary, she may enjoy staying with us at Pemberley for a few months without the company of your younger sisters. Georgiana might enjoy someone to practice her music with. I could hire a music teacher to travel to Pemberley for the two of them during your sister's stay."

Elizabeth slightly shook her head in the negative at Mr Darcy's last comment. She had accepted his terms and could not fault him for trying. It seemed that he planned to speak of their future as an inevitable consequence of their time together. She did promise not to stifle his comments. She only hoped that he would not be too disappointed at her refusal if he chose to propose once again. Seeing no easy way to respond, she ignored his request and continue.

"Kitty is content to follow whatever scheme Lydia concocts. She will generally not find herself in mischief without Lydia's prodding. She displays some talent at drawing but refuses to practice because Lydia doesn't want Kitty's attention to be distracted from what she is currently doing. I would be interested to see what her reaction would be to Lady Catherine's insistence that she practice more. In some ways, I think Lady Catherine's instruction might be good for her. However, she would soon take it much too far and be afraid to pack her own trunk if Lady Catherine gave her alternate directions. Kitty is a young and impressionable girl, but she has a good heart."

"And finally, I must reintroduce you to Lydia. She is as headstrong and willful as the day is long. Trying to persuade Lydia to admit fault or change her position is an almost useless cause. Only once when our father yelled at her to stop crying about a new bonnet, did she immediately acquiesce. Of course, my father also turned redder than any of the tomatoes in our garden and I think even Lydia was frightened of him at that moment. She was disciplined even less as a child than the other four of her sisters which is a difficult standard to achieve. She also possesses an amazing ability to turn any occasion into a party. She is exuberant, lively, and exciting to be around when she is in a good mood. Few people can boast to a disagreeable evening when Lydia is in her finest form. She always seems to find herself in difficult scrapes which she devises the most unusual methods of extracting herself from. Usually, the process involves at least two of her sisters and three of the neighbours. The last one also included the use of a cow."

Elizabeth laughed out loud at the memory of her sister trying to jump off a branch onto the back of one of the Lucas' cows after being too afraid to climb down the tree that John Lucas dared her to climb.

"Now that you understand each of my younger sisters better, we shall return to my elder sister." Elizabeth believed the last hour and a half provided the foundation for Mr Darcy to believe her appraisal of her sister and hoped she had said enough. "Jane became the recipient of my mother's constant attention due to her incomparable beauty and sweet disposition which never seemed to tire of my mother's frequent nerve attacks. However, each piece of praise my mother bestowed, especially in company, only made Jane more reserved in that same company. Simply stated, she is uncomfortable being the centre of attention which my mother repeatedly tries to thrust her into. After all, beauty does not lead to an extroverted personality any more than I believe wealth leads to the same. Although I am sure that society expects for each to do so regardless of the individual's inclination." Elizabeth allowed her last comment to hang for a moment knowing full well that the man walking beside her knew who she specifically directed the comment toward. She knew her next discourse would bring much more discomfort to her than to her companion. Selfishly, she wanted him to feel a little uneasiness at the same time she knew she would.

"Several of Jane's former marital prospects shied away because of our lack of fortune. Each time our mother lamented about Jane's heartache to the entire neighbourhood. Jane learned two very valuable lessons from the experiences. The first lesson was not to display her emotions openly for the world to later laugh about when our mother's hopes did not come to fruition. She wanted no one to see if her heart was truly touched when our mother was determined to display its broken state to all of our acquaintances. The second lesson was that although men may initially show an interest in her, her lack of fortune made them soon leave, regardless of their affection for her." Elizabeth felt her voice changed from an explanatory to an almost desperation when she moved on to Jane's relationship with Mr Bingley. "When she met Mr Bingley, these lessons were thoroughly ingrained in her. What she displayed to a non-intimate acquaintance and what she felt were two very different emotions. I can promise you that my sister felt your friend's departure deeply. I can tell that she still feels his absence when I read her letters. Can you fault her for trying to maintain her privacy regarding her heartache?"

She knew when she asked the question that Mr Darcy would not verbally answer. Elizabeth also knew she said all that she needed to say to make him realise the gravity of his error. For a man so completely committed to maintaining his own privacy, surely he could sympathise with another trying to do the same. While continuing to walk, she observed how he avoided her gaze. He stared intently at the path in front of them although that was the focus of his gaze. She knew he was contemplating her last question and wanted to give him ample time for reflection; her sister's happiness depended on his decision. After he finally glanced at her, she knew from his dejected look that it was time to finish their walk. She said enough for one day.

Taking a deep breath and standing a little straighter than she had for the past several minutes, she provided the final part to answer his question. "Now it seems that you are much better acquainted with the members of my family than you had any inclination of when you met me this morning. I hope you see that each may have their faults, as do members of any family, but they are my family and deserving of my steadfast devotion. I love each one of them dearly, just as they love me despite my many faults."

Motioning to the end of the path with her free arm, for her other had not left Mr Darcy's arm for some time, Elizabeth tried to lighten the mood to end their discourse. "Well Mr Darcy, it seems we have spent the last several hours in each other's company and neither of us seems to be missing any limbs. I would venture that this walk could be counted as a success. Would you agree?"

He answered in a teasing tone that Elizabeth found refreshing and rather surprising after his continued silence. Did he make his decision regarding Mr Bingley so quickly? If so, what was his decision? Unfortunately for Elizabeth, he did not reveal his intentions to her.

"Miss Elizabeth, is your only qualification for a successful exchange is for both parties to return with all their arms and legs? If so, I would be willing to wager a considerable amount that each of our walks will be successful."

"If we continue to walk, yes, I too would venture that each of our walks will be successful. If you ever decide to ride your horse, I am not sure I would be willing to take your bet."

Mr Darcy couldn't help but release a small laugh. For the first time, Elizabeth saw the flash of his dimple. How did he possibly manage to stay unmarried for all those years in the ton with a smile and dimple like that? Then she remembered that very few ladies were the lucky recipients of his good humour. It was probably a good thing for any number of ladies would likely try to compromise him and force him to marry. But that was a topic better saved for another day.

She looked up as Mr Darcy interrupted her thoughts. “Ahh, that must be a conversation for a different day. I would dearly love to know why you refuse to ride a horse. Perhaps I will be able to teach you one day. Pemberley is known around the country for its horses. I am sure I could find one suited to you.”

She couldn’t help but return his good humour with a smile of her own. “I see you already decided on your next question.”

“Is your answer worthy of an entire conversation? I have only five questions and no desire to waste one if your answer could be summarised in five minutes or less.”

“Perhaps I will let you have a free question. It will all depend on your mood when I next see you.”

“For that I thank you.” Seeing the edge of the woods from the path they walked on, Darcy began his goodbye. “Will I see you at the same time tomorrow?” When Elizabeth nodded her head in agreement, Mr Darcy continued, “Where shall we meet? I confess I am not comfortable with the thought of you walking alone before sunrise each morning to the pond. If we could meet somewhere closer to the parsonage, it would ease my mind considerably.”

“What if we meet a few hundred yards farther in the wood from where we stand now? We each will be able to take a different path leading here, so no one should see us meet. Once we are in the woods, it should be simple enough to avoid anyone else."

"I suppose I should be thankful that Lady Catherine deals with illegal hunters so harshly. Her tenants do not dare enter these woods for fear of her wrath if caught. Tenants innocently walking through the woods fear of being wrongly accused of an illegal act if discovered."

"Although Lady Catherine does love to be valuable, perhaps we should refrain from thanking her upon our next meeting," Elizabeth answered with a light-hearted smile. She could scarcely believe that her morning started and ended in such different manners. How could this man make her experience such a wide range of emotions in such a short amount of time?

Mr Darcy thanked her for their walk, expressed his anticipation of the next day's meeting, and quickly told her goodbye. Elizabeth did not have a chance to say anything other than her own rushed goodbye before the gentleman headed on the lane toward Rosings and left her alone in the wood.

Chapter 7

What people Darcy encountered on his return to Rosings, he could not recall. His mind remained singularly preoccupied with only one matter, Elizabeth. How different the morning ended than what he had planned several hours earlier. He meant to return to Rosings as an engaged gentleman. Now his hopes and dreams floated in limbo and he remained completely unsure of where they might finally land.

In a manner of hours, the infuriatingly perfect woman held his heart, shattered it, and then offered to temporarily possess it for one week, and one week only. If she discarded it, how could he live?

Their conversation circled in his mind. He knew that Elizabeth spoke honestly of her family, but thoughts of their outrageous behaviour at the Netherfield Ball always followed any allowance he felt he might allow toward their individual characters and actions. Could he think of any reason why Miss Bennet was not a suitable wife for his friend? If he was willing to accept the Bennets as in-laws, couldn't Bingley? Together the two gentlemen might even be able to mould the other

Bennets into a more socially acceptable family. After all, Mr Bennet is a gentleman with an adequate estate. They could never associate with the Bennets in London of course, but he could withstand their company at Hertfordshire during short biannual visits.

Even after Elizabeth's explanation, he couldn't help but wonder how Elizabeth and Miss Bennet escaped their mother's training. His greatest accusation against Miss Bennet was her seeming indifference to his friend. But undoubtedly Elizabeth knew her sister's heart better than he. If Miss Bennet still keenly felt the loss of his friend, it must mean her attachment was far greater than he originally allowed himself to believe. He knew Bingley still displayed the unquestionable signs of a broken heart when he left town. Bingley's usual zest for life withered the longer he remained away from Netherfield. Darcy thought the pain might lessen with time; but did his own longing for Elizabeth ever go away?

Elizabeth's unasked question remained – now that he knew the truth, what would he do to remedy the situation? If he immediately wrote to Bingley to inform him of the deception and misjudgement, Bingley might never forgive him for separating him from Miss Bennet. His friend might decide it was too late to remedy the situation and leave circumstances as they currently stood. He might waste his life pining away for the same woman who loved him equally but could not seek him out to show it. And if Bingley did not reconcile with

Miss Bennet, his deception might lead to the loss of his closest friend and his hope of making Elizabeth his wife. He needed another option that didn't involve losing Elizabeth and Bingley.

But what if Bingley did call upon Miss Bennet and she accepted his return? Their reconciliation might help to promote Elizabeth's favourable examination of his character. If he proved the instigator of their renewed relationship, Elizabeth would see how prodigiously he took care of his friends and family. Still, Bingley's return to Miss Bennet did not necessarily lead to Bingley or Miss Bennet's forgiveness of him. Could Bingley forgive him if Miss Bennet could not? When Miss Bennet learned the truth, would she ever forgive him? His sins might prove unpardonable, even for a woman as forgiving as Miss Bennet.

As Elizabeth's dearest sister, he already knew he could not win Elizabeth's affection if it drove a wedge between her and Miss Bennet. He took a deep breath to pause his rapidly circulating thoughts. Then he remembered what Elizabeth told him scarcely an hour ago. Miss Bennet possessed a caring soul and likely would not carry a grudge even if deserved. Yes, if Elizabeth's faith in her sister proved justifiable, he might be granted forgiveness by both Bingley and Miss Bennet.

But Darcy could not allow himself to rejoice over the prospect of his friend's marriage to Miss Bennet.

Despite all the benefits of reconciliation, one drawback loomed over his happiness. If Elizabeth never accepted him, as Bingley's closest friend, he would observe Bingley and Elizabeth's sister sharing the same marital felicity that he longed for. How could he watch over the children of Miss Bennet and not think of the children that should belong to him and Elizabeth? What if the Bingley's had a daughter who looked like Elizabeth? How could he spend the holidays with the Bingleys and not think of where Elizabeth spent her holiday? What if she married and her new family planned to spend the holiday with the Bingleys, while he also visited them?

He forced himself to stop walking when nausea almost overwhelmed him. His heartbeat quickened, but not from the same emotion that followed her hand gripping his arm. He took off his hat to wipe the sweat trickling down his forehead and made his decision. Elizabeth's marriage to someone else could not be tolerated. He would not allow it; he could not see her happiness without sharing it. He needed some assurance of a shared future with her before he could face saving the hearts of both his friend and Elizabeth's sister. Surely she must understand. His decision would be in both of their best interest.

Before walking within plain sight of Rosings, Darcy stopped by the side of the road to calm himself. After his heart returned to a normal pace, he finally walked up the front steps of Rosings prepared for the admonishments from his Aunt for missing breakfast. His stomach made an ungentlemanly growl from hunger when he remembered his decision to not eat prior to his walk; the nerves in his stomach before he departed made even the thought of eating unbearable. He headed for the parlour where Lady Catherine often preferred to eat breakfast to see if any food remained.

Chapter 8

Elizabeth returned to the parsonage with considerable less angst than she left it a few hours before. For better or worse, she told Mr Darcy the truth about her family. She could think of nothing else to convince him of her sister's affection for his friend; her words must suffice. She felt she left him with enough knowledge to justify the reconciliation between her sister and his friend. Now he only had to realise the error of his decision and take the proper steps to remedy the situation.

One glaring problem remained with her plan – it relied on Mr Darcy. Her past prejudices against his character prevented her from completely believing he would tell his friend of his mistake. For him to tell Mr Bingley would require him to admit a fault in judgement. The truth might also lead to a loss of his friendship with Mr Bingley. Would he be willing to put it in jeopardy to save her sister? He had no assurance of what might happen after he told Mr Bingley of his deception.

She walked into the parsonage to find Charlotte finishing the last remnants of her breakfast. Lizzy bid her friend good morning and explained her decision to enjoy the beautiful weather on a walk this morning.

"I had no doubt you were enjoying the beautiful spring morning when you did not arrive to break your fast with me, Lizzy. Did you have a restful sleep last night? I hope your early morning exercise was not due to a restless night."

"I easily fell asleep after I retired early last night. I awoke rather early and decided to go for a walk instead of interrupting the rest of the household. Where is Mr Collins? I did not see him working in his garden when I returned to the parsonage."

"Mr Collins is fervently researching his sermon for this Sunday. He knows Lady Catherine will be in a foul mood after the departure of her nephews. He is combing through sermons to find one pertaining to the return of family members. Somehow I don't think the prodigal son would be an appropriate text for this occasion. I do hope he is able to find another more appropriate selection. I cannot imagine that comparing Mr Darcy or Colonel Fitzwilliam to the son that gambled away his fortune would not be appreciated by Lady Catherine. Anyway, I believe the search will keep him occupied for a majority of the day. Is there anything, in particular, you would like to accomplish during this time, Lizzy?"

Elizabeth couldn't help but allow a small smile to escape her lips at Charlotte's mention of Mr Darcy as the prodigal son. Not believing that teasing Charlotte about her husband would be in anyone's best interest, Elizabeth continued. "As I was already the fortunate recipient of a beautiful morning for my extended walk, I cannot imagine having any more selfish desires fulfilled today. Surely there must be something which you might require my assistance with. I am afraid I have been a most troublesome houseguest with my rambles throughout the woods at all hours of the day. You must let me assist you with something to make it up to you."

"Lizzy, if I kept you cooped up inside the parsonage for a month, you would be a fearsome thing to behold. I dare say it would severely vex even my nerves." Charlotte and Elizabeth both laughed at the obvious reference to Mrs Bennet. If anyone else dared to tease Lizzy about her mother, she would feel mortified. Being teased by one's closest friend who knew Mrs Bennet almost her entire life was an entirely different matter. Charlotte took her friend's hand and continued, "Your walks make you the best of houseguests for I know that I can leave you for several hours a day without worry of your entertainment. If you aren't too tired, I was going to walk to the village for some fabric after breakfast. I would greatly enjoy your and Maria's company. I will miss you both dearly when you leave."

"A walk will be a delightful way for the three of us to spend a few hours together reminiscing about doing the same activity only a few months ago in Hertfordshire. I am sure I will be ready for a trip in an hour after I partake of these delicious rolls and eggs. I admit that I am famished. I walked far longer than I originally intended but the beautiful weather encouraged me to keep going without regards to my stomach." After taking a few bites of the bread she buttered, Elizabeth continued. "Are you sure Mr Collins will not miss us if we are gone this afternoon? I should warn you that once you are in the sunshine, you are not likely to want to return inside anytime soon."

"If he is able, I am sure he will call upon Rosings to impart his dismay that Lady Catherine's nephews departed. In fact, I am surprised that he has not announced their departure as yet. He knew that Lady Catherine believed Mr Darcy would finally allow a public announcement regarding the engagement of him with her daughter. I'm afraid that her displeasure will be fully evident for the next few weeks."

Suddenly swallowing her bread proved increasingly difficult. How did it manage to get stuck in her throat at such an inopportune moment? Elizabeth picked up her teacup and drank the entire contents, hoping to stop the coughing fit she knew was coming. Once she cleared her throat, she took a deep breath to calm herself. She didn't want to talk about Mr Darcy. The gentleman intruded on her thoughts enough that she didn't need to make him the subject of conversation when in the company of her dear friend.

"We must make the most of the next few days so you will have plenty of happy memories to reflect upon."

Elizabeth finished her breakfast while Charlotte sipped tea. They continued to talk of childhood memories while Elizabeth purposefully refrained from any subject that might interrupt their happy banter.

The ladies rose from the table to retrieve Maria from the parlour for their walk to the village. Unfortunately, it was at the same time that Mr Collins hurried into the dining room from his study. Although he saw Elizabeth pass through the door at the last moment and was able to put his hands up in an attempt to stop himself from running into his cousin, the man, in an uninspiring display of grace, still managed to run directly into her. His hands, which he intended to use to shield himself from running directly into her, instead hit her directly at her bosom.

"Mr Collins!" Elizabeth yelled as she batted his hands down, well after he could have reasonably removed them from her person. She wrapped her arms around her chest and stared at him with a horrified look on her face. She could not understand why he still had his hands positioned in front of her, seemingly trying to decide whether to perform the same act again would meet with equal admonishment. Surely he didn't mean to do it again? Would Charlotte forgive her if she hit the offending man? She looked at her friend's shocked expression. Yes, quite likely Charlotte would forgive her.

All members of the room looked at each other, each turning an unnatural shade of red, and proved unable to speak for several moments. Elizabeth continued to look at her cousin in mortification as he continued to stare intently at the two breasts that his face betrayed his enjoyment at touching.

Eventually, he sputtered, "My dear cousin, I am monumentally sorry for, ah, for placing, touching, umm, feeling, ah--."

Thankfully Charlotte quickly interrupted her husband's awkward apology, "Mr Collins, what is it that you came to ask me?"

Elizabeth sighed from relief as Mr Collins dropped his hands back to his side and turned his extremely focused attention away from her chest.

"My dear Charlotte, have you noticed Mr Darcy's carriage passing by the parsonage? I feel sure I would not have overlooked such a magnificent conveyance, but they should have left Rosings by now. Something must have happened to them. I am sure of it. I was on my way to visit Lady Catherine to offer any assistance and would like for you to accompany me."

“Mr Collins, perhaps you might give them a little more time. It is possible that you simply missed them pass when you were combing through sermons. Did you happen to find one that would ease Lady Catherine?”

“I was fortunate to find the most perfect sermon about the prodigal son who returned to his family after a considerable absence.”

After the ladies exchanged a knowing glance, Charlotte asked her friend if she might see if Maria wanted to join them on their walk. Realising that her friend needed a moment to convince her husband of the inappropriateness of such a topic, Elizabeth readily agreed and left the dining room in no particular hurry to find Maria. By the time she returned with the girl in tow, Charlotte had persuaded her husband to continue searching for a more appropriate sermon, but could not dissuade him from visiting Rosings.

***

Mr Collins not so reluctantly parted ways with the female trio on the road between Rosings and the parsonage. Being sure to make haste, for his benefactress would surely be relieved by his presence, he made record time to arrive at Rosings. Seeing Lady Catherine sipping tea sitting on the most expensive sofa in the east parlour, Mr Collins made sure to impart a bow worthy of the lady of the room. Upon recognition of his gesture by his magnificent counsellor, he immediately imparted his sorrow for the departure of Mr Darcy and Colonel Fitzwilliam and offered his apologies for not bidding them a final farewell as they passed by the parsonage.

"Lady Catherine, I wished to call upon you to provide whatever comfort you need following the departure of your dear nephews. But I feel it shall not be long before they return for an extended visit. Who could depart the pleasure of your company without immediately feeling the loss? I know that even my short visits to Hertfordshire to find and marry my dear wife were marred only by the loss of your constant guidance."

"Mr Collins, Mr Darcy and Colonel Fitzwilliam did not leave today. They have postponed their departure until Monday. I was correct; their attachment to Rosings grows greater than ever before. Darcy seems particularly reluctant to return to his responsibilities in town. I feel it will not be long before a happy event occurs."

Mr Collins felt his eyes widen at confirmation to the information he already took as fact. "When did he impart this glorious news? I did not observe his carriage pass down the lane this morning and feared I missed being able to bid him a final farewell."

"At breakfast this morning I advised him it would be dangerous for him to depart so late in the morning. Immediately recognising the soundness of my advice, he agreed to delay his departure for one more day. Once he agreed to change his departure by one day, of course, I could not allow him to depart in the middle of the week. It is so inconvenient to change locations in the middle of the week and interrupt schedules. It is much better to depart on Monday, to ensure there is a clear break between both locations and schedules. I told Darcy as much."

Lady Catherine was so wise. In fact, she had the wisdom equal to that of any gentleman. How had Mr Collins survived for so many years without her guidance? "How could any gentleman not recognise the soundness of your guidance, your Ladyship? Mr Darcy is fortunate indeed to be the constant recipient of such advice. How many other young men would benefit from such an opportunity? I am sure we would not have many of the problems in England if only your wisdom could be dispersed throughout the country."

Lady Catherine narrowed her eyebrows and raised the volume of her voice in annoyance. "Mr Collins, how could you think I could possibly have the time to mentor all of England? Do you think so little of my family that you should want to limit my time with them? Several evenings ago, I even had to inform Colonel Fitzwilliam of the errors in Napoleon's strategy. I may limit my advice to a few selected individuals, but I am sure it will be attended to properly by those it is bestowed upon."

Mr Collins eyes grew wide at her ladyship's response to his unintended insult. He would never intentionally insult Lady Catherine! He would sacrifice almost anything in his life before making a mistake of such a magnitude! The clergyman needed to repair the problem and quickly. "Lady Catherine, I could never intentionally make such a blasphemous remark. I only meant to relay how blessed I feel to be given such wisdom from you and how rich my life became from your attention. Your family is the most fortunate of all the families in England. How lucky to be born into such a family as yours! The gracious Lord continues to smile upon each new generation of the Fitzwilliam family. And with you at the forefront, how could the good Lord not continue his blessing? I know the small acquaintance that my dear Charlotte and I possess has brought us more pleasure than we can possibly relate."

Lady Catherine smiled slightly and lowered her voice. "And how is your wife, Mr Collins? Is she prepared for the departure of her sister and friend? You must bring them all by for dinner tomorrow night so I may ensure they are properly prepared for their departure. It would ease my mind greatly to know they are being taken care of along their journey."

"Lady Catherine, that is so gracious of you to give your time and your wisdom to my dear family. Your goodness knows no bounds. I am sure that all the members of the parsonage will be honoured to join you and your lovely family for dinner. There can be nothing more important to my small family than doing whatever we may ease your mind."

Chapter 9

Marcus woke his master prior to sunrise for the second day in a row. As he bathed the previous night, the valet's job to prepare his master for inspection by the world, or at least the one person in the world that mattered, required less effort than normal.

He quietly left Rosings, careful to avoid as many servants as possible. He wanted to limit any reports to his aunt of his early morning rambles. Although early morning activity was not unusual for him, Darcy feared his Aunt might devise another way for him to spend his time if given the chance. Thankful for another morning free of inclement weather, he began the trek toward his appointed meeting place with Elizabeth where he waited until the woman he loved arrived.

He watched as she timidly approached from the opposite direction. Why would she be unsure of her reception? He certainly hadn't made a secret of his intentions. He just needed time to convince her of their suitability and her plan provided him with the perfect mechanism. He had one week to change the entire course of his future. He needed everything to be perfect.

Fortunately for him, Elizabeth wore his favourite dress without a spencer due to the morning's rather mild weather; the day definitely started off well. Darcy couldn't help but smile as she came within arm's length. The gentleman bowed and immediately took the lady's hand inside his own. Almost instinctively, he carefully brought it higher and caressed it lightly with his lips. It was the first time she allowed him to touch her with his lips. He noticed her involuntarily blush at his touch. Without releasing his prize, he tucked it safely into the crook of his arm and urged her to begin down their appointed path.

"Good morning, Miss Elizabeth. It seems we have a beautiful morning for our walk. I feared what bad weather would do to our plan." Darcy could not help but feel gratified that Elizabeth's cheeks had not yet returned to their normal colour.

"Good morning to you, Mr Darcy. You certainly seem to be in a very good mood. But who could not be on this beautiful day? Perhaps God is doing his best to help our quest to improve our characters."

"Perhaps God is making sure we have a chance to learn how perfectly suited we are to one another." He watched as her cheeks became even redder and she nervously laughed. "Miss Elizabeth, I hope you don't find what I said humorously. I assure you I was quite serious."

"I have no doubt that your words were heartfelt. My mind made a few mental leaps that led me to laugh at something unrelated. I did promise never to ridicule what is wise or good. I hope that you are not offended by laughing, otherwise, we will find these mornings very taxing indeed. I shall have to gather my strength before embarking each morning for our meeting if no happiness can ever be derived from our spending time together."

"I hope to never suspend any pleasure of yours," Darcy paused for a moment and quietly added, "as long as the beliefs I hold most dear do not provide the basis for your amusement."

"We are agreed, sir. I will only tease at follies, nonsense, whims and inconsistencies. If you happen to be the reason for such merriment, you cannot fault me for teasing in response. Besides, you need never fear being teased for inconsistency; that is one character trait I do not believe you capable of."

Darcy thought for a moment before responding, "I can live with that. It seems Miss Elizabeth that you have a question to ask me."

"Mmm. I must admit I spent most of the night thinking about it. I think I finally found the one that will give me the insight into your character. I want you to tell me about your favourite childhood memory."

"There are a number of subjects I thought you might ask me about, but I never even considered this one."

"So I succeeded in asking you something you did not prepare for? I must admit that makes me just a little proud of myself." Seeing a quizzical look on his face, she clarified her last statement. "I want to know what you truly felt about something without giving you an opportunity to say what you think I want to hear. Without proper time to prepare, you are left with only the truth to guide you. I thought of some other questions that might explain your behaviour while at Netherfield and Rosings, but for my first question, I wanted you to reveal some background information which will probably give greater clarity to your behaviour as an adult. I must admit that the thought of learning about the trials the young Mr Darcy encountered held certain pleasures in itself."

"So you want to know about me as a young boy?"

Her eyes sparkled at him; he loved the fact that she did not bow to his wishes.

"Currently I have an image in my mind of the adult you. The only difference is that you are considerably shorter, but you are still impeccably dressed and reserved in all your mannerisms. Tell me, do they make beaver hats for two-year-olds? Were you born knowing how to stand at ease with one hand behind your back? I wish to know if at any point young Mr Darcy found himself stuck in a tree, or with a bleeding knee from climbing too many rocks, or perhaps bringing a frog to present to his mother for her birthday. So, Mr Darcy, were you born the gentleman you are today, knowing every rule of polite society or were you once known for playing pranks on your poor housekeeper?"

Darcy smiled at her joke. How did she manage to put him at ease so quickly after distressing him? He didn't need any more reasons to love her, but this one certainly took a permanent place on his list.

"My housekeeper, Mrs Reynolds, is likely a better source of information on all my misdeeds as a child than I am. When you come to Pemberley, you must remember to ask her for a complete listing of all my misdeeds." He looked to see her reaction, but she didn't even seem surprised by his references any more. Was that a good sign or a bad sign?

"But to give your curiosity just a taste, I will tell you about one of my most notable instances of mischief. I must warn you this is all hearsay as I was unfortunately too young to remember. When I was barely four years old, I climbed up to one of the mid-level branches on one of the oaks near the house. I am told that I was perfectly content until I made the mistake of looking down and realised I was terrified of heights. As any four-year-old boy would do, I started screaming at the top of my lungs for help. This, of course, made my mother and Mrs Reynolds run frantically out the front door where they saw me desperately clinging to a branch about twenty feet in the air."

"Not waiting for any of the men to reach the tree, even though several of the gardeners were only about a half mile away and a few footmen even closer, my mother climbed up the tree after me. She scampered up the tree while wearing a silk dress with a pearl necklace and diamond earrings and didn't care when her dress ripped in several places on her way to reach me. She finally climbed to the branch which held me, pushed on it to test its weight and then sat down next to me. My mother held me until I stopped crying, which apparently took some time. When I finally looked down, I saw most of the household returning to the house. Only my father remained standing firmly at the base of the tree."

"Even as a young child, I knew that my father and mother both held their positions as master and mistress of Pemberley with great care. I thought my father would be furious with me and started to cry all over again. My mother motioned for my father to join us in the tree. He took off his jacket and waistcoat and made his way up the tree to sit on a branch below the one holding my mother and me. When she would tell me the story which she would at least a few times every year, I heard how she and my father sat there with me for almost an hour. We talked about anything and everything while they tried to make me comfortable with the height we sat at. My stomach began to rumble and my mother asked me if I preferred to eat in the tree alone or the dining room with them. I was rarely allowed to eat in the dining room with my parents, so I readily accepted their invitation."

"My father climbed down the tree and waited for the two of us to follow. My mother asked me if I wanted to race her and of course, I agreed. I managed to win and when we got to the bottom, my mother and father each knelt down to my level, took me by the hand and made me look at that tree branch I spent the better part of the afternoon sitting in. They told me I couldn't let my fears dictate what I could do. When I was older, I couldn't always count on my parents being there to talk me down, but they knew I could conquer whatever the problem, just as I got myself out of the tree."

When Darcy finished telling the story, he quietly added, "I haven't thought about that story since my mother died. I never realised why she kept telling it to me. I always thought she enjoyed laughing about my being stuck in the tree, but it was to remind me to face my problems and to use the lessons my parents taught me."

They walked in companionable silence for about ten minutes observing the woodland animals and sights before she finally broke the silence with her laughter.

"May I be let in on the joke this time?"

"I am sorry. I just pictured Lady Catherine trying to climb up a tree after your cousin with Mr Collins valiantly trying to assist her."

With his dimples prominently displayed for Elizabeth to see, he replied, "I am happy to say that my mother and Lady Catherine held few similar characteristics. If you want to imagine what my mother looked like climbing a tree, you will have to meet Georgiana. It is remarkable to see the resemblance between them. In fact, as you have already confessed to your tree climbing abilities, that same oak is still there and waiting for someone to climb it. Maybe we can get stuck in it together when I am able to take you to Pemberley."

"Are you going to force your poor sister to rescue you so I am able to fully see what the Darcy family looked like stuck in a tree for the afternoon?"

"I look enough like my father that I could easily fill his role. I believe we will need a four-year-old son to properly complete the picture though." He looked at Elizabeth before deciding whether to continue. Seeing her obvious enjoyment at the levity of their conversation, he couldn't help himself. "I would be fully amenable to helping to accomplish the production of a Darcy child for just such an occasion. I must warn you it may take several attempts to make the picture exactly perfect, for it would not be the same with a green-eyed daughter with unruly hair or a blue-eyed boy with the same blonde hair as his aunt." He lifted her hand from his arm and once again caressed it with his lips. "I feel ready to do whatever is necessary to complete the task of producing a young boy with my height and equally unruly hair. If he happens to have green eyes like his mother's, I hope you will indulge me in the slight change to the picture."

Elizabeth could only laugh. "If persistence ever proved to be a problem when you were a child, I would like to inform you that you have conquered that obstacle completely."

Darcy pretended to look affronted at her accusation. "I am only trying to improve your mind. I cannot see how you can fault me for trying to give you an accurate picture of the scene I described."

"I think the one in my head will suffice, but I appreciate your willingness to do whatever is necessary to present me with an accurate representation of the Darcy family sitting in a tree."

"As for my other bouts with mischief, I will rely on Mrs Reynolds to give you a full recounting when you meet her."

Elizabeth raised her eyebrow in amusement and smiled unexpectedly. She spoke quickly, making him wonder if she had time to even think first. "I think we have done quite well, Mr Darcy. We just managed to have a conversation full of liveliness, laughter and the recounting of a favourite story and you haven't even answered my question. If this course continues, I will no longer need to fear to have to gather strength before our meetings. They might turn out to be the favourite part of my day."

***

Elizabeth's eyes widened and then shut tightly, realising what she just stated. She could do nothing but silently censure herself. How could she blame him for making statements about a shared future when she only encouraged him? Was she actually enjoying their time together? What did that mean? She could not possibly morph from hating the man to looking forward to time alone with him in less than three days! That was not the goal at all of these morning exchanges. Instead of discovering how she misjudged two people so completely, she found herself following the goals he set. She needed to focus! She must understand why she so grossly misunderstood him and forget any thoughts of enjoying herself, no matter how glorious his dimples looked when he smiled fully. Oh! Where did those nasty thoughts keep coming from?

Mr Darcy interrupted her inner dialogue, "You asked for my favourite childhood memory and I think I have it."

Elizabeth had nothing to add and let Mr Darcy continue, eager to stop the thoughts flowing through her mind. "When I was twelve years old, Georgiana had barely reached her second birthday. My mother never fully recovered from her birth and her health steadily declined from the time of her confinement. That Christmas my mother ensured the entire house was decorated for the season. The decorations at Pemberley during Christmas always brought visitors, but that year, my mother never put so much effort into guaranteeing that every aspect was perfect. She had the entryway covered in garland and wreaths. It seemed like hundreds of lights, ornaments, and multi-coloured bows covered the tree in our family's private sitting room. Perhaps it is just the memory of a child, but I have never seen or felt anything as inviting since. I remember on the night before Christmas, I snuck downstairs to see if any presents were under the tree. My father promised me a new hunting saddle and ice skates if I behaved that year."

Elizabeth looked to see if he would mind a quick interruption to his tale. He didn't seem particularly intent on racing forward, so she took a chance. "And did you manage to behave that year, or did you find yourself stuck in a pond without the means to get out?"

He laughed quietly, so Elizabeth could barely hear him. After he rewarded her with a brilliant smile, he told her, "You seem to have a spectacular method for guessing my most embarrassing moments. I was actually very well-behaved that year if you don't include a minor incident in which Richard and I got in a fight while in my father's skiff. If I remember correctly, he tried to steal a fish I rightfully caught. When I tried to take it back, the ensuing fight caused a rather large hole in the bottom of our small vessel. Unfortunately for you, I was not stuck in the pond, as Richard and I are both excellent swimmers. We did, however, have to tell my father that we ruined his skiff. As punishment, we spent the next week building him a new one and working in the stables."

She smiled at his memory. "This time I feel perfectly safe in my vision of a shorter version of your current self-dealing with the muck in the stables."

"I suppose it might surprise you I spent many, many hours working in the stables and in the fields."

"I don't believe it. The formidable Mr Darcy throwing manure over his shoulder would certainly be a sight to see."

"My father wouldn't let me have my own horse until I learned to properly care for one. He ensured I took almost complete responsibility for my first horse. I wasn't allowed to do the more dangerous tasks until I was bigger, but I learned quickly that you don't have to be very strong to shovel manure. Midnight always held a special place in my heart, perhaps because I worked so hard to be trusted with him."

"Your parents certainly ensured you understood the importance of being responsible for what you are entrusted with."

"I take that trust very seriously. I would never forgive myself if something horrible happened to someone I loved." Elizabeth felt his opposite hand clasp down on hers. She felt the promise he made even if he didn't say it. He included her in his realm of responsibility whether she accepted her place in it.

"I know."

Both seemed content to walk along the path loss in their own thoughts and listening to the relaxing sounds of the forest. After walking alongside the pond they met on the previous morning, they found a place to sit and watch the wildlife. After Elizabeth broke their silence by laughing at two ducks battling over a leaf, she realised that her questions interrupted Darcy's Christmas tale.

Guessing that he would likely be content to sit in silence for the remainder of their time together if left to his own devices, Elizabeth took the initiative. "Are you ready to continue? I believe you were about to tell me of your new saddle and ice skates. I can only guess what problems those got you into."

"I never made it to the Christmas tree that night to look. Instead, when I was sneaking along the hallway, I found my father kissing my mother underneath the mistletoe. I stood there watching them for some time; I am not sure how long. I remember how the candles lit the hallway so I could barely see them, but I will never forget how happy they looked. Eventually, my father picked up my mother in his arms and walked with her down the hallway to his room. I quietly returned to bed and looked at the stars. That night I discovered what I wanted for my own marriage; I wanted one like theirs. My parents loved each other. They were perfect for one another in so many ways. They were equally fortunate that both families supported the union. The Fitzwilliams approved of my father's fortune and the Darcy's were eager for a connection with the Fitzwilliams."

"When I awoke the next morning, my mother and father already sat in the family parlour by the tree. Georgiana scampered around the room trying to tear the paper on everything beneath the tree. Her laughter was contagious and neither of our parents ever tried to quiet or subdue her enthusiasm. I had as much fun watching her unwrap my presents as I had to unwrap the few she begrudgingly let me open myself. My father did get me the saddle and the skates, along with a few books he thought I needed to read. After I thought I received everything I would, my mother handed me a small package containing the pocket watch I still use."

Darcy momentarily took his hand from Elizabeth's and reached into his jacket. He handed her the well-used gold pocket watch. Elizabeth opened it and read the inscription aloud. "To my son, I will love you always." She returned the pocket watch to him and reached for his hand to return to her own; she needed to find some way to reassure him of her continued presence by his side. She couldn't help the tears welling in her eyes for his loss. She couldn't imagine how hard it would be to lose the person you love most; she wouldn't know what to do if she lost Jane or her father.

"I remember sitting there looking around my family and thinking I must be the most fortunate boy alive. But then my mother died a few weeks later. That Christmas was the last time my family was together and happy."

Elizabeth listened to the silence following his confession, wondering what else he might say. She only heard the sounds of the ducks playing in the pond. She leaned closer to him, hoping to entice him into continuing. As his silence continued, she couldn't help but wonder if allowing her into his life, privy to his most private thoughts would be extraordinarily difficult for him. She chastised herself for such an unfeeling thought; of course, it would be difficult to talk of his deceased mother. She knew enough of him to know he did not easily discuss his private thoughts and feelings; now she demanded complete honesty from him in regard to a highly emotional time in his life. She needed to give him time. He would speak when ready, so she sat patiently beside him, waiting for Mr Darcy to reach that time on his own.

At what seemed with great personal pain, he forced himself to continue while looking into the distance. "When my mother passed away, my father lost a large part of himself. Seeing Georgiana brought back memories of my mother and it became painful for him to spend a great deal of time with her. He also gained an all-encompassing fear he would lose her too. Consequently, Georgiana spent much of her early childhood in the nursery without free access to Pemberley, as I had. It was slightly less painful for him to spend time with me, but I could tell that it hurt him, nonetheless. After my mother's death, my interactions with my father largely centred on expectations, behaviour and my future responsibilities."

"Not that either of my parents were overly affectionate when I was younger, but I felt the loss of my mother's affections, and subsequently my father's, deeply. I did what I could to gain his attention and affection. That meant diligently following the lessons he imparted to me. With my mother's loss, I was largely left to my own devices. I chose to spend time outdoors or in the library reading."

Not wanting to interrupt, but wanting to make sure she didn't misunderstand him, she squeezed his arm and waited for him to pause before she spoke. "You preferred activities that allowed you to escape."

He nodded in agreement. "I didn't think of it that way when I was younger, but I recognised it later at university. I suppose that is one reason that Bingley and I became such close friends. We both saw something in the other which our own lives lacked. His own parents lacked in providing him direction, largely because they didn't know everything that society expected of him. I easily provided him with the knowledge of what being a gentleman encompassed; it was all my father taught me in the last few years of his life. I lacked the company of someone who was openly affectionate and outgoing."

Elizabeth thought she finally started to understand the gentleman. She understood what he lost at such a young age. She could see why he took his responsibilities seriously and how difficult it was to reconcile his upbringing with loving a country gentleman's daughter without connections. She could only imagine how hurtful her words in the defence of George Wickham were. He never mentioned Wickham's name, but she guessed the role he played in the life of Darcy's father. Wickham brought some happiness to him that was wholly unconnected to Darcy's mother. His father divided his already limited attentions between Wickham and his son.

"It seems I am the one to leave today's walk with a great deal to think of this afternoon," she whispered after the long moment of silence.

Chapter 10

When Elizabeth finally returned to the parsonage, she found Mr Collins dutifully working in his garden, preparing the beds for the spring flowers. Still not overly comfortable in his presence, but realising she did not want the awkwardness of the day before to mar the rest of her trip, she sincerely complimented him on his efforts and entered the house to find her friend. Once again, she found Charlotte sitting in the dining room, eating breakfast.

"Did you have a pleasant walk this morning, Lizzy?"

"I did. I am certainly going to miss the scenery here. You are very fortunate to have access to it whenever you wish."

"You know you are welcome to visit whenever you are able. You are just as welcome here as any member of my family. Maria is already speaking of returning next spring. If you are able, I would love for you to join her."

"I greatly appreciate the invitation, Charlotte. If I am able, I would dearly love to see you again. I daresay I will look forward to it all winter."

"It is settled then. Whenever you are available in the springtime, you must come to visit."

After allowing Elizabeth to eat some breakfast rolls and meats that remained on the table, Charlotte asked if she looked forward to that night's dinner at Rosings. Elizabeth answered honestly that her mind had been preoccupied with other matters. She knew the finality of her statement caused Charlotte to leave her alone for the remainder of the day.

The party from Hunsford made the same walk to Rosings that they made ten times on previous occasions. The self-important butler escorted them to the parlour where all the members of the Fitzwilliam family sat or stood waiting for their company to begin their party. Mr Collins made his usual overly gallant bow to each of the members already in the room. Could she blame Mr Darcy for thinking her family unacceptable? But as his family contained Lady Catherine, could he fault her for Mr Collins? Being sure to not follow his lead, the ladies of his party curtseyed with none of the exaggerated manners of their male protector and took the position they occupied on each of their prior visits.

Elizabeth wondered at Lady Catherine's invitation as only Colonel Fitzwilliam showed his obvious enjoyment at the addition of their company. From his usual seat next to her, he entertained his audience with tales of his latest campaign exploits. She laughed when appropriate and gasped when needed, but her mind was otherwise preoccupied with the gentleman standing behind Mrs Collins and Miss De Bourgh. Mr Darcy's head was tilted slightly away from the two ladies in front of him. It took Elizabeth some time to understand that he strained to hear exactly how his cousin entertained her before dinner. She simply wasn't prepared to deal with his temper at the moment. Mr Darcy would have to find a way to calm himself down; she didn't have the energy.

Their party continued as such until dinner was announced. Lady Catherine pointedly suggested that Mr Darcy escort Anne and the Colonel escort herself, as befitting their positions in the household. The gentleman from Derbyshire seemed none too pleased with his placement during dinner; he sat between Lady Catherine and Mr Collins and directly across from his female cousin. Elizabeth occupied the position next to the Colonel; a position that made it almost impossible to hold a conversation with anyone at Mr Darcy's end of the table. As she suspected, the meal passed rather slowly and the mistress of the house spent her time directing her nephew's attention to her daughter instead of allowing for discussion with anyone else at the table.

When they finally returned to the parlour after dinner, Elizabeth noticed that Mr Darcy's mood turned even more taciturn than was his norm. He looked like he might explode when Colonel Fitzwilliam once again sat next to her. She felt a sudden need for a headache to end their party quickly. Just when she lifted her hand to her head to feign the pain, Lady Catherine interrupted Elizabeth's discussion with the Colonel to remark that she seemed out of spirits. The great lady immediately accounted for it herself, supposing that Miss Bennet did not like to go home again so soon and suggested she remain another month.

"Thank you for your kindness, Lady Catherine, but I am afraid I must return to town by Saturday next. My uncle is sending a servant to accompany us on the post."

"Two young ladies should not ride in a post when I have the power to deliver you to town next month."

"Thank you again Lady Catherine, but I must abide by my original plans to return to town next week. My father and uncle's plans demand it."

Out of the corner of her eye, she saw Mr Darcy's mood suddenly improve. For that reason, she wasn't surprised when he interrupted their discussion. "I must agree with my Aunt, Miss Elizabeth. It is an unnecessary danger for you and Miss Lucas to travel by post when you could travel in the safety of a private carriage instead."

After letting out a small chuckle that only Elizabeth noticed, Colonel Fitzwilliam echoed his cousin's sentiments. "I agree. Darcy and I plan to ride our horses back to town when we leave on Monday. Neither of us enjoys being cramped in a coach when we could enjoy the fresh air. You and Miss Lucas must travel with us in Darcy's coach. You will certainly have ample room and it will be infinitely more comfortable and safer than the post."

Before Elizabeth responded, her cousin took the liberty of answering for her. "Colonel Fitzwilliam, my cousin and sister appreciate your overly generous offer, but it simply wouldn't be proper."

"Mr Collins, do you mean to say that two young ladies are not safe in the company of my cousin and me?" Asked Mr Darcy. "If this is the case, I will have to let my sister know of the unfit and dastardly nature of her two guardians. I hate to think of your opinion of my family if you believe two of its members are unable to ensure the safe return of your own family members." Every member of the room watched as the colour in Mr Collins' face drained, leaving him a pasty white. For a moment, Elizabeth feared she needed to find some smelling salts to revive the man.

She looked around the room to see the reaction of the other members of the Fitzwilliam family. In an acting display worthy of any Bennet sister, she heard Miss De Bourgh innocently interject, "Mr Collins, Mr

Darcy and Colonel Fitzwilliam escorted me on a number of occasions when I stayed at Pemberley and Glenmore. I can assure you, they were the epitome of propriety."

If Elizabeth hadn't used the same expression when she feigned innocence on more than one occasion, she might mistake Miss de Bourgh's comment for true sincerity. Instead, Anne seemed amused by her cousin's quick retort to Mr Collins and merely wanted her chance to add to the game.

Furious that Mr Collins insulted her favourite nephew and somehow managed to challenge the honour of her entire family, Lady Catherine stood up to address the entire room. She spoke in a voice that brokered no opposition. "Miss Lucas and Miss Bennet will travel with my nephews to town on Monday. No one has any cause to doubt the reputation of my family."

Charlotte thanked Lady Catherine, Mr Darcy and the Colonel for their kindness and accepted on behalf of her sister and friend. She then suggested that the members of the parsonage return as she suddenly felt unwell. Miss De Bourgh looked fondly at all of her guests and then ensured they returned safely and without physical exertion by ordering her mother's carriage to take them home.

During their ride back, Elizabeth's thoughts reverted to the smirk on Darcy's face after his aunt announced Elizabeth's travel plans. He knew exactly what he was doing. If she wasn't the uncooperative prize of such a venture, she might congratulate him on his success at their next meeting. But once again, he got just what he wanted in a remarkable display of manipulation.

She could not help but wonder what other tricks Mr Darcy might use to arrange her life according to his wishes. Was anything ever denied to him? No wonder he hadn't married. The matchmaking mothers of the ton met their equal and likely didn't even know it. Fitzwilliam Darcy wasn't going to marry until he was ready and now that he decided, he wasn't about to let anything stand in his way, even the desires of his intended bride.

Chapter 11

The altercation between Mr Collins and Lady Catherine's family allowed the members of the parsonage to return earlier than normal from a dinner at Rosings, thereby allowing Elizabeth ample time to sleep before her early morning appointment. As was becoming almost a habit, she awoke in plenty of time to dress and arrange her hair as best she could alerting no one else in the household.

At least she regained some confidence in her air. After her tumultuous week, her spirit showed signs of a remarkable comeback. She convinced herself that she was ready to see him again. After all, he spent most of the night in her thoughts, anyway. As an added benefit, his actions in person were considerably less intimate than those in her dream. For once, she wished she hadn't read some of the hidden books in her father's library; her imagination combined with some risqué dialogue found in the books kept her dreams entirely too vivid for her comfort. Until last night, no man ever invaded her dreams and now Mr Darcy seemed to dominate her thoughts, both those waking and asleep.

On her way to the meeting spot, she wondered on the state of her future walking companion's mood. Except for the very end of their dinner at Rosings, she recognised the tell-tale signs of his displeasure. She easily guessed their source, but as neither wanted to alert Lady Catherine to their growing friendship, she could do nothing but continue to act in the same past manner as she usually did. This meant she spent her time conversing pleasantly with Colonel Fitzwilliam and doing all she could to avoid any interaction with Mr Darcy. She hoped the outcome of the evening's final conversation provided him with sufficient happiness to outweigh the earlier problems. Even with the painful revelations made and occasional moments of awkwardness, she found herself looking forward to seeing him, as evidenced by her growing desire throughout the night to speed the rise of the sun.

Seeing a large black mare with one white boot and its rider approaching, Elizabeth ducked quickly behind a tree, hoping he didn't see her. As the horse and its rider approached, she heard the horse stop and its rider dismount. She heard the footsteps of both draw closer. She hoped it wasn't Colonel Fitzwilliam or one of the men from the village. How would she explain her presence there so early in the morning? She did not relish the thought of listening to Lady Catherine chastise her walking habits.

The voice from behind the tree where she stood interrupted the one running through her head. "Miss

Elizabeth, if you choose to hide, I would recommend wearing a dress in a colour other than red. I likely saw you before you even heard me approach." Darcy walked from behind the tree to face her. Saying nothing else, he took her bare hand and as tenderly as the day before, caressed it with his lips before placing it on his arm away from the substantial animal beside him.

"I wasn't aware that hiding from an unknown gentleman riding a large beast would be called for on my walk this morning. If I had, I am sure a green dress would be much better suited to camouflage my position. Although I must admit that my mother will be very disappointed that I own any dress designed to blend in with the forest. I don't ever remember her giving the modiste those specific instructions."

The rakish grin provided by Darcy in response to her comment made her blush. He seemed unwilling to let the opportunity to tease her pass. "And what directions does your mother give the dressmaker?" The continued crimson on her cheeks provided the only answer she chose to give. She saw his dimple make an appearance before he spoke again. "I admit I am very fond of your mother's style selection. Although the one you are wearing today is much better suited for my plans this morning."

She needed to change this topic of conversation. The discussion of her mother's desire to parade her physical attributes was not her topic of choice for the morning. "I wasn't aware that answering a question required certain attire. Perhaps you should have warned me."

"And give you time to think about your answer? No, I believe I will use your own method against you. My question for you today has two parts. Are you ready?"

"Am I correct in assuming your question deals somehow with the third companion on our walk this morning?"

"That depends."

"On what?"

"On how you answer the first part of my question."

She raised her chin in mock superiority. "I am not frightened of you, Mr Darcy. Do your worst."

They stopped walking, and he turned to her, focusing intently on her eyes. The intensity made her lose all levity derived from the opening of their conversation. She waited breathlessly for him to speak.

"Do you trust me?"

She arched her eyebrow with suspicion, "With what?"

"Oh, no. Remember the rules. You must answer honestly holding nothing back, imposing caveats, or trying to avoid parts of the question. So I will ask you my simple question again. Do you trust me?"

She wondered how he could sound so confident while asking a question so full of meaning. He just stood there patiently waiting for her to answer. Unable to look away, she imagined all the implications of such a question. Could she trust the man who stood before her? Even a week ago, she had no reason not to believe the things he said. Her issue always stood with the manner of his statement, not the veracity of the statement itself. After the confessions made in his letter and the day prior, she knew the responsibility he levied on himself with regard to those he cared about. In truth, the one instance which negated her reply in the affirmative was his action regarding Mr Bingley and her sister.

She looked away from him, no longer able to look into his dark eyes. They clouded her judgement. How could she be expected to say anything with such a gaze focused intently on her person? She bit her lip from continued indecision. He revealed so much of himself to her yesterday, but she still felt a pull on her heart reminding her of their past. Elizabeth felt a warm hand lift her chin, forcing her to return her eyes to his face. He looked at her with such sincerity and hope. But she must answer him honestly.

Finally, she answered, knowing it would cause him pain. He asked for her honesty and she refused to lie to spare his feelings. "In most instances, my answer is yes. However, as long as a certain issue between us remains unresolved, I am afraid I cannot answer that I have complete faith in you."

Elizabeth saw the pain in his eyes; he tried to hide it, but it appeared too quickly. He took a deep breath, seemingly unwilling to let her negative answer dissuade him. "I am hoping that this will be one of those instances. I would like to teach you to ride."

Her eyes widened upon studying the horse further. "On that beast?"

Darcy looked affronted at her characterization of his riding companion. "He is one of the finest horses at Pemberley. I raised him from a colt. His sire was Midnight and when Midnight became too old to ride, I began to ride Erebes, named for the Greek God of the Darkness and Shadow." Changing his tone, he said more gently. "I promise I will let nothing happen to you. That is why I wanted to know if you trusted me."

Elizabeth alternated between looking at Darcy and the immense animal following behind them. "You don't have a side saddle on your horse. How do you propose we begin my lesson?"

"You can sit with both legs draped over one side. It isn't the ideal condition, but at least you will be able to become comfortable with Erebes." He obviously saw the continued indecision on her face, for he added, "I will make sure you are completely safe."

Elizabeth looked tentatively from the horse to the equally imposing gentleman before her, "You promise?"

He smiled and looked down into eyes that she knew betrayed her apprehension, "I promise." He allowed a slight pause. "Well then, it is time to begin your first lesson." Instead of leading her to the saddle where she expected her lesson to begin, Darcy led her to stand in front of the horse. "You must become acquainted first with Erebes. Bring your hand up to his nose."

He stood next to her, took the hand still connected to his and brought it to his horse's nose. "There you go." Frightened at the horse's decision to aggressively smell her hand in response to their introduction, she immediately withdrew her hand from Darcy's and brought it back to her side.

"He won't bite you. You need to let him get used to your scent." He brought a carrot from his pocket and gave it to her. "I wasn't sure if we would need some help. Give this to him and I promise you will have a friend for life."

He seemed so sure of himself, but she couldn't understand why. His question held massive implications. Now he planned to lead her through something he knew she feared, but he seemed so calm. The massive animal terrified her and her reaction did not even seem to faze him. Of course, he knew Erebes from the time he was born. Likely the horses knew the gentleman beside her better than she ever would. She sighed in resignation. Well, in order to get to know Mr Darcy, she supposed she needed to become properly acquainted with his horse first.

Elizabeth broke the carrot in two and held the larger part in her hand about a foot from the horse's nose. Erebes immediately reached his neck to take the treat from her hand. The animal licked and nudged her hand hoping to find more carrots. Shyly, Elizabeth brought her other hand with the smaller piece to the horse's mouth. Erebes retrieved his treat and licked both her hands hoping to find if she somehow possessed a third hand with more vegetables for him.

Elizabeth held up both her hands to the horse's nose and apologised in jest. "I am sorry but I have nothing left to give."

Darcy reached out to stroke Erebes gently on the nose. "Don't worry. He knows you will take care of him now. Are you ready to ride?"

"I don't suppose I have much choice now that we are all properly acquainted."

"I suppose you don't. Would you allow me to assist you in the saddle?"

"Yes, please." Darcy waited for Elizabeth to turn around and face him. She didn't think of the position this placed her in when she agreed. Oh well, it was too late now. She turned and took a deep breath before he placed his hands around her waist. No man ever touched her like that before. His touch was so light at first she barely felt it through all her layers of clothing, but it was still enough to make her heart beat faster. When her breathing calmed, his grip tightened; she knew he could feel almost every curve of her form. She felt the heat creep up her face. John Lucas helped her many times into and out of trees, but the only other time she felt the current tightening in her stomach was after jumping off a rope into the pond behind Longbourn. Why did an action that simultaneously scared and excited her cause the same physical reaction as Mr Darcy intimately touching her?

After what seemed like far too short a time, he lifted her onto the beast. She arranged her legs as comfortably as she could on the saddle intended for a male occupant. She imagined that riding astride would certainly prove more comfortable, but the amount of leg she must expose made the idea completely unfathomable. Once she stopped wriggling around on the seat, she expected

Mr Darcy to walk in front of the horse to lead her and Erebes around the riding trails in the woods. When he grabbed a free area on the back of the saddle with one hand and kept the reins in his other palm, she could not help but wonder what he planned to do. He certainly didn't intend on doing what she imagined his preparations would logically lead to. When he placed his foot in the stirrup, swung his opposite leg behind Elizabeth, and hoisted himself on Erebes' bareback, only inches behind where she sat, she had no choice but to laugh at her own delusion.

Even though his body could easily engulf hers, he seemed careful to avoid touching her, even though his arms were only a few inches above hers, Darcy finally asked, “And what, may I ask, is the subject of your merriment this morning, Miss Bennet?"

"Simply that it is not wise to underestimate the determination of one's opponent."

"Is that what I am, your opponent? Are we waging war?"

Hearing the lightness in his voice, she turned around. When she saw the amusement in his eyes, she couldn't help enjoying their closeness. "I did warn you that if you ever dare to bring your horse, escaping the morning with all your limbs intact is no longer a certainty. Judging by our current position, it seems we are well on our way to all the usual consequences of warfare."

In an intimate whisper in Elizabeth's ear, Darcy answered her teasing question with a much more serious response. "I promised not to let anything happen to you." He moved his face away from her ear and continued in a somewhat louder voice and a faked innocent expression, "How am I to do that if I do not have control of the horse? I am merely ensuring that your request is fulfilled."

Making sure not to let her guard down, she resorted to usual response in a tense situation, she teased him. "Mr Darcy, I must warn you. When I try to ride a horse, the person sitting on the beast's back is never in charge."

"Is that the reason you never ride?"

"The pitiful and rather short story is that one afternoon when my father tried to teach me how to ride, the horse ran away from my father with me on its back. I fell off about a half mile from where we started and succeeded in hurting my shoulder. I had to stay in bed for several weeks recovering from my fall. After that, I always felt safer when my own two feet were responsible for taking me to my destination."

Darcy allowed his arms to relax slightly against Elizabeth's frame, not even fooling himself that his supposed reason centred on his desire to better handle the reins. "Well, we must get started then. I hate to think you refuse to change your opinion of something once it is formed."

***

He knew he needed to tread very carefully; he felt her entire body tense when he surrounded her. But he refused to let go. This was what he wanted. For the first time, the woman he loved was in his arms. She placed herself under his protection. Whether she realised it, she trusted him. He needed to find a way to morph her trust into love. He just needed to be patient.

Not knowing what else to say or do, Darcy lightly flicked the reins that lay in both their hands, indicating to Erebes that he needed to start at a slow walk. Elizabeth's body tensed at the horse's first movement. In a quiet voice, he reminded her, "You will be safe, I promised. Remember? Just relax and enjoy the scenery before you. See how a different point of view makes something familiar look and feel an entirely new?" Sensing that he said enough, Darcy quietly held her as they made their way through the forest.

Eventually, time led to a certain familiarity between Elizabeth and him. As Darcy allowed his arms to rest and entrap his partner a little more, he felt her fall back slightly touching his chest. He needed to keep her there, but before he could tighten his arms, she instantly sat even straighter than before.

"If you want, now might be an ideal opportunity to ask me another question."

With an unsteady voice, Elizabeth answered. "This is certainly an unusual day. It could be the first time the reserved Mr Darcy ever volunteered to take command of the conversation."

"There must be a first time for everything. Now about that question."

"You never asked me the second part of yours. I think it only fair that I fully answer yours first."

"I asked you to let me teach you to ride, and you accepted. That was the second part."

"I thought that was more a directive than a question."

"I think we both may readily agree that I lack the capability to make you do anything you do not want to do."

"Very well, Mr Darcy, since you are helping me to conquer one of my fears, I feel I should do the same for you. I want to know why you spend so much time looking out windows when in a company. What is it you fear so much when in a parlour? Perhaps you would rather I ask you about your favourite book. But alas, I am afraid that will do nothing to help me understand how I misjudged you."

Darcy tightened his arms around her. Truthfully, he had hoped she would ask something as innocuous as his favourite book or play. But of course, she would choose the subject of what he feared most. Well, almost feared most. He would play parlour games for years with every lady of the ton if it meant he could keep the ones he loved safe. But that would be a discussion for another day.

Instead of indulging her question, he asked one of his own. "Why do you think I am uncomfortable in a social situation? I believe my cousin and I already tried to answer this for you several weeks ago at Rosings."

"I think you held something back. You claim shyness, but you seem just as reserved in the company of your aunt and cousins as you did in Hertfordshire. I thought you would at least be comfortable around your family. I find it hard to believe that the addition of the parsonage inhabitants significantly changes your demeanour at Rosings."

Deciding that his own distress would likely alleviate Elizabeth's, he finally answered her question in a slow and steady voice. "Even as a young child, I was shy. My parents rarely forced me to participate in social situations that would push me to overcome my introversion. Growing up as the future master of

Pemberley, my access to the other children in the area proved limited. I spent more time with Richard and Wickham than anyone else. After my mother died, our entire household became quieter and almost void of female company. Unlike you, I grew up without the benefit of a lively household to prepare me for the realities of society."

Elizabeth turned her head to look at him, encouraging him to continue talking; she did not seem satisfied with his answer. Apparently, he wasn't the only one with a persistent streak; she already possessed the dominant Darcy characteristic, and they weren't even married yet. He smiled slightly and continued. "While at university, Bingley and Richard possessed enough charm for all three of us. My name ensured I never had to exert myself to gain entrance to a society or club. I generally kept only the company of other young men who never minded if I limited my participation in conversation as long as I kept my fencing and riding skills on par with the others. Then I turned twenty-two and unexpectedly found myself in sole possession of Pemberley, guardian to my sister, and without the expertise to successfully guide myself through society."

Darcy urged Erebes into a quicker walk, and continued, "During my first season, Lord and Lady Matlock tried when they could, but they had three of their own children to watch over. Richard spent much of his time with his regiment and was not available to accompany me to my social engagements. I did not pine for lack of social invitations and you can well imagine why I received the invitations I did. It only took a few weeks to realise that every invitation I received was from a family with a daughter of marriageable age who inevitably I found myself partnered with for the night. Undoubtedly after dinner, instead of the gentlemen removing themselves to a separate room, the father thought that remaining with the females would be much more enjoyable. For a young man who loathed being the centre of attention, you can well imagine my enjoyment. As it was entirely improper to excuse myself early or to sit in silence by a lady, I stood by the window; the very place most people prefer to avoid when in a company."

"My behaviour became cemented after my first season when I returned to Pemberley. I began to have nightmares of being placed on an auction block. All the mothers of the marriageable ladies lined up to examine me. They gossiped with their friends about my many attributes and imperfections. I vividly remember one mother inspecting my back teeth to check my health. Mostly they just asked for a full accounting of my assets. Toward the end of the dream, the bidding began. The feeling of dread when one of the more vocal and aggressive mothers finally won usually woke me. After several nights of that dream in succession, I decided to accept few invitations when I returned to town and even then, only when I was particularly acquainted with the gentleman. I still get that same feeling of dread whenever I am in a room with a mother who has intentions for her daughter and me."

Elizabeth's stomach tightened in response to his story. Darcy used one of his thumbs to gently rub her forearm in an intimate circular pattern. His ministrations did nothing to relieve her discomfort; it only made it worse. She dropped the reins and lifted her hands to cover her mouth.

Darcy talked to her softly, "Now you understand why I feel so uncomfortable in certain situations?" He seemed to need for her to understand his fear.

Finally gaining her composure, Elizabeth answered. "I understand how you must have felt on the night of the assembly in Hertfordshire. It was everything you fear. All the gossiping that started as soon as you entered. At least in the ton, everyone already knows who you are and they have no need to discuss it anymore."

"I must admit that I did not expect you to become so sympathetic to my plight." His voice betrayed his obvious pleasure at Elizabeth's compassion.

Elizabeth bit her bottom lip. "Would you like the complete truth, or can we keep our peace and leave things as they stand for the moment?"

"I would prefer the truth."

"I wasn't distressed entirely due to sympathy; I was also trying not to laugh. I imagined my mother, Lady

Catherine, Miss Bingley, and a number of other nameless ladies dragging you out of a doctor's chair and fighting over who had the right to bid on you first. You must admit, it would be humorous to watch as a third party." Seeing that Darcy was not responding, she had to continue. "I felt terrible for laughing, which is why I tried so hard to hold it in. I was completely sincere when I expressed remorse for the way the people of Hertfordshire made you feel upon your initial introduction to our society. I know how uneasy Jane is whenever she meets a new group of people who initially show interest due to her beauty and then the knowledge of our lack of fortune is spread just as quickly as the rumours of the enormity of yours. It seems the people who want the limelight the least are thrust into it most often."

Not hearing any response to her admission, she continued. "May I tell you the end of my mind's accounting of the events?" Seeing him nod out of the corner of her eye, she continued. "You managed to escape while all the women tried to pounce on top of you. They ended up fighting with each other until they reached the bottom of the pile only to find your greatcoat. When they looked up, they saw you riding away into the distance with a full smile gracing your face."

She saw that Mr Darcy still made no reaction to her speech. Suddenly feeling uncomfortable again, Elizabeth tried to straighten her back to remove at least part of the connection between herself and the man who held her allowed no part of her attempt. Instead, he held her even closer, but Elizabeth felt the loss of tenderness in his embrace. She felt thankful when she saw the point they usually parted company at.

Trying once more to return the ease they felt earlier, she thanked him for the first ride which the horse obeyed its rider. Alas, she still received no response. He carefully got off the horse and put his hands around Elizabeth's waist in order to help her down as well. He quickly thanked her for the ride and left quickly and without ceremony. And he didn't even kiss her hand after he spent the better part of the morning with his arms around her.

As Mr Darcy rode away, he left Elizabeth wondering if she would find herself as alone in the morning as she found herself now. Could she regret her actions? She certainly didn't mean to laugh and almost made herself sick trying to keep it inside. But Mr Darcy opened up to her, and she betrayed that confidence. Yet she couldn't wholly blame herself. What would life be like with a man who could not laugh at himself?

Chapter 12

Darcy sat quietly with his cousin in his sitting room after all the occupants of Rosings retired for the evening. Richard had invited himself to Darcy's room after dinner, and as always, invited himself to a healthy dose of scotch.

Both gentlemen drank in silence. Every time Darcy looked up from staring into the fire, he noticed his cousin's intense gaze upon him. The Colonel likely wanted to know about the source of his mood but Darcy refused to break their silence.

"You are quiet, even more so than usual. What's on your mind?"

Darcy contemplated telling his cousin and his closest confidant of his dilemma. But he promised Elizabeth he wouldn't tell anyone of their meetings and he couldn't break that trust. He took another substantial drink of scotch, relishing in the warmth that burned his throat and stomach before it settled. He reached over and poured himself another tumbler full.

"Even if you can't relay specifics, you obviously need someone to talk to."

"There is a rather serious matter which is causing me considerable grief." He paused, trying to find the right words to continue. "Have you ever had a dream that scares you?"

Richard looked at him in surprise. Apparently talking about dreams was not the topic he anticipated. "Of course. Every man who values something fears losing it. Often my own fears and demons manifest themselves in my dreams."

"There is one recurring dream in particular which is caused me considerable anguish." With great difficulty, Darcy proceeded to tell Richard of the same dream he told Elizabeth. When he looked up from swirling the scotch in his glass after summarising the dream, he found Richard clutching his glass with both hands and letting out a hearty laugh, causing his face to colour several shades of red. Darcy felt the heat creep up on his cheeks and wondered if it matched the crimson colour of his cousin's.

"What humour do you find in my pain?"

"Darcy, you never cease to surprise me. I expected a dream that frightened you to contain no less than a scoundrel kidnapping Georgiana or an ogre that you must wrestle to maintain control of Pemberley. I certainly did not expect something as innocuous as matrons putting you on an auction block. If you find anyone that does not find that dream comical, you must do one of two things. Your first task is to check him for a pulse. If surprisingly he does have one, your second task is to cast him out of your circle because the man obviously has no personality or sense of humour. The idea of the proud and dignified master of Pemberley being inspected for fleas with magnifying glasses by the women of the ton should make anyone laugh." He watched as Richard took another large drink from his glass and commenced his laughter all over again.

"I said nothing about fleas."

Through his fits of laughter, Richard managed to spurt out, "Well in my imagination you certainly did. You should see the places that Lady Catherine wanted to have you examined. I believe she even took the time to inspect the length of the hairs on your arse!" Richard paused for a moment before finishing. "Darcy, if you miraculously find someone who manages or even tries to check his laughter for the sake of your feelings, you should make him a permanent part of your life. That person cares more about you than even I do, and I do not know of anyone who holds you in a higher regard than I do."

Darcy waited while Richard continued in a slightly less amused tone. "Darcy, I am not laughing to mock you. I like to think I am amongst your dearest friends, but clearly, even I was unaware of the extent to which your fear of a parlour extended. You cannot hold a grudge when no offence was meant. I would hate to find myself bereft of your company for the remainder of our time at Rosings because of a misunderstanding, especially one as ridiculous as this. I don't think either of us would choose to play billiards or ride with Lady Catherine if presented the opportunity."

Darcy felt more than a slight twinge at Richard's words. He would never hold a grudge longer than a few days against his closest friend. They had too much history and blood between them to throw away a friendship over this night. Still, that didn't mean he couldn't brood about it for a while. Besides, what was so wrong with veiling one's feelings or being afraid of finding himself trapped in a life with a wife completely unsuited to his desires? His fear and reaction seemed perfectly natural. Why was his cousin still laughing? He took another drink while glaring at his cousin. That was the last night he would allow his cousin to raid his selection of scotch.

Continuing to laugh, although much more softly as time progressed, Richard remarked that he couldn't believe this dream caused them both so much worry. He then asked whether Lady Catherine's rather pointed demands regarding signing the marriage contract between him and Anne brought this dream to light again. He couldn't help the snort that escaped his mouth. When his cousin smiled slightly at his response, a fleeing thought passed through his mind, but as he had other things to worry about, he pushed the tiny voice away. Before the Colonel stood to leave, Darcy listened as his cousin told him of the worries he felt as he watched Darcy experience more mood swings during the past winter and since they arrived at Rosings than in the entirety of their acquaintance.

Darcy said nothing in return; he knew his cousin was right. Elizabeth Bennet made him crazy and had ever since she stayed at Netherfield to care for her sister. A much more tempered reaction by Elizabeth seared his soul while Richard's much more vocal reaction to the same dream merely annoyed him. He put his glass down and held his head in his hands as he realised the solution. Only when he finally could express his love and receive hers in return, would he finally regain his sanity.

Until then, his extreme mood swings would likely continue. At least he knew enough of his cousin that he would be forgiven for his cross mood in the morning; Elizabeth would not be so easy to convince. He would use the next morning to clarify his reaction to Elizabeth and he would be one step closer to gaining control of his mental faculties.

As his cousin left, he poured himself another glass of scotch and continued to stare at the fire hoping that the lightly flickering flames would calm him enough to finally drift into sleep.

Chapter 13

The sunlight from his bedroom window began to peak through, causing an unwelcome interruption to Darcy's slumber. He placed the pillow that lay beside him over his head, hoping to drown out the light reaching his face. How many glasses of scotch did he have after Richard left? He sat there for most of the night trying to reconcile Richard's traitorous reaction and words. When he realised he had to meet Elizabeth in only a few more hours, he finally stumbled from his chair to the bed, not bothering to remove the remainder of his dinner attire.

Elizabeth! Darcy sat straight up in his bed. The sun was already rising, and he left her alone for their morning walk. Damn it to hell!

"Marcus! Where are you? I need to get dressed now!"

The servant hurried in, "I am sorry, sir. I did not expect you to wake for several hours."

Darcy growled to the servant who offered to help him out of bed. "Why didn't you wake me before sunrise like I asked?"

Shifting nervously from foot to foot, the valet answered with the truth. "I tried, sir. You told me to leave you alone."

"I wasn't thinking properly. From now on, if I tell you I need to be up at a certain time, make sure that I am properly awoken. Now hurry up! I need to be gone in the next ten minutes."

"I am sorry sir, but there isn't any water for a bath. I should be able to at least have you shaved and dressed properly though. There is some water in the basin if you wish to wash your face and hands while I retrieve your clothing."

Elizabeth would never forgive him. He needed to see her and he needed to see her quickly.

"Just get on with it. Also, have one of the footmen get my horse ready. I need him to be saddled and by the front door by the time I am ready."

"Yes, sir. I will return in a moment."

Darcy splashed water on his face and looked up to face his tired reflection in the mirror. After how he left

Elizabeth yesterday, he knew she would believe he deserted her. How was he ever going to explain himself?

***

He recognised that stance. It was the same he saw the first time he approached her by the pond. This did not bode well for Elizabeth's mood. Darcy took a deep breath, dismounted from Erebes, and walked tentatively to the lady's side. He knew she must have heard him, but she chose not to face him.

"Miss Elizabeth, please forgive me. I overslept this morning. As soon as I realised the time, I dressed and rode Erebes through the woods trying to find you. I thought you might be here."

She turned slightly but did not face him. Finally, she answered icily, "You made a fortunate guess. If you will please excuse me, I need to return to the parsonage as the weather may not cooperate much longer with outdoor activity." She turned completely away from him again.

He moved to step in front of her. He wasn't going to let her shut him out of her life. He was hurt, but he wasn't about to lose her because of it. He made a mistake, but so did she. She couldn't just discard him as if he were a toy that lost its ability to amuse her. He worked too hard and came too close yesterday to getting what he wanted. She wanted to understand him and walking away without discussing their problems certainly wasn't going to help her. He already made that mistake once; well actually twice if he counted his miserable proposal.

Maybe he should harness the same strength she did when intimidated; he needed to say what she least expected him to. To do that, he needed to temper the frustration he felt when he opened his mouth to speak to her again. "You can ride Erebes. It will certainly take us less time to return if we ride horseback."

Obviously realising the hidden aspects of the offer, Elizabeth's eyes flashed in anger as she glared menacingly at him. "I assure you I am capable of walking back. Please be assured I won't keep you from riding Erebes to Rosings so you are able to return before it begins to rain."

That idea certainly backfired. The glare from her eyes was worse than when he first arrived. He remembered that same look in her eyes; it was an exact replica of when they last sat in the parsonage together. That was a scene he did not want repeated for anything. He had come so far in the last week, he couldn't lose it all. Darcy knew he needed to tread very carefully, but he certainly wasn't about to retreat. He promised himself when they began this endeavour that he would not fail.

He took a deep breath and spoke again, "I would prefer to escort you back if you will permit me."

"I have no cause to prevent you from walking where you choose while on your aunt's property." Elizabeth turned and began to walk determinedly on the same path they always used to arrive at the pond. Darcy watched for a moment as she turned her head in his direction, sent him a scathing look, and continued walking. He was determined not to let her get away from him. Even if she didn't mean that look as an invitation, he meant to take it as one. He hurried to return to her side, knowing full well she likely did not want his company.

"I believe you still have three questions left to ask me. As neither of us is in a mood for idle conversation, the answer to one of your questions might be used to pass the time."

Elizabeth stopped her purposeful stride, looked him straight in the eye and arched one eyebrow. If he thought walking for a few minutes might help her anger to subside, he was sadly mistaken.

"I want to know why."

No further clarification was offered or required; he understood her meaning perfectly well.

"Because I was hurt and didn't know how to respond to your laughter. You were laughing at one of my greatest fears. I opened up my heart to you and your reaction felt like a knife cut sliced it open."

Elizabeth's face softened slightly from the anger that covered it. "I am sorry that I laughed. I truly am. I told you that when it happened. I wasn't laughing at your pain. I had a difficult time forcing the thought of you being inspected by the ladies of the ton out of my head."

"I suppose the thought of the Master of Pemberley being inspected for fleas may be humorous to some. At least that was what Richard told me last night when I revealed my dream to him."

She spoke quickly. "And what was his reaction?"

"He didn't even try to withhold his laughter as you did. Apparently, I do not take anyone laughing at my attempts to hold on to what I value most. He also said I should not let a misunderstanding harm a relationship that was very important to me. He also told me that anyone who would try to temper their laughter to spare my feelings must care for me a great deal."

He watched as the softening of her countenance reversed when she spoke again. "So it is acceptable for him to laugh, but not for me?"

Why wasn't she listening to him?

"I am not pouring my heart out trying to win Richard's love or affection. I know where we stand. I know that he will be by my side through whatever trouble I encounter. No matter how much I wish it, I cannot say the same for my relationship with you."

He took several deep breaths before continuing, trying to find some patience hidden somewhere deep inside. He tried a different tactic. "I want you to think about something. How would you feel if you told your sister a dream about your forced marriage to a man like Mr Collins? Would you forgive Miss Bennet for laughing at the absurdities that you must endure for your entire life? For I can assure that I find no pleasure in the thought of you married to that man."

"That is a ridiculous question. Jane and I teased each other about what a horrible match he might be. She would have helped me to see the absurdity of it myself."

"Very well, pretend that you dreamt that you had to fetch help for your mother and that the only way to reach a doctor in time was on horseback. Oh, and add to the vision, it was midnight with no moon and you must race through an unfamiliar forest. How would you feel, after relaying this terrifying ordeal, if your sister laughed at you since she has no fear of riding horseback?"

Elizabeth shot back at him with a vengeance. "Jane would never laugh at that."

"And why would she not?"

"Because she loves me and she could not hurt someone she loved."

He couldn't help the sharp intake of breath when he understood what she said. Elizabeth didn't love him. To hear her say what thoughts plagued him for the last week was more painful than he imagined. He hoped that after he opened up to her, it would change her mind. But she proved through her laughter that his honesty did not bring him her love.

He needed to get away; his heart was pounding too hard in his chest. A wave of nausea swept over him. It hurt too much to stay. He gazed deeply into her eyes for what he feared might be the last time.

But before he walked away, he felt a hand firmly grab his arm and Elizabeth's stern voice berating his behaviour. "Why do you always walk away? Why do you never stay to finish what you start?" He couldn't answer her; he couldn't even look at her. Honesty at this point was simply too difficult. He needed to get away. He jerked his arm away from her grasp.

After he walked several paces away from her, he heard her ask him a final question in a frightened voice. "Is this the last time I will ever see you?"

He turned to face her. When he saw her bottom lip quiver as her hands clenched in solid fists, he did not understand what she wanted from him. In seeming defeat, he answered in the same quiet voice that she used, "I don't know if I can. You will know my answer in the morning." He had nothing else to give.

Chapter 14

"Darcy, you have been entirely too quiet today. I am sure I know what the problem is. You need to spend some more time outdoors. The rain today forced you to cut short your exercise routine." The gentleman could bring himself to do nothing but nod in response to his Aunt's inquiry. He had not the energy to disagree with her or anyone else that day. His aunt continued. "I know just how to improve your mood tomorrow. You will take Anne in her phaeton first thing tomorrow morning. I am sure the both of you will need the fresh air after being inside all day today."

He didn't know how much she knew, but she knew enough to know he had other plans for the morning. He needed to somehow excuse himself from the task but had no idea how without raising more suspicion. Darcy certainly didn't need to be left alone with Anne; he had no idea how Lady Catherine planned for their time alone to end. But, he was fairly sure it would be with a forced marriage proposal.

He had to meet with Elizabeth in the morning. They needed to sit by the pond and stay there until every possible misunderstanding between them was clarified. There would be no more miscommunications. Tomorrow, they would leave the woods together and in peace.

"I would be privileged to do so later in the afternoon, but I feel I will need to give Erebes some additional exercise tomorrow morning, as I had to shorten my ride today."

"Nonsense Darcy, your horse received plenty of exercises yesterday and earlier in the week. You had plenty of time during your morning excursions. What else could have occupied your time besides riding around the countryside?" Darcy eyed his Aunt; she definitely knew. "Besides, the weather may not permit Anne to leave the house tomorrow afternoon so it must be done tomorrow morning at sunrise." She looked her nephew straight in the eye. "I insist."

Lady Catherine had eyes just like his mothers, yet they held such different expressions. While his mother's held laughter and love, her sister's were filled with contempt. And she trapped him rather neatly into complying with her wishes. No matter what, he couldn't be left alone with Anne for an entire morning; he knew his aunt was desperate. He looked to his female cousin, curious to see her reaction to her mother's insistence.

"Darcy, I know how much exercise and care Erebes requires. Perhaps you could ride alongside Richard and me in the phaeton? The three of us used to have such fun when we were younger." Anne looked pointedly at Colonel Fitzwilliam, who answered quickly.

"Anne, that sounds like a wonderful idea. I would be pleased to drive you tomorrow morning while Darcy rides alongside of us." Turning to Darcy, Richard looked at him with equal meaning.

"Lady Catherine, since Fitzwilliam agreed to escort our cousin in my place, I will be able to meet with them after breakfast."

Obviously not appreciating the direction of the conversation, Lady Catherine directed her most authoritative voice at her nephew, snapping him out of his thoughts. Her anger was obviously about to boil over. "Darcy, unless you give me your reason why you cannot spend the morning with your cousins, you will be there alongside them for their entire ride. You will leave at sunrise." Without allowing anyone else to respond, she rose from her chair, glowered at both of her nephews with disdain, and retired for the night.

Chapter 15

The three cousins arrived in the foyer as planned; Darcy purposely waited to hear Anne leave her room before he left his. He looked around the entranceway and saw no less than four footmen and the butler all taking careful note of the three cousins' movements.

They looked at the marked discomfort of the others; at least Richard and Anne felt as uneasy as he did with their situation. He might have to make a concerted effort to pass on his foul mood if one of them appeared pleased with their forced togetherness. But as none of the three retained a choice in their activity, he led the other two outside. The sooner it began, the sooner the charade could end.

Richard looked up at the sky, "It looks like Lady Catherine's forecast regarding the weather was correct. If we didn't ride this morning, we may not get the opportunity later in the day." He then helped Anne into the black phaeton and entered on the opposite side. "Are you ready, Darcy?"

Darcy looked behind him as the sound of more than a few horses trotted up to the house. He watched as four groomsmen rode up beside the phaeton. Apparently, his aunt wanted to ensure he could find no way to see Elizabeth that morning. He knew he would be followed if he tried to take off and leave his cousins behind. What would Elizabeth think after the answer that he gave her when they last spoke? She would believe he never wanted to see her again.

Darcy mounted his horse, nodded, and the three began their forced activity on the road between the parsonage and Rosings. He should be riding into the woods right now to meet Elizabeth instead of alongside his cousins. He strained his eyes to see if he could make out her position in the woods. He wanted to know if she was waiting for him.

What would she do if she saw him with Anne instead of spending the morning with her? Would she be jealous? Would she be hurt? Would she even care? Would she recognise that he had no choice unless he exposed their pre-arranged meeting? Would she leap to an ill-formed conclusion? As the phaeton was not suited for driving along the same wooded paths designed for people and lone horses, he was thankful he needn't worry about the questions for long. As soon as he passed the parsonage, the chances for Elizabeth to spy him decreased exponentially.

"Darcy!"

He turned his head to glare at the Colonel. "Fitzwilliam, you don't need to yell."

Darcy watched as Richard's smug grin graced his face before answering. "Then perhaps you can tell me what I just asked you."

Darcy refused to be a source of amusement for his cousin. He was in no mood to be Richard's dancing monkey. In a cold tone, he responded, "Please repeat the question."

"I asked when you plan to return to Pemberley."

"My plans at the moment are not fixed." Darcy ended the conversation in the most efficient means he knew how; he urged Erebes to gallop enough ahead of the phaeton to make conversation almost impossible. He heard an occasional laugh from Richard or an exclamation from Anne but felt no need to be part of or pay attention to their merriment. Just because they changed their minds and chose to make good use of time away from Lady Catherine did not mean that he would pretend to be equally pleased. Maybe he did need to do something to temper their pleasure.

"Darcy!" Richard waited for Darcy to turn his head in acknowledgement. "I think we better turn back, the rain might start sooner than we thought."

Finally, his cousin chose to speak some words of sense. They definitely needed to end this mockery of an outing. Darcy pulled on the reins and indicated for Erebes to turn around. In his hurry to return to Rosings, he momentarily forgot that he needed to pass by the parsonage to return to Rosings. And in perfect concert with his luck of the past twenty-four hours, he remembered that particular problem just in time to see Elizabeth emerging from the woods.

Anne changed the focus of his attention as she exclaimed loud enough for everyone to hear, "Look, Richard, there is Miss Elizabeth. She is certainly out very early for a walk."

Without interrupting their conversation, Darcy heard Richard's response. "I remember her telling me she always started her day with an early morning ramble when possible. It seems not even dark clouds can dissuade her from her walk."

"I would like to speak to her for a moment. Do you think we can stop? The rain should wait until we return to Rosings."

Richard looked at his male cousin, still riding by their side. "Darcy, we are going to wait here for a moment. Anne wants to speak to Miss Elizabeth. You don't mind, do you?"

Darcy's nightmare situation just materialised. All the questions he managed to suppress now confronted him. He saw Elizabeth acknowledge Anne's wave and approach the phaeton parked near the gate to the parsonage. If only his original plan for the morning worked out; he could be trying to convince Elizabeth of his contrition for his behaviour over the past few days. Now, not only did not have a moment to speak with her, he needed to silently communicate why he couldn't meet her but could find time to spend with the woman who Lady Catherine wanted him to marry.

He noticed several pieces of her hair flowing around her shoulders, just as he loved it. Not only did she take his breath away, her distinctly rigid manner of walking betrayed her desire to strangle him if given the chance. As she grew closer, his attention strayed from the curls on her head to her face. Even from this distance, he could see the puffiness in her eyes and the redness colouring her cheeks and neck. She looked like she spent the morning crying. He could do nothing but try to ignore her dishevelled appearance. Could he be tasked with a more impossible assignment when he was undoubtedly at fault? Maybe it meant that she cared for him? No, that was too much to hope for. Now his sudden appearance likely only exacerbated his cause to gain her forgiveness one day.

He watched as she carefully avoided eye contact with any of the three. Finally, she cleared her throat and addressed the Fitzwilliam cousins. "Good morning Miss de Bourgh, Colonel Fitzwilliam, Mr Darcy." Did he imagine it or did she seem especially pained just having to mention his name? "I see you are taking advantage of the reprieve of rain to enjoy some fresh air as well. I was just returning to the parsonage for fear the rain might begin any moment."

As Anne initiated the contact, she took the privilege of answering from Darcy or Richard. "We were returning for the same reason. Before you return inside, I want to invite the members of the parsonage to tea after the service tomorrow. I hoped to extend the invitation to Mrs Collins personally, but I fear the weather may keep us from calling on you this afternoon."

Darcy looked at the strain on Elizabeth's face; he knew she didn't want to attend. He also knew she had no choice but to accept. Soon, he heard her accept on her party's behalf as she knew of no prior engagements. She thanked Anne for the invitation and begged them to return to Rosings as Lady Catherine would never forgive her for making them travel in the rain.

As soon as his cousin urged the horse pulling the phaeton to continue, he watched as Elizabeth hurried for the parsonage door, seemingly eager to escape his notice. If only she looked behind her, he might show her some sign to display his remorse for not keeping their appointment. Seeing her quickly shut the door behind her, he urged Erebes to catch the phaeton and continued back to Rosings, just in time to beat the thunderstorm.

Instead of joining his cousins for breakfast with Lady Catherine, Darcy excused himself, citing a letter of business which needed his immediate attention. He shut the door to his sitting room and told Marcus he was not to be disturbed. He sat in the chair behind the large desk, looking out the window, unsure of what he expected to find. After some time of seeing nothing of interest, he swore he saw staring back at him with a slight reflection the wounded expression on Elizabeth's face.

He would never do anything to purposely hurt her. How could he? How could she think him capable of injuring her? He loved her with everything in his being. He was hurt when he left her the previous two mornings. She had to understand that. At the time, the pain that she didn't love him was just too difficult to manage. But he wouldn't purposefully hurt her.

And then he remembered. He already hurt her and willingly did so again. As long as he remained undecided regarding Bingley and her sister's situation, he put his own happiness above Elizabeth's. How could he possibly accuse Miss Bennet of not feeling something for his friend because she did not make her feelings openly known? He never felt more hypocritical than at that time.

He realised he had to tell his friend the entire truth as soon as he returned to town. Even if it meant seeing Elizabeth happily married to someone else when they became godparents to the Bingley's children, he could not trade his own comfort for the happiness of her beloved sister. Darcy didn't know if Bingley would forgive him for the transgression, but it no longer mattered. He saw the grief that his actions already caused the woman he loved. If he had within his power to remedy any of the offences, she rightfully held against him, he must do it, no matter the personal cost to himself.

He ran his both his hands through his hair, pulling at the tips in frustration. He had to see her but knew it to be impossible. He must wait until tomorrow. Even though he knew it was hopeless for her to meet him before church services, he would still go to their spot to wait, just in case. How could she forgive him for not being there a third time?

Chapter 16

Darcy ensured Marcus knew he needed to awaken by sunrise no matter what time Lady Catherine wanted to leave for services. He demanded that he dress for church, knowing full well the inappropriateness of his clothing choice for an early morning walk in the wood, especially since the rain lasted the entire day before soaked the ground. But clothing or mud was the last problem on his mind. He needed to know he could stay there as long as possible to wait for her, just in case she decided to join him. Her pained expression and redness of her eyes haunted him; he saw them every time he closed his eyes. He caused that pain. He must find a way to remedy the hurtfulness of his actions.

He quietly opened his door and sneaked down the hallway, similar to the method he used as a child to escape Lady Catherine's tirades. He needed to remember to thank Marcus for hurrying that morning; his aunt's servants wouldn't be up for some time. He quickly glanced around the foyer, checking to see if anyone was already awake; his initial scan revealed no one else's presence. He reached the front door, but before he had a chance to open it, he heard the butler call his name from the shadows behind the staircase.

The butler eyed him with obvious suspicion. "Mr Darcy, is there anything that you require?"

He didn't even try to temper his curt reply, "I'm fine." Why should he have to report his actions to the butler?

Before he could hurry through the door, he heard the butler replied, "I only ask sir because Lady Catherine asked if one of the grooms might accompany you on your morning exercise. She is very concerned for your welfare."

"I am sure she is. A groom will not be necessary. I will speak to Lady Catherine at breakfast. That will be all." He exited through the door before the butler could say anything else. He needed to get out of there quickly before any of the grooms could follow him. That was the last thing he needed if Elizabeth did decide to meet him. He went to the stables and saddled Erebes himself.

Darcy rode around the countryside for some time to make sure that no one followed him. Finally, he took an alternate route to their usual meeting place. The gentleman arrived a little past sunrise but knew it wasn't long enough for Elizabeth to leave without his notice. But he already made his plans for the morning; he would wait. And wait he did. Unfortunately, his only company other than Erebes proved to be several squirrels that ran by him, throwing angry glances at him as they scurried by. What was their problem? He sighed in disgust with himself; he certainly couldn't blame his current predicament on the furry rodents. His mess was of his own making and only he could clean it up.

After observing the sun make its way entirely too quickly across the sky, he checked his pocket watch that now held memories of both his mother and Elizabeth and knew he had to return to Rosings for breakfast. He didn't need the added ire of Lady Catherine if he also missed the family breakfast. If only Elizabeth agreed to meet him, he could explain his actions. He might even be able to relieve her distress from the morning before, and well, the morning before that. But the day wasn't over. Anne invited her to tea after services, but he needed a chance to explain himself before then. He couldn't make her face Lady Catherine without knowing she had his full support. The butler's warning this morning gave him plenty of forewarning as to his aunt's mood. Maybe he could arrange to speak to her for a few moments at church. He needed to try again.

Breakfast proved to be as strained an affair as he imagined. Anne and Richard seemed determined to avoid talking or having any interaction with anyone else at the table that wasn't absolutely necessary. Lady Catherine moved past mere insinuations of a union between him and her daughter. As much as he tried, he could not dissuade her from her continual pestering. For once, Anne seemed as determined as he to change the course of the conversation. Maybe she didn't want to marry him either. That would certainly simplify his life. But his current streak of luck didn't lead him to believe that would happen. For now, he would concentrate on his role and hope he could continue eating enough food to disallow Lady Catherine from speaking to him.

By the time the members of Rosings departed for the church, Darcy recognised the lateness of their arrival. He lost yet another opportunity to contact Elizabeth or convey some silent message. Knowing Mr Collins would never start until she arrived, he watched as Lady Catherine took her time, making an entrance befitting Mr Collins' enthusiastic greeting he was sure was coming. How could he chastise Elizabeth's family when Lady Catherine was an integral part of his?

Darcy followed the rest of his family down the aisle of the small church. All the members of the church, except the one he wanted to face him, turned around to look at the late arrivals. Unfortunately, Mr Collins did not follow Elizabeth's example by avoiding his gaze. He watched as the clergyman broke from talking to several members at the front of the church to barrel down the aisle to greet his party.

With a bow worthy of greeting the king, the clergyman addressed the group. "Lady Catherine, Miss De Bourgh, Mr Darcy, Colonel Fitzwilliam, it is such an honour to have you grace our humble establishment. I know that I speak for all my parishioners when I say your presence serves to magnify the importance and significance of my sermons."

"Mr Collins, I believe it is very important to show the people under my guidance the importance of following the morality imposed by the church. It teaches them to properly follow the words and teachings of those appointed over them."

He stood straighter and squared his shoulders even more as his aunt glared at him. If only she knew he considered Elizabeth far above her, despite their differences in fortune. His aunt could definitely take a few lessons from the woman he loved how to treat others. But now was not the time for that talk. In fact, he just needed to make it twenty-four more hours before he could wait another year before seeing the lady.

As he remembered Elizabeth's reproofs, he nodded in recognition to Mr Collins and even attempted a polite smile. It proved an unfortunate mistake, for it gave the parson entirely too much encouragement. The additional greeting he received in return was worse than the ones he usually heard in the parlour of Rosings. He couldn't even stand to listen to the inane words uttered; he only cared about one person right now and it certainly wasn't Mr Collins. He promised himself that he would do better when he finally had Elizabeth beside him.

When he finally walked past her pew, he hoped to catch her eye, but she refused to turn from staring at the empty pulpit. He looked over his shoulder and noticed the lady's eyes and cheeks still seemed an unnaturally red colour. More strands than normal fell around her shoulders. Apparently, her hair fit her mood, uncontrollable and frustrating. But that was exactly the way he loved her curly locks. If only he could be the one to offer her comfort and relieve the distress.

He watched intently as Elizabeth remained with her emerald eyes locked on her cousin the entire service no matter how many times he turned his head, hoping to make eye contact with her. He knew she was avoiding him; the only times her attention remained focused on her cousin was out of amusement and there was certainly nothing amusing about whatever topic his sermon centred on this morning. He needed to talk to her; if only her idiotic cousin would finish the sermon which, after glancing around the room, no one seemed to pay any attention to anyway.

Finally! Mr Collins said the concluding prayer signalling the imminence of their departure. Why couldn't his aunt slow down! He hurried more than he wanted to as Lady Catherine walked out after the conclusion of the sermon with a much greater sense of urgency than she arrived with. Mrs Collins politely, but awkwardly due to the speed with which his aunt tried to depart, stopped Lady Catherine to thank her for Anne's kind invitation to tea that afternoon.

Elizabeth certainly didn't seem excited at the prospect; she stood cautiously behind her friend's back. He had never known her to hide from a confrontation before. Instead of catching his eye, she seemed completely focused on a tree in the background, over his cousin's shoulder. After everything that happened this week, it seemed she finally had enough. Tomorrow, he would take her away from all this.

Lady Catherine's voice brought him out of his thoughts of Elizabeth. "Mrs Collins, I am sure that Anne felt compelled to make the invitation as it was only proper as your guests will finally be departing after their prolonged visit."

He watched Elizabeth as Mrs Collins answered. "Your daughter has always been very kind to us, Lady Catherine. I am sure Miss Elizabeth and Maria are very grateful to be able to spend one last afternoon in the company of your family."

His aunt spoke in a tone which left no one, except possibly Mr Collins, to doubt her meaning. "As it is the last afternoon that your friend will ever see any member of my family, I will look forward to bidding them farewell this afternoon."

After taking a deep breath, Mrs Collins tactfully answered, "We look forward to seeing you shortly Lady Catherine."

Lady Catherine turned to her family and demanded their immediate departure, under the guise of making the most of their limited time together. After their breakfast that morning, he couldn't imagine wanting to spend any more time in the same room. As he could not help it, back to Rosings they would go.

***

Elizabeth finally moved her intense gaze from the distant tree to watch the Fitzwilliam family depart, wondering if there was any way that she could possibly avoid meeting them for tea. Lady Catherine was the last person she wanted to face. Well, almost the last person. A certain nephew of hers currently held the revered spot of the last person she wanted to talk to.

At least she managed to avoid eye contact with the gentleman she desperately wanted to avoid; she couldn't bear to see his disdain and hatred. His refusal to meet her yesterday proved that she permanently lost his good opinion. She didn't need further proof through seeing a lack of affection in his eyes. Besides, if she looked into them, she may cry from knowing she would never see their flash again.

After the members of the congregation all departed, the inhabitants of the parsonage made their way to Rosings. As Mr Collins spoke enough for the entire group, Elizabeth felt it unnecessary to contribute beyond the occasional head nod or agreement to whatever absurd comment he mentioned next. If she heard about the cost of the hideous fireplace one more time, she might scream! She doubted that Charlotte would forgive her for that particular transgression. She touched her temples lightly with her fingers. Thankfully Charlotte didn't seem to notice as she was preoccupied with Maria's questions about living so close to Lady Catherine. It was a good thing she didn't ask Elizabeth's opinion; she doubted she could select a diplomatic answer to the question.

When they arrived for their final visit to Rosings, Mr Collins led them into the parlour where Lady Catherine and her family waited, making sure to take the opportunity one last time to point out several particularly ostentatious, and rather hideous, ornaments in the entryway and hallway. As she saw Lady Catherine's intense gaze focused on her, she tried to hide slightly behind her friend; this was not the time to challenge the older woman. She just needed to survive the tea. Her emotions were still too raw to face Mr Darcy's aunt. Almost too afraid to even look at the other members of the party, Elizabeth immediately focused on Colonel Fitzwilliam and took a seat next to him.

After they exchanged their usual pleasantries which she gallantly soldiered through, the Colonel commented: "You must be anxiously anticipating your return to town and Hertfordshire, Miss Bennet. Have you ever been away from Longbourn for such a lengthy time?"

"My elder sister and I often visit our aunt and uncle in town for several months at a time. But I confess that I have never been away from Jane for such a long period. She spent the winter with our aunt and uncle while I remained at Longbourn. Sisters shouldn't be separated for such lengthy periods."

At the mention of her sister's name, Mr Darcy interrupted her private conversation with the Colonel. "I believe Mr Bingley will be most anxious to see your sister. I will be sure to relay her location as soon as I return to town. It is unfortunate they missed seeing one another this winter. I hope that problem is soon remedied to everyone's satisfaction."

She felt the teacup almost fall out of her hands. It was fortunate that she already drank most of its contents. Of all the subjects she expected to hear while at Rosings, Mr Darcy's agreement to reunite her sister with Mr Bingley never entered her mind. After being rejected yesterday, she felt sure that he would never make amends. After all, without using her good opinion to coerce his decision, she gave up hope.

She looked up at Darcy with a tentative and confused smile that even with its timidity, she knew reflected a complete change her entire demeanour. Its recipient returned her glance, even allowing a slight display of his dimple, something she could not remember ever seeing in the parlour of Rosings. And those eyes, they made her want to melt into his arms.

But as quickly as her smile appeared, it vanished when she remembered that she lost the respect and friendship of the handsome gentleman behind her. Why did he smile at her after she already lost his good opinion? Why did he look at her like that as though they were walking alone in the woods again? Was reuniting Jane with Mr Bingley a consolation prize for completely giving up on her?

She didn't return the same emotions that he claimed to feel for her, or at least to the extent that he felt for her, but she certainly felt something for him. She didn't know if it was love that she felt, but she felt a large amount of respect and admiration for the gentleman. Her dreams over the past week proved that respect and admiration weren't the only feelings he inspired in her. Besides, the veracity of the tears she shed the day before as she waited for him in the wood proved that her emotions certainly changed from the same time the week before.

Certainly, he had his flaws, but who did not? Could she claim perfection? She learned enough over the past week to know that claim to be impossible. She was as stubborn and foolish as he! But despite his pleas, that did not guarantee their marital happiness, not that it mattered anymore for his good opinion was lost to her for all eternity. When she gained the courage to look at him again, his pained expression conveyed enough. That was the proof she needed. The thought of having to see her in town caused him to grimace.

The next comment that Elizabeth heard startled her from continuing with her thoughts. Miss de Bourgh did something she had never done during any of their visits; she led the conversation in a voice louder than Elizabeth ever heard her use. The young lady remarked to the group at large how much she enjoyed her morning ride on the day prior. "My mother was kind enough to suggest that the three of us enjoy the fresh air before adverse weather conditions kept us inside for the remainder of the day."

Lady Catherine interrupted her daughter to address Elizabeth. "I am very aware of everything that goes on at Rosings. I always do what is needed to ensure the continued welfare of my family."

If Elizabeth doubted Lady Catherine's knowledge of her relationship with Darcy before, she no longer did. She dreaded what humiliation Lady Catherine had in store for her. At least she could rely on the fact that the lady would never expose her former relationship with Mr Darcy; it would mean the end of her hopes to unite her own daughter and nephew. But her interference with Lady Catherine's plans no longer existed. She wondered when and if the gentleman would ever let his aunt know. Now that she no longer prevented Lady Catherine's plans, would Mr Darcy marry his cousin?

Before she could form a coherent thought to the one looming in her mind, Anne addressed her. "Miss Elizabeth, wasn't my mother most attentive to our needs by making sure I spent time with my cousins?"

"Yes, your mother is most attentive." Wonderful, Elizabeth thought. Now she must endure chastisement from both mother and daughter. How could she deal with another hour of this torture?

"Darcy preferred to ride on his own yesterday morning, but mother wouldn't hear of it; she absolutely insisted that we ride together at sunrise. I think he would have been much better off being allowed to ride where he wished as he held a fearsome mood for the rest of the day. Perhaps whatever he might have found during his morning exercise would have soothed his temper if he was not absolutely forced to ride with Colonel Fitzwilliam and me."

Elizabeth eyed Mr Darcy's female cousin suspiciously. Could she know too? If Anne did, why would she try to explain his reason for not meeting her? Obviously, Miss de Bourgh didn't know everything. If only she knew that Mr Darcy no longer wanted her, the daughter of Lady Catherine would have no reason to provide that explanation. But what if Mr Darcy didn't hate her? What if he tried to meet her and Anne was trying to let her know what happened?

This simply did not make any sense! She further examined the young woman's face and saw an absence of malice; the woman seemed sincere in her remarks. There must be another explanation. But the only one that came to mind was that Anne wasn't trying to hurt her; she was trying to convey Mr Darcy's reason for missing their morning meeting. Elizabeth felt utterly confused. She already spent the greater part of two days crying and cursing the man behind her, whose face she wasn't sure she wanted to see. She did not need any more reasons to add to her confusion about him. As such, the only words she could muster implied that exercise in the morning always helped her mood throughout the day.

Anne opened her mouth to speak, but the menacing voice Elizabeth heard belonged to the girl's mother. "Miss Bennet, I believe you were observed walking unescorted yesterday."

She thought she escaped Lady Catherine's wrath; apparently, she didn't.

"I often walk unescorted in the morning, Lady Catherine."

The great lady stared at her without blinking for what felt like an eternity before the mistress of Rosings Park finally spoke in a tone that bordered on cruelty. "I don't approve of young women traipsing around the countryside unescorted. I would never allow Anne to do such a thing. Who would want to align themselves with a girl whose only recommendation is that she is an excellent walker? No decent gentleman will marry you if you cannot curb your wild behaviour and your shocking attitude toward respect for one's superiors. It is obvious you still need considerable guidance before you are ready to join a proper society."

Elizabeth felt her cheeks immediately flush and her chest constricts beyond anything she previously knew. Lady Catherine vocalised the same thoughts she had only the day before when Mr Darcy failed to show for their meeting. Her mind immediately raced back to yesterdays' solitary walk. As she walked alone in silence, she knew he decided he could not tolerate a woman who could not check her tongue and behaviour; she pushed him too far. Only with that admission did she forgive the man who inhabited her dreams for his quiet and pained withdrawal, for in truth he did nothing to need her forgiveness other than leaving abruptly. And if placed in the same situation, could she claim to have stayed to see through to the conclusion of their problems and misunderstandings? If she told him of her fears relating to a life with Mr Collins and he laughed at the absurdities she must endure, would she have stayed as long as he did after her laughter? Undoubtedly, she admitted the answer was no. She would have spat out several harsh words to pain him and left without allowing him a chance to explain. But when he acted even better than she, she chastised his behaviour and pushed him further.

She recalled that after her revelation at the end of her walk, Elizabeth found the same piece of moss on which she read his letter only a week before, sat down on it once again, and cried. She lost the chance to understand how she could so egregiously misjudge gentlemen that she met. Would her heart ever find what it longed for? She longed to find a gentleman who would open his heart and life to her. But when Mr Darcy opened his soul, she betrayed him. The formidable man who searched so long for someone to share his troubles and provide him comfort saw the woman he loved laugh when confronted with his fears. She then allowed her own hurt at his dismissal to colour their next meeting. How could he forgive her?

Now, only one day later she felt as though she reinjured a wound that had not even begun to heal. Faced with hearing the same revelation she internalised only the day before and knowing she could not prevent the tears from once again forming in her eyes, she excused herself from the chair and walked to the window where Mr Darcy usually stood. She would never see the flash of his dimples or feel the warmth and security of his arms around her. She would never feel the strength of his chest supporting her. He would never discuss his favourite book with her while passing the time on a rainy Sunday afternoon. She would never feel the safety that his mere presence provided. She had no one to blame but herself and the thought made the tears flow down her cheeks. She lifted her hand to wipe away their moisture, hoping that no one would speak to her;

she could not rely on her voice or anybody part to properly function.

She glanced up from the window just in time to see Mr Darcy's face turn a shade of red she hadn't thought possible. She saw Colonel Fitzwilliam forcefully grab his arm and whisper something quietly to his taller cousin. As she watched, Mr Darcy's face calmed slightly. What did the Colonel say to him? Well, it didn't matter. She lost his good opinion even if he was enough of a gentleman to defend her honour. For now, she needed to discover a way to make it through the rest of this miserable tea without fleeing the room; an option that looked more tempting as the afternoon progressed.

***

Darcy watched as Elizabeth turned back toward the window. He tried to control his temper as he made an attempt to consider his cousin's advice. If Richard hadn't spoken, he might've chosen to cut ties with his aunt right then, but that certainly was not going to help Elizabeth at this moment. He wasn't sure at what point his entire family learned his personal affair, but he recognised the soundness of Richard's advice, even if it went against his every instinct. She needed his support, but she needed to keep her dignity in the process. He had to do something. He noticed that Lady Catherine made a point to direct her next question to Mrs Collins to deny Elizabeth any support from her family or friend. At least his cousin couldn't stop him from providing the woman he loved with at least some comfort.

He walked to the same window where Elizabeth stood and watched as her shoulders moved significantly with every laboured breath. He saw the tears stream down his beloved's face as she looked into the same woods that each held so dear. Knowing every eye in the room focused on their backs, he had to restrain his hands from moving to her shoulders and drawing her close to him to offer her his strength. Instead, he spoke slowly, in a voice only she could hear. "To me, you are perfect." Seeing her bite her bottom lip as confirmation that she heard him, he waited until the depths of her breaths eased and the tears stopped flowing before he left the window and returned to where Mr Collins stood.

Making sure that Mr Collins felt the full effect of his height, importance, and fury when he finally spoke, Darcy looked down at the little, scared man in front of him. "Mr Collins, I believe Miss Elizabeth is not feeling well. She would benefit from returning to the parsonage at this time. Please use my carriage as walking might further exhaust her."

Seemingly not yet satisfied that she inflicted enough pain, his aunt continued with her tirade and had the audacity to address him. "Darcy, you are certainly very considerate to concern yourself with the health of my parson's poor relation. Since Miss Elizabeth is feeling so poorly, I would hate for her to further exert herself by travelling tomorrow. She will stay with Mrs Collins and take the post later in the week. You have no need to delay your travel plans to meet the needs of someone so wholly unconnected to you."

The Colonel grabbed Darcy's arm and interrupted him before he responded. "Miss Bennet's distress is obviously due to the loss of her sister's company. The sooner they are reunited, the sooner she will feel better. As gentlemen, it will be our privilege to be of assistance to a gentleman's daughter. She and Miss Lucas will return with us tomorrow as planned."

Richard changed his position to stand between Darcy and their aunt.

"Darcy, don't you have some preparations to make for our journey tomorrow? I am sure that everyone will excuse you from tea to take care of any details which are sure to keep you occupied until we leave early tomorrow morning."

Darcy wondered if his cousin would actually stop him from attacking their aunt. Certainly, Mr Collins couldn't stop him. The pitiful man looked like he might faint as he alternated looking between Darcy, his cousin and his aunt. He wasn't given much chance to decide.

As Mr Collins looked up to the two men who would allow no opposition, he answered quickly in a shaky voice. "Mr Darcy, Colonel Fitzwilliam, once again you are incredibly thoughtful to show such consideration for my poor cousin."

Oh yes, removing Mr Collins from his view would barely take any trouble. The poor man may even run away before the confrontation even truly started. Would he take the time to continue their battle? No, the pitiful man would soon have no hold over the woman he loved.

Before anyone else in the room could say or do anything else, Mrs Collins excused herself from Lady Catherine's side, walked to the window, retrieved her friend, persuaded her husband and sister to walk very quickly out the door and wait for Mr Darcy's carriage to take them back to the parsonage. Satisfied that Elizabeth would be taken care of by Mrs Collins, he felt that she would not need his protection in the next few hours. But once she left the parsonage tomorrow, he vowed that no matter what, she would be in his care. They would work out everything that needed to be before he allowed her out of his care.

Chapter 17

He heard his cousin's booming voice from the bottom of the stairs. "Darcy, are you ready to go? Your man already went to the parsonage to let them know of our arrival in a few minutes."

Fitzwilliam Darcy curtly nodded his head to his cousin who stood at the grand entrance in confirmation he was more than ready to leave. He walked out with his cousin to see his Aunt, standing there, ready to pounce on him one final time. With a paler complexion than she seemed to possess earlier in the week, Anne cowered slightly behind his aunt looking more upset than usual at his departure. Was he mistaken in his belief she no longer desired a union with him? For her sake, he hoped she would simply miss having two other family members to draw away her mother's attention.

"Lady Catherine, your hospitality to your guests was remarkable. I bid you farewell."

The lady glared at him; not an easy feat for someone her height trying to intimidate someone a foot taller and almost a hundred pounds heavier. But then again, his aunt never backed down. He defiantly stared back at her; he wasn't about to let her arrange or feign control over his life anymore.

When she spoke, she used the same voice that used to make him run away from her as a little boy. Too bad he was a grown man now and would not be lectured to as a child. "Darcy, your behaviour during this visit was abominable. Your mother would be seriously displeased. I demand you return as soon as you regain your sense and ability to adhere to the obligations of this family."

"Lady Catherine, I am sorry to let you know I will not be able to return to Rosings for some time in the future. Once again, I bid you farewell." He looked over his aunt's shoulder to address his female cousin. "Anne, I wish you the best. I am sure that Georgiana will enjoy seeing you if you are in town visiting Richard's parents. Until then, I am sure she will continue to correspond with you regularly."

Lady Catherine rudely interrupted his goodbye to Anne. "The air in town is hazardous to Anne's health. The air at Pemberley would be much more suited to her well-being. She will visit Georgiana early this summer at Pemberley. By then, you will have your priorities in order."

"Georgiana has always been dear to me. I trust we will be able to continue our friendship wherever we are able to meet." With an added amount of feeling betrayed in her voice, Anne added, "I wish you all the joy in the world, cousin."

"Thank you."

Darcy did not forget the dragon for a long, for she whipped the back of her dress as she would a tail, and snatched his cousin's fragile arm. His aunt turned her back to him and marched up the stairs, dragging Anne with her. He saw his female cousin turn her head sharply to catch Richard's eye and mouth the word "Goodbye" to him.

Fully ready to leave Rosings, two cousins climbed on their respective horses and made their way down the lane to retrieve Miss Bennet and Miss Lucas. It didn't take long for the quaint parsonage to come into view, but it felt like an eternity. He had enough of waiting. Starting now, Elizabeth would be under his care. Certainly, they still had more than a few details to work out, but he pledged his love to her once again while she stood at the window in Lady Catherine's parlour. She seemed so relieved at his confession. He just needed a little more time. Perhaps they could come close to settling their problems during their private discussion that Fitzwilliam promised to arrange during their return to town.

Not even waiting for the Colonel, Darcy immediately dismounted his horse when they arrived at the front gate of the parsonage. He walked through the gate, knocked on the door, and found his way to the sitting room where the members of the parsonage waited for him expectantly. Elizabeth still looked withdrawn and pale, no doubt from her ordeal over the past several days. She sat wearing the same red dress she wore a few days before. He wasn't sure if the red in her dress made her cheeks appear more flushed than normal or if she was still in considerable distress. Whatever the reason, he needed to hurry and get her away from this horrible place.

He addressed the group with as short a comment as he could muster. "Good morning. I trust everyone is in good health this morning." He heard Mrs Collins' short answer that Elizabeth felt better after her return to the parsonage yesterday. Apparently, Mr Collins was still scared of him and left his wife to confront his opponent.

Although Mrs Collins answered his last question, Darcy directed his focus and next question to one lady in particular.

"Are you ready to depart, Miss Bennet?"

Elizabeth sat in silence. What had Lady Catherine's tirade done to her?

Mrs Collins looked at her sister and friend before once again answering; apparently realising that Elizabeth could not bring herself to speak that morning. "Thank you for all of your assistance, Mr Darcy. My husband and I both feel much safer knowing Lizzy and Maria will be safe during their travel back to London. They are both prepared to leave.

"My cousin and I will make sure they are protected and arrive safely to their families. If Miss Lucas and Miss Bennet are ready, we shall depart as soon as possible. Colonel Fitzwilliam is already ensuring their belongings are properly packed."

He wished Elizabeth would say something. He needed to know she was alright. At least if he could see her eyes, he could be sure of her state, but she hadn't made eye contact with him yet. How he wished he could sit in the carriage with her instead of riding alongside.

Two ladies made their final goodbyes to Mr and Mrs Collins. Both Charlotte and Elizabeth said a tearful goodbye. Neither made any comment about when they would next meet. He assumed that Mrs Collins came to the same conclusion about the effects of Elizabeth's presence in Kent on her disposition.

Darcy first helped Miss Lucas in the carriage and then performed the same act for Elizabeth, holding her hand longer than necessary, trying to persuade her to look at him. As he finally locked his focus on her troubled green eyes, he squeezed her hand to silently let her know of his continued affection. When she quickly looked away, he knew it wasn't enough. But he couldn't do anything else until they stopped at the inn. He mounted his horse and began the journey to bring the woman he loved away from Lady Catherine and closer to her new life with him.

Chapter 18

He saw her gaze out the window for long periods, but nothing seemed to hold her interest. Every time he rode next to her window, she seemed to stare right past him, almost as though she didn't even see him. Obviously her distress from the day before clouded her thoughts. She couldn't have possibly missed seeing him. He was right next to her! What was going through her mind? He certainly didn't want to make any guesses this time. They would openly talk to limit any and all misunderstandings. If he learned one thing over the last week that was the fact he and Elizabeth had no problems misinterpreting the other's actions.

After a time, through the window, he saw her open a letter and begin to read it. He wondered what it said although the content mattered little since it seemed to perk Elizabeth's attention. He watched as her countenance lightened; maybe she finally began to feel better. She seemed less upset than when they began their journey that morning. She didn't look overjoyed at the letter's contents, but she wasn't further distressed and that in itself was a small victory.

Just then, she locked eyes with him from inside the carriage. He saw a small smile grace her lovely, red lips. Although it didn't stay long, for it vanished when she broke eye contact with him, it was enough to give him hope. And if that wasn't enough, when he passed by her window, on several occasions she noticed his proximity and the same small smile appeared once more. He was thankful for whatever that letter said if it made her willing to communicate with him affectionately.

Thankfully they were almost done with half of their journey back to town. Darcy told the driver to stop at the inn ahead, aware the horses needed a slight break and it provided him with an opportunity to speak to Elizabeth. He didn't want to wait any longer. When the carriage finally stopped, Elizabeth jerked her head, seeming to refocus her attention on the inside of the carriage. At least stopping the coach finally snapped her out of her reverie, hopefully, this time for good.

Darcy waited for the footmen to open the carriage door, but took the opportunity to help the ladies down himself. The next moment reminded him why his cousin was his closest friend.

"Ladies, would either of you care to accompany me to the inn? Or if you would prefer, there is a little path that takes you to a river. Darcy used it many times to stretch his legs and can vouch for its pleasant views. You would be in full view of the coach at all times."

As he suspected, Miss Lucas admitted she preferred to eat something light at the inn with Colonel Fitzwilliam, allowing him the chance to escort Elizabeth to the river in privacy.

"Miss Elizabeth, may I persuade you to walk with me? I assure you it is very refreshing after sitting so long in one attitude."

"Are you sure you wish to join me or would you rather stay by your horse and be content to watch?"

"In this instance, I will be able to admire you much better from your side than at a distance so far I could barely make out your figure."

Elizabeth's cheeks returned to the same redness he saw earlier that day, this time he knew they coloured for a different reason. He felt quite pleased with his efforts as she didn't appear upset by his comment.

"I have since learned I can do little to dissuade you once your mind is set." When she finally looked at him again, she gave him a half-hearted smile that helped him to slightly push away his fear he said too much.

"I hardly expected you to concede so quickly. I shall take advantage of your unusual bout of complacency and offer you my arm before you change your mind."

While Darcy surmised various reasons behind Elizabeth's mood, they set off on their short walk. Possibly, she just needed to increase the distance between herself and Lady Catherine. The closer they came to London, the better her mood became; whatever information the letter held certainly seemed to help. Things were starting to look up already for him and he barely spoke more than a few sentences to her.

“Are you looking forward to returning to Hertfordshire next week? It must seem an eternity since you last saw your father."

She looked momentarily around her surroundings as if lost before she answered him casually. "Actually I will not be returning to Hertfordshire for another several weeks."

"Will you be staying in London that entire time?"

Still not looking directly at him and instead to the dense woods in the distance, she answered revealing nothing at all. "What makes you ask that, Mr Darcy? Do you think I would have somewhere else to be?"

"I only hoped to ascertain the direction of your plans, as I am sure they will influence my own."

With his last statement, her eyes fell to the bare ground. She dropped her hand from his arm and took a step away from him. He immediately felt the loss of the pressure on his arm. With the loss of their physical connection, he felt their emotional one slipping as well. This did not bode well for him at all. In a small voice, he heard her say, "Mr Darcy, I do not know what to expect when we return to town. So much has happened between us in such a short amount of time. I admit I am utterly confused about what the future holds."

"Miss Elizabeth, the last time we had a moment alone, you asked me why I never finish what I start. I am telling you now, with no uncertainty that my deep affection and love for you has not and will not change. I realise that we still have much to discuss and many more issues to resolve, but I believe you and I are perfectly suited to one another if only we can overcome our respective pride, tempers, and propensity to misunderstand one another." He saw her take yet another step away from him. He needed to change tactics. "But I can see you are still not ready and for that reason only, I will remain silent. I must ask your permission to continue as we have in the last week. I cannot return to pretending to be indifferent to you. Please do not ask it of me. Please. Don't give up on us." He took a deep breath before continuing. "Unless you are completely decided against me, I cannot give up on you."

"Everything changed so quickly between us, Mr Darcy. So much has happened in just one week. My mind and my heart are in a constant state of chaos and confusion. I believe I have felt every emotion and sensation known to mankind over the course of only seven days. I have not had time to accept or understand these changes. I can promise you absolutely nothing at this time."

She refocused her eyes to stare directly into the depths of his. She needed to know if he understood, but the intensity radiating from his dark eyes caused her to look away once more. He needed an answer, but she had none to give. He wanted so much of her, but she was not prepared to decide. She realised that if she did not make up her own mind, her decision would be taken from her, one way or the other. She could not expect him to wait forever with no assurances of their future marital felicity. But she could not agree to marry him, not yet anyway. Nor could she expect to keep meeting in secret with no one becoming the wiser. But this was the most important decision of her life; she needed time to be sure about it, whatever she decided.

He looked at her tentatively and when he finally spoke, his voice seemed easier than before. "And time is still needed? If that is what you want, I will make sure you have it. But I must ask you again, please do not ask me to silently give you up and pretend there is nothing between us."

Despite their proximity to the servants, Darcy took several steps toward her and tenderly placed one hand below her chin to force her to look at him. At first, she tried to resist, but he would not allow her. Even when gentle, his strength and determination were evident.

She could not accept him, but neither could she reject him. Darcy wasn't ridiculous like Mr Collins, a childhood friend like John Lucas, or lacking in strength of a character like Mr Bingley. Before her stood a man who knew what he wanted and wasn't afraid to fight for it, no matter how many barriers they built between them. They both deserved to see it through wherever that path might lead.

"I could not ask you to display a disguise to the world that you do not believe. I know enough of you to know that would not be fair." Without breaking their eye contact, he asked. "How long will you be in London?"

She had to look away; his gaze caused her to become dizzy. Instead of standing there, she continued walking along the riverbank, causing him to break the lock of his hands around her back. After some time, she quietly answered, "I will not be in London after this week."

He looked at her quizzically, "If you will not be in Hertfordshire or London, where will you be?"

"Before I arrived at Kent, my uncle and aunt invited me to join them on a tour for the Lakes this summer. Yesterday my aunt wrote me that such a trip this summer will be impossible. Instead, they plan to travel to see sights in the North as soon as I return. Jane will be joining us."

He firmly held her arm, forcing her to stop walking. She glanced at him quickly to see the excitement in his eyes that brightly shone. She could almost hear the wheels in his head turning. As such, she was surprised to hear the lightness of his answer. "Where exactly in the North will you be travelling? There are many beautiful sights to see."

He trapped her quite effectively, but she refused to give up. "My aunt wants to spend a week where she grew up, amongst other locations." She looked away from him; she didn't want him to see her deception.

Darcy once again brought her chin to face him. "Miss Elizabeth, look at me." She moved her eyes from his mouth to his eyes. When she finally did, he continued. "In what town did your aunt grow up?"

She should have known better than to try to dissuade him from his course. So she chose to answer simply, "Lambton." She planned to spend a week not five miles from Pemberley. Only a fool could not guess what his plans now held.

"Well, I believe you still owe me the answer to three more questions and I would like to ask you for one of the answers now."

"I am afraid we have little time. Will this require a long response?"

He leaned in closer to her. If he wanted to kiss her, he would only have to move a fraction. She felt an invisible pull bringing her closer to him. She was afraid to breathe for fear he would feel her slightest movement against him.

"Just a word."

She felt her entire body immediately stiffen. He just promised to stay silent on the question of marriage and now he wanted to ask her a question that required only one word for an answer. There was not much she could do to stop him from asking it even though he just promised to remain quiet on the subject. It took her a moment to find her voice. When she did, she was surprised by its strength. "Go on."

"You asked me for a time to sort out what you are feeling. I want to ask you if you will stay at Pemberley during your trip to Lambton and possibly even when you are visiting some other estates?"

"Mr Darcy, I appreciate the offer, but I cannot accept."

He stared at her directly. Gone were the tenderness and intimacy of his voice. "Why? And remember, you promised me honesty."

"My aunt and uncle are not of the same society as your family. If given permission, I will ask my family if we might call on you, but that is all we may do."

He answered quickly and with slightly more compassion than before. "If your aunt and uncle mean as much to you as I believe they do, it will be a privilege to host them during their journey. Is there no other reason?"

"It is not my decision where we stay, Mr Darcy. My uncle will make our travel arrangements."

It worked; either her tone or her words made him seem easier. He brought one of his hands to caress her cheek lightly with his fingertips, making her entire body shiver. "If I can persuade your uncle, will you agree?"

The tenderness of his touch made her lose almost all thoughts. But still, one thought remained to circle through her mind. "Why are you asking this of me?"

His voice dripped with honesty as he lowered its tone and returned to whispering softly in her ear. "You want time and I want to make sure you have it. You will finally have the uninterrupted time you need to decide what you want. But you need to make a completely informed decision. I want you to see Pemberley; I want you to feel it. I want you to know what it means to me. I want you to know all of me. That is why I want you to come to Pemberley."

Instead of the discomfort she thought it would bring, it seemed to calm her. The realisation of what he asked her didn't bring the pain she feared. She took the moment to look inside herself. She had a decision to make right then whether she felt prepared to make it. He was right; they could no longer meet as indifferent acquaintances. She felt too much for him. A week ago she abused him abominably and now the thought of his pain made her own soul hurt. She wanted to provide him with the ultimate comfort she knew he longed for. If she just fell into his chest and let him completely engulf her in his arms, she knew the anxiety that ate away at his soul would vanish. Hers might as well, but she still was not sure. Alas, she couldn't do that, not yet. She still needed the time she requested of him and he freely offered. She was not prepared to decide her future that day. But she was prepared to take another step toward it.

"I thank you for your invitation, Mr Darcy. But it will be up to you to persuade my uncle."

He moved his head to look at her once more; she could see the fire of ecstasy in his eyes. Then again, she expected no less. "I warn you, Miss Elizabeth, I can be a very persuasive and determined man."

"That, Mr Darcy, is no surprise at all." He flashed his dimples at her response. "Perhaps we should go back to the carriage. I would like some refreshment before we continue our journey. After we eat, will you be ready to begin the next stage?"

Lightly, he brought one of her hands to his lips, and even though the glove, she swore she felt the warmth from his lips. When he captured her full attention, he promised with no uncertainty in his voice, "No matter where you go, I will be at your side."
.

Chapter 19

From the view on top of his horse, Darcy saw the large brick home of Mr and Mrs Edward Gardiner nestled by the docks in Cheapside. From the outside, it seemed a perfectly respectable habitation. In fact, it was far above anything he would have guessed prior to their arrival. What sort of people lived there? Elizabeth certainly thought the world of them. A month ago, he feared being associated with such a residence and the people that resided there; now he hoped for their lifelong acceptance and friendship.

He thought back to the several subjects that he schooled himself on during the remaining hours of their travel. He needed to show Elizabeth the man he was, not the one she used to think him to be. When he greeted Mr and Mrs Gardiner, he would do his best to be polite and entice them to accept his offer to stay at Pemberley. He could not accept no for an answer, but neither could he be forceful or too direct.

He let the footman open the carriage door, but took the opportunity to help Elizabeth down safely, as Colonel Fitzwilliam already did the same for Miss

Lucas. He almost forgot Mrs Collin's sister was in the carriage. Thank goodness his cousin seemed to understand his anxiousness.

A young maid opened the door before any of them even reached the first step. He felt the tight squeeze on his arm but knew it had nothing to do with his presence. While escorting her up the stairs, he thought Elizabeth's excitement might cause her to take the steps two at a time. One reason he loved her so was due to her love of her family.

He immediately felt the loss of pressure on his arm as Elizabeth flew into the welcoming embrace of her elder sister waiting anxiously in the hallway. As Miss Bennet looked up from her sister's shoulder to see him, Miss Lucas, and an unknown gentleman, she dropped her arms and immediately looked uncomfortable from showing such an open display of affection outside her immediate family. He tried to smile to ease her embarrassment but wondered if such an unusual emotional display from him might cause equal uneasiness.

After Jane whispered something to her sister, Elizabeth turned around and looked to the two gentlemen she unexpectedly brought with her. He hoped she didn't regret her decision to allow him to persuade her uncle and aunt to travel to Pemberley. With a slight blush to her cheeks, Elizabeth grabbed and squeezed

Miss Bennet's hand with both of her own and addressed the group that stood behind her.

"Jane, you remember Mr Darcy? Behind him is Mr Darcy's cousin, Colonel Fitzwilliam who I had the opportunity to meet while in Kent."

Miss Bennet curtseyed in acknowledgement of the introduction. Elizabeth continued the introductions. "Colonel Fitzwilliam, allow me the honour of introducing my elder sister, Miss Bennet. She spent the last few months in town with my uncle and aunt." The man bowed in acknowledgement.

If Darcy was going to start, he supposed he should start first with the most acceptable of her family members. "Miss Bennet, it is a pleasure to see you again. Your sister spoke many times of her anxiousness to see you. It is a pleasure to see a family with such obvious affection for each other."

Miss Bennet smiled at his compliment and looked at the gentleman with a mixture of anticipation and warmth. "It is a pleasure to see you too, Mr Darcy. I must thank you and Colonel Fitzwilliam for ensuring my sister and Maria's safety." His heart warmed further as Elizabeth affectionately kissed her sister on the cheek. The joy between them seemed to warm the entire room.

Miss Bennet smiled at her sister and continued to address the group in the hallway. "My aunt and uncle are currently with Sir William helping him with some last-minute purchases before he and Maria depart this afternoon. I know they would like to express their appreciation in person if you are able to stay for tea until they return. It shouldn't be more than fifteen minutes."

"Thank you for your hospitality, Miss Bennet." Darcy turned to his cousin and saw a slight head nod. "My cousin and I have no prior engagements and would appreciate the opportunity to meet your aunt and uncle. If you would please excuse me for a moment, I will let my driver know we will be not be departing yet." Darcy bowed to the ladies still standing in the hallway and left through the front door.

By the time he returned, he found his cousin in the nicely apportioned parlour laughing at a detail regarding the much-famed fireplace at Rosings. He could certainly be more comfortable in this room than at any room in Rosings. Mrs Gardiner had excellent taste in furnishings even if she did not use the same stores he frequented. Then again, he had almost the same subtle side table in Georgiana's music room. Maybe they did frequent a few of the same vendors.

Instead of taking his usual place by the window, Darcy gathered his courage and took a spot standing next to his cousin, doing his best to take part in the conversation. As he caught Elizabeth's eye, she rewarded him with a half-smile when everyone else was distracted. He felt his breathing passages return to a normal size when she let her appreciation known, but his comfort proved short-lived. He heard voices in the hallway and one of them he remembered well.

He watched as Miss Lucas' face brightened after hearing her father's voice. With a single word of greeting, she quickly stepped into her father's open arms. Sir William showed equal affection for his youngest daughter but stiffened slightly when he eyed the two additional gentlemen in the room, one known and one unknown. Once again Elizabeth took the opportunity to introduce the parties previously unknown to each other.

Mr and Mrs Gardiner seemed surprised by his presence. If Elizabeth mentioned to them the nature of their acquaintance in Hertfordshire, he could easily guess the reason to their surprise. He walked over them and began to discuss the pleasure of their niece's company while at Rosings and his offer to escort her and Miss Lucas back to town, as his own plans demanded he returned today. He soon found himself pleasantly surprised at the manners and decorum of Mr and Mrs Gardiner, despite their connections to both Mrs Bennet and trade. If he met them at a dinner, he might easily mistake them for people of fashion. When Mrs Gardiner came to offer him another cup of tea, he took the opportunity to ask what he desperately hoped for.

"Mrs Gardiner, I heard from Miss Elizabeth you grew up in Lambton."

"Why yes. I spent much of my childhood there and met my husband when he travelled to the area for business."

"It is a lovely town. I spent many happy days playing on its outskirts." He took a deep breath; this was it. "I heard from Miss Elizabeth that you planned to visit there next week."

"Yes, we planned to travel to the Lake District this summer but my husband's business needs to be changed and we find ourselves having to adjust the itinerary."

"I am sorry to hear it; the Lake District should be lovely this time of year. But perhaps I could offer a slight compensation for missing your tour of the Lakes. I would like to invite you and your family to stay at Pemberley during your travels in the area. It is a perfect location from which to journey to the surrounding estates. I hope you won't mind if my sister and I join you as your guides when my business will allow. We are quite fond of the area and would appreciate the opportunity to show you the parts most visitors overlook."

Mr Gardiner answered for his wife who looked to Darcy as though she might be speechless.

"Mr Darcy, that is very kind of you, but we could never intrude on your privacy. You must be looking forward to spending time with your family after being gone so long from her company."

Darcy wasn't about to let them off that easily. "I assure you, Mr and Mrs Gardiner, my sister will heartily join me in this invitation as soon as she is granted the opportunity to meet you. It will be our pleasure to continue and deepen our acquaintance with your family." In a moment of either brilliance or lunacy, Darcy added, "Please, I ask you to reconsider for I will have to disappoint my sister by staying here for the next several hours trying to persuade you and I know she is anticipating my arrival home."

After Mr Gardiner looked to his wife and received an encouraging smile, he bowed his head slightly in acceptance. "In that case Mr Darcy, I cannot see how we can refuse such a generous offer."

Mrs Gardiner took the opportunity to ask about his sister. "Is there a time we might be able to call on your sister? I know my nieces and I would appreciate the chance to thank her for your family's kind invitation."

"If it isn't too much to ask, I have a rather delicate request." He saw Mrs Gardiner nod in permission to continue. "I hope you might be able to call on her tomorrow. I would bring her with me to call on you, but my sister is very reserved. I hope that if you are able to meet her in familiar surroundings, she might be more comfortable."

Mrs Gardiner smiled in seemingly complete understanding, setting Darcy at ease for asking such an intimate request. "It would be our pleasure. Is ten o'clock an acceptable time?"

"I will let her know to expect you then." He heard the clock chime in the hallway. "I am afraid I must be going; I know she is awaiting my return."

"Of course, Mr Darcy. Please give your sister our regards and again, our thanks. Sir William and Miss Lucas will need to depart as well if they wish to return to Hertfordshire at a reasonable hour. If you will excuse me, I promised to keep him aware of the time." Mr and Mrs Gardiner left the side of the room where they spoke with Mr Darcy to attend their other guests.

***

Elizabeth couldn't hear anything of Darcy's conversation with her aunt and uncle, although their discussion was at the forefront of her thoughts. As she sat with the rest of the party, Elizabeth tried to focus on hearing the latest gossip from Lucas Lodge and Longbourn. She rejoiced at the departure of the militia but lamented Lydia's invitation to join Mrs Forster starting on Sunday in Brighton. She wished she could speak to her father about Lydia's behaviour, but she knew it would be a futile task. However dear her father, he would not curb his daughters' behaviour until it began to negatively affect the sanctuary of his library.

When she finally looked up from Sir William's latest tale, she saw a smile evidently printed on Mr Darcy's face. She knew that look. It was the same he wore whenever he got what he wanted. She pitied her aunt and uncle; she did not know how far he would go to persuade them to accept his invitation, but he certainly wasn't going to accept a refusal from them. Of all people, she knew it was almost impossible to deny him anything he desperately wanted, and he desperately wanted her at Pemberley. At that moment, her heart fluttered as she realised she wanted it just as much.

She looked up when she saw him approach their group to address his cousin. "Fitzwilliam, we should be going. Georgiana is likely anticipating our return." Both cousins turned to Jane, Elizabeth, and Mr and Mrs Gardiner to bid them goodbye. After his cousin finished, Darcy added that he looked forward to their visit tomorrow to Darcy House. Elizabeth laughed slightly to herself as she realised she wasn't the slightest bit surprised that Darcy managed to arrange an opportunity to see her tomorrow as well. Truthfully, she expected nothing less. The cousins then wished Sir William and Miss Lucas a pleasant and safe journey home and left Cheapside.

After all the guests departed, the Gardiners sat alone with their favourite nieces. The carefully made observations by her aunt and uncle now began; each of them pronounced Mr Darcy's to be infinitely superior to anything they expected.

"He is perfectly well behaved, polite and unassuming," said Mr Gardiner.

"There is something a little stately in him, to be sure," added his wife; "but it is confined to his air and is not unbecoming. Though some people may call him proud, I have seen nothing of it."

"I was never more surprised than by his behaviour to us. It was more than civil. It was really attentive, and there was no necessity for such attention."

"To be sure, Lizzy," said her aunt, "he is not so handsome as Wickham; or rather he has not Wickham's countenance, for his features are perfectly good. But how did you come to tell us he was so disagreeable when in Hertfordshire?"

Elizabeth tried to control the colour in her cheeks but knew it was useless. She excused herself as well as she could and said that she had liked him better when they met in Kent than before.

"But, perhaps, he may be a little whimsical in his civilities," replied her uncle. "Young great men often are. I admit to a certain amount of trepidation accepting his offer to stay at Pemberley during our trip. Elizabeth do you think him sincere in his invitation?"

Elizabeth answered that she harboured no doubt regarding the genuineness of his invitation. She saw the knowing glance exchanged between her aunt and uncle. How did they both come to the same conclusion? She refused to claim a much more intimate acquaintance with Mr Darcy than she initially revealed. But at least her answer proved that Mr Darcy would not regret his invitation for their stay at Pemberley.

Chapter 20

Georgiana Darcy looked up from her roll when she noticed her brother walking to his place at the head of the table. He leaned down to kiss her on the cheek before he sat down.

"Good morning, Georgiana. I hope you slept well."

"I always sleep better knowing you are home and safe."

She waited until he found the jam he preferred on his roll. She wanted to wait until his attention was somewhat distracted before she continued. He didn't need to know how much she worried about his answer. "Will you be here until Mrs Gardiner, Miss Bennet and Miss Elizabeth call and then stay through their visit?"

He stopped eating and brought his napkin to his face.

"Georgiana, I have to see Bingley this morning. I am afraid I am long overdue for this visit and I can put it off no longer. I will do everything I can to return by ten o'clock but I cannot make a firm promise."

Her nervousness turned into terror. "You mean you may not be here for the first time I meet your new friends?"

Georgiana knew he never introduced her to ladies whose opinions he did not value, other than Miss Bingley's of course, as he could not escape that relationship no matter how hard he tried. In fact, he never introduced her to any single ladies of his acquaintance; she always assumed when he did, he meant to finally marry. To confirm her suspicion, she realised that her brother invited no one to Pemberley unless they were of a long-standing and intimate acquaintance. To invite the Gardiners, who he admitted having just met when he escorted Miss Elizabeth from Rosings, meant he must hold one of the Miss Bennets in particularly high regard. Since he wrote of Miss Elizabeth while in Hertfordshire and just spent nearly a month in her company, she could only reason that he meant to marry the lady.

Now he wanted her to meet his future wife without Mrs Annesley or him by her side? How could her brother allow her companion to visit her sick daughter when he knew how much this day meant to his future? But of course, he should give Mrs Annesley the time off. She was horrid for thinking of her own needs above her companion's. She wouldn't have asked for time off if her daughter wasn't quite ill. Every girl, no matter her age, should have the loving comfort of a mother when sick.

But how could she possibly accomplish such a feat completely alone without embarrassing herself? If Miss Elizabeth proved as witty a conversationalist as her brother claimed, how could this lady like a girl who could barely speak in public? She would embarrass her brother and possibly ruin his chances for a happy marriage, all because she could not properly fill her role as Miss Darcy! She couldn't help the beginnings of hyperventilation.

Her brother grabbed her hand and talked in the same calm voice he always used when she became upset. "Georgiana, calm down. Please, it will be alright. I promise I will return by ten o'clock. But if I do that, I must leave now. Will you be alright until I return?"

Georgiana's breathing slowed. She needed to change clothes; the corset with this dress felt entirely too tight. "Thank you, Fitzwilliam. I will be fine in a moment. Please give Mr Bingley my best wishes."

***

Darcy arrived at Bingley's while he knew his friend would still be at breakfast. Possibly, his friend wasn't even awake yet. Since Georgiana needed him home, he needed to take the chance.

Bingley looked up from the poached egg on his plate to see his oldest friend walk through his dining room door. Upon seeing his visitor, the young man immediately stood and grabbed Darcy's hand.

"Darcy! I thought you would be back last week. I called at your house expecting to see you and was told you wouldn't be returning for another week." He smiled slyly before finishing, "I guess you had a better time at Rosings than you usually do."

"It was a very pleasant trip, thank you."

"Good morning, Mr Darcy," Miss Bingley purred. "I am so pleased you have returned home and called on your dearest friends so quickly. May I offer you some breakfast or tea? You prefer a little lemon and sugar in your tea if I remember properly."

He almost forgot about his friend’s sister until she spoke.

"Good morning, Miss Bingley. I thank you for your offer, but I am fine. Charles, I hoped I could speak to you in private this morning and I am afraid I need to return to Georgiana as soon as possible."

"Dear Georgiana, I do dote on her. She is just like a sister to me. How is she?"

"Georgiana is doing well and looking forward to returning to Pemberley for the rest of the spring."

"Well, I must take this opportunity to call on her. Would you let her know I will call on Darcy House this afternoon?"

"I am sorry to disappoint you, but my sister's calendar is full for the day. I am not sure how much time she will have available this week. Perhaps you will be able to call on her when we return to town again."

Darcy watched as Bingley alternated between looking at his friend and sister. After a few rotations, he offered to finish his breakfast and then show Darcy into the study.

After Bingley settled into his favourite chair, he offered the opposite one to Darcy, who chose to stand instead. "Sorry about that Darcy. You know Caroline. She has been at me all week to find out when you were returning. I am surprised we escaped that easily."

"I appreciate you finishing your breakfast in four bites or less. You looked like Fitzwilliam after a long campaign."

Bingley laughed appreciatively at his friend's humour. "Since I doubt you came to see me about my eating habits, what is it that you needed to speak to me so urgently about?"

Darcy looked at his friend knowing his next words were likely to bring him both great joy and great pain. He needed to rely on Bingley's eventual willingness to forgive him.

"Miss Bennet." There, he could not go back.

Bingley eyed his friend carefully. Darcy felt his waistcoat tightening under his friend's scrutiny. "What about Miss Bennet?"

"I have some news which will likely cause you pain, and I beg of you to let me finish or else I may not get through it all."

After his usual jovial mood vanished, Bingley answered, "Go on."

"Miss Bennet spent the winter in town with her aunt and uncle. Your sisters and I intentionally withheld the information from you, knowing you would want to continue your relationship with her. I thought her mother was forcing her, hoping to secure your fortune. I saw no particular regard on her part for you while in Hertfordshire and I didn't want to see you trapped in a marriage of unequal affection. I forgot to account for Miss Bennet's reserved nature and the indications she gave to you alone. Recently, I learned how deeply mistaken I was. Miss Bennet felt the loss of your company deeply, and if I had to make an educated guess, I would say she still feels the loss."

“What?”

Bingley did the same thing Darcy would have done after hearing such a declaration. He stood from his chair, approached his dearest friend.

"How do you know that Miss Bennet misses me as much as I miss her?"

"I have the information on good authority."

"Don't you dare choose this time to be cryptic with your answers, Darcy!"

"Her sister, Miss Elizabeth, told me when I saw her in Kent over Easter."

"Why would Miss Elizabeth let you know something so personal?"

"We were in a heated argument and I believe we both lost momentary control over the civility of our speeches."

"What were you arguing about?"

"It doesn't make a difference."

"It damn well does, Darcy. I asked you a question and if you value our friendship, you will answer anything I ask."

Darcy finally sat down in a chair, unable to stare down at his friend. He placed his head inside his hands. "I asked her to marry me. When she refused, I wanted to know the reason. At that time, she informed me of my mistake in separating you from her sister."

Bingley sat back down in the chair he recently vacated, poured himself a glass of scotch, drank a few small sips, and took several more moments before he answered. "I don't know what is more unbelievable, that you proposed to Miss Elizabeth or that a woman actually refused you." Much to Darcy's surprise, his friend then laughed in an almost wicked manner. Seeing Darcy's glare, Bingley retorted, "Don't you dare give me that look, Darcy. That little piece of information is the only thing encouraging me to forgive you. If you suffered even part of what I have since the end of November, you have felt enough grief and I did not need to inflict more."

"I do not deserve your forgiveness, but I will heartily accept any that you offer." He didn't stand yet. He still needed to tell his friend one more important piece of information. "I also came to tell you something else. Miss Bennet, Miss Elizabeth and their aunt will be at Darcy House today at ten o'clock to call on

Georgiana. I would like for you to join us if you are able."

"I am surprised you want anything to do with the Bennets, especially after Miss Elizabeth refused you. What prompted the call?"

"Miss Elizabeth gave me an opportunity to repair some of our misunderstandings. I also invited her, Miss Bennet, and their aunt and uncle to Pemberley next week. I would be pleased if you were included in our party as well."

Bingley sat in silence, considering the offer carefully. "I will decide after I see Miss Bennet. I wouldn't want to cause her any more pain if she cannot forgive me." After Darcy stood up to leave, Bingley laughed slightly and added, "Caroline will strangle me if she finds out I turned down an invitation to Pemberley." Until that point, Darcy realised that Bingley forgot about his sisters. "What were my sisters' motivations in helping you separate me from Jane?"

Darcy wasn't ready to answer for anyone else. Bingley's sisters dug their own grave and now they must lie in it. "I am afraid only they can answer that and you must discern their sincerity for yourself. I must tell you though that your sisters will not be included in my invitation. I want to make the Bennets feel welcome and I am afraid the presence of certain people will make that extremely difficult."

Bingley finally stood up and walked his friend to the door.

"Darcy, I will meet you at Darcy House by ten o'clock. It seems that I need to speak in private to my sister about a matter of some import first."

Chapter 21

Georgiana breathed a sigh of relief when the maid told her Mr Darcy had returned. By the time he arrived to check on her, she felt the model of decorum and ease, or at least that was the picture she wanted to present.

"How is Mr Bingley, Fitzwilliam?"

"He is doing well and will be joining us for tea with Mrs Gardiner and her nieces as soon as he is able." Darcy paused before continuing. "I should probably let you know so you aren't surprised that Mr Bingley paid Miss Bennet considerable attention while in Hertfordshire. And I am not positive about the reception he will receive as he left rather unexpectedly last fall."

Georgiana's ease vanished. She certainly didn't need any other sources which might lead her to say the wrong thing at the worst possible moment. "What should I do?"

Her brother looked at her with understanding. "Just try to let Mrs Gardiner and Miss Elizabeth's behaviour guide your own. I am sure they will do everything they can to ease any tension which may still exist. If things become too awkward, I will ask Mr Bingley if he wants to join me in another area of the house."

Georgiana's worry lessened. "Thank you, Fitzwilliam. I desperately want to be a good hostess for your guests."

"They are our guests Georgiana, not only mine. They are looking forward to meeting you. Now, is there anything you need assistance with before they call?"

"I already ordered tea, fruit and cake and asked Mrs Blaine to make sure they were brought soon after your, our, guests arrive. If I forget something, will you make sure to remind me?"

"I am sure you will be fine. I have faith in you, my dear." Darcy then suggested she practice her music until their guests arrived. Her brother took his seat on the bench next to her and turned the pages while she lost her thoughts to Mozart and managed to forget for long spans of time about the importance of her visitors.

***

When the housekeeper finally announced the guests, Elizabeth couldn't help but be enchanted by the picture the brother and sister presented sitting at the gorgeous pianoforte. Before she greeted Mr Darcy and his sister, she quickly gazed around the elegant, albeit comfortably arranged room. Each piece of furniture was well-matched and obviously expensive, although not of the same design or colour. If she saw each piece of furniture separately, she would never have decided to place them in close proximity. Somehow the subtle accent vases and landscape paintings tied the room together, although she couldn't understand how. The room obviously wasn't designed by someone who was solely interested in the latest fashion or trend. The designer knew what she liked and brought it all together in a manner that didn't seem forced or awkwardly manipulated.

When Mr Darcy and his sister stood from the piano a little too quickly to be called graceful, her attention was drawn back from her thoughts. She greeted them both with a warm smile, wondering what was going on in the mind of the girl standing next to Mr Darcy, staring at her with obvious interest. The ends of her otherwise straight blonde hair were carefully curled and arranged in fashionable style, framing her oval face and girlish lips. Her eyes were the mirror image of her elder brother's; that could prove very dangerous for some young man in years to come.

Each of the women curtseyed while the master of the house bowed. The timid girl certainly didn't seem very comfortable with the position of the hostess. Of course, she wouldn't, she was a Darcy after all.

Miss Darcy offered seats to each of them and immediately called for the refreshments. Elizabeth looked around to each of the seats, not sure which to occupy. Mrs Gardiner accepted the chair that demanded the greatest attention to the conversation, saving either her or Georgiana from taking it. Elizabeth took the one between Miss Darcy and her aunt. Jane sat opposite of her, looking over her shoulder to stare at the door every few moments.

Almost immediately after they sat down, the maid brought in the tea and placed it in front of Miss Darcy. Elizabeth watched as the girl's hand shook slightly when she poured the tea for her guests. When the tea was poured, and the refreshments offered, the young hostess looked up and took a deep breath, signalling her intention to begin the conversation. Thankfully led by Mrs Gardiner, the group exchanged the usual pleasantries, including the discussion of the return trip from Rosings, the weather, and each person's health.

"That was a beautiful piece you were playing, Miss Darcy. I don't believe I have ever heard it played more perfectly."

Georgiana blushed. "Thank you, Miss Elizabeth. My brother encourages me to practice whenever I can. And I heard from Fitzwilliam that you play and sing so well. He said he rarely heard anything which gave him more pleasure."

Elizabeth couldn't help her cheeks from blushing a rosy colour upon Miss Darcy's unintended disclosure.

"Miss Darcy, we want to thank you and your brother for your generous offer to visit Pemberley," said Mrs Gardiner. "I grew up in Lambton and always admired your home as the most beautiful I could imagine. My nieces and I could not stop speaking of our excitement on our way to see you this morning."

Georgiana didn't answer immediately. Thankfully, Jane tried to help their aunt's cause. "We have heard so much of Derbyshire from Mr Darcy and my aunt. I know that Elizabeth is particularly excited to discover new walking paths. Do you have any suggestions for her?"

"There are several beautiful paths. There is one in particular in the wood which has a lovely view of the valleys and streams. Many of the sites can only be seen by horseback though."

Jane responded with a warm and welcoming smile, "Are you a horsewoman, Miss Darcy?"

"I do enjoy spending much of my time riding while at Pemberley. Do you either you or your sister ride, Miss Bennet?"

"I ride a little, but I am not a great rider. Unless Lizzy changed her mind while at Kent, she avoids riding whenever she can."

Darcy didn't seem to be able to help himself. "Miss Elizabeth, I hope you will make an exception while at Pemberley. I am sure that Georgiana and I can find a horse who will behave properly. If needed, I will even offer my services to help improve your riding ability."

"Fitzwilliam taught me to ride many years ago. He is an excellent teacher."

Her heart began to beat faster in remembrance their ride together as she met the gentleman's intense gaze.

"I will make an exception, but only if you find an exceptionally docile horse that will promise to obey its rider, Mr Darcy."

"Do not fear Miss Elizabeth, I will make sure you are properly introduced to your horse. I am sure there is at least one mare at Pemberley which you need not fear. If needed, I will even offer my own for your use."

She laughed lightly at his joke. "I will trust your choice, Mr Darcy."

Self-satisfied with this little conversation, the gentleman changed the subject, likely for the benefit of other guests.

"Mrs Gardiner, have you any plans for tomorrow night? The King's Theater is showing 'A Midsummer Night's Dream'. The troupe is one of the best in London.

I was planning on attending tomorrow night and hoped you, your husband, and your nieces might join me in my private box and then at dinner with Georgiana and me afterwards."

Elizabeth took a sip of tea, hoping to gain a few more moments to think. She did love the theatre.

"My family and I have no plans for tomorrow evening and gladly accept your offer, Mr Darcy," answered Mrs Gardiner.

Upon hearing her aunt's words, Elizabeth felt her face fall; she completely forgot something in the excitement of seeing the play. She brought nothing suitable to wear to the theatre. What if she had a dress made today? That wouldn't work. No seamstress worthy of the occasion could finish a dress in less than twenty-four hours. What was she going to do? Ordinarily, she might borrow one from her sister, but Jane was much too tall and with an entirely different figure. If needed, she usually chose one of Kitty's dresses to borrow. When she packed for Kent, she only planned on going to the parsonage and then home to Longbourn. Her original plans certainly did not include social outings with one of the most eligible bachelors of the ton and then a trip with that same gentleman to his grand estate.

She needed to find a way to refuse the offer without appearing ungrateful. She needed to tell her aunt. Maybe she would know how to renege on their acceptance. She leaned over and tried to quietly and discreetly explain her problem to her aunt.

Before she finished, she heard Miss Darcy's voice. "Don't worry Miss Elizabeth, you look to be my same size. If you don't own any suitable dresses, you can borrow a dress from me for tomorrow night. I have more than enough."

Elizabeth's face fell in disgrace. Did Miss Darcy think she couldn't afford anything better than the dress she currently wore? What had Mr Darcy told her about Bennet's fortune? Certainly, the fabric wasn't the same as the one that Georgiana wore, but it surely wasn't of a material she should feel embarrassed to be seen in. She knew the girl didn't say it maliciously. In fact, she probably just wanted to help. Despite what her mind tried to convince her emotions of, Elizabeth couldn't help it when her entire body seemed to blush a bright red.

She looked to Mr Darcy who wasn't paying any attention to her; his focus centred solely on his little sister. Elizabeth watched as the girl clutched her stomach in pain. As Georgiana looked around the room, her breathing seemed to become laboured. Her face was drained of colour. She took a quick glimpse around the room before she stood from the chair and fled from the parlour, nearly running directly into Mr Bingley who stood in the doorway, taking in the scene.

Elizabeth sat there stunned, not sure what to do. After Mr Darcy took a measure of the situation and ran past Bingley, who just came in, Elizabeth clutched her skirt and chose to follow closely behind him. Both tried to catch his sister who ran up the stairway but proved unsuccessful. Darcy reached Georgiana's bedroom door only a few seconds after the girl and she followed only a few steps behind him. She watched as he shook the handle several times trying to open it, but found the lock turned.

"Georgiana, please let me in. I need to talk to you."

Between sobs, they heard a loud, "No!"

Darcy dropped his head fall against the door and tried to speak to her again, this time in a much calmer voice. "Georgiana, please, it will be all right. I am not going to be mad at you. Just please let me talk to you."

"I messed up everything! Miss Elizabeth will never marry you and it is my fault! I failed you! Please, just leave me alone."

Elizabeth placed a hand lightly on Darcy's bicep. He turned and in a very soft voice, he pleaded with her. "I am sorry. I never told her anything or gave her any idea of my hopes for us. Please believe me."

"I do believe you." She thought for a moment before speaking again. "Would you let me try to speak to your sister? I have some experience dealing with sixteen-year-old girls." Seeing him nod his head, she continued. "If you could go back downstairs and let my aunt know, I would appreciate it. I am sure that Jane would appreciate someone else in the room to help the conversation if it becomes awkward as Mr Bingley just arrived." Elizabeth just realised the irony of sending Mr Darcy to the parlour in hopes he would ease the discomfort of others. At least he might take Mr Bingley with him to some other part of the house if the circumstance dictated it.

Elizabeth tried knocking on the door with a much softer force than Mr Darcy. Instead of yelling to make sure Georgiana could hear her, she used a normal, but tender, tone of voice, trying to coax the girl to the door. "Miss Darcy, it is Miss Elizabeth. I was hoping you might let me talk to you for a few minutes. Could you please let me in?"

Elizabeth heard footsteps coming closer to the door on the other side, but the door remained closed. "What about my brother?"

"Your brother returned downstairs. It is just the two of us now and it will remain that way as long as you want."

"Please don't make me. I am so embarrassed and ashamed."

"You have nothing to be ashamed of. Please, Miss Darcy, I promised your brother I would try to talk to you. You don't want me to return to him as a failure, do you?"

Lizzy heard the turn of the lock on the door and saw the handle turn downwards. She saw Georgiana's red eyes and face partially covered by the handkerchief that she used to wipe the tears from her cheeks.

Without saying anything else, the girl returned to sit on the bed, which Elizabeth could tell by its rumpled appearance that she laid on before she opened the door. She remembered Wickham's words about the girl. How could she ever believe this fragile and shy girl in front of her was proud and disagreeable?

Elizabeth climbed on the bed next to Georgiana and tried to hold her. Soon she felt her shift from holding her pillow to laying on Elizabeth's shoulder for support.

"Miss Darcy--"

Georgiana looked up. Her eyes looked so much like her brother's when he was upset. How could she refuse whatever she wanted?

"Please don't call me that."

Unsure where this was going to lead, Elizabeth was willing to try any conversation topic to encourage her to release her anxiety. "What would you like me to call you?"

"Georgiana."

"In that case, you must call me Elizabeth." Elizabeth thought for a moment, "Actually, I would prefer that you call me Lizzy. This is how my family and friends call me."

"I wish I had a friend. Most of the females I am around want something from Fitzwilliam or just want to be associated with Darcy family. They don't really care about me."

Elizabeth looked at this girl who she already knew was largely sheltered from the world. She didn't realise the extent of it until now. Most of her female companionship was with paid companions, one of whom betrayed her. No wonder she craves affection and strives so hard to please her brother. No sixteen-year-old should have so much pressure thrust upon them. Then she remembered how much Darcy dealt with at two and twenty. After he confessed his childhood memory, she thought she understood him. But now, after meeting his sister, she finally did understand his sense of responsibility and the loneliness resulting from trying to meet his family's expectations.

"Doesn't your brother ever call you something other than Georgiana?"

"He used to call me Georgie, but it reminded me of someone else..." She added quietly, "He doesn't call me that anymore."

"Well, what if we found a new name for you? Only people you invite may use it."

Georgiana's breathing seemed to ease. "I would like that." She looked up to face the older girl, "Do you have any ideas?"

Elizabeth hoped to take the chance to see if she could coax a smile from Georgiana. "How about Ana?"

"I already have a cousin named Anne. I want a name all my own."

"How about just G? I know none other girls that go by a single letter. You would be an original." Finally, she saw the true beginnings of a smile.

"That is horrible."

"All right, all right. Let me think of something else. Mmmm. What about Giana?"

"Giana?" The girl's partial smile finally became full. "I like it."

"I hope that you feel comfortable around me now."

Georgiana looked at her tentatively and dropped her voice back down to almost a whisper; Elizabeth had to strain to hear her. "Aren't you mad at me?"

"I was never mad at you, Giana."

"But I saw the way you looked. So upset and it was because of something I said. I just wanted you to like me."

"Let me ask you something and I want you to tell me the truth." She waited for Georgiana to nod. "What do you think I told my aunt?"

"I thought you said you didn't own any dresses."

"I said I didn't bring any dresses with me. I planned to spend time at Kent and immediately return to my home in Hertfordshire. I didn't know I would spend time in town until a few weeks ago. I thought I would just have something made when I arrived in town if the situation arose. Unfortunately, Jane and I cannot wear the same dresses, as she has a much different figure than I do. So you were right, I don't have any dresses, but I do own them." Elizabeth paused. "Now I need to ask you something else. Did you offer me a dress to wear because you wanted me to be embarrassed about my wardrobe or because you wanted to help me?"

Georgiana's innocence seemed to exude from her entire being when she answered. "I wanted to help. I know how much Fitzwilliam wanted to escort you to the theatre."

"So your heart was in the right place. Now, let me ask you one more thing. Are you going to forgive me for not following the rules of propriety by coming to see you?"

Georgiana looked at her, with eyes full of questioning. "There is nothing to forgive. This was wonderful of you."

"And why do you feel that way?"

"I think you did it because you care about me. Fitzwilliam already loves you, so you have nothing to gain from being nice to me."

Elizabeth, too stunned to speak, allowed Georgiana to reflect on her own words, hoping to forget her final comment. "Now you see why I have no need to forgive you? Your heart being in the right place is the most important requirement." She watched as Georgiana nodded her head. "So you think your brother still wants to escort my family to the theatre?"

"I am sure he does."

Elizabeth put on a sheepish grin of her own. "Then I suppose I need to find a dress in a hurry. I don't suppose you have any ideas, do you?"

The girl beamed at her new friend. "I have the perfect dress for you. My Aunt Eleanor persuaded me to buy some dresses in case I decided to come out this season; she wanted me to have at least a few dresses ready. I don't think that is such a good idea. After today I don't feel ready to come out yet; maybe next year."

Georgiana grabbed Elizabeth's hand and walked them both to a closet almost the size of Lizzy's bedroom at Longbourn. She never even imagined that one girl, especially one who wasn't even out yet, would own so many gorgeous creations. Many of them seemed to be works of art more than dresses. She must have a different dress for every day of the year. Her own wardrobe could not even be compared to the one in front of her. Lydia and Kitty would faint if they ever saw the dress selection. Of course, Lydia would also strangle Kitty when she found out she was too tall to fit in any of Miss Darcy's dresses.

After a few minutes of carefully searching through the right side of the room which housed her clothes, Georgiana brought out a beautiful forest green dress. She held it up for Elizabeth to touch; the silk felt like butter. Two inches of intricate pearl beading could be seen just below the breast and a slightly larger row with the same pearl beading design completed the bottom and the slender straps.

Elizabeth drew her hand away and shook her head at her new friend. "Giana, I couldn't possibly wear this. It is the most beautiful dress I have ever seen. I am sure you had a special occasion in mind when you helped to design this dress."

"I want you to have it. Please at least try it on."

The girl's longing eyes begged Lizzy to at least grant the request to try on the dress. "All right, I will try it on, but only if you are sure."

Elizabeth was rewarded with a beaming smile from Georgiana. "I am sure. Let me call my maid to help you."

"Please don't Giana. I don't want the servants to get the wrong idea if they see me going through your clothes."

"I don't understand, Lizzy. Won't you be marrying my brother soon?"

Elizabeth had to mind her expression before she just lost all the progress she made over the past hour with the girl. "Giana, why would you think I am marrying your brother?"

"Fitzwilliam never encourages me to become friendly with single ladies of his acquaintance; in fact, I don't know if he has any other single ladies that he is closely acquainted with. And he invited you to Pemberley; he never does that with people who he isn't very familiar with. But most importantly, I saw the way he looked at you. It is completely obvious that he is in love with you."

She took the younger girl's hand and answered carefully. "Giana, I am not engaged to your brother."

"But you will be soon, right?"

"Your brother and I have a rather tumultuous relationship. I am not sure what our future holds."

Georgiana's voice returned to the timid and shy level of their time in the parlour. "But how could you not love my brother? He is the most wonderful man in the world. I worry I will never find a man who will live up to the standard he set."

"Your brother is a very good man who loves you very much. But no one knows what the future holds for your brother and me. We have a lot of obstacles to work out."

Instead of questioning Elizabeth further, Georgiana moved on and pleaded with her to try on the dress she selected. Lizzy raised her eyebrow at her request questioningly. With a confidence she hadn't seen in her until that time, Miss Darcy stood behind her and placed a large green feather in her hair that matched the dress perfectly.

"A night at the theatre with dinner afterwards at Darcy House is just the way to work out some of those obstacles."

As Elizabeth stared at herself in the mirror with Georgiana behind her, she once again wondered if she would be granted the time she needed or if events might take on a course of their own, without regard to her opinions.

Chapter 22

Mrs Gardiner was the only occupant of the parlour that looked to the doorway when Mr Darcy walked back in. As he examined the other two sitting on the sofa in rather close proximity, they made no indication they had any knowledge of anyone else in their midst. Although their body language seemed somewhat stifled, neither appeared distraught nor unhappy at their proximity.

He walked over to join the lady who stood by a small table next to the pianoforte holding several books. He had planned to read one of them that afternoon while he listened to Georgiana practice, but it seemed that plan was now for nought.

He politely greeted Mrs Gardiner in a quiet voice, trying not to interrupt the progress of his friend. "I apologise for leaving so abruptly, Mrs Gardiner. Georgiana isn't feeling well. Miss Elizabeth is tending to her now."

"I am sure she will be fine. We do have another appointment that we need to keep in an hour though."

"If Miss Elizabeth has not yet returned, may I offer to ensure she is returned safely to your home? I am afraid that I am relying rather heavily on her to relieve my sister's ailment."

"Thank you for your offer, sir. If you are able, when you escort Elizabeth to our home, my husband and I would like to invite you and your sister to stay for dinner. It will be a quiet affair with just my nieces, you, and your sister, if she is feeling better tonight. I also planned to invite Mr Bingley and his sister, but have not had the proper moment yet."

"If Georgiana is recovered, we would be delighted. I have a feeling the only way I will be able to persuade my sister to let go of Miss Elizabeth's company is with the promise of being able to dine with her tonight."

"Then it is settled. We look forward to seeing both you and your sister tonight."

Darcy and Mrs Gardiner turned their attention back to the books on the table.

"You have an interesting collection of books here, Mr Darcy. Are these some of your favourites?"

"Actually I have not read any of them yet. Colonel Fitzwilliam brought them back for me after he returned from his last trip to the continent."

She held up one and responded, "This one seems to have caught my interest. Would you mind if I took a few minutes to look through it?"

"Of course not. Please consider it on loan until you finish it. When you visit Pemberley, I am sure there are several other books from my library which you might enjoy."

Mrs Gardiner responded that she looked forward to the tour and took a seat on a chair close enough to Miss Bennet and Bingley to overhear their conversation. He took the seat opposite of her and tried to concentrate on his own book he selected from the pile on the table, trying to give his friend some privacy that he too would want to enjoy.

All too soon, he heard Mrs Gardiner remind her niece they needed to leave to make their next appointment. Before they left, Bingley heartily accepted the invitation to dinner at the Gardiners and apologised for his sister not being able to join them, as she was leaving for Scarborough that very morning for an extended visit. When he saw the fully evident smile emerge on Miss Bennet's face at Bingley's answer, he felt much more secure in his decision to exclude Bingley's sister from their time at Pemberley. Miss Bingley and Mrs Hurst were the last people that either of the two eldest Bennet sisters needed to spend time with.

After all of his guests left, Darcy sat alone in his parlour, patiently waiting for Elizabeth and Georgiana to re-emerge. The morning's tea certainly did not progress in the manner he planned, but he could not feel completely disappointed with its direction. Bingley and Miss Bennet seemed to have become reacquainted quite nicely. Mrs Gardiner proved that she would present her nieces with at least some leeway; that might prove very helpful next week at Pemberley.

Chapter 23

Elizabeth collapsed on the bed, feigning exasperation, but with an amused smile on her face. "Giana, I only need one dress for tomorrow night and we decided from the beginning it should be the first one you selected. I think you made me still try on half of your wardrobe."

Georgiana couldn't seem to help the worried look plaguing her eyes. "But you had fun, didn't you?"

Lizzy needed to remember to check her teasing around the girl who was still too apprehensive about their friendship to tease Elizabeth in return. So, she grabbed Georgiana's arm and gave it a slight yank, hoping to make her fall on the bed next to her, just as she would do to one of her sisters.

"I had a wonderful time. I don't remember ever seeing such beautiful gowns. Although now I think I may have to warn my father to send more funds to my uncle. I don't see how I can leave town without several new dresses. Your taste certainly inspired me."

The girl's entire face lit with excitement. "Lizzy, we must go shopping. It will be wonderful! I know the best modistes. It will be such fun. I have never gone shopping with someone younger than my aunt. Oh, I am so excited!"

"I see I found the key to your interests. Let me speak to my aunt and I will let you know when would be a good time to order some new clothes. You are officially a necessary part of our outing."

Both ladies turned toward the door to the hallway as they heard the large clock outside Georgiana's room strike one o'clock. Miss Darcy put an arm around her stomach and asked, "Lizzy, would you like something to eat? I am rather hungry. I was too nervous to eat much at breakfast."

"I admit I am."

Georgiana sat up on the bed and took Elizabeth with her. "Come, let's find Mrs Blaine. I know she can help us."

With Georgiana's assistance, Elizabeth put back on the dress she arrived in. She felt a pang of disappointment at seeing her reflection in the mirror when fully dressed. After trying on the most beautiful dresses she ever saw, her own wardrobe seemed rather plain and inadequate.

Then she remembered Georgiana's difficulties. Maybe she wouldn't trade the beautiful dresses for the girl's set of problems. Her own kept her quite busy, she needed no more. What a pair they were. But her vanity shouldn't keep her from satisfying her stomach; a girl had priorities after all.

Georgiana led her down the upstairs hallway which Elizabeth did not take the time to look at closely earlier. The wallpaper certainly wasn't ostentatious. She didn't doubt its expense, but it seemed to fit the house and its occupants. Unlike at Rosings, she didn't see furniture or paintings displayed to make the viewer appreciate the owner's wealth. The décor was subtle and more comfortable than she imagined. The inhabitants of Darcy House wanted it to feel like a home. Why did she feel surprised, especially after seeing the parlour where they had tea? Didn't Mr Darcy's confessions over the last week destroy her misperceptions about him? There was so much more to him than his wealth. He was a man who valued his family above all things. Whoever decorated the house wanted its inhabitants to live within its walls, not just exist. It seemed there was still much to discover about the master of this house.

Georgiana brought her down the staircase to the housekeeper's small office on the first floor. She knocked on the door but heard none response. They then walked to the dining room to see if Mrs Blaine might make arrangements for dinner. Elizabeth followed Georgiana's lead to yet another unknown destination after finding the dining room empty. Eventually, Lizzy found herself in the same room she first became acquainted with Giana in. There weren't any remnants or indications of the small party gathered there only a few hours before. She wondered if her aunt and Jane left to call on Mrs Gardiner's friend. Georgiana grabbed her hand to lead her to a different parlour in a different part of the house.

Miss Darcy knocked on a set of large wooden doors that looked well-designed at excluding any unwanted guests. Upon hearing her brother's permission to enter, Georgiana opened the heavy door and allowed Elizabeth her first glimpse of Mr Darcy's sanctuary. The furniture differed greatly from what she originally suspected; it was neither gaudy nor uselessly fine. It had less splendour and more real elegance than the furniture of Rosings. Would she ever move beyond her prejudice against his aunt? She certainly needed to make more of an effort; maybe it would come with time. The man whose home she stood in was far superior to his aunt. In fact, he was superior to most of her acquaintances.

Her mind quickly wandered back to the room in front of her. Each of the chairs looked extremely comfortable; just the type she would spend hours sitting in and read a book on a cold winter day. The selected colours were dark and masculine, but not uninviting or cold. The papers on his rather impressive desk provided evidence of its considerable use. It seemed Miss Bingley's comments about Darcy's extensive letters of business were correct. For once, Caroline Bingley seemed not to exaggerate to impress the gentleman. She wondered if Mr Darcy himself decorated the rest of the house or whether it reflected his mother's tastes. No matter, for this room was clearly his; it was a perfect reflection of the gentleman and she had to admit that she rather liked it.

***

Fitzwilliam Darcy stood upon seeing the two ladies he loved to enter. He waited for his sister to speak, unsure as to the direction of the conversation. He didn't want to do anything to upset her again. Georgiana certainly looked better than when he last saw her running through the hallway.

"Fitzwilliam, we were looking for Mrs Blaine. Lizzy and I wanted something to eat."

Lizzy?

"I believe Mrs Blaine is looking into another matter. Why didn't you just call one of the maids? I am sure they could have arranged for something."

Georgiana blushed slightly and confessed, "Looking for Mrs Blaine gave me an excuse to give Lizzy an unofficial tour of our home."

"I am sure we can give Miss Elizabeth the official tour whenever she wants. But until that time, we can find something in the kitchen to keep the two of you from tearing apart the house."

Elizabeth raised her eyebrow. She didn't think he knew his way to the kitchen. Certainly, he could ring a bell for a maid to bring them something to eat.

He led the two ladies down a small hallway to an entirely separate part of the house. Once they entered the kitchen, he asked one of the scullery maids where the head cook was. After finding the woman, he requested a small selection of food for the three of them to be brought to the library.

Once back in the room, he offered Elizabeth the chair. He took the one next to her and watched as she lightly fingered the leather, swirling it around the tuft before lightly dipping her finger in the indentation. He imagined her sitting that exact chair so many times reading a book last winter.

He looked at his sister. "It shouldn't be too much longer before the two of you are properly fed."

Georgiana blushed and glared at him. "Fitzwilliam, you know I become rather irritable when I don't eat. It isn't fair to tease me in front of Lizzy about my appetite."

"Giana, I guess now is as good of a time to tell you as any. If you ever visit Longbourn, you will find yourself in the very good company. I don't think there has ever been a missed meal at my home. My sisters and I would never allow it."

Giana? How did Elizabeth manage to rename his sister in the course of one afternoon?

"I see I shall have to send a note to my cook at Pemberley. She should expect several hearty appetites at the supper table next week." Elizabeth looked at him with a spark of humour in her eyes and he finished with an evident smile directed at the woman he loved. "I meant for the Colonel and Mr Bingley of course. I daresay that the two of you are nothing to my cousin. Even on your worst day, you could not best him, especially when I am serving a particularly fine meal. Bingley, however, gave him a run this morning."

With the mention of Bingley, Darcy unconsciously rubbed his finger around his tender jaw. It was probably in his best interest to change the subject even though the two ladies across from him were smiling. "I suppose I should be thankful for Georgiana's stomach. I was wondering if I would ever see you two again when you came downstairs."

"We found the perfect dress for Elizabeth to wear to the theatre tomorrow night, brother." Her eyes widened and then hurriedly added, "She left all the dresses she normally wears to evening parties and events at Longbourn."

He smiled gratefully at his sister. Maybe something in red would accentuate Elizabeth's dark features.

"I see you found my sister's passion, Miss Elizabeth. I am pleased to see her efforts benefited someone else as well."

"I should warn you, Mr Darcy. Your sister demanded that I try on half of her wardrobe. I think she is looking for an excuse to do some more shopping."

"Fitzwilliam, Lizzy wanted to know if I could go shopping with her this week. She wanted to buy some more dresses before she left for Longbourn."

Once again, he turned to Elizabeth. "I hope you understand what a feat you are undertaking by taking Georgiana shopping. I trust you have planned nothing else for that week."

The lady looked at him with mocked superiority. "I will be happy to take Georgiana for an entire week. I dare say you could not separate us even if you tried." She reached over and affectionately grabbed the girl's hand.

"I don't think I am ready to give her up just yet," he smiled. "Yesterday, I saw her for the first time in several weeks. The two of you will have to plan your escape for sometime after Miss Elizabeth's visit to Pemberley."

Recognising this was a dangerous conversation for him to continue, he told the ladies about the invitation to the Gardiner's for dinner. He was pleased that Elizabeth looked as excited about their time together as Georgiana.

Chapter 24

Darcy left his home the next day to pick up the Gardiners and the Bennet sisters for the theatre; he could barely contain his excitement. Marcus must have made him try on ten jackets that evening. The one they finally decided on was an excellent choice although he couldn't say why it was any different from the other nine. It didn't matter. It made him feel ready to face the ton.

They would see Elizabeth on his arm at a very public location; it was as good as announcing his intentions. In all his years in society, he made sure never to show his preference for a lady. Now, all the ton would see that Fitzwilliam Darcy was no longer an eligible bachelor, and he didn't even need to enter a parlour to announce it. For a bonus, he would spend several hours sitting in a dark room next to the woman he loved. It was perfect.

He knocked on the door and waited for an answer. After a moment, a red-haired maid opened the door for him and motioned for him to enter. He walked in the hallway and strained his eyes to see Bingley already sitting in the parlour talking to Mr Gardiner, Mrs

Gardiner, and Miss Bennet. Darcy wondered where Elizabeth was. He jerked his head to stare at the top of the stairs when he heard a melodic voice on the brink of laughter.

"I hope your countenance is not an indication of your mood tonight, Mr Darcy. I would hate for Georgiana's beautiful dress to be put on display next to such an unpleasant companion. People might think I forced you to be seen with me just so I could wear this exquisite gown."

If it wasn't for the mischievous smile and arch of her eyebrow, he thought about falling to his knee to ask her forgiveness. He had never seen her look more beautiful. On second thought, beautiful didn't even accurately describe her. He lost himself. Her eyes showed the happiness that seemed to radiate from her soul; the happiness that came from spending the evening with him. He brought her that happiness.

He took the time to take in the rest of her. Her dark curls surrounded her shoulders; the rest of the curls were held in a fashionable twist with a large feather. The dress displayed her every physical attribute to perfection.

***

When Elizabeth walked out of her room to the top of the staircase, she couldn't decipher why Mr Darcy didn't even look pleased to see her. She didn't think for more than a passing moment that he was unhappy to escort her to the theatre. Even though their real goodbye the night before at Gardiner's door was not the passionate one she dreamt of later that night, it still displayed his anticipation for tonight. But as she slowly descended the stairs, the countenance on his face morphed from one of disappointment to one of sheer ecstasy. Elizabeth almost tasted the darkening of his eyes and the dimples he subtly displayed for only her to see. That was the look she waited for. She loved that look. She wanted to keep it as a sacred treasure that no one else would ever see.

"I see that you are going to be rather quiet this evening, Mr Darcy."

He responded by taking the stairs two at a time to take his place next to her. When he arrived, he lifted not one, but both of her hands to his lips and didn't return them to her side. Instead, he kept her gaze, and in a soft voice that hypnotised her, "Forgive me, Miss Elizabeth. Your beauty stunned me into silence."

With his words went any thoughts of maintaining her emotions at a manageable level. She barely found the air to breathe in order to respond, but eventually, she did. "How could I not forgive such an excellent reason?" She needed to keep her wits about her tonight. She was going to face the ton with only Mr Darcy for protection.

Her aunt's greeting from the doorway of the parlour snapped her out of her thoughts of the gentleman. The rest of the party interrupted their all too brief moment together to greet her and her suitor. Mr Darcy dropped one of her hands, but kept the other one close to him, firmly placed on his arm, under his opposite hand.

He greeted her family and Bingley and then said, "I apologise for being late. There were several interruptions to the traffic flow on the way here. I suggest we leave as soon as possible if everyone is ready. I would hate to make anyone miss the opening act."

Mr Gardiner looked to the other members of his family. "Thank you again, Mr Darcy. We cannot tell you how much we appreciate this invitation. Mrs Gardiner and I have been trying to find the proper time to attend the play for several weeks. And now that Elizabeth joined us, I believe both of my nieces are now ready." Her uncle took his wife's hand, and soon the party left the house.

***

When they arrived at the theatre, Mr Darcy looked around to see how many people currently watched him. Seeing that he held most of the room's attention, he turned to face the woman on his arm, causing her to drop her hand from his arm and into his open palm. Gently, he lifted her hand to his lips, and instead of returning it to his arm, he lightly caressed it with his thumb and kissed it again. He smiled at her with an authenticity that few saw from Darcy during his years amongst society. He couldn't have announced his intentions with any more clarity than if he granted the famed Times' gossip columnist a private interview to discuss his marital plans.

He needed to remember to keep Elizabeth away from Mrs Markham if she happened to be there tonight. He was wary of the woman's constant attempts to corner him into conversation; surely every word would be twisted and displayed on the front page of the society section for the world to read. He wanted his intentions known, but not in that manner.

His actions garnered the attention he hoped for. Every woman in the theatre was either looking at him and Elizabeth or talking to another woman that was. It seemed his display provided more entertainment than doing a backflip in the middle of the lobby. Elizabeth didn't even seem fazed by his display. He watched as she appraised the room with a confident smile but the increased pressure on his arm made him nervous. Was the confident smile just a display for the ton or did she mean it?

"Mr and Mrs Gardiner, would you like any refreshment? The theatre has an excellent wine selection. Or if you prefer, we can wait until we arrive at my box."

"A glass of red wine would be wonderful, thank you, Mr Darcy."

The gentleman indicated a waiter to bring his party a selection of his favourite red wine imported from Rome; he hoped it might help to relax Mrs Gardiner slightly. He didn't want her attention directed to his actions all night instead of the play.

Darcy waited for an usher to show them to his private box. Seeing that the chairs were arranged in clusters of two, just as he directed, he made sure Elizabeth sat in the chair next to him on the right side. He did not plan this evening so he could spend the night sitting in proximity to Bingley. Fortunately, his friend had the same idea and took Miss Bennet to the two seats in the centre. That meant that Mr and Mrs Gardiner would not be able to see him or Elizabeth once the lights lowered. And if he stroked the back of her hand, certainly no one could blame him. What a perfect night.

Chapter 25

Darcy was pleased to see Bingley's luggage already loaded on the cart with the rest of their belongings. He climbed off his horse and walked to the carriage to help his sister step down. He revelled in the idea that this would be the last time he would enter Gardiner's house without Elizabeth as his fiancée. He planned for this trip to be a very memorable journey indeed. He had to stop himself from taking the steps two at a time.

He, Colonel Fitzwilliam, and Georgiana immediately saw Mr and Mrs Gardiner in the hallway. They all exchanged pleasantries and expressed their anticipation for their trip. Darcy looked up to see Elizabeth and Jane descend from the stairs; he couldn't keep the smile from taking over his face.

He looked up the woman he loved addressing him from the stairs. "Well Mr Darcy, it seems you are about to allow several lively women to descend upon Pemberley in one swoop. I hope that you warned your staff for you may not recognise your drawing room by the end of the week."

He lifted her hand to lightly kiss it. "I am willing to take my chances. I feel safe that at least my stables will remain free from tampering."

"I wouldn't bet too much on that. You did promise to introduce me to your horses."

"I believe that I even promised to let you ride Erebes and many of my family can tell you how unusual that is." As he now stood next to her, he lowered his voice so the others would have a difficult time hearing him. "I welcome any changes to my life and home that make you accept it as your own."

***

"This is so much nicer than riding in the covered carriage by myself." Georgiana looked to the other ladies in Gardiner's open carriage. She saw her brother and the other gentlemen riding ahead, enjoying the freedom of being able to ride their horses instead of confined in a carriage. Usually, she rode by herself or with her paid companion. She got along well with her companions, but she always remembered that her brother paid them to accompany her. For once, she travelled to Pemberley with people who cared about her and not about the money her brother paid them to converse with her.

"Giana, I completely agree. Even though our trip just began, it is already proving to be one of the most enjoyable I ever experienced. I could not ask for a better company to share it with." Elizabeth squeezed the hand of the girl next to her. They both looked as Darcy turned his horse around to ride next to their carriage. He pointed to a clump of trees in the distance. "There is a lake ahead. Would you like to stop for a short break? We are not far from the inn where I made arrangements for us to spend the night."

The ladies looked to one another trying to discern the opinions of the others without revealing their own. Finally, Mrs Gardiner made the decision that as they left early to enjoy the scenery, they should take as much time as they wanted to enjoy it. Darcy told the driver to prepare to stop ahead and pointed to the lake. He rode ahead to the other gentlemen to let them know of the change in plans.

After they stopped, Georgiana brought out the remainder of the food that Mrs Blaine packed for the first part of their journey.

"Would anyone like a light snack before we explore the lake?"

Although the other members of the carriage politely declined, her cousin commented, "You know I never turn down a meal."

"I would hate for you to break a perfect streak, Richard."

"Georgiana, there are two things the military taught me. The first being that a man should never turn down the opportunity to sleep in a warm bed and the second that a soldier should always eat, for he doesn't know when he will get the chance again."

The girl laughed as she handed him a selection of carefully wrapped pastries. "Now I know why you always accept an invitation to Pemberley. Fitzwilliam and I make sure you are always provided with both."

The group spent an hour in each other's company walking and admiring the lake and its scenery. After they strolled around the lake, Mr Gardiner pointed to some dark clouds in the same direction as the inn they planned to stay in. Mr Darcy suggested that they begin their drive again immediately, but with the ladies in Darcy's covered carriage instead.

Chapter 26

As she sat on the sofa in front of a small fire in the bedroom of the inn where Mr Darcy arranged for them to stay for the night, Elizabeth couldn't help but be impressed with his commitment to the well-being of everyone in his party. She surprised herself when she recognised that she almost expected that type of behaviour from him. From their conversations over the past two weeks, she knew he would always be concerned with the welfare of not only those he loved but those that worked for him as well. Whatever she learned of him over the past few weeks, he certainly wasn't the last man in the world she could ever be prevailed upon to marry.

Jane interrupted her thoughts as she remarked that, "Oh look, the rain stopped already. I can't believe it passed after such a short time."

Elizabeth walked over to the window her elder sister sat by the windowsill. "In that case, I am going for a walk around the periphery of the inn. Would either of you like to join me?" Georgiana and Jane both confessed they wanted to rest in their shared room until dinner, but reminded her to stay close to the inn. Elizabeth bid the two lazy blondes goodbye and began to walk down the hallway to the stairs.

Before she reached the staircase, she heard the door next to her open and natural curiosity persuaded her to look in the room as Mr Darcy's manservant walked out. But before his servant could shut the door, Elizabeth's eyes locked with the gentleman's sapphire ones. There she saw him sitting in a chair, still wet from helping with their luggage and horses. His hair dripped onto his shoulders, but she barely saw that. She changed her focus to his upper body clad in a soaking white shirt that was opened halfway down his chest, allowing his dark chest hair to peek out. His boots already sat beside him, allowing her the first glimpse of his muscular legs.

Elizabeth felt a wave of heat overwhelm her entire body; her breathing immediately deepened as she seemed to have to fight for each gasp of air. By accident, she once saw the Lucas brothers swimming in the pond in a similar state of undress, but it did not affect her like this. Seeing John Lucas' chest and calf muscles amused her; she had to hide her laughter from behind a tree. Laughter was the last emotion swelling inside her when she saw Mr Darcy for the first time without his full attire.

The colour on her cheeks deepened when the gentleman noticed her staring at him. In two long strides, Mr Darcy came to the door, grabbed Elizabeth's hand and gently brought her into his room, shutting the door soundly behind them.

***

Was it his imagination or had she not blinked ever since they locked eyes?

He took Elizabeth's hand, still inside his own, and slowly brought it up to allow her fingertips to caress his face. She tried to pull her hand away, but he wouldn't let her. Darcy clenched her fingers inside his own. He needed her to touch him; he needed to have this moment; he waited so long for this chance. He closed his eyes and gently moved his other hand to her arm when she finally took over the gentle ministrations on her own. Her fingers ran along his jawline and felt the stubble of his afternoon beard. He wished he shaved so he could properly savour the sensation. She moved to stroke the tips of his hair and the edges of his ear. As her fingers shyly ran across his mouth, he couldn't help but allow himself to lightly kiss each one as it passed. He was about to lose all control and he knew it.

He reached his hand back up to take her down from his face pressed it against his chest, so she could feel his heartbeat.

"I know my fourth question, but I do not want an answer right away. Are you ready?" He whispered and waited for her tentative nod before he continued. "I want you to think about what you want from your future. You need to decide where your life will lead you. What will make you happy? What is it you desire most?" He took her hands once more to his lips and after kissing each one and then placing them over his heart and holding them there, he continued. "Who do you want beside you in that life? Who do you want to be the father of your children? Whose arms do you want to hold you when you need comfort or affection?" He couldn't help adding in one more question. "Who do you want to love you with their entire being till death do you part?"

He took her hands to his lips one final time and then allowed them to gently drop to her sides. Then he walked to the door, opened it, and checked if the hallway was empty for Elizabeth to leave his place without being seen.

He waited for her to leave, but she remained frozen. Darcy closed the door again and moved back to her. He couldn't decide what to do. Could he trust himself any longer in a bedroom alone with the woman he loved so passionately? He gazed into her eyes, searching for an answer.

***

She couldn't understand why Mr Darcy was just staring at her. Was it possible to read minds? What if he could read hers at that exact moment? She had tried to walk to the door, but her legs felt so heavy. She couldn't control them. Her mind demanded that they move, but they wouldn't comply. She knew she had to leave or risk being discovered, but she wanted to touch him, just one more time. She needed to feel just a little bit more. Just a little more time was all she needed. Immediately after, she could leave and no one would ever know.

Elizabeth closed her eyes for a moment and could feel his breath on her cheek. She watched as his chest rose and fell in a perfect rhythm. She knew he wanted to kiss her. She wanted to be kissed...

She couldn't bring her eyes to meet his; she needed to keep them focused elsewhere. Starting tentatively at first, she gained confidence allowing her hand to feel his chest through his shirt, a single fold of the cloth that separated his naked chest from her hand. She never felt anything like this on her own body; he looked and felt like the perfect sculptures she saw in the London museums. She could only wonder if the rest of him also mimicked the sculptures she studied.

She bit her bottom lip in indecision; it was the first time she questioned the rationale of her activities since she stayed in his room. If she reached out to softly touch him with another hand, would this be the breaking point? Could she stop herself or him from anything further?

***

Fitzwilliam Darcy found heaven. Nothing that God created could be more perfect than Elizabeth Bennet's hand exploring his body. He couldn't believe this was happening; he wouldn't stop her for anything. Whatever she wanted, she would find in him a willing participant. If it resulted in their immediate marriage, he could no longer regret the circumstance; he would only rejoice at their union. He lifted his own hands to caress her arms while she remained focused on his chest. Then slowly, he moved his hands to her back, to bring her breasts against his chest. For the first time, he felt their fullness press perfectly against him.

He wanted to crush her to him; he wanted to feel what her own bare skin felt like against his. He wanted to kiss her. And once he finally claimed her lips, he would only let them go long enough to bring her to his bed...

"Darcy, have you seen... DARCY!"

Darcy jerked his head up as he heard his cousin's voice hissing at him from the door. He immediately stepped in front of Elizabeth, trying to expand the width of his body to the greatest extent possible to shield her from Richard's prying eyes. Suddenly he felt her break away from his grasp. He turned to see her dash for the door. Colonel Fitzwilliam reacted immediately, stopped her flee by placing himself in front of the closed door.

"Miss Elizabeth, please take a moment to calm down. No one needs to see you leaving this room..."

***

Elizabeth put her hands up to her face. What had she done!? She had to get out of there!

Since she had no other options, she sat in relative privacy in the chair so recently occupied by the scantily attired gentleman now standing on the other side of the room. With the face covered by her hands, she reflected on her actions, which she soon discovered did not lessen her discomfort in the slightest. How could she allow this to happen? How did this man to cause her to lose all sense of propriety? She could not even fault him as she initiated it. She did everything. It was completely her fault! She didn't even know if he enjoyed it. He must have lost all respect for her. What would his family think of her when Colonel Fitzwilliam revealed the truth?

He had wanted her to leave, and she refused! She still was not completely sure of her feelings toward the gentleman, but how could she refuse his offer of marriage after such a display? Would he even offer? Of course, he would, he would feel bound by honour to do so. His cousin saw her as a willing participant in their actions; alone in his room. The truth would be well-known.

She knew she liked and appreciated him far more than a few weeks ago, but that did not mean she loved him enough to bind her life with his. She could not deny the passion she felt for the man, but Romeo and Juliet also felt passion. The young fabled lovers let their passion overwhelm them, but she believed they never felt real love. Was she about to fall into the same trap? Would her future end in a similar manner as theirs, just over the course of many years instead of only a few days? Did he hate her for putting him in such a position?

Darcy immediately walked over to her and knelt down on both knees in front of her.

"I am so sorry. I should never have taken such liberties with you. Will you ever forgive me?"

The tears formed in her eyes, she took some time to force out the words in one breath, "How can I offer you forgiveness for what I created?"

He gently wiped the tears from one of her cheeks before taking her hand that he soon felt shake inside of his. He moved his head so he could stare directly into her eyes.

"I must take responsibility. Because of my actions, I must ask you something you are not yet prepared to answer."

She put her hand up to his mouth, stopping him from speaking further. The desperation poured from her voice when she pleaded with him, "Then do not ask it yet. Please, give me a chance to consider your fourth question before you ask your next."

He hung his head and squeezed both of her hands that he protected inside his own.

"I will keep silent. The Colonel will remain the same; he is not only my cousin but also my best friend and I trust him with my life." He needed a deep breath before he could continue. "I do not want your acceptance just to protect your reputation. I want your heart given freely and I will give you the time you ask for, but I hope for my sanity, that you do not take too long." He kissed her hand and let her sit until she felt well enough to stand without assistance and the tears stopped running down her cheeks. He checked the hallway once more before Elizabeth quietly slipped out of his bedroom.

Chapter 27

Elizabeth caught her aunt's worried glance, as Mrs Gardiner continued to pass concerned looks her way ever since they entered the carriage. It was no wonder she was still doing so, as they had travelled for several hours, during which she only contributed a passing yes or no to the conversation and said just as little during supper the evening before. Her aunt must have realised that the quiet and withdrawn Elizabeth of today differed greatly from the merry one of yesterday morning.

"Lizzy, you look like you have the weight of the world on your mind. What is troubling you, my dear?"

She gave her aunt a small smile, trying to dissuade her from further conversation. "'Tis nothing. I am just distracted by the beautiful scenery."

Mrs Gardiner looked at her with understanding and sympathy. "Lizzy, you never were a very good liar. It is not in your nature to be deceitful. Please talk to me. You have been so quiet ever since we arrived at the inn yesterday. Did something happen?"

There was no chance of her answering that question with the truth. If she did, they would be on their way back to London to get a marriage licence instead of to Pemberley, where Mr Darcy offered her time to be sure of her choice. Elizabeth glanced at the other females in the carriage who each looked at her with apprehension. If she couldn't share her troubles with her dear aunt, her favourite sister, and the girl, who would be likely her future sister, who could provide her with comfort? She felt lost and overwhelmed. She needed guidance and who could she possibly place more trust in? The only other person she trusted as much as the others in the carriage provided the source of her heart's conflict. With a sigh of resignation, she finally gave in.

And once the words started, she couldn't stop their steady flow. Everything in her mind poured from her lips. "I was just thinking about Shakespeare. So many of his plays are about love, but what really is love? In fiction, there is always some great defining moment where the hero or heroine is instantly aware of their newfound attachment. But how are such things determined in real life? When do people know they are in love? And what is love? What is the difference between love and lust? Romeo and Juliet had lust and passion, but did they ever find true love? If two families are very different, can the two lovers live happily? Or is the love just a trick of our imaginations, like what happened to Helena and Demetrius in A Midsummer Night's Dream? Could a fairy goddess fall in love with a rascal if she no longer has control of her mind? Is love just a spell that can be taken away at any time? And in the Taming of the Shrew, what about Katherina and Petruchio? Can you love someone that changes you or do you need to change to fall in love? Is submission by the wife a requirement of love? Can two strong personalities ever mesh and unite as one in happiness? Does love have to be difficult to be great?"

She took a deep breath and finally stopped when she saw Jane staring at her in concern with her blue eyes wide open. At least her aunt gave her an affectionate smile that she appreciated more than she could express.

"It seems like you do have the weight of the world on your mind after all, Lizzy. I cannot tell you exactly what love is; that is something that each person needs to determine for themselves." Elizabeth felt her momentary ease that arose from her aunt's calming voice suddenly vanish. But her aunt immediately continued. "I can tell you how I knew I loved your uncle. Would you like to know?"

Lizzy looked at Georgiana and Jane, both of who looked just as interested in the conversation. Maybe it wasn't the most appropriate conversation for Georgiana to have at her age, but as the girl almost married the year before, it might be better for her to hear it as well from someone like her aunt. In fact, they could all glean some value from this conversation. And as she started this, she might as well follow through. "I think we would all like that very much."

In a motherly tone which Elizabeth heard her aunt use on many occasions to soothe her nieces and nephews, Mrs Gardiner spoke clearly and with obvious affection for the other ladies in the carriage. "I should begin by answering one of your first questions. From my experience, I believe love can be differentiated from lust through sacrifice. Passion alone does not lead to sacrifice; passion is often a selfish emotion. When you are willing to forgo your own passion or desire for the man you love, that is a sacrifice; you care more about him than you do yourself. I do not mean that two people in love should not be passionate; I think that is a necessary and vital component to a happy marriage. But both participants should be more concerned with their shared passion than simply their own." Mrs Gardiner looked at each of them before continuing. "Do you all understand what I mean?"

Passion. Elizabeth's thoughts on that particular subject were definitely not ones she felt willing to share with anyone.

She felt physically drawn to Mr Darcy, and he seemed to enjoy what happened as well. But was their mutual passion and physical connection enough for a successful marriage lasting for the rest of their lives? She needed more information, but how could she ask without accidentally revealing what happened? What if the tale just poured out as her questions did? She physically bit her tongue to force it to remain silent and hoped that her aunt continued with no prodding.

Thankfully, her sister saved her. "So, it is acceptable for a woman to enjoy, and at times more than enjoy, holding the arm of the man she loves?"

Elizabeth's cheeks flushed instantly; she felt so completely wonton! While her dear and innocent sister feared to hold Bingley's hand, she touched Mr Darcy's chest! And did she stop there? No! She wanted to touch more of his body. She wanted to be touched by... Who knew where it would have stopped if Colonel Fitzwilliam hadn't interrupted them?

Thankfully, everyone else in the carriage watched as Jane's cheeks turned a rosy red from embarrassment. For once, Elizabeth held no thoughts of teasing her sister to ease the awkward question. She wanted the group's attention to stay with her sister as long as possible. Her own heart raced just from the thought of what happened at the inn.

"I hope she does. If she does not feel that connection, their union will not be what either hope for from life," answered Mrs Gardiner.

Jane continued very shyly, "But what does it mean when he kisses your hand and you..."

"You want more? I might ask if you ever felt the same when another young man held or kissed your hand. Is it one man in particular that causes your heart to beat faster or your cheeks to fill with colour? When you hold his hand during a dance, is it the same as the set before with a different young man? If it is just one man that causes you to experience such emotion, it might be love, or it might be lust. I must then refer back to my question of sacrifice. Are you both willing to sacrifice for your common happiness? If the answer is yes, I would be more inclined to believe that love has become the guide of your heart and emotions."

No other man ever made Elizabeth feel remotely similar to what Mr Darcy inspired. She enjoyed dancing with John Lucas and the several of the other boys from Hertfordshire, but she never felt the heat from their hand long after the dance ended. No other man made her heart beat faster just from thinking of him. And when his eyes pierced her soul, her entire body became flushed. It was a fact she couldn't deny; no other man came close to making her feel like Mr Darcy.

Elizabeth looked anxiously at her aunt; she wanted her to continue with the story of how her aunt met her uncle. Mrs Gardiner must have guessed her desire because she quickly complied when their eyes met.

"When Mr Gardiner came to Lambton on business, I had no intention of ever leaving Derbyshire. It is the most beautiful area in England. But, I fell in love with your uncle when he travelled there. When I thought of him leaving to return to London without me, I realised that being with him, anywhere, was more important than my selfish desire to remain in Lambton. And without my asking him to do so, your uncle even set up several business contracts with merchants in the area to make sure we always had a reason to return to Derbyshire, even though he may have gotten a better price from other areas of England."

"Now Lizzy, we will return to some of your original questions. For some, love may come only after many months of a gradual change in estimation; you might even be in the middle before you knew it began. For others, it may come along suddenly, like a bolt of lightning. And maybe even for others, they may wake up one day after a wonderful dream and realise they are in love. I don't believe there is any one way to know you are in love."

Frustrated that her aunt refused to give a firm answer to her question, Lizzy countered. "But if it does come slowly, when do you know your relationship evolved into something further?"

"It may be a momentous and emotional event, maybe a separation, or possibly just a moment when you look at him as though you never saw him before. I am sure it is different for everyone. For me, it was the thought of your uncle leaving and never being able to see him again. I knew then how much I loved him."

Jane looked at her sister and changed her facial expression to match the same she usually reserved for moments late at night when the rest of the household was fast asleep. "Lizzy, I think that we both fear marriage to a man we don't love. Deciding who to marry is the most important decision a woman can make. Once wed, it cannot be rescinded and must be accepted. We have plenty of examples of poorly matched couples in unions not rooted in love and respect, even among our closest friends and family. But Lizzy, I hope that your fear of an unhappy match isn't closing your heart and your mind to the possibility of finding real love having the happiest of marriages. Love isn't always easy and you can't always choose who you love." Jane took a deep breath; Elizabeth knew that look. It was the same that Jane wore when Mr Bingley left Netherfield. She grabbed Jane's hand and encouraged her to continue.

"I knew I was in love with Mr Bingley when he left Netherfield last fall. I felt as though a part of me left with him. I wanted to stop loving him, especially when I thought I would never see him again. But when I saw him again, it was as though I felt complete again. I am not sure how else to describe it."

Elizabeth looked at her sister with compassion on her face. She knew how much Jane suffered from Mr Bingley's departure, although she never admitted the extent of her grief until that time. She almost envied her sister the heartbreak; at least she knew her heart. If Mr

Darcy left her, would she be affected? Would she care? Would she cry into her pillow at night? Would she feel as though a part of her soul was severed from her interminably? Was he undoubtedly an integral part of her future? Could she imagine her future without him? He made her feel more emotions than she ever imagined, but were they founded in love, lust, passion, anger, or possibly a combination of all of them?

Georgiana's voice broke her stream of thoughts. "I know I haven't ever been in love, but I think I know at least part of what it is; trust. If you cannot trust the man you love, you don't really love him. You know you can always trust the people you love to support and protect you, even when something horrible happens. You can trust them to act in your best interest, instead of their own. And if you do something wrong, you know they will forgive you." Elizabeth gave Georgiana an encouraging smile; she knew she spoke of her experience with Mr Wickham. Her brother, who did love her, protected her from the man who only acted in his own self-interest. Georgiana Darcy was a very fortunate girl; she knew her brother would stand by her through anything.

But did she trust Mr Darcy? He asked her that question almost two weeks ago. By his own choice, he remedied the only offence which forced her to withhold complete trust in his character. Now that Jane and Mr Bingley were reunited, and she was sure, shortly to be engaged, did she trust him absolutely? Did he complete her heart? Could she carry on contently with her life if he was no longer a part of it? Would he be the biggest regret in her life if she left Pemberley without accepting him? Could she ever feel this way about another man? What would she sacrifice for him? Were his needs more important to her than her own? No other man made her feel remote like Mr Darcy did. But was it him or was it just the feeling of being wanted by such an extraordinary man? She didn't need to decide today as much as she wanted to; the gentleman that caught her eye as he travelled past the carriage promised her the time she needed while at Pemberley. He was so thoughtful...

***

That same gentleman of Elizabeth's thoughts eventually found himself in a conversation he preferred to avoid. Bingley and Colonel Fitzwilliam rode ahead of the group while he lagged behind with Mr Gardiner. The events of yesterday continued to plague his mind.

Eventually, he noticed that Gardiner slowed his horse slightly and gave him a small head nod, indicating Gardiner's desire for him to join the tradesman. Not knowing the reason, he slowed his horse to the same speed. His companion seemed to be distressed over something.

"Mr Darcy, I hope we might take this moment to discuss a topic of some importance before we arrive at Pemberley." Gardiner waited for him to look the older gentleman in the eye before continuing. "Elizabeth's father isn't here and I feel the responsibility to act in his place. First, I need to know if you already asked my niece to marry you."

Darcy eyed the man to his left. "We are not engaged."

"I know that I will not be able to watch Elizabeth every moment during our time at Pemberley. Undoubtedly if you desire time alone with her, you will find a place and time that will accommodate your plans without anyone else being the wiser. I need your word that you will not do anything to take away Elizabeth's choice regarding her future."

"I hope you do not doubt my intentions toward your niece, Mr Gardiner. They are entirely honourable."

Darcy watched as Gardiner urged his horse to catch up to Bingley and Fitzwilliam. After yesterday, he would never give Elizabeth up. He was sure she loved him, even if she would not yet admit it. He promised himself that when she left Pemberley, it would be as his fiancée. And most importantly, she would anticipate their union with a desire equal to his.

Chapter 28

Pemberley House looked extremely impressive from the carriage window. How could someone who matured here, not feel a sense of pride in their home and heritage? It certainly explained one more aspect about the man who consumed Elizabeth's thoughts. The closer she came, the more insignificant she felt. If she was mistress of the house, would she still feel inconsequential or would she feel a sense of pride at maintaining and watching over such an establishment?

When they finally arrived at the doorsteps, Elizabeth once again waited for Mr Darcy to help her out of the carriage. She wanted him to have the moment that she knew he longed for - to escort her himself into his home. But what would the servants think to see him escort her instead of his sister? She tried to let go of his arm as they traversed the granite stairs, but he put his hand over hers, refusing to sever their entrance together. What was she thinking trying to take away that moment that Darcy wanted so badly? If the servants didn't already know, they certainly would know soon of her relationship with their master, anyway.

As they walked inside, Elizabeth didn't even hear the words he uttered in her ear; she could only hear faint tones in the distance as her mind was preoccupied with the splendour in front of her. Fortunately, she managed to keep her mouth closed. She must have stood in complete stillness for some time, for she finally heard her aunt tell Mr Darcy that she appreciated the offer to see their rooms, as her nieces seemed tired. Georgiana lightly took her other arm and led both her and Jane to their rooms while Darcy reluctantly dropped her arm to escort her aunt and uncle to their respective chambers.

***

She took a moment from trying not to gawk at her surroundings, when she heard Georgiana's voice.

"Lizzy, are you feeling well?"

"I am embarrassed to say I feel fine. This is simply the most exquisite home I have ever seen. To say that I feel overwhelmed would be an understatement."

"Oh. Well, we can fix that. Instead of going to your rooms, would you and Jane like to come and spend some time in mine so you can relax in the company? If you feel as I do when I go to Rosings, being alone won't make you feel any more comfortable in your surroundings."

Jane answered for her. "I think that is the soundest advice I have ever heard. I will speak for my sister and gladly accept the invitation."

"Wonderful. Jane, Lizzy, I have a whole new closet full of dresses that you simply must try on!"

And after several hours and what seemed like a hundred dresses later, with Jane and Georgiana's constant attention, she finally felt almost as comfortable at Pemberley as she did at Longbourn. But she couldn't help but wonder whether that feeling would stay when she left the comfort of Georgiana's room and equally impressive wardrobe. Then again, did she ever feel a more incredible mixture of vitality and safety than when alone with Mr Darcy? But when she arrived at Pemberley, once she was entirely surrounded in his world, she felt overwhelmed. She just needed a few minutes alone with him to recoup that feeling of assurance; then she might feel the permanent relief she hoped to find.

But when she was alone with him, she forgot about the impropriety of the situation. It seemed so natural. She forgot about the consequences of their situation and thrilled at the connection they shared. But there were consequences to their actions; she already imagined their severity when Colonel Fitzwilliam interrupted them yesterday. Thankfully, the damage was not permanent or public. However, now done, she could not take back what she did, nor after careful reflection of her aunt's words this morning, could she honestly admit to herself that she wholly wished to.

Didn't her aunt say that a marriage should have passion? In fact, it was a necessity for the couple's happiness. Could she be fortunate enough to have found both love and passion with a gentleman who felt the same for her? Or did they both have personalities too strong to ever completely reconcile into a lifetime of happiness together? She wanted that moment where she finally knew she loved him beyond all reason and did not simply feel passion or admiration for him. She needed that moment to be completely sure of the most important decision she would ever make.

At least she had time to consider his fourth question. What did she want from her life? Could she live happily without that feeling that only existed when he smiled solely at her and held her tightly in his arms? She just needed to find a way to talk to him; somehow, he would make sure that the feeling of belonging at Pemberley extended farther than Georgiana's room. She only hoped that the feeling of comfort didn't extend into another Mr Darcy's bedroom. Whether he might invite her in if given the chance was a question she need not ask as she already knew the answer. Unfortunately for her sensibilities, she didn't doubt the answer of whether she would accept the invitation if asked to enter.

***

Elizabeth, closely followed by Jane, walked in Georgiana's footsteps, back down the stairs to the parlour. This time, she tried to take note of the hallways and the decorations which Georgiana pointed out. But the farther they went, the more uncomfortable she felt in comparison to the grandness Pemberley. Once again, she felt like an outsider, insignificant when compared to the manor and its occupants who seemed so at ease within its walls. She tried to calm herself with the one rational thought that circled in her mind; who wouldn't feel the magnitude of the responsibility of being mistress of such a house? Elizabeth couldn't deny that the path she travelled certainly led in that direction.

The three ladies walked into the parlour where Elizabeth immediately focused her gaze on Mr Darcy, who sat comfortably talking to his cousin, Mr Bingley and the Gardiners. She tried to return his tentative smile, but she knew it must appear forced to those who noticed it.

While she sat relatively quietly, the others fell into easy conversation, which she was surprised that Mr Darcy joined, and even led, on more than one occasion. Was he truly this much more comfortable at Pemberley than at Rosings or Hertfordshire?

After the gentleman finished discussing with her uncle the merits of the pond for fishing, he glanced at her from the side of his eyes. She barely noticed as she was still fiddling with a loose string on her dress that held her attention for most of the conversation so far. It seemed like a much easier task to manage than facing the magnitude of Pemberley and the decision that lay before her about its owner.

And as he could read her mind, Mr Darcy suggested, "Mr Gardiner, may I invite you to join me, and whoever else would like, on a short walk around the pond? We still have a few hours of daylight and I think the exercise might do everyone some good after being inside the carriage for much of the day."

She might find a chance to talk to him alone. For almost the first time since she entered the parlour, she spoke in a voice that betrayed her excitement and enthusiasm for the idea. "Mr Darcy, that sounds like a wonderful idea. I know I would enjoy a short walk and the chance to soak up some fresh air."

The smile he gave her in return vanquished any doubts that her response was not exactly what he hoped for.

It was then she heard her aunt's voice, "Edward, I think a walk would be lovely. Would you mind if I joined the three of you?"

Her uncle stood and walked to his wife. "I think that is an excellent idea." He then addressed the group at large, "Will anyone else be joining us?"

To Elizabeth's surprise, Georgiana stood next to her and admitted she would enjoy the walk too. Apparently, her idea of a private moment with Mr Darcy would not be as simple as she hoped. Of all the people she expected to hinder her hopes for time alone with him, Georgiana was certainly not on the list. Jane and Mr Bingley both admitted they would prefer to stay in the parlour, and Colonel Fitzwilliam tactfully offered to remain to act as their chaperone while the rest of the party went outside.

Mr Darcy offered her his arm, which she readily accepted, and the five walked out the front doors and around to the side of the house. Elizabeth lifted her face to the sky to feel the sunlight shine on her face. The cool breeze against her arms did nothing to dissuade her enthusiasm; besides, the heat from Mr Darcy's body left her slightly warmer than normal.

And then, there she saw it; the only place that Mr Darcy could possibly be leading her towards. A magnificent oak tree stood proudly in front of her. The green leaves already formed, expanding its already significant size. Its trunk a symbol to its longevity; Darcy's ancestors must have planted it when they built the house. This was the tree where Mr Darcy's parents taught him one of the most valuable lessons he ever learned. And he made sure that he took her to see it.

She leaned over to whisper to him, "Please tell me that is the infamous tree of your youth."

He gave her a small smile that did not betray to others the delight that only she saw in his eyes. "Of course it is. The question that remains is whether we will be able to persuade Georgiana to climb it with me. Shall we ask her?"

She couldn't help the teasing smile that emerged, "I think she would be a sight to see climbing all the way to the top. I don't doubt she could though."

Upon hearing her name, Georgiana walked closer to them and asked what caused them to laugh.

"Miss Elizabeth and I were wondering if you would mind climbing the tree with me for some additional exercise."

The girl looked sceptically at her brother, "Fitzwilliam, are you sure that is the first thing that you want to show our guests? Our climbing abilities are usually not part of the tour."

He winked at his younger sister before answering, "Perhaps we can save it for day two of their visit. But I am indebted to Miss Elizabeth a promise to show her the Darcy siblings climbing that particular tree, and you know I hate to go back on my word."

Georgiana looked at Elizabeth in feigned frustration. "Lizzy, why in the world would you want to see Fitzwilliam and me climb a tree?"

"Because once I see the master of Pemberley climbing a tree, I hope to finally see Pemberley as you do, as your home."

"Well, if that is all it will take," her voice trailed off as she tilted her head up to look at the highest branch. "Fitzwilliam, will you help me make it on to the first branch? I should be fine from that point."

Elizabeth laughed as she had not done in several days. Nothing could make her see Pemberley as a home, more than the girl's face twisted in determination to do anything to make her feel at ease. Now that she saw the tree in question, the mental image of the Darcy siblings climbing to the highest point did nothing to hurt her merriment. Between breaths, she assured them that no demonstration would be necessary right now, but she did not want to take away the option later in the week. She felt Mr Darcy move his other hand to caress her hand, now clutching his arm even tighter as she stood entirely too close to him for propriety's sake. Even if they weren't alone, somehow he still managed to make her world right. If only she knew what the rest of the week held. Not that it mattered, because for now, she only needed to enjoy the walk in a place she was beginning to love.

Chapter 29

After her guests retired for the night, Georgiana roamed the same hallways that she and her brother showed to their guests only a few hours before. She initially feared for Lizzy once they left her sitting room that afternoon, she seemed so quiet. Thankfully, her brother asked Lizzy to join him for a walk around the outside of the house. Her brother was so thoughtful; fresh air was just what Lizzy needed after so many hours inside.

She never had a friend stay at Pemberley. All the young ladies that stayed at Pemberley were there as her relations or as relations of her brother's guests. They didn't come to Pemberley to see her; usually, they avoided her unless she was spending time with Fitzwilliam. Elizabeth was different and hopefully, her friend would be her sister soon. And if there was one thing she was sure of in her heart, it was that sisters always said goodnight to one another before falling asleep. She gained the confidence to knock on Elizabeth's door. She waited to hear Lizzy's voice invite her in before she entered.

Elizabeth was sitting comfortably in her nightgown on the bed with Jane next to her. The youngest Bennet sister patted the pillow and signalled for her to join them on the bed. "Giana, have you come to stay up with us tonight? You are always a very welcome addition to our merriment."

This is what she hoped for - a night of gossiping with two young ladies that truly welcomed her comments, insights, and laughter. Even so, she shyly sat on the bed next to Lizzy and waited for them to start the conversation. She hoped she wouldn't say anything to mar their happy time.

"I hope I didn't interrupt anything. What were you laughing about when I came in?" She watched as Jane and Elizabeth exchanged a glance. Elizabeth gave an embarrassed looked to her elder sister.

"Jane, I suppose we need to tell her."

Georgiana looked at Jane to encourage her to reveal their discussion.

"I was just doing an impression of Mr Collins describing the exterior of Pemberley."

Now she felt confused. Did Elizabeth not like Pemberley? Who couldn't be impressed by Pemberley? "Who is Mr Collins and why would he not like Pemberley?"

"Mr Collins is our cousin and the parson of your aunt, Lady Catherine. I don't think that even Jane would begrudge me mentioning that he is, shall we say, utterly ridiculous? One evening while at Longbourn, he held an entire conversation about the fireplace at Rosings. I never felt less anxious to see a fireplace in my life as when I dined at Rosings. I felt as though I already knew more about it than the one at Longbourn that I saw every day of my life." Georgiana looked at Lizzy to encourage her to continue. "I fear that if he ever saw Pemberley he might faint for he could never begin to relay all of its loveliness to every person he met from that point forth. Unfortunately, I fear he would admire and praise the very things that mean the least to its inhabitants."

"And what do you think of Pemberley, Lizzy? What do you admire?"

Jane piped in with an obviously feigned innocent expression before Elizabeth could answer. "Yes, Elizabeth, do tell us what you admire most about Pemberley?"

Lizzy lightly kicked her elder sister, pursed her lips and remained silent. Mimicking Jane's expression, Georgiana dramatically fluttered her eyelashes, looked at Elizabeth, and asked once more, "Lizzy, I do believe you owe me an answer. What aspect of Pemberley have you come to love? Please don't limit yourself to the house itself. The walls of Pemberley contain many treasures that are beloved."

Elizabeth dropped her head back against the headboard with a resounding thud and a large smile upon her face. "How can I win when the two of you gang up against me? Well, I will only say that Pemberley is the most welcoming home I have ever be welcomed to. And as for the treasures inside, I admit that they are truly priceless and irreplaceable."

"Is that all? I fear little sister that you left out which treasures you value the most."

"How can I not love everything about Pemberley when it gave me such a wonderful addition to my life, Jane?"

"I think I will accept that answer for now. I hope though you find at least one other prize that you make a permanent addition in your life while here at Pemberley."

Elizabeth looked back at Jane who gave her a hopeful smile. She knew Jane would allow her answer to remain where she left it. She said enough for one night on that subject.

"Giana, would you like to play a game with Jane and me?"

"Of course."

"First, you must promise to not think any less of us once we tell you what the game."

Miss Darcy looked affronted at her accusation. "I could never think ill of either of you."

"Let's hope you feel the same after I tell you the game. The Bennet sisters meet a few nights a week to play a game taught to us by the brother of a good friend. It is called Three Card Brag."

Instead of the confused look she expected to see, she saw Georgiana's face immediately perk up. "I know how to play that. One of my companions taught me. I didn't know it wasn't a proper game until I already realised how much I enjoyed it. She said she played it growing up, so I didn't think it was improper at all - until Mr Bingley inadvertently mentioned it one night and my brother gave him a wary look."

"Well, that certainly makes this easier. Jane and I travel with a box of buttons and we just use those for chips instead of money. At the end of the night, whoever wins is allowed to choose two ribbons from the collection of one of the losers. The person that comes in the second is allowed to choose one ribbon from amongst the losers. Mary likes to tell us it is the same as the sin of gambling, but when she wins, she never turns down an opportunity to take a ribbon from Lydia. She claims she is just trying to teach us a lesson, but I think she gets more joy out of playing than the rest of us. Would you like to play with us?"

"Of course I would. I have some ribbons that would look beautiful on either of you."

In a caring, but firm voice, Jane spoke before she was able to clarify a few unofficial rules to Miss Darcy. "Wait a minute, Georgiana. You can't lose on purpose just so that you are able to accessorize Lizzy or me."

The girl's face fell so suddenly that Lizzy felt the need to do something to change the mood. She arched her eyebrow and answered her sister with mock superiority. "Speak for yourself, Jane. I have had my eye on several of Giana's ribbons since she took us on the tour of her rooms. I believe there was a green one with silver borders that would suit me perfectly. Now, since there are only three of us playing, how about if the winner selects two ribbons from either one of the other two, and the second place selects one from the one that finishes third? That way we will each have a reason to try to place either first or second." Elizabeth watched as both girls nodded in agreement.

"Just so we know we are playing by the same rules, here are the ones taught to us by our friend. Everyone is dealt three cards and everyone has to bet the same amount as the lead bid each round if they want to stay in. When there are only two players left, one player usually must double the bet of the other to force the end of the betting. But since we play with buttons, we often just skip that part because by the end, no one actually has any reason to keep any buttons safe; that is one disadvantage to playing without real money. The order of hand rankings is: three of a kind, straight flush, straight, flush, pair and finally just high card." She looked to Georgiana to make sure she played by the same rules. "Do you have any questions?"

"My companion and I usually just played with very small amounts of change and kept the max bid very low so that neither one of us ever felt too disappointed at losing. But there is one question I want to ask, do you play ace-two-three as the high running flush or ace-king-queen?"

"We always play with ace-two-three high, if that won't confuse you too much."

"That is fine. My companion told me that it differed depending on who played, so I just wanted to make sure when I make my bet."

With a full smile, she asked the younger girl, "Rather confident, aren't you? Already counting on getting the high hand?"

"I just want to make sure I have a chance at the red ribbon I saw you wear in your hair yesterday. I would hate to overbid without knowing the rules."

Elizabeth couldn't help but laugh. Finally, it seemed the Georgiana felt comfortable around her and Jane. The girl's current attitude was much more conducive to the manner she wanted to pass the time tonight; with sisterly affection between all three of them. From the beginning of the first game, Elizabeth and her two companions settled into a happy conversation of life at Pemberley, Longbourn and the delight of living with other sisters. After more hands than Elizabeth cared to count, for she was enjoying her time with Jane and Georgiana, she let out an involuntary yawn when she heard the clock chime from the hallway. She could see Georgiana's blinks taking longer and longer as she rested her head comfortably against the pillow in between deals. Although she knew that Jane could stay up longer without a problem, after her lack of sleep the night before, a little more tonight would be welcome.

When Elizabeth mentioned it, the other two agreed it was time to retire for the night, but they would play one final hand to determine the winner. Elizabeth dealt the cards and couldn't help but hope that she did, in fact, have the winning hand. The green ribbon she mentioned earlier would look spectacular with her emerald green dress. She bit her lip in anticipation of seeing her cards. After a quick peak, she immediately tried to mask the smile she felt appear by biting the inside of her cheeks. But when she looked up, she saw that Georgiana already noticed her tell. After years of practice, she still hadn't learned to check that habit.

They went around once with each betting two buttons. On the second round, Jane folded. As usual, Jane didn't want to risk being one of the final two. She never liked the competition that always existed between the last two in. Inevitably, someone always lost almost all their buttons in the final round. And if it happened to be her, it was worth the chance. It was a beautiful green ribbon. As she predicted, both she and Georgiana continued bidding until she ran out of buttons, forcing the end of the betting. Once again, the whole game came down to the final hand, a situation that neither one could actually affect.

Elizabeth turned over her cards to display two jacks and a ten. Instead of turning her cards over, Georgiana exclaimed with a sly smile, "Drat! You beat me. I guess you will have to take that green ribbon after all."

Lizzy didn't want to win; not like that anyway. In her best authoritative voice and a raised eyebrow, "Giana, let me see your cards."

Instead of flipping them over, the girl quickly slipped them back into the pile. "Lizzy, I told you you beat me. Why would you need to see the cards? Now, before I go to bed, I will get that ribbon and bring it to you."

With a resigned shake of her head, she answered, "There isn't any use in fighting a Darcy, is there?"

Georgiana gave her a small smirk that resembled her brother's entirely too closely. "The sooner you accept that the sooner you will make all of us very happy." Quickly, but affectionately, she hugged both her and Jane before she left to get the much-disputed ribbon.

Chapter 30

Sitting completely alone in the family dining room, Darcy looked up from his morning coffee and papers when Elizabeth entered the room, wearing the same green ribbon that she won from Georgiana, prominently displayed on her favourite emerald green dress. Her eyes met his as she walked toward his spot at the head of the table.

"Good morning, Elizabeth. I thought you might sleep late this morning. I don't believe anyone else will wake for several hours."

Choosing to ignore the familiarity of his greeting which she had not yet given him explicit permission to use, she kept her good humour and smiled at him. Did her heart not beat a little faster when he spoke her name before her mind told her that it wasn't proper?

"I saw the sun begin to shine through my window and my desire to start the day was too great. Are there any walks you can recommend, Mr Darcy?"

"I believe there are one or two paths which you might find acceptable."

"If you could send me in the right direction, I will let you get back to your papers. I am sure these are only a few of the matters that await your attention."

Instead of answering her, he stood with the papers in his hand and gave them to one of the footmen waiting in the hallway. He walked back in, offered his arm to her. "Elizabeth, you can't believe I would give up this opportunity to spend time alone with you and show you my home. The papers can wait for another hour."

After picking up a piece of bread to take with her to hold her over until they returned, Elizabeth dutifully walked with him out the front door. She was not surprised when he led her to the stall that contained the only other being allowed to accompany them on their walks. With a simple nod of his head, he dismissed the groom that came to saddle his riding companion.

"Am I to have my second riding lesson?"

"I hoped that I could persuade you to join me. I want to show you one of my favourite places and it is much easier to reach on horseback."

Elizabeth surveyed the house around her, feeling suddenly very uncomfortable. "Are you sure that we should be seen riding off together? I don't want anyone on your estate to get the wrong idea." Rather, she didn't want them to get the correct idea.

"Elizabeth, my staff is very loyal to me. This is my home. I hope it will be your home very soon, as well. I don't want to spend your first days at Pemberley worried about what the servants will think of you spending time with me."

His words didn't ease her discomfort. She twisted her mouth in indecision.

"But if it will make you feel more comfortable, I will ride in a different direction from your walking path. Once the path goes down the hill, it will fork; wait for me there. When we return, I will make sure to continue to ride for sometime after in order to spread apart our return times."

She smiled in relief. "Thank you."

She bid him a quick goodbye and walked toward the dirt path that led from the garden into a nearby wood that he pointed out to her as she broke apart pieces of the bread that she brought with her. The garden certainly was lovely. His mother seemed to prefer flowers and plants that grew in concert with the landscape instead of trying to improve the gardens to fit society's expectations. In whole, she felt entirely satisfied with the current arrangement. Maybe she would plant a little more lavender, but that certainly didn't need to be changed anytime soon. She laughed quietly to herself when she realised that she already began to think of how to make Pemberley more familiar to her. She did promise herself that she would use this time to think about her future and decide what she wanted. It seemed her mind was accomplishing the feat anyway, even without her demanding it to consider the possibilities.

By the time they met at the fork in the road, Elizabeth felt her easiness restored and flashed Mr Darcy a welcoming smile as she saw him approach. He dismounted from his horse and stood next to her; his own good humour seemed apparent after she greeted him so warmly. When he brought her hand to his lips, she could only widen her smile in response. Even if she wasn't sure that she was in love with him, it still felt intoxicating to be loved by him.

All too quickly, Mr Darcy released her hand to give Elizabeth a carrot to feed to Erebes, just in case she needed to become reacquainted. Once she felt ready to begin, she stood by the gentleman and without invitation, put her hands on his shoulders, silently inviting him to put his hands around her waist. She knew she surprised him with her forwardness, but at that moment she didn't care. She made a decision the night before and was determined to follow it.

After spending time with Georgiana and Jane, Elizabeth examined her feelings for Georgiana's elder brother, trying to use what her Aunt, sister and friend discussed with her in the carriage. When she tried to think of any reason she should not accept him, the only reason she considered for more than a minute or two centred on his behaviour at Hertfordshire. Ever since she took the time to know him better, holding his past offences, even those at Hertfordshire, against him became increasingly difficult.

As such, when she felt Darcy's warm hands surround her waist to lift her on Erebes, instead of embarrassment, she allowed herself to revel in their closeness. When she situated herself as comfortably as possible on the saddle designed for a male rider, she looked down to the gentleman, and with a teasing smile on her lips.

"Are you going to stay down there all morning or are you planning to join me?"

With a pronounced smile but without a word, he lifted himself on the horse directly behind her. He took the reins in both hands and let his arms rest comfortably against her waist. As she already made her decision the night before how she planned to act around Darcy, as soon as he lightly kicked Erebes to indicate the beginning of their ride, Elizabeth sighed contently and allowed her back to fall into the masculine chest of the man behind her. Mr Darcy left the reins in his hands that surrounded her. The proximity of his body was quickly causing her to lose all rational thought.

After spending time admiring the views of Pemberley in perfect peace and quiet, Elizabeth's mind ventured to the last time they found themselves alone and together. He asked her about her future. He wanted to know if she loved him. She thought again about what her aunt told her. Suddenly his hand felt slightly more constricting than before.

"Is something on your mind?"

Elizabeth answered as simply as she could. "Love."

"And what about love?"

"I am trying to decipher it, but it still seems so mysterious." She wanted to hear if he had any response. When she heard only silence, she continued, "I am not sure how to ask this," she remained silent and then finally blurted out her question, "But how did you know when you were in love?"

"Is this your fourth question?"

She smiled. "Do I need to make it one of my five to gain an answer? I hate to think that I can only expect an answer to two more questions for the remainder of our acquaintance." In a voice of mocked superiority, she finished, "Besides, this is in response to the question you asked me yesterday, so I should not have this count for one of my five."

One of his dimples showed. "I think I will let you leave your last two questions for another occasion. After all, that allows me to look forward to having three more private conversations with you."

She hoped he wouldn't be offended by her question, but she desperately wanted to know the answer, so she repeated it. "So, how did you know you were in love?"

He waited for several moments before answering. When he finally did, his tone partially matched the lightness that hers displayed, but she could still hear more than a tint of seriousness behind his words. "I cannot fix on the hour, the spot, the look, or the words, which laid the foundation. It is too long ago. I was in the middle before I knew that I had begun."

She took a chance in teasing him. She desperately hoped he would not be offended, for she wanted to continue in their semi-peaceful existence that morning. His arms felt too wonderful around her to wish he would stop.

"My beauty you had early withstood, and as for my manners - my behaviour to you was at least always bordering on the uncivil, and I never spoke to you without rather wishing to give you pain than not. Now be sincere; did you admire me for my impertinence?" She felt his chest rise with a small laugh. Her plan worked, he didn't seem upset with her.

He simply answered, "For the liveliness of your mind I did."

Elizabeth could not help but laugh and turn to him. "You may as well call it impertinence at once. It was very little less." She turned back to face the horse. If she was perfectly at ease with him and their relationship was already decided, what would she say? When she devised her answer, she took a chance. "The fact is that you were sick of civility, of deference, of officious attention. You were disgusted with the women who were always speaking and looking and thinking for your approbation alone. I roused and interested you because I was so unlike them. Had you not been really amiable you would have hated me for it: but in spite of the pain you took to disguise yourself, your feelings were always noble and just; and in your heart, you thoroughly despised the persons who so assiduously courted you. There - I have saved you the trouble of accounting for it; and really, all things considered, I now begin to think it perfectly reasonable."

"I would never dare disagree with you."

Elizabeth could not help but laugh again at his attempt at a joke. She couldn't believe how easy this conversation felt. If they tried this same conversation two weeks ago, it would have continued in a much different stream of emotions.

"But I must at least expound upon one area. I finally recognised my love for you when I realised that you consumed almost my every thought. You filled my dreams, both in night and day. I could no longer imagine my future without you in it."

If possible, she relaxed even farther into his chest, drinking in his musky scent. She draped both of her arms over the one still holding her waist. She felt a peace previously unknown and didn't want it to end. A future with the formidable Mr Darcy? Could she still deny that she hadn't spent much of the last two weeks constantly thinking about that question? He consumed almost her every thought. He filled her dreams, both in night and day. But was it love? She could no longer convince herself it wasn't, but did that mean it was? If this wasn't love, what was? Shakespeare never wrote anything as perfect as how she felt in the security and warmth of Mr Darcy's arms.

They continued their ride in a similar companionable silence, only interrupted by Mr Darcy pointing out a particularly interesting site along the way. When they reached the same fork in the road where their ride began, she felt Mr Darcy drop the reins and use his arm to fully engulf her body next to his. The smoothness of his freshly shaved cheek pressed next to hers. Oddly, she felt the overwhelming feeling was over all too soon when he loosened his arms from around her.

She heard his sigh as Mr Darcy dropped his arms from around her waist and upper chest and carefully swung his leg over the hind end of Erebes. Once safely on the ground, he lifted his arms to her waist in order to help her down. But once down on the ground, he did not release her. As he looked at her standing in front of him, she couldn't help the laugh that escaped her lips.

She felt her entire body glow with happiness. This was going to be a very good day indeed.

***

Elizabeth sat by the edge of the pond under the shade of a large tree watching from a distance Jane walk with Mr Bingley, Mr Gardiner fishing happily with Colonel Fitzwilliam, and Georgiana deep in discussion with Mrs Gardiner. She wished Mr Darcy was there; she envied the intimacy that Jane shared with Mr Bingley. She felt positive Jane's engagement would be announced before their party left Pemberley. But what of her own? Her ride with Mr Darcy the day before was no less than perfect. She did not want to alter a single moment. Did their cosiness and comfort that morning serve as a sign for things to come?

If only she could just sit beside him; she wanted the peace that came with his presence, that same peace that she found that morning and the afternoon before. Elizabeth looked into the distance, allowing her mind to continue its aimless wandering, curious where it might take her on this beautiful day. A moment later she heard his voice.

"Elizabeth?"

The gentleman of her very thoughts sat next to her, allowing her to remain comfortably leaning against the tree. "Mr Darcy, did you finish your business?"

"I did. I apologise for not accompanying you at the start of the picnic, but when I met with my steward, he told me of a matter that could not be put off any longer."

"I understand. But that does mean you belong to us for the rest of the day." Her eyes sparkled at him as she smiled for him alone.

"I willfully submit to your demand. Did I interrupt you? You looked like you were deep in thought when I came upon you."

Her cheeks blushed as she answered him, "I was just daydreaming."

"And what did you see in your reverie?"

"A man." She whispered.

"A man?" He slightly raised the eyebrows "And what did he do?"

Her cheeks blushed a deeper red. "He sat down next to a woman."

In a soft voice, he whispered, "Did she lean against him for comfort?"

"She did." Elizabeth looked around to see if her family was watching them. The tree hid their closeness to one another from the rest of the party. Mr Darcy took the opportunity to move his arm over her shoulders and helped her to learn intimately against him. Their bodies were almost one.

Not moving his mouth from the close proximity to her ear, he asked his next question. "What did he do next?"

In a raspy voice, she answered, "He whispered something to her."

He waited breathlessly. "And what did he say?"

Elizabeth only blushed further; she couldn't seem to find her voice.

"Did he tell her that he loved the way her eyes sparkled when she looked at him?" She nodded slowly, seeming to drink in his every word. "Did he tell her that he loved it when she argued with him?" She smiled coyly and nodded again. "Did he tell her that her laugh sounded like the voice of an angel?" She leaned in even closer to him and nodded.

Mr Darcy moved his head slightly to kiss the soft hair above her ear and then moved his lips to the base of her neck; he allowed the heat from his breath to caress the exposed skin above her dress. When she seemed sufficiently engrossed at the moment they would remember for the rest of their lives, he allowed his mouth to travel back to her ear. "Did he tell her that he loved her and wanted to spend the rest of his life by her side?"

She slowly nodded and moved her head so that her mouth was temptingly close to his. Their eyes met. They reflected a softness and pure joy he had never seen before. With just one more question, he would finally claim her lips and her vow to be tied with him forever. He was so close.

"Elizabeth, my love--"

***

"LIZZY! Lizzy! I am so excited!" Elizabeth forcefully jerked her head up and her body away from him to see Miss Bennet running towards her. Darcy's arms immediately felt empty and his stomach turned from the resentment he felt at the lost moment. He wanted to grab her back to him and magically rewind time, but he knew that he could not. Elizabeth already gave her complete attention to her elder sister, still running eagerly towards them.

Jane Bennet finally reached Elizabeth and took her hands, encouraging her younger sister to stand next to her. The elder Miss Bennet had no reserves from her sister where confidence would give pleasure; and instantly embracing her, acknowledged, with the liveliest emotion, that she was the happiest creature in the world. "'Tis too much! Charles and I are engaged." Elizabeth did not withhold the sincerity of her congratulations; they were given with a warmth and delight which words could but poorly express. "I do not deserve it. Oh, why is not everyone as happy?"

Darcy thought the same question. He was only seconds from finally gaining Elizabeth's acceptance as his wife. He just needed time to say four little words. They weren't even the four-syllable words Bingley usually accused him of using. He only needed four short words to secure what he wanted most in life. He had planned on using several others, but really, if he knew about the coming interruption, he would have settled for the four. His question only required fourteen letters and her response, but three! Now he must wait; he knew Elizabeth would not want to take away anything from the day that now belonged to her sister. He could not help hanging his head in frustration; it seemed the more polite of the two options before him; he didn't believe Bingley would appreciate being strangled for not waiting just a few more minutes so he could have ensured his own happiness as well.

Hearing the commotion, soon all the members of the picnic assembled around the tree which Darcy hoped to make a sacred place which he could return to with his wife and relive the moment where they finally found happiness. Seeing the joy on his friend's face and that of Miss Bennet's, he could no longer begrudge them the profuse congratulations of the Gardiners, Richard or Georgiana. He vowed to have his time with Elizabeth; he would find a way and soon. He just needed to find a place without any people or doors that people could walk through whenever they wanted. Once he found that place, she would finally be his.

The party reassembled together by the impressive lunch spread which Georgiana ordered for the day. They ate, laughed, and continued to offer Miss Bennet and Bingley their hopes for a most joyous future. Only when a chill from the late afternoon breeze arrived, did the party finally decide to go back to Pemberley and prepare for the evening.

Darcy walked with Elizabeth in a short distance from the rest of the party, using the last opportunity to talk with her privately that day.

"Elizabeth, I hope I may persuade you to take a walk with me in the morning. I believe I received a satisfactory answer to my fourth question, and it seems I am finally able to ask my fifth and the final one."

She gave him a welcoming smile and nodded with agreement.

"Would seven o'clock be satisfactory? Would you prefer to eat breakfast before or when we return?"

"I prefer a morning walk before the breakfast," Elizabeth answered a little shyly.

"Six o'clock tomorrow morning in the foyer then. I will be waiting for you." He whispered to her before they walk to the house and joined the rest of the party.

***

Darcy was ready almost thirty minutes before six; for once, he awoke Marcus to begin his morning preparations as he didn't want to be late. Trying to pass the time, he sat in the large chair behind his desk and noticed the post on the silver tray that came the previous night. He glanced through the addresses and saw nothing important until the last one. It had Longbourn as the return address, but it was addressed to him; on the back was written "Urgent." If it hadn't been from Longbourn, he likely would have still waited until he took his walk with Elizabeth. As he had some time to spare, and he needed to know if something happened to her father or mother, he opened the letter.

Darcy,

I am sure you are surprised to find my handwriting instead of Mr Bennet's in a letter from Longbourn. I heard the rumours about you and Miss Elizabeth and wanted to wish you joy in your upcoming marriage. I admit though that I am surprised you found the lady worthy as a wife when even I moved on to someone more suitable. Unfortunately, I have found it exceedingly difficult to marry where my interests lie due to my lack of funds available. Luckily, I found just the opportunity to reclaim what I am owed.

I persuaded Miss Lydia to run away with me to marry; we left Hertfordshire at the same time you are receiving this letter. You know me well enough to know I have no plans of marrying such an annoying and destitute girl. If you want your beloved's sister returned to her family unharmed and possibly with her reputation intact, you will pay me 30,000 pounds. I realise that Lydia is not worth what dear, sweet Georgiana was, but I am sure you will agree that to you, her sister is. If you do not comply, I will make sure that Lydia's reputation will be undoubtedly ruined in the most public and dastardly manner imaginable and for good measure, I may even announce my near-elopement with Georgiana.

The longer you wait, the harder it will be to repair Lydia's reputation or explain her disappearance. I suggest you make haste for your house in town, for that is where you will receive your next set of instructions.

You know me well enough to know I do not make idle threats.

G. Wickham

Chapter 31

Elizabeth walked quickly down the staircase, anticipating her morning walk and the future she dreamt of the night before. She only stopped when on the third step from the bottom she heard the sound of glass shattering against the wall and the slamming of a door in the distance. Without thinking, she rushed towards the sound, and found herself at the door she knew to be for Mr Darcy's study. Without having time to knock, the door swung violently open, revealing the gentleman on the other side. He looked past her; she wasn't sure if he even saw her.

"Mr Darcy?"

For the first time, she noticed the anger radiating from his eyes; she had never seen him, or anyone for that matter, look that furious. When her father lost his temper, he never approached the level of quiet fury staring back at her. Even after Mr Darcy's failed proposal, he kept some demeanour of his composure.

He answered her, in a tone without any of the gentleness or love she hoped to hear from his lips that morning. "I have to go to London immediately. If you will excuse me, I need to wake your uncle and the other gentlemen; they will be joining me."

"Please, please tell me what happened." She could hear the desperation in her own voice.

He paused for a moment while his face softened. Before he answered, the rage in his countenance returned. "I can't." He turned to walk from her.

This could not be happening! Not when she finally made up her mind to accept him! She felt her chest tighten before she spat out, "No! You cannot do this to me. You cannot just leave something without finishing it. You promised that you wouldn't make the same mistake again."

Her words reached him. His entire face softened and his shoulders relaxed slightly. He carefully led her into his study, closed the door, and brought both of his hands up to cup her cheeks.

"Elizabeth, please don't ask me. You won't want to know once you hear it."

But she needed to know. If this matter was going to ruin her life, she had the right to know the reason. And suddenly she remembered; she still had two questions remaining.

"I still have two more questions which you promised to answer no matter how difficult it may be; let this be one of them."

He stroked her cheeks with his thumbs before answering in a slightly louder and stronger voice, but it still held the same sincerity. "I am not trying to protect myself. I am trying to protect you."

She couldn't help the tears forming in her eyes. "But if this is taking you away from me, now at all times, I need to know. I need to understand."

Without any more words, Darcy looked deep into her watery eyes and then leaned in to kiss her forehead. He moved his hands from her face to bring her whole body to him, closing the already slight space between them. As she listened to the strong beat of his heart, she couldn't help feeling the hopelessness of her situation. She whispered again and again that she needed to know. If this would be the last time she felt his arms around her, she had to know what drove them apart. How would she live with the uncertainty and confusion?

"Wickham convinced your sister Lydia to elope with him. Now he is refusing to marry her. He wants money to save her reputation. He wrote me a letter."

She pulled her face away from his strong chest and gazed up at the mask he presented. That meant there was more. "You promised to tell me the entire truth."

In a strong, but firm voice, he answered her. "Elizabeth, I am sorry, but I cannot tell you any more." He tilted her face to make her look him squarely. "Please understand. You cannot forget some things once you hear them."

Elizabeth returned her head to his chest and considered her options. She needed to trust this man who held her in his arms and who she planned to marry. She already pledged her heart to him. Although not said aloud yet, it did not make her vow any less sacred. Now, fate gave her a chance to prove that pledge before she made it publicly. She wiped the tears falling down her cheek with her hand, looked up to the gentleman that stood before her, and said as simply as she could, "I trust you. Please help my sister."

With a relieved sigh, he answered, "Elizabeth, thank you." He squeezed her to him once more before releasing her, kissed her tenderly on the forehead, and left her alone in his study. She could only watch his painful trek up the stairs, wondering if her entire future just vanished with him.

***

After several hours in private conversation, Darcy and the other gentlemen assembled in the entranceway to bid the ladies farewell. He already gave direction to Marcus to ensure their luggage would be packed and sent after them; he didn't need anything to slow them down. Whatever they needed could be procured in town anyway. Speed was the most important factor now. He had to reach Wickham before the scoundrel could carry out his threat. He didn't even want to think what would happen to his life if Elizabeth's entire family was ruined.

He looked around the room quickly while Elizabeth stood in front of him. With a nod of his head, he quietly dismissed all the servants in the hallway. Colonel Fitzwilliam, with Georgiana close behind him, already went outside to ensure their horses were prepared.

Elizabeth looked at him with her eyes full of angst and allowed him to begin. "I need to ask something of you before I leave."

She squeezed his hands that fit so perfectly intertwined with his own before promising, "Anything."

"Will you watch over Georgiana for me? She already loves you so much; there isn't anyone else that I would trust her care to. I know that she seems very easy to watch over, but she is very headstrong. When her mind is set along a path, there is little that can be done to dissuade her. She will always find a way to do what she believes is best. I need to know that you will stand by her and protect her as best you can."

The determination in her voice put his mind at ease as he heard her words. "You will not be able to separate us. I already love her as a sister."

"I promised, we will take a walk when I see you next after your sister is safe with your family."

The tears that formed in her eyes cut at his heart. She brought up her hand to his face. "I will look forward to it every day."

"Elizabeth, you are the most important person in the world to me. Never forget that."

"I won't."

Darcy looked to see if the Gardiners or Jane and Bingley were watching. Seeing both couples preoccupied with their own goodbyes, Darcy leaned in and kissed Elizabeth tenderly on the forehead. He then moved to her ear and gently whispered, "Remember that there is nothing that can keep me from asking you the question I have waited so long to ask. The next time I see you, my love for you will be perfectly clear to everyone who sees us. And when that time comes, I will finally claim your lips for my own."

He lightly fingered her cheeks once more and went out the front door to meet his sister and cousin, leaving a still speechless Elizabeth in the foyer.

***

Elizabeth turned her attention to Jane's stressed voice as soon as the four ladies returned to the house from watching the gentlemen ride away in haste. "Aunt, what in the world is going on? Charles refused to tell me. Please, something terrible must have happened. Uncle must have told you."

Mrs Gardiner looked at them all for some time before finally responding. "Perhaps we should sit down somewhere. I have a feeling we are all in need of some tea. Georgiana, is there anywhere, in particular, that is especially pleasant this time of day?"

"The conservatory is quite nice with all the flowers beginning to bloom. I will have one of the maids bring us tea there."

"That sounds like an excellent suggestion. Would you show us the way?"

Miss Darcy took them through several hallways where Elizabeth nervously looked up to see Darcy's ancestors hang majestically on the wall. Why did each one appear to glare at her in menacing stares? Were all Darcys so tall or was it just a requirement for the artist to paint them so? Was there ever one whose portrait should not be hung in a museum for scores to view in awe? Surely one Darcy out of a hundred must be awkward or gangly.

As she passed her Darcy, he seemed to fit perfectly in with his family line. Would they have approved of her even if not in her current situation? What if her sister's reputation was ruined? Would Mr Darcy disparage his entire family's reputation to marry her? His family left him so many obligations to fulfil and he refused to run from any of them. Would he discard her to protect his family's past and future? Would she let him leave her without a fight? But, could she force him to go against every fibre of his being that demanded the protection of his family's good name just for her?

Oh, Lydia! How could she be so selfish and stupid! If only someone had taken the effort to curb her wild behaviour as a child. But then, wouldn't that make her almost as guilty as her parents? Perhaps if she and Jane had taken the time, Lydia would be much different and not have placed them in such dire straits. It was no use assigning blame now. She needed to trust Mr Darcy and the others to return Lydia safely to her family. She needed to trust Mr Darcy. But why did that infinitesimal nagging doubt still plague her when she thought about their future? Would she ever be sure about a future with that imposing man that looked down on her from the wall? His eyes seemed to see right through her, even from a lifeless painting.

After they reached the conservatory where each settled into one of the comfortable chairs, Lizzy looked around and wondered if the others felt as ill at ease. She kept squirming in her seat, but no matter how many times she readjusted herself, it made no difference. None of the three unmarried ladies would find any peace until they heard what Mrs Gardiner said. Elizabeth's mind was swimming. What did Mr Darcy plan to do? What could they possibly tell Georgiana? Did her aunt even know of the girl's connection to Wickham?

They sat in awkward silence until the maids brought in several pots of tea and plates of fruit. Elizabeth slowly sipped of her tea, but she couldn't force any food down her throat, no matter how tempting the array of delicacies looked. When she set her tea down, she surveyed the room and saw that each of the other ladies looked the same way she felt. Finally, her sister's voice broke the silence.

"Aunt, please, please tell us what has happened."

Elizabeth watched as her aunt carefully placed the china teacup on the table and examined Jane, Georgiana and her.

"Mr Darcy received word this morning that Lydia ran away from Longbourn to be married. To make matters worse, he does not believe the wedding will take place. He and the other men went to town to track down the scoundrel that she left with and return Lydia to her family before the damage is too great to be concealed."

Elizabeth watched as the slight colour that remained drained from Jane's face. Her sister now knew what she already realised; that their family would be ruined if the gentlemen did not reach Lydia in time for the scandal to be hidden. What would happen to Jane's engagement only formed the day prior? Would Mr Bingley honour his word? Would Jane be the victim of a broken engagement? How could their family possibly survive another scandal? All five Bennet sisters would be forced to live on the charity of Mr Collins!

If only she prevented this terrible tragedy from ever occurring! She alone knew the kind of man that Wickham was and she did not relay the truth to her father who might have stopped this supposed engagement from forming. And now, her entire world turned upside down because she did not take the proper measures to protect her family. When in the same situation, Mr Darcy managed to protect his sister from the scoundrel. He somehow knew he should be with Georgiana at Ramsgate and then saved her from a horrific fate. At least Wickham would have married Georgiana; he would feel no such eagerness to do the same with Lydia.

"Who is this terrible man that would do such a dastardly act to our family?" Asked Jane.

"It was Mr Wickham."

Georgiana gasped and reached to tightly grab Lizzy's hand. Elizabeth wrapped her arms around the girl and tried to offer her that same comfort as during their first meeting. She took her hand in hers and left her aunt and Jane sitting in the conservatory. But before she left, she mouthed the words, "I will explain later" to the two women who remained. She saw them nod in understanding although still in confusion.

When she settled Georgiana on her bed, she took out the pins that held her hair, and gently stroked the blonde locks the fell in an unruly mess around her shoulders.

"Lizzy, how could I have let this happen?"

"Giana, this is in no way your fault."

"Of course it is my fault. If my brother was not so concerned with my reputation, Mr Wickham would be known for the cad and scoundrel that he is."

"Giana, this is not your fault. The fault belongs to me. I knew what kind of man Wickham is and I did not warn my family."

"Oh, Lizzy! You cannot possibly blame yourself for this." Giana lay quietly in her arms for several minutes before she spoke again. "We must do something."

"We are doing something. We are waiting for your brother, your cousin, Mr Bingley and my uncle to recover Lydia. We are not giving them one more thing to worry about by bounding off for London to recover Lydia ourselves."

Instantly Georgiana perked up. "Lizzy, what a wonderful idea! We will go to town to rescue Lydia."

Elizabeth spoke quickly, trying to head off Georgiana's plan before it became too firmly embedded in her mind. "Giana, I just said we should stay here and not worry your brother. He wants to find us safely here when he returns."

"But Lizzy, I know where to find Wickham!"

"How in the world do you know that?"

"I have my sources. Besides, I am not going to tell you unless you go with me to London."

"It isn't that easy. I promised your brother."

Giana smiled at her and answered, "You promised him you would look after me, didn't you?"

"How did you know that?"

Giana's voice suddenly became quieter. "I guessed; he never leaves anymore without someone he trusts implicitly to look after me; especially what happened after Ramsgate." Then with more strength and conviction, she continued. "How are you going to look after me if you don't go to town with me?"

She arched her eyebrow and looked at her young ward while trying to display some semblance of authority. "You are staying put Miss Georgiana Darcy. You will be at Pemberley when your brother sees you next."

Georgiana narrowed her eyes and brow and explained in a voice that brokered no opposition, "I am not staying put and we both know that you can't stop a Darcy when they put their mind to something."

"Giana, how do you plan to leave here on your own? You must know that my aunt would feel terribly responsible if something happened to you while in her care."

"Then don't make me do anything drastic. I know plenty of ways to sneak out of this house without anyone knowing. I have access to plenty of money and jewellery to make sure that I am not found." Giana paused for a long moment before continuing and softened the determination in her face. "Lizzy, please don't make me do that. Come with me."

She sighed in resignation. "How do you suppose that we convince my aunt of this? You know that you are not going to get me to go without her and Jane."

The girl smiled widely at her and answered rather quickly as though she knew what Lizzy's answer would be long before she finally gave in. "I know. I already have that part worked out."

"Now will you tell me how we are going to find Wickham?"

"I will tell you when we get to town. Otherwise, I am sure you will try to find a way to stop me. This way, I know you will go with me."

"I suppose you better tell me your plan so I can help you to convince my aunt."

And with that, they spent the next hour rehearsing their parts to make sure they could battle any argument that Jane or Mrs Gardiner made against their plan to travel to town early the next morning.

***

Georgiana led her by the hand through the same hallway they walked through only an hour before. The glare from Darcy's ancestors didn't seem to lessen; in fact, they seemed to admonish her even more than previously.

They returned to the conservatory to find her aunt Gardiner and Jane sitting on the sofa together, neither one speaking. Even though they went over the details of the plan in upstairs, it didn't mean that she was prepared to deceive her aunt.

"Aunt? Georgiana and I need to talk to you about something."

Her aunt waved them to join her and Jane on the sofa.

"We need to go to London."

"Lizzy, your uncle and Mr Darcy both told me that they wanted us to stay here and wait for them to return. They do not need any extra worry."

Elizabeth answered uncertainly, "But they left without knowing how to find Mr Wickham."

Her aunt looked at her incredulously, "How do you know how to find the man?"

"Because during one of our conversations at Longbourn he told me that he never felt safer than when in Bath. He spent much of his time there before he joined the Army. The gentlemen are on their way to the wrong place if they want to find him."

Her aunt's eyes shut in hopelessness. "Lizzy, we can simply write them."

"But aunt, what if there is other information that we don't realise that we know and would be of value to them? I know that Mr Darcy and he used to spend a lot of time together, but that was several years ago. They will need our help when they find Lydia. You know as well as I do that only one of her sisters will be able to control her. Uncle will need our help." She watched as her aunt seemed to resign herself to the idea. "Please, we cannot sit here and wait when we might be of use."

"Well, I suppose we should go to town. We must inform Mr Darcy's stuff as his servants must escort us. We will leave first thing in the morning."

Chapter 32

Darcy handed his long, dusty riding jacket to the footman who finally answered after he forcefully hit the metal knocker several times. He tried to ignore the obvious look of surprise on the servant's face when he and the other gentlemen stood at the front door of Darcy House, well past darkness and without any forewarning.

"I need to see Mrs Blaine in my study right away." With that order, he immediately directed the other gentleman to follow him to his study. They needed a place away from the servants and any prying ears to plan their next course of action. He hoped that the ride would have allowed a coherent plan to form, but his anger quelled all other rational or fruitful thoughts.

Before they had a chance to sit, Darcy heard a knock on his door and Mrs Blaine's voice behind it. He quickly invited her in, letting her observe the seriousness of the four gentlemen in front of her, and then immediately began with his purpose. "Mrs Blaine, I need to know if there have been any messages left for me in the last few days."

"Yes sir, there are usual calling cards left for you. You also had numerous invitations to supper parties. Per your instructions, we told the callers that we did not know when you expected to return from Pemberley."

"And have you seen Mr Wickham at any time in the last week?"

The housekeeper looked shocked as she answered him, "Of course not, sir. We have strict instructions to not let him near this home."

If Wickham did not leave them any messages, there was not much left he, nor anyone else, could do tonight. He hated being at Wickham's mercy; it grated on nerves he did not know existed before today. "Mrs Blaine, if Mr Wickham or any unusual messenger comes to the house, please invite him in and ensure he is not allowed to leave without my knowledge. It is of the utmost importance that no one is simply allowed to drop off a message and leave, no matter what time or in what manner the message is delivered."

She bit her top and bottom lip momentarily together and then answered, " Mr Darcy, what would you consider an unusual messenger?"

He thought for a moment before responding, "Anyone that I would not normally associate with."

She nodded, "That should be simple enough. I will let the footmen know to detain anyone unusual that comes to the house."

"Thank you, Mrs Blaine. Also, Colonel Fitzwilliam will have his usual room. Please show Mr Bingley and Mr Gardiner to two of the other spare bedrooms. I am not sure when we will be departing, but I need for our things to be ready for travel with no prior notice given. That will be all for the night." With a nod of his head, he dismissed her.

Mrs Blaine left the room as quickly as she entered, leaving the gentlemen looking at each other in silence. He couldn't stand to be around anyone right now. He needed time to calm the horrible variations of his future that he could not stop thinking about. Finally, he suggested they should all retire for the night and wake up early in hopes that they had some starting point from which to make a plan. And if they didn't, hopefully, one of the four would have an idea of where to begin the search. For one, he had no idea where to begin the search; he relied on Wickham finding him to begin negotiations for the blackmail payment. And until Wickham contacted him, he and Miss Lydia could be anywhere in England, possibly even Scotland.

After the others retired to their bedrooms, and he sent his servants to the gentlemen's respective homes for clothing and personal items, Darcy once again returned to his study, hoping for some peace of mind that eluded him ever since he opened that damn letter. As soon as he sat down in the same leather chair where Elizabeth sat only a week before, he brought his fingers to his temples, once again contemplating the evils of the circumstances that lay before him. The one thought that kept circulating was that he should have asked Elizabeth to marry him before he left, regardless of the situation with her sister. He needed to have that happiness to hold on to in order to refrain from strangling Wickham within the first moments of their meeting. Now, he was left without any guarantee of the future that he determinedly clung to.

But what if he married Elizabeth, and it ruined Georgiana? Could he put his own happiness above that of his beloved sister? The irony that he now contemplated the same issue that she held against him two weeks ago didn't escape him. But would Georgiana also choose Elizabeth over her own place in society? Fortunately for him, he believed the answer was yes. But would Elizabeth even allow Georgiana to make that sacrifice? It didn't matter; once he and Georgiana joined forces to persuade her that the only acceptable future for her was as Mrs Darcy, Elizabeth would eventually capitulate. He had to believe that. Damn Wickham for making him doubt it.

***

He walked into the dining room to see his cousin, his closest friend, and the uncle of his beloved eating breakfast without any servants in the room. Apparently, they had been there for some time as Gardiner was already finished and Richard already began to attack the second plate of food by his place. Bingley's mood seemed to fit his own better; his friend barely touched the food in front of him, except to make an occasional angry jab at a sausage that continually slipped from his fork.

When he took the seat next to his cousin and poured some coffee from the pot, Richard finally stopped eating long enough to stare at him and examine his mood. He hadn't said a word in response to the silent inquisition or even begun to eat before Richard spoke in a voice he usually reserved for those subordinate to his command. "Don't take that mood with me, Darcy. Every man at this table will do whatever is possible to save Miss Lydia and ensure that Wickham is not ever able to do this to any other young lady ever again."

The master of the house stared back at his cousin and dropped his fork that he was ready to use. The words flowed quickly from his mouth, albeit a little quicker and louder than he planned. "I have no idea what you are talking about. My mood should be the same as every other man here."

"And it is, cousin. But we cannot risk allowing your personal anger and vendetta to cloud your judgement and our collective decision making. Wickham will count on your rage to sway the situation in his favour. I have no idea how, but you know as well as I do that he will."

He sat there in silence knowing Richard was right. Wickham knew him too well.

Instead of answering, he speared one of the sausages on his plate and tore apart several pieces of bread that he proceeded to devour.

Finally, Bingley friend put down the fork he used to attack the remaining food on his plate and spoke in a significantly more determined voice that was his norm. "Darcy, we will get Miss Lydia back. Failure will not be an option. And God helps that bastard when we find him because there is not much that will stop any man in this room from destroying him." And with that, Bingley rose from the table and walked to a chair on the other side of the room where he sat alone and in silence.

Yes, his friend was in the exact same mood that he was. That was what he needed. Destruction at this point was the only option. He knew Richard would not fail to inflict as much pain as possible on Wickham when they had the chance, no matter how many years of military training allowed him to express the calm demeanour he now displayed. He wasn't sure about Gardiner, but as the man's own children would suffer the consequences if Miss Lydia was not returned with some semblance of respectability, he believed that Gardiner would follow the other three if needed. He gave Bingley a half smile from across the room and proceeded to use the table manners that even his aunt would find acceptable for the rest of their rather quiet meal. Now they just had to wait for Wickham's messenger.

***

He wasn't sure how much time passed when Mrs Blaine knocked on the library door, interrupting gentlemen's forced silence. Darcy shut the book he had open but wasn't reading to answer the door. With a movement of his head, he indicated that she should enter; he carefully closed the door behind her.

He took a deep breath in before speaking. "Is there something you need to tell me?"

Mrs Blaine looked anxiously at him and fiddled with the small silver wedding ring on her left hand. "Sir, there is a young man, a boy no more than ten years old, here with a message for you."

He took another deep breath before answering. "And what is the message?"

"He has a sealed note that he was told to deliver specifically to you."

He looked to Richard who gave him an encouraging nod before he answered. "Then bring him in, but give us a few minutes first."

He looked to the other gentlemen, silently inquiring if they had any idea of how to approach the boy. Richard spoke first. "Darcy, I suggest that the first thing we need to do is see the note. From there, whatever we do, we show unity in the decision. We don't know how well this boy knows Wickham and we can't let him think that we are split in our decisions."

He watched as Gardiner nodded in agreement.

Mr Darcy moved to stand behind the desk in the library. The Colonel stood on this right, his face trained on the door, watching for the approaching enemy, just as a battle-hardened soldier should. Bingley stood with his arms crossed in front of his chest and with his head tilted slightly upwards, but eyes trained on the door; his face wore the same mask that Darcy often saw in the mirror; apparently, he taught his friend well without knowing it. Finally, Gardiner took the spot next to Bingley on his left.

After what seemed like an hour, Darcy heard the doorknob turn and saw the door open slightly. The boy with curly brown hair who stood no more than four and a half feet tall, weighing even less than Georgiana had at that age, stood before him. With dirt covering his face and shabby clothing, he held a battered hat in one hand and a sealed message in the other. The boy nervously eyed each of the men standing with him; obviously not sure of the reception that Darcy and the other men would offer.

"I heard you have a message for me." He purposely used his more authoritative demeanour and was pleased to see it garnered the intended effect; the boy cowered by the door and meekly held out the message.

The boy's voice matched the frightened look on his face and he tilted his head back to stare up at Darcy. "Sir, I was told to deliver this to Mr Darcy personally. Are you him?"

"I am." He swiftly took the note from the boy's hand. Once he held it, he took more time to consider the child in front of him. He couldn't talk with the other gentlemen while the boy stood there with him, nor did he want to release him yet. Without opening the letter first, he walked over to one of the cords and pulled it to request the service of a maid.

He met the maid at the door and closed it behind him; he didn't want the boy to hear their conversation. When he finished giving her direction, he walked back into the library and turned to the boy who hadn't looked up from staring at the titles of the books on the wall closest to him in some time.

Without much emotion, he asked, "Are you hungry?"

The boy looked back from the books and stared directly at him before finally answering, "Yes, sir. Very."

While tapping the note against his palm, he spoke in an easier tone, but still, one which the boy wouldn't be likely to argue with, "Go with Brigitte. She will make sure the cook finds something for you."

He and the other gentlemen watched as the boy walked out; Darcy couldn't help but notice the number of patches on the pants that were several sizes too large. Where did Wickham find that boy?

"Darcy, are you going to open it?"

With that, he hurriedly broke the seal and read aloud,

Darcy,

I hope you are enjoying your unexpected visit to town. I realise you would much rather be enjoying the sight of a pair of enchanting eyes staring back at you - those same eyes that I saw my own reflection in on a number of occasions, but some inconveniences cannot be helped. I am sure you understand. Since I am such an old friend, I know how you detest town, and I hate to delay the next leg of your journey. I find that I wish to move the playing field to somewhere more comfortable to me and less familiar to you. You will receive your last set of instructions at Bath. And do not fear for the company - I will ensure you are met at the Pump Room tomorrow. I do hope you will enjoy the wait; I am sure your presence there will cause quite the stir and I know how you love to be the centre of attention at any social gathering.

Until we meet again,

G. Wickham

Wickham knew perfectly how to torture him! After all, his childhood companion did have years of practise and time to think about the different ways to annoy him. But it was his fault that he still let that rogue worm its way under his skin. Would he ever be truly rid of that parasite? He had to believe so. At the end of this, somehow, he and that bastard would never have to face one another again. He finally looked up from the letter and glanced at the other two who knew first-hand the distasteful actions which always resulted from dealing with Wickham.

"Well, Darcy, it seems as though we are off to Bath," Richard spoke first.

Darcy looked to the gentleman whose face remained stoic ever since he looked up from reading the letter. "Gardiner, what are your thoughts?"

"I am afraid that in this case, there is no good answer. As you stated this morning, Wickham has to actually meet with you at some point to get his money and that is his ultimate purpose. But, the longer he keeps us running around, the harder my niece's reputation will be to salvage. In this case, I do believe that we are damned if we do and damned if we don't."

He felt his face twist in indecision as he took in Gardiner's all too perceptive words. Damned if they do and damned if they don't. That was exactly the situation that Wickham wanted to put them in. He looked at the other gentlemen and made the decision, "We go to Bath and we leave immediately. But first, we need to have a little talk with our young messenger who I believe will prove very valuable."

Instead of taking Richard and Bingley with him to the kitchen where he sent the boy, he decided he may be able to find out more information from the one who actually spent a considerable amount of time around children. He led Gardiner down the same hallway and through the same corridors he led Elizabeth only the week before...

They found the boy sitting at the table, devouring the loaf of bread and soup that the cook put in front of him. He took the seat next to the boy at the small rectangular table while Gardiner sat across from the child; Gardiner already warned him that they didn't want to surround their guest and further intimidate him; not when they needed his help. He wondered how close to sit, fortunately, the boy's smell kept him from deciding to crowd the boy any further.

He started off slowly and with an easy question, "How do you like the soup?"

The boy took another bite of bread and quickly chewed it before answering, being careful not to look at Darcy or Gardiner. "It's very good."

"I thought you might like it. I see that you are already almost done with the bowl in front of you. Would you like some more or perhaps you might like some pork or some other meat to go with your bread?"

The ruffian immediately eyed him with suspicion, but then looked to the tray of food the cook was preparing and silently agreed.

Darcy looked to Gardiner and opened his mouth to begin speaking, but before he could, he saw Gardiner shake his head, causing him to stop before the first words came out.

The tradesman took control of questioning the boy now. "We are happy to see you enjoying the food. But you don't have to eat it all now; you can take some with you when you leave. Would you like that?"

They both watched as the boy nodded and stuffed the last piece of the bread in the otherwise empty trouser pocket. Immediately, the boy went back to consuming more of the soup, which the cook just added to his bowl.

Once again Gardiner spoke, trying not to distract the boy too greatly from the mass of food in front of him. "When you were upstairs in the library, you looked as though you were searching for a particular title." Gardiner and he both waited, hoping the boy would offer some information.

The boy simply answered, "Yes."

Darcy decided to use Gardiner's tactic from before. "Did you see any books you liked in the library?"

"I was looking for a book of Shakespeare's sonnets."

The master of the house couldn't hide his surprise or his awe that the homeless boy read Shakespeare. He asked simply, "Why Shakespeare?"

"My father read it to me before he died last year."

"And you haven't had any chance to read it since?"

The boy hung his head and shook it back and forth.

"Would like a copy of the sonnets?"

"Very much."

In a soft and careful voice, Darcy answered. "I have a bargain for you then. I was wondering if you remember what the man looked like who brought you that note. Could you describe him for me?"

"He was tall but not as tall as you. He wasn't dressed nicely like you either. He had brown hair if that helps."

"It does, but was there anything that you remember in particular about him."

The boy thought for a minute and answered, "He had a scar on his cheek."

"Was it a new scar or was it an old one?"

The boy answered, "It wasn't pink like a new one."

Darcy saw Wickham last winter and there was no scar on his almost flawless face. Whoever delivered the note wasn't Wickham, which meant there was a decent chance that Wickham really was in Bath. He immediately felt more at ease with his decision.

He looked at the boy and thought about another option. "I will make sure that one of my servants brings you a copy of the book as I promised. But I wonder if you wouldn't be willing to make another deal for two weeks worth of breakfast and dinner at my home." The light in the boy's eye clearly showed he had the child's full attention. "I need to know if you see that man again who delivered the note. And if you find out where he lives or works, I will make sure that you are given some extra compensation for your efforts. And most importantly," he took a miniature out of his coat pocket, "if you see this man at all, please tell one of my servants right away."

"What do I have to do for the food?"

"Just watch for either of the two men and let me know if you see them."

"And I can come by every day for food, just for watching for him?"

"Yes. And, if we are going to have a deal, I would like to know your name, as you already know mine."

"Matthew, Matthew Jarrods, sir."

"Well then Matthew Jarrods, we will shake on it and we have a deal." He brought out his hand to the boy who eagerly returned it and for the first time, looked him square in the eye. The boy shaking his hand barely resembled the one who walked through his library door over an hour before. Darcy gave him another smile, before standing up from the table, walking out of the kitchen, and leaving the cook to fuss over the boy for a little bit longer.

As they walked back through the corridor, he looked to Gardiner, who followed closely behind him, "Gardiner, I am surprised you didn't say more."

"Quite frankly, so am I. But Matthew and you seemed to work things out between the two of you rather well. I do believe you have a devoted follower."

"If nothing else, the boy will get a few good meals. And now I feel much better about leaving for Bath immediately."

***

After the carriage ride that seemed endless due to Jane's occasional crying and Georgiana's silence, Elizabeth took Georgiana by the hand as soon as they arrived at Gracechurch Street. She led the younger girl straight up to the bedroom that Elizabeth usually occupied. "Alright Giana, we are now in town and have already tried to find your brother at his home with no success. You heard Mrs Blaine, they left the day before, and she doesn't know where. Now, tell me what you know."

The girl's eyes glowed at her as she answered rather excitedly. "I know of a contact that can help us find Wickham."

After trying to gain a small height advantage on Georgiana, she raised her eyebrow and asked, "Georgiana, I want to know who your contact is and where we can find him."

The girl raised her head and looked Elizabeth in the eye, "Not yet."

"Georgiana, that is not the deal we reached. You said you would tell me how to find Wickham when we arrived in town. Now, I want to know how to find Wickham."

"Lizzy, I am sorry, but I will only tell Fitzwilliam."

"We were just at Darcy House. You heard the housekeeper; your brother left yesterday and told no one of his destination or of his planned to return. Now tell me what you know!"

"I will do no such thing. We may need to do something ourselves if I am not able to tell Fitzwilliam the information I know. If I tell you now, you will surely tell your aunt and ruin any hopes we have of finding Lydia."

"Georgiana, there is no plan for us to find and rescue Lydia. I promised your brother to protect you. We will not be doing anything that will put you in a situation where I must follow through on that promise. I need you to tell me what you know so that we can tell my aunt and come to a sensible course of action."

The girl looked at her in pity, "Lizzy, I am sorry but I will not tell you. Besides, if I told you now, you wouldn't believe me, anyway. You would simply believe I was lying to appease you. Please believe me that whatever happens, everything will be fine in the end."

Elizabeth closed her eyes and took a deep breath feeling her heart still pound, wishing she felt Georgiana's confidence about the safety of their future. She had to trust Mr Darcy; she didn't have any other choice. After all, he promised that when he saw her next, his final question would finally be asked. If only she could be sure that nothing would get in the way of that promised time together. Wherever he was, she hoped that he was closer to recovering Lydia. She knew that she couldn't control his younger sister for much longer, and if something happened to the girl while under her protection, neither Mr Darcy nor she could ever forgive herself.

Chapter 33

Darcy threw his coat, hat, and gloves to the ground of his sitting room in the inn, not caring who would have to pick them up later. For over twelve hours he stayed at that ridiculous tea room that smelt of cheap perfume and body odour. No matter how much the people of Bath wanted to pretend they were of the highest social class, their smell gave them away instantly. And what did he discover after his misery of being engaged by every mother and her child in that horribly cramped space? Nothing! Only that Wickham still enjoyed making him miserable.

And to compound his already insatiable anger at the situation - Wickham made him stay in the place he hated most - completely surrounded and preyed upon by society mothers. When he left for Pemberley only a few days ago, he thought he would never again have to endure such treatment and phoney interest in his business and person. The mothers there were only interested in one subject, his marital status. He felt his back teeth grind together every time someone new approached him; he had to consciously force himself to stop, otherwise, the headache that began at the beginning of the day would only get worse. If only he could simply explain that it was already decided even though he had not announced it or finalised that status with the lady!

He poured himself a full glass of scotch from the small bar and before he sat down he heard a strong knock on the door. He stormed to the door and wasn't surprised to see his cousin. Without a word, he motioned for Richard to join him and returned to the small bar. He silently poured another glass of alcohol, shoved it in the hand of his cousin and sat down in front of the small fire in one of the two lumpy leather chairs.

Darcy used the next half hour in what he considered a very taxing endeavour, drinking the scotch in his glass and not taking his anger out on his cousin, who he knew did not deserve his wrath, but might be forced to deal with it due to his unfortunate proximity.

"Today was nothing short of a perfect calamity." With that short sentence, he finished the last of the scotch in his glass, revelling in the burning sensation flowing down his throat. The scotch he found in his hotel room proved a godsend - especially after spending all day at the Pump Room. If he ever had to drink another ounce of that blasted spa water, he would spit it out on the person that gave it to him. Why people spent time there by choice he would never understand.

Richard looked at him and took a small sip of his scotch; still half of the drink remained. "Yes, it was."

Darcy turned from the fire to face his cousin, "So, do we leave Bath and return to town, or do we stay here?"

"I think we should stay here. Wickham needed to have his fun with you, Darcy. But as you know, he has to meet with you to eventually collect his ransom. Unless you can definitively say you know where he is, we need to stay here - no matter how taxing and miserable it is for you. Bingley and I tried to keep our distance because we didn't know what Wickham had planned and how we might interfere with those plans."

He glared at his cousin, realising the soundness of his advice. But why did he feel as though he needed to return to town in a hurry? At least Georgiana and Elizabeth were safe at Pemberley; that was one less thing he needed to worry about. He sat back in the chair and ran his fingers through his hair, trying to make a decision. He loathed being at the mercy of his nemesis, but what else could he do? He would spend one more day on display at the Pump Room, but that was it. And he would find a way not to drink any more of that damned water, even if offered by the king himself! If Wickham did not show his face by tomorrow night, they would return to town the next morning and he would find a way to tear apart the city.

***

Matthew walked quietly on the street, lightly kicking pebbles as he waited for the sun to rise, signalling his welcome to arrive at Darcy House for breakfast. After the last three meals from Mr Darcy's cook, his hunger hadn't diminished; it only grew with each serving. He could barely see Mr Darcy's house from where he stood, but he did not want to risk anyone making him leave for dirtying the street with his presence. As if he could help not being able to take a bath in almost a year!

Not seeing anyone else on the street that would mind his being there, the boy sat near the corner and watched the taxis driving by, occupied by the drunks as they left the pubs.

He looked up as a young and obviously drunk couple, judging from the raucous language coming from the carriage, urged the driver to stop several yards from where he sat in the shadows. He heard the lady laugh after she asked the gentleman what house he would get for them once they were married. He heard the gentleman answer that it was five houses down and that the owner owed him something - it was the one with the blue door; he would point it out as they drove past. Immediately, the driver complied when the lady yelled for the driver to drive by the house on the way back to their hotel.

Matthew couldn't see the gentleman's face and didn't recognise the voice, but he did know that the man just referred to Mr Darcy's house as the one that the girl planned to move in to. The carriage drove much too quickly for him to chase them, but something in his gut told him that Mr Darcy would be interested to find out what happened. And as he took the small book of sonnets out of his pocket and lightly fingered the cover, he knew that Mr Darcy would keep his word to keep letting him eat at Darcy House, even if he tracked down the gentleman from the miniature sooner than the end of the two weeks. He ran down the street to see the cook and let her know of what happened. There may even be some extra reward if what he told her turned out to help Mr Darcy. He couldn't help but smile when he thought of what a delicious reward the cook would have for him. She may even find some chocolate for him.

***

Elizabeth awoke to two small hands grasping and shaking her shoulders. She slowly opened her eyes to see Georgiana still dressed in her nightgown and with one hand still resting on Elizabeth's shoulder.

"Lizzy! Lizzy! Fitzwilliam and Richard still haven't returned. Something terrible has happened. I know it! We have sat here for a full day waiting for them to return. We must do something - anything! I can't let Wickham harm them. He has done too much to my family already. I won't let him ruin yours as well. We have to find your sister and Wickham! We simply must do something. Lizzy, wake UP!"

Now fully awake and sitting up against the pillows, Elizabeth questioned her friend with as much compassion as she could muster that early in the morning, "Georgiana, what do you expect us to do? Although you might know how to find someone with knowledge of Wickham's location, you still won't tell me who that is. And once you do, how do you think that we could get the information from that person?

"My same reasons for not telling you still apply Lizzy. And I already figured out the last question - we will pay him. I know where Fitzwilliam keeps extra money for emergencies. Surely a few hundred pounds would be enough to buy the information we want."

"Georgiana, you are not going to persuade me to go to an unknown location with a purse full of money and ask a complete stranger where my sister and Wickham are. That is a lunacy. If you want me to participate in this idea in any way, you have to start giving me some details."

Georgiana eyed her for some time and finally laid down on the bed next to her. It only took a moment for the girl tightly closed her eyes and tensed her face. Elizabeth began to slowly stroke her hair and back, hoping to relax the girl enough to finally reveal the information that Georgiana guarded so closely.

When the girl finally spoke, Elizabeth had to lean down to hear the girl's words. "We have to go to a tavern. That is where we will find Wickham's contact."

She couldn't have possibly heard her correctly. Georgiana could not possibly think they could saunter into a pub and demand the unnamed contact reveal Wickham's whereabouts.

She couldn't help the spark of fear in her voice at hearing the barest of details of the girl's plan. "Giana, you know as well as I do that if we walk in to there with a fist of money, it will be immediately taken from us and we will be forced to leave without information, the money, or our reputations intact." She paused for a long minute, and then continued, "In the worst case, we may not be able to leave at all. Even if we could escape in the same condition as we arrived, we need to have some reason that will make him tell us."

Georgiana remained silent for several minutes thinking about what Elizabeth had said.

"Elizabeth, what is it that almost all men believe?"

"That they should be king?"

The same devilish smile stayed on Georgiana's lips. "Other than that; be serious, Lizzy. They believe they are smarter than women. But what if we beat him at his own game? In the end, we might be able to make a deal that would allow him to save his dignity and reputation and we would learn where Wickham is."

"Georgiana, what are you planning for us to do? Your brother left you to my care. If I let you do this, he would never forgive me. Please, let us think of another way to help."

The girl looked at Elizabeth, with a look of defiance that she had never before seen equalled, even from Lydia. In a voice that could not have possibly belonged to the same girl who only one week ago ran from the parlour in fear, Georgiana spoke clearly and without emotion, "I am going to do this. You promised my brother to look after me. If you want to keep your promise, you will help me and stand by me."

"Please, Giana, don't say that."

"Lizzy, I will not let Wickham hurt anyone else. I will not sacrifice your sister for my brother's peace of mind. I will not live with that guilt. Besides, by the time he returns to town, we will be safely returned with the information needed; we may even have recovered Lydia."

"Guilt goes more than one way, Giana. What if something happens? Do you think your brother will forgive himself or us? He should not have to bear that burden. He worries enough without adding to it."

The cold, confident voice now gone; Georgiana answered in a hesitant loud whisper, "So you choose my brother over me?"

"Giana, I didn't say that either."

"Then say you will help me. I will do this with or without your help. You know that even if you lock me in a room, I will find a way to get out. You know my brother too well to think you can keep a Darcy from something they want to do. I will be much safer if I have you beside me. Please, Lizzy, I need you." Elizabeth couldn't help but notice that her voice gained confidence again when she spoke of the Darcy legacy of stubbornness.

If anything happened to Georgiana who insisted on following through with this lunacy on her own, Elizabeth would never forgive herself. She laughed at the irony; she already adopted the main Darcy family trait and wasn't even an official member of the family yet. Her stomach hit the floor; if their plan went badly, she would never be a Darcy. But if she did nothing, Georgiana would do something terrible on her own; that she could never allow.

Eventually, she sighed in resignation. "Alright Giana, tell me more of your plan."

By the end of the next hour, Elizabeth began to see promise in Georgiana's idea, but more than a slight fear of the consequence kept her stomach tightened and slightly nauseated. But if something did go wrong, she needed to be by her side; she promised Darcy and she could not go back on her word, not when he promised that he would save her own sister.

She and her co-conspirator sat on the bed deep in conversation, planning for each detail they needed to accomplish in the next twenty-four hours to save Lydia. And although Georgiana still failed to give her the all-important details of the contact's name or their exact destination, she was ashamed to admit that she felt relieved to finally do something to help her family, instead of waiting impatiently for some news that others saved her sister. But as her stomach had yet to agree with her mind, she knew that their plan was far from perfect.

***

They finally dressed and met Jane and her aunt Gardiner at the breakfast table much later than Elizabeth usually ate. She sat down with Georgiana and tried to appear calm, not giving away the apprehension she felt as soon as she saw her sister and aunt. In this, she took Georgiana's lead and simply began to eat whatever food sat in front of them, hoping that Jane and Mrs Gardiner would continue to discuss their plans for entertaining the children that day. She couldn't believe her good luck.

They couldn't agree on a way to occupy Jane during the course of the day; they couldn't bring her along as much as she wanted to have her older sister by her side. Now it seemed as though they wouldn't have to choose or tell yet another lie.

Georgiana gave her a sideways glance once there was a long pause in her sister and aunt's conversation. The girl carefully put down the piece of bread she buttered, and asked, "Mrs Gardiner, may Elizabeth and I go to Darcy House in order to collect a few of my things? I also wanted to find a few books that I believe Elizabeth would enjoy reading while in London. I fear we need something to keep our minds occupied while waiting for the men to return."

Her aunt's face lit with obvious satisfaction at Georgiana's idea and immediately let her know so. "That sounds like a very good idea. I noticed you three sitting around with worried faces all day yesterday and would like to avoid that if possible." Mrs Gardiner caressed Georgiana's cheek lovingly before continuing. "Your brother will not be pleased with me if I return you to his care with several worry lines on your brow. He would much rather find you reading a book or practising your music than waiting anxiously by the door."

With more eagerness than she posed her first question, Georgiana responded happily to Mrs Gardiner. "There are also a few shops I would like to take Lizzy to if I may. There are some lovely new dress designs that I wanted her opinion on before I ordered anything else. That would likely keep us occupied for almost the entire day if you agree."

Mrs Gardiner alternated between looking at Georgiana and her. Elizabeth couldn't help but feel the deceit upset the food she just forced herself to eat. How could she do this to her aunt and sister? Equally disastrous would be to let Georgiana tread down this path alone; she could not allow that to happen, no matter how much it went against her better judgement.

After looking for her approval, which she silently gave, her aunt's face lightened and her aunt Gardiner agreed to Georgiana's plan.

"Thank you for this. I am afraid we need to do something to divert our attention from other issues," Elizabeth said to her aunt.

"I would have agreed to almost anything that would lighten your moods after I watched you wander in quiet incense about the house yesterday. If shopping will help to prevent that mood from lurking about this home, I would not dare to discourage your outing."

Georgiana and Elizabeth looked at each other, shared a smile, and returned to the food in front of them. Elizabeth didn't know where she found the ability to eat more, but she couldn't risk her aunt wondering why she couldn't finish breakfast after planning an afternoon that should ease her worry. She couldn't possibly tell her aunt that their plans that afternoon would bring her aunt and sister more worry than even Lydia's tenuous fate.

***

Georgiana left with Elizabeth and Maggie, one of Gardiner's maids, soon after they finished breakfast. She watched as the footman opened the door for Elizabeth while she told Tom, the driver, that they planned to go to Darcy House and then shopping for the rest of the afternoon. The man looked at her curiously although she could not understand why; it was the same expression he gave her when she told him they were leaving Pemberley on Monday.

Tom had driven her since her father died; her brother trusted him implicitly with her care. And now she must deceive him. Would Tom forgive her? Would her brother forgive him in time? She closed her eyes and took a deep breath, trying to control her breathing; she needed to think about Lizzy's sister; she needed to do anything she could to make Lizzy her true sister. She would think about everything else later; she couldn't lose her nerve, not when she finally managed to convince Lizzy of the possibilities of her plan.

They rode in relative silence to Darcy House, her own mind full of the plan. She immediately took Elizabeth's hand and escorted her friend quickly through the house to her room on the second floor. Without discussion, she looked through several of her drawers and in her closet until she finally found what she searched for; she gave a set to Lizzy and put the others on herself. Georgiana hoped that the maids wouldn't notice what she took, but the items were innocuous enough, she had to count on the maids not discovering the missing garments for several more hours. It would all be over by the end of the night, anyway. She took Lizzy's discarded things and hid them under the mattress with her own.

While Elizabeth sat on her sofa, Georgiana took the time to pen two carefully worded notes; she spent the ride to Darcy House trying to decide on the exact phrasing. She couldn't say too much, nor could she say too little for it to work. She glanced at Lizzy, still sitting on the sofa, wishing she could ask her friend to read them over, but she knew as soon as she did, Elizabeth would tell her aunt the truth. On the outside of each letter, she wrote a time and put them in the absurdly large purse that she found under several hat boxes. If anyone asked about its odd appearance, she would simply say that Caroline Bingley told her it was the newest fashion in Paris. It would serve the lady right for chasing Fitzwilliam all of those years. Once they both carefully checked over the other to make sure their outer appearance remained unchanged, the two ladies went down the stairs to Darcy's library.

Georgiana led the way to Darcy's library and opened the door to the room filled with books lining three of the four walls in the room. Without giving Lizzy time to examine the titles or number of volumes, Georgiana took her friend's arm and guided her to the western wall of the large room. She looked through several of the volumes and finally decided on a set of particularly thick ones. Just as her brother told her last year, she took out each of volumes in the set but the final three and set them on the floor in a neatly stacked pile. When a portion of the wall was exposed, she wedged her fingers between two of the wooden panes, causing the panel to swing open. The safe where her brother kept spare cash was finally exposed.

"Fitzwilliam told me the combination in case I ever needed additional funds in an emergency. At the time I could not think of any situation I would need to act without my brother next to me, but that same girl would never have conceived the plan we are about to carry out either. I feel that I have grown up more in the past few days than I have in the past few years." She turned to look at Elizabeth in the eyes; she needed for her to understand this. "Having you and Jane near me gave me a confidence I never knew I possessed. I will never be able to thank you enough. It is no wonder that your courage rises with every attempt to intimidate you with four sisters to stand behind you. I have only the two of you and already it changed my outlook on the world. I cannot and will not lose you, not for anything, and certainly not because of George Wickham." With that, she turned the dial, took a stack of bills from the safe and placed them in her purse.

When she bent down to pick up the remaining books on the floor, Elizabeth grabbed her arm, forced her to stand, and then spoke in a quiet voice that more than worried her. "Georgiana, this doesn't feel right. I feel as though I am stealing from your brother. We don't know if we will be able to return this money. It may be lost forever. This is more than I or my family can ever repay him."

"Lizzy, the money doesn't matter to Fitzwilliam. The family is what matters." Seeing the worried expression on her friend's face, she knew Elizabeth wasn't convinced. Georgiana could do nothing but wait. If they didn't take the money, they would never be able to find Wickham. She knew that she had no chance of finding Lydia or even going through with part of the plan if she did not have Lizzy next to her. Up until that point, she believed that Elizabeth would eventually see her way; that gave her the confidence she needed to convince Elizabeth that she would follow through with her idea, regardless of her friend's participation.

After several minutes of staring at one another, she watched as Elizabeth grabbed the garnet cross that she always saw hang loosely around her friend's neck. Elizabeth reached behind her neck, unfastened the clasp, and held it out to her.

"We should both leave him something in place of the money. It will be something that is valuable to each of us. When he finds the money is gone, he will be able to choose whether to return the objects we left, or keep them in exchange to repay him for the theft. It will also serve to remind us of our decision each day we feel the loss of the object we leave behind."

While Elizabeth held the cross in her palm, Georgiana looked down to her own hand to see the ruby ring sparkling at her; it belonged to her mother. With a deep breath, she pulled off the ring which hadn't left her hand since her brother gave it to her. She squeezed the ring once in her palm, took the cross that Lizzy now held in an open palm, and placed both treasures at the front of the safe; they would be the first things her brother would see when he opened it. She wondered if he would keep them as a reminder of the insanity of her actions that day, but she still would not refuse to give up her mother's ring for the chance to be Elizabeth's sister, nor would her mother want her to.

With Elizabeth not looking; Georgiana took the object hidden behind the last three volumes and shoved it in her purse. As she returned the last of the books to their designated place, she silently prayed they would not encounter any situation where the object weighing down her purse might be needed.

Chapter 34

For the hundredth time that day, Darcy stood alone, examining the assortment of gentlemen and ladies carelessly socialising in the hell where Wickham forced him to wait for news of Elizabeth's reckless sister. This morning proved just as exasperating as the day before. How much more could he possibly take? He turned to see Richard and Bingley conversing rather animatedly with several gentlemen on the other side of the room. Damn both of them! How could they feign perfect ease amongst complete strangers when he knew that deep inside, each felt a rage similar to his own? At least Gardiner sat down in the opposite corner of the room, carefully watching anyone that entered the door to guess at their purpose.

He consciously stopped himself when he realised that once again he began to alternate between grinding his back molars and tensing his jaw every time he began a new survey of the room. He could only take so much more of this pretence. Darcy reached in his coat and flipped open the pocket watch that now reminded him as much of Elizabeth as his mother; the smaller hand hovered slightly past the second-hour mark. He wasted another entire morning and part of the afternoon on this fool's errand. Damn!

One more hour; after that, he would not wait a minute longer to begin the rest of his search.

As soon as he sat against the bench of the coach, Richard leaned forward and began the verbal assault that he knew was coming. "Darcy, we shouldn't have left. We may have just lost our best chance to find Wickham. Could you not have made at least some effort to converse with anyone? And before you even say it - of course, no one came up to you. Everyone in that room was scared to death that the invisible beast you carried on your back would be unleashed on them if they approached you. You could not have appeared any more conspicuous, unapproachable, and self-important if you explicitly tried to reach that goal."

"What about you and Bingley socialising and carrying on for hours! How did that help find Wickham!?"

"Did you not notice that between Bingley and me, we managed to speak to almost every person in that room? How else were we going to determine if Wickham and Lydia had been in Bath? You know Wickham as well as I do, if not better; you know he would have found some way to make a spectacle of himself. I cannot imagine that Miss Lydia would have tempered him. She likely only made the display even more flamboyant, ridiculous, and fortunately for us, memorable. Darcy, you have let your anger take over your better judgement."

"And what did you find out? Nothing! That is all the more reason to leave Bath! Richard, I am not returning to that place! You may go back if you wish, but I will no longer be made into Wickham's puppet. He will not pull any more of my strings. I will act as my conscience and instincts dictate. As you so aptly said before, Wickham has to find me if he wants to be paid. And if I control the details of that meeting, it will be that much better for me."

The four gentlemen sat in a tense silence until Bingley leaned over to speak to him, in a voice that the others could still hear. "Darcy, do not forget what I told you at your house before we left. We may disagree, but we stand together as one. Keep that in mind when you think we are against you."

Bingley was right. He could not let their internal differences impact their mission. "I know."

It was at that moment that the coach jolted to a stop in front of their inn. All four left the carriage and walked inside; all followed him in an unspoken understanding. Before he led the way to his room, he stopped by the front desk to ask for any messages. The young clerk reached behind the counter and handed him two sealed letters, stating they both only arrived in the last hour.

Staring at one letter for a moment before grabbing it, he motioned for the rest to follow him up the stairs.

Quickly skimming the short note, he read what he both feared and hoped for. They needed to return to town immediately; it did not matter that they would not reach until well after nightfall, even with riding their horses without adequate rest. He looked around the room, trying to focus on the other men's reactions as they read the letter he passed around. But he could not force himself to concentrate on his companions, not when the sudden nauseous feeling in stomach made his entire body shutter.

***

Elizabeth looked anxiously at her young friend as they stood in the entrance Darcy House, waiting for Maggie to accompany them to their next destination. She couldn't help but feel guilty when she saw Maggie's innocent smile greet her as she returned from talking to Mrs Blaine. She tried to catch Georgiana's eyes, but they were already focused on the ground. At least she felt badly too, but unfortunately not enough to stop. Once they walked out this door, it would soon be one step further from turning back. They both knew that, but it did not stop her from following Georgiana out the door when all three were ready to leave.

She waited by Georgiana's side in front of the luxurious carriage as they told Tom they planned to look for a few items in Cheapside at Gardiner's World Goods and then would decide later what shop to visit next. Tom smiled, nodded, looked curiously at the large bag that Miss Darcy held with both hands in front of her, and waited for the footman to help them into the carriage before he took the reins.

When they arrived at the destination, Elizabeth exited the carriage first, but instead of Georgiana following her, she purposely left the bag in the carriage and spoke to the driver in a voice too low to be overheard. She watched as the driver nodded in seeming to understand and was soon joined by her friend that gave her a confident smile. Finally, the three women walked through the large front doors of Gardiner's store. Without thinking, she breathed in deeply when she walked into the shop, inhaling the spicy and foreign atmosphere. She and Jane loved the aroma from the worldwide wonders that her uncle sold. But she was not here on a pleasure trip today. She had a very specific mission, and for her, that meant going straight to the ribbon section, after Georgiana mentioned that she wanted to look at the feathers on the other side of the store to accessorised some of her new dresses.

After several minutes of standing at the ribbon counter, Elizabeth saw the maid inching away from her to check on Georgiana. She leaned over and whispered to her that she wanted to find a present for Miss Darcy and desperately needed Maggie's advice between the four that she held. The servant examined each one of them carefully, mentioning that one might go better with Miss Darcy's eyes while another complimented her friend's complexion. Elizabeth carefully played on the girl's indecision, hoping to draw out the decision as long as possible.

Finally, Georgiana's voice that came from behind her startled her from her thoughts. "Lizzy, I think the green one in your hand is the prettiest of the group."

"Do you really think so?"

Georgiana smiled confidently at her. "Absolutely."

"Well, then, I suppose I should buy it. It would go nicely with my green and white flowered dress."

Georgiana stayed with Maggie while Elizabeth walked to a clerk only about ten yards from where they stood and told him that she wished to purchase the ribbon and to have it charged to the account. The clerk nodded, and she left the store, with Georgiana and the maid following behind her, less than a minute later.

She glanced quickly at Georgiana sitting on the seat next to her. It was now or never. They needed to begin work on task number three.

"Maggie, I am rather hungry and I am sure that Miss Darcy is as well." She waited for Georgiana to nod excitedly in agreement. "I know of a wonderful bakery about a ten-minute drive away. They sell the most delightful biscuits and the bakery should open again in just a few minutes. Would you mind terribly if we made a stop? I am sure that Mrs Gardiner would appreciate a few brought back for her children. And if the three of us happen to sample more than a few, no one could possibly hold it against us." She gave the servant girl a wicked smile.

"I believe Mrs Gardiner would be very pleased if you brought back some treats for the children." And with that statement, Maggie knocked on the top of the carriage, indicating to the driver that they needed to stop. The coach halted and the Darcy's driver opened the door to ask if they changed their plans. She gave the driver directions to the bakery and settled back against the velvet seat, waiting for the ride to begin.

As they neared the bakery, Elizabeth exclaimed, "There it is Georgiana! I am ashamed at how excited I am about the biscuits. You are about to experience one of the greatest treasures of London, hidden away in Cheapside."

"Miss Elizabeth, it seems everyone in Cheapside had the same idea," said the servant girl.

"Oh, I hate to wait in line for so long, but I feel terrible that I raised Georgiana's hopes only to dash them." She needed Maggie to come to the conclusion on her own.

Maggie's smile suddenly reappeared. "Miss Bennet, if you and Miss Darcy stay here in the carriage, I will wait in line for you. It shouldn't take more than thirty minutes if you don't mind the wait."

"Thank you so much, Maggie. I am sure that Miss Darcy and I can keep each other entertained here in the carriage." She reached in her small purse and took out several shillings. "Please buy some extra for yourself, Tom, and David - a thank you for your troubles."

They waited for Maggie to exit before Elizabeth turned to her younger friend and whispered, "Now, how are you expecting for us to be able to escape this carriage without your driver and footman noticing?"

"We are not going to escape. We are going to tell them that we are going to the milliner shop a few stores down from the goods store." She leaned over Elizabeth's lap to look out the window; she smiled when she saw Maggie talking in line with the young footman a few years older than she. "And it seems we just had another stroke of good luck. David should keep Maggie entertained. There are two fewer people who will worry about what we are doing. Now we only have to worry about Tom. Lizzy, it is time to go."

They left the carriage on the side opposite of the bakery, to keep Maggie from noticing their departure.

"Tom, we are just going to go into the milliner store across the street. See the one with the blue bonnet in the window? There are so many just in the window that I want to see, I cannot help myself. Miss Bennet and I will not take too long."

Tom moved as if to step down from the front.

"Tom, you don't need to do that. Miss Bennet and I will be just across the street. Surely you can trust her, can't you?"

That did it; Elizabeth thought she might lose her breakfast standing right there on the street. How could Georgiana say that? The girl's words continually replayed in her head. But did not Mr Darcy say something similar? She must remember that was why she chose to follow his sister on this ridiculous path. They would be fine. They would take care of each other. Yes, Tom could trust Miss Darcy to her care. She would keep the girl safe. Mr Darcy trusted her with Georgiana's safety and she would not disappoint him for anything; not when he was trying to save her sister.

"Tom, I will keep her very safe this afternoon."

Tom alternated between looking at the two of them and finally nodded and retook the reins in his hands. Elizabeth swore she could feel his eyes boring holes in their backs as they walked away, each with their purse in hand.

They walked into the store and looked around for a few minutes, before Elizabeth turned to her friend and asked, "Now what? How do we get out of here?"

"With new hats and cloaks of course!"

Georgiana picked up two of the gaudiest hats that Elizabeth had ever seen and promptly carried them over to one of the ladies there to assist customers. She told the girl that she wanted to purchase the creations and did not need them fitted, as she and her sister were in a terrible hurry. And if she had any cloaks for purchase, she needed two of those as well, explaining that they forget to buy their other sisters anything from town and they would be just devastated if they returned without any presents. The shop girl returned with two cloaks, one with varying shades of blue stripes on a black background that miraculously matched the peacock blue feathers in on the hat and a second cloak with pink borders surrounding the brown fabric that might, in a remote Japanese village, be considered a match for the hat with red and pink ribbons intertwined.

Of all the creations to select, she couldn't believe that the girl with one of the most stylish wardrobes in all of England would pick these atrocities. She couldn't help but look at her friend while narrowing her eyebrows.

Georgiana leaned over and whispered to Elizabeth, "Tom knows I would never wear anything like this. He will be on the lookout for anyone plainly dressed or how we are currently dressed if he suspects anything. The best disguise is to be noticeable; that is the last thing he would suspect."

She did not know whether to be proud of the girl's cleverness or incredibly worried about her potentially deceitful nature. Elizabeth couldn't help but think that she and Mr Darcy needed to have a very long and detailed discussion about right and wrong after tonight with his sister. Of course, as she was Georgiana's accomplice, Mr Darcy may wonder the same thing about her. She would think about that tomorrow; she did not have the energy or brainpower to deal with it today. She needed to concentrate her efforts on protecting Georgiana.

Georgiana turned to the salesgirl and with a huge smile said, "I don't have the heart to give these away to our sisters. We love them too much. Would you mind helping me with the blue one and then my sister with the pink one? Our sisters will just have to do without presents from this trip. We will have them properly fitted later."

Before Lizzy could do anything else, she found herself walking next to her friend to the rather large General Store, dressed in a pink hat and brown and pink cloak that she hoped to never see again after this day. They walked quickly around the store. She alternated between watching Georgiana's next move and looking for Darcy's driver to follow them. It was hard to believe that the girl's plan actually worked. She followed her through the bolts of fabric until they found a small section where several cheaply pre-made dresses hung. Elizabeth looked at Georgiana who shrugged and shoved a burgundy dress into her arms; the girl selected an equally unfortunate blue one for herself. If nothing else, at least their dresses would somewhat match their monstrous hats. What was she thinking? Was she truly vain enough to worry about fashion at a time like this! Even so, she couldn't help but roll her eyes as she held up the dress to examine it. Georgiana grabbed her arm and led her to the nearest clerk to pay for the newest additions to their wardrobe.

She felt uncomfortable as the clerk's eyes examined their figures before he took the money from Miss Darcy. How she wished she could berate him for his ungentlemanly behaviour. But not only did she need something from him, they were the two young ladies that shopped in a strange store without any type of escort. For the first time, and she feared not the last today, she wished that Tom was with them.

Elizabeth took a deep breath and asked the same bothersome clerk, "Is there a room in the back which we might be able to use for a few moments? We promise to only be a few minutes and won't cause any problems." She forced a smile at the young man who now unabashedly ogled her breasts. Thankfully before she could no longer stop her arm from slapping the man, he escorted them into the back office.

He spoke quickly as he escorted them to the office. "The owner is gone today, but he won't mind two ladies using his office for a few minutes."

"Thank you so much. We appreciate your assistance." Georgiana smiled quickly at him and closed the door separating them from the rest of the store.

"Well, Lizzy, these are certainly the ugliest dresses I have ever purchased. Mine is too long, and yours is going to be too short and the material feels like it is going to itch terribly. They aren't even slightly fitted. But now I see why you made me put on my worst petticoat at Darcy House. If anyone saw the ones I normally wear in combination with this dress, they would know we weren't as we say."

Elizabeth raised her eyebrow and kept silent that she believed it was better if no one else noticed Giana's figure for the rest of the night. Instead, she said, "Hurry and dress Georgiana, we don't have much time. Most people can't afford to have dresses designed and specifically made for them; these dresses are made for someone to alter later. Now, can you help me with these buttons?"

With her direction, Miss Darcy quickly returned to her mission which required them to change quickly.

Carefully, they helped each other out of their own clothing, on with their new dresses, and put on the hideous cloaks overtop the rather unattractive dresses. Elizabeth went to put on the hat, but Georgiana stopped her.

"We can't bring the hats with us. They are too expensive. We can't wear them with these cheap dresses. We are much better off putting up the hoods of the cloaks. There are more girls walking around London without hats than with, particularly amongst the group that we want to blend with."

She narrowed her eyebrows and then smiled slightly. "Giana, you never cease to surprise me. What other observations of human nature and interaction have you made recently?"

"Plenty, but we will wait for another time to go over those."

"What are we going to do with the dresses we wore here?"

"Unfortunately I think we are going to have to leave them here. I don't see how we are going to be able to take them with us. The owner's wife is certainly going to be given the nicest dress she ever owned when he finds them in his office tomorrow. Maybe there will be a miracle and she will even like the hats." Georgiana motioned to the corner. "We will put them in the corner, under that cloth, where they won't be immediately obvious to the clerk if he returns for some reason."

Squirming in her newest purchase, the girl looked to Elizabeth, "I guess it is time to go. Which way do we need to leave to make it to the delivery service?"

"We need to go out of the store and to the right, in the opposite direction of the bakery. Make sure to walk quickly, but not too quickly. Keep going until we reach the end of the road and take a left. We must try to avoid being recognised by Tom. If he sees us, we are done without even getting a chance to start." Lizzy took Georgiana's hands in her own and looked intently at her. "Once we do this, there is no going back. Are you ready?"

They walked quickly, but not too hurriedly, out of the store. Elizabeth kept Georgiana to her immediate left, hoping it might appear they were one person instead of two for someone watching on the other side of the street. She silently thanked the cool weather which allowed them to put up their hoods without drawing undue notice. She was too afraid to speak for fear that somehow her voice might carry straight to Tom's ears.

When they turned the corner from the street where they started, Elizabeth grabbed Georgiana's arm and felt confident enough to finally speak. "We need to follow this street until it ends in a mile or so. We will then walk for about ten more minutes until we see the delivery service on the right. We should be able to post our notes there."

Georgiana turned towards her, "I know that I shouldn't be saying this, but this is all rather exciting. I daresay that this plan is the most exhilarating thing that has ever happened to me. I realise we are doing something for the good of your sister, but I wonder if it is wrong for me to feel pride in what we are doing."

Elizabeth thought carefully before replying; she knew this would not be a good time for teasing. "I think that as long as you are feeling pride for the right reason, it is a good thing. Pride, under good regulation, is acceptable. If you are feeling pride because you are helping a fellow human being, I believe that is always acceptable. If your emotions stem from the thrill of the role you are playing or because of the excitement without consideration for the good of the action to others than I believe your pride is misguided. Only you know your heart."

They continued walking in silence until Miss Darcy finally stopped walking and turned to face her. "I feel happy that I am finally able to do something to combat Wickham and help your sister at the same time. I feel as though I am restoring my confidence; something which I never had in large quantities, and even less after Ramsgate. But I can say I would not do this if saving your sister was not the ultimate cause of our actions.

Protecting someone else is somehow easier and more important than saving myself."

"If that is the case, I believe your motives and your heart are in the right place. I believe that God makes us feel good for helping others to encourage us to continue. It would certainly be a bleak world if we were all inherently evil. And I know for a fact that you, Giana, have the heart of an angel underneath your rather determined Darcy shell."

"Thank you, Lizzy."

With that, they continued walking, with the older lady leading the way.

"Do you have the letters?"

"They are in my purse." Georgiana lightly shook the immense accessory that she held with both hands.

"Good. We must be very sure to keep hold of your purse. If anyone knew what it held, we would be robbed before moving another twenty steps." She leaned back, hoping to avoid attracting any attention.

After another few minutes of walking in silence, Georgiana asked her, "How did you learn your way around Cheapside so well?"

"Jane and I were permitted to visit our aunt and uncle rather often. When we would visit, we would not have use of the carriage on most days. My aunt also made sure that we knew her favourite haunts before she would allow us to wander. As long as we kept a maid with us, my aunt and uncle would allow us relative freedom. Until now, I have never given them any cause to question whether I would choose the most responsible course of action."

Georgiana looked over and gave her a half-hearted smile, "I hope that when all of this is done, their faith in you will be restored. Who could not love a niece that would do anything to save her family? If you had to select a reason to be dishonest, I believe this would rank amongst the most honourable."

She thought about what Georgiana said. But only one thought came to mind. "But what about your family? Will they forgive you?"

"One good thing about my family is that I know that any problems I cause will be contained within my immediate family as much as possible. It is quite likely that no one other than Fitzwilliam and Richard will ever know what I did. My brother's level of anger will directly correlate to how much danger we encounter and how he finds out what we did. If we are able to tell him next week while sitting safely on the sofa in my music room, his anger will dissipate rather quickly. If he finds out another way, I don't know if he will ever truly forgive me for putting myself and you in harm's way, no matter how little the threat. But I could not live a satisfactory life knowing I could do something to help your sister and simply sat waiting for someone else to help. As long as I return safely, Richard will forgive me. He has never been able to stay cross with me for long."

Despite being on a public street, Elizabeth reached out to Georgiana and gave her a sisterly hug. She held her until both of their rate of breathing returned to normal and she was sure they could safely continue. They continued with linked arms until they reached the delivery service. Upon arrival at the counter, Georgiana carefully took out the two letters from her purse; Lizzy did not want any of the other contents to spill out. Taking the notes from her hand, the young clerk asked for the house address and the delivery date.

Georgiana pointed to the first letter and said, "I need this letter delivered at exactly 5 o'clock today. I need the second letter delivered at exactly 11 o'clock tonight."

"Miss, the second time is outside our normal delivery hours. Would a few hours earlier be acceptable?"

Georgiana looked worriedly at Elizabeth, unsure as to how to answer. Elizabeth took the liberty of answering the clerk's question herself. "Actually, we need these letters to be delivered at the exact time we specified. You see, we are playing a game with our cousins and if they receive the letters early, we will surely lose. Is there an extra fee that we might be able to pay to compensate the messenger for his time? We would be so appreciative for your assistance." Georgiana followed Elizabeth's lead and took considerable effort to smile innocently and affectionately at the clerk, eventually causing him to blush and stammer a reply.

With a red face, the clerk eventually answered, "Well, I suppose I could deliver the second letter for you myself. I wouldn't want you to lose the game on my account."

"That is so kind of you. You have no idea how much we appreciate your help." Georgiana took out a half-crown over the specified cost of the delivery from her purse.

He absent-mindedly took the money and continually stared at Georgiana.

"I hope that if you ladies have any other letters to be delivered, you will be sure to see me. I will personally make sure that you are taken care of. I will send your first letter with the messenger leaving here in a few minutes." Georgiana blushed and thanked him for his kindness. She assured him that if they need anything else, they would visit his business first.

They left the store and began to walk toward their final destination for the night. The only path available was the one they conceived of that very morning. If only Elizabeth felt better about the sanity of their endeavour. But as they already escaped from Tom and Maggie, mailed the letters, and took the money from Mr Darcy, they could do nothing else but face the future they created. She wondered how their actions today would shape the rest of their lives. Would Mr Darcy still be in her life or was his good opinion lost forever after her actions this day?

Chapter 35

Tom Connell looked over at Maggie and the footman laughing at a joke he could not hear, waiting patiently for the biscuits that it seemed all of London knew of. But how could they not? The smell was intoxicating, even from where he sat. He couldn't keep his eyes off of Maggie's place in line, trying to use sheer willpower to move her forward. Finally, only three more people remained between the maid and the counter. It would not be much longer now.

He looked over his other shoulder to the milliner's shop where Miss Darcy and Miss Bennet went. How long could Miss Darcy and Miss Bennet spend in such a small hat store? Even with his limited interest in Miss Darcy's shopping trips, he knew that most of the stores she visited were of a much higher calibre with a much larger selection than the small one that they entered. He hoped that it would not take them too much longer. After the mad rush in which Mr Darcy left Pemberley, he could not help but feel the need to carefully watch his employer's younger sister. It went against his better judgement to let them shop alone, but how could he go against the wishes and assurances of his future mistress?

Only a blind man would miss Mr Darcy's intentions for Miss Bennet. He certainly did not believe that Mr Darcy would fire him for refusing to allow Miss Darcy and the future Mrs Darcy to shop in privacy, but it certainly would not lead to a pleasant interaction between him and the Master. Besides, Miss Bennet truly did seem concerned for Miss Darcy whenever he saw them together. She would not let anything happen to Miss Darcy. Yes, he made the right decision. They would be fine.

Tom breathed in just as a group left with their baskets full of bread and sweets. His eyes immediately focused on Maggie. Finally! She handed money over to the cashier, while the footman took a bag easily large enough to feed all the Gardiners, plus the three of them. He could not wait. He jumped down from the carriage to open the door for her, allowing the footman, David, who was relatively new in his employment by the Darcys to carefully set the bag on one of the benches.

The maid girl asked him as she settled herself in the carriage, "Tom, where did Miss Darcy and Miss Elizabeth go?"

"Over there," he pointed over to the hat shop.

"I will go to them," stated the maid.

The driver watched as Maggie crossed the street, dodging the carriages and horse riders near her while he climbed back to the driver's bench. Several minutes later he heard the maid's voice call to him from the other side of the carriage. She motioned for him to lean down, so she did not have to yell.

He leaned over as she looked up at him. "Are you sure they went to find new bonnets? They are nowhere in the store. I looked all over and it is not a large shop at all."

"I am sure that is what Miss Darcy said."

He jumped down again from the carriage and took Maggie by the arm to walk back to the milliners, leaving the footman in possession of the carriage. It did not take him long to look behind each of the displays and in the corners, hoping to find the two young ladies.

His face hardened before he finally spoke in a hushed voice, "Maybe they went to another shop in the area. We will search them all until we find them. There is no reason to worry. I have known Miss Darcy since she was ten years old and has never proven to be even the slightest trouble." The words trailed off as he quickly remembered the bit of information he acquainted after Ramsgate. But George Wickham had not been near Miss Darcy, of that he was positive. "I am sure that everything is fine. We cannot let David know that there is a problem. Mr Darcy would not want anyone to know of the private doings of his family. Do you understand?"

"I understand."

"Good, now we need to start calmly searching the stores. I will go right and you go left from the front of this one. We will meet at the carriage in fifteen minutes, or just return as soon as one of us finds them."

Tom's father always boasted of Tom's ability to stay calm in any crisis. He never fancied himself as a man to worry needlessly, but he knew that if he returned without either of the two young ladies from their afternoon excursion, the lack of recommendation for his next place of employment would be the least of his problems. Mr Darcy might string him up from the nearest tree and leave him there for the vultures to pick at his bones. Quite frankly, he could not blame his employer if that was exactly what happened.

He first went to the lace store next to the milliners, but it did not take long to realise that neither of the young ladies stood in the small store. He next went to the bookstore and spent considerably longer looking through it, hoping that Miss Bennet was simply searching for a new novel and lost track of time. He walked up and down each aisle, making sure that he did not miss any area. Still, he found nothing, so he left for the next store before he would have to meet Maggie. He glanced at the carriage but saw only the footman sitting at the back, looking aimlessly around the street, waiting for them to return.

He walked into the General Store, hoping to find something, anything. Once again, he searched the store but found nothing. A young clerk noticed his exasperation and asked, "Is there anything that I might be able to help you with? We have a wide variety of goods here."

"Yes, I am looking for two young ladies. The slightly elder one has brown hair and wore a green dress. The other, nearly the same height, has blonde hair and wore a pretty blue dress. Have you seen them by any chance?"

The clerk gave him a half smirk. "Yes, they were here about half an hour ago."

"Did you see where they went?" Tom tried not to appear too anxious.

"They each bought a new dress. Then they went into the back office for a few moments. They didn't look like the type to steal anything, so I didn't think my boss would mind. I didn't hear anything from them after that. I knocked on the door about fifteen minutes later and didn't hear anything. When I checked the room, they were gone and nothing seemed out of place. I guess they were able to do what they needed and left."

Having no other clues as to their whereabouts, Tom asked if he could see the back room. The clerk eyed him suspiciously, but his instinct told him that he needed to know and take the risk. Eventually, with some prodding and uncomfortable glares given, the clerk let him in the back room. He quickly searched the musty office, under the careful supervision of the clerk. Suddenly when he lifted a sheet, he found the dresses that Miss Elizabeth and Miss Darcy wore earlier that day hidden carelessly underneath the sheet. Nothing good could come from this discovery. Something bad happened, and he had no clue as to what.

Trying to regain his composure, he took a minute to pick up the dresses.

"You said they bought dresses in here. What did they look like?"

"One was red and I can't remember what the other one looked like. I can recognise material of quality when I see it and neither dress they bought was close to the ones in your hand."

"Thank you for your help." Tom gathered the dresses in his hands and tried to smash them in as small a ball as possible and covered them in the old sheet.

The servant hurried back to the carriage, quickly opened the door, and shoved both the dresses and Maggie inside. How would he explain this! He could not tell Mrs Gardiner that her niece and Miss Darcy disappeared from Cheapside without any trace as to their location and in completely different clothing. Then again, he felt grateful he was explaining it to Mrs Gardiner and not Mr Darcy. How long was his Master planning to be away? He silently prayed the ladies were found before his employer's return.

Through the open carriage door, he took only a moment to tell the maid in a quiet voice that they needed to return to the Gardiners right away. He did not want the footman to realise the gravity of the situation. In a louder voice, he told her that Miss Bennet and Miss Darcy saw a friend of Miss Darcy's at the millinery and decided to go to tea with her that afternoon and had no more use of the carriage. It was a terrible lie, but he could not think of a better reason right then.

Just as he suspected they would be, he found Miss Bennet's aunt and the elder Miss Bennet on the parlour. Noting the two servants, Mrs Gardiner dropped the book she held and stood, addressing her questions to the driver. "Is there something wrong? Where are Miss Elizabeth and Miss Darcy?"

"Mrs Gardiner, there is something we must tell you. Miss Elizabeth and Miss Darcy are gone. We can't find them anywhere. We went to Walbrook Street to buy some baked goods to bring back to you for tea. Maggie stood in line while the two ladies went across the street to look at a bonnet. After about thirty minutes, Maggie went to the store to look for them, but they were nowhere to be found. We then searched each of the surrounding stores. I got desperate and finally asked the store clerk if he saw a young lady matching Miss Bennet or Miss Darcy's description. He told me they bought two cheap and ugly dresses. I found the dresses they wore this morning pushed into a corner of a back office. When we couldn't find any more traces of them, we headed straight back here to tell you."

Both Jane and Mrs Gardiner sat speechless, clutching on to one another for sanity. After several minutes, Miss Bennet looked up from staring at her lap to observe her aunt whose face was ghostly white.

After what seemed like an eternity, Mrs Gardiner looked at the young woman and spoke in a clear and decisive voice. "Jane, will find Elizabeth and Georgiana. They are two smart young women that would not do anything unsafe or irrational. We will trust in their judgement."

"But Aunt, they ALREADY did something that is both unsafe and irrational."

"Jane, they wouldn't leave us to worry needlessly. I am sure they will walk through the front door at any time. When they do, they will offer us a perfectly reasonable explanation. We will not sit here in hysterics until that time. We will not search aimlessly around London and put ourselves in danger causing your uncle and Mr Darcy, even more, worry when they return. Until we have some clue where they went, we will wait for word from them."

With great difficulty, Jane separated her aunt's hands from her own, stood, and walked past the two servants who quickly moved out of her way.

"Jane, where are you going?"

"Aunt, you said that we need to have some idea where they went. Well, I am going to search Lizzy and Georgiana's room to see if they left anything for us."

"That is an excellent idea. I will be up momentarily to help you." Mrs Gardiner stood up and turned her attention to the driver. "Please do not alert the rest of the household with what you have told us. While we search their bedroom, please search the carriage to see if anything was dropped or left. Did you take them anywhere else today?"

He answered quickly. "Yes, ma'am. I took them to Darcy House and then to Mr Gardiner's store."

"Very well. Go to the World Goods and find out if they bought anything there. We need to know if it was part of their plan or merely a way to waste time waiting to slip away. Find out if they spent any more time in one area of the store than another. In fact, wait a few minutes for Maggie to collect herself and then take her with you. She can take you to the parts of the store where the girls spent their time. If you find out anything of value, immediately return here and let us know. If not, please go to Darcy House and ask the housekeeper to search Miss Darcy's room to see if any notes or information was left."

Happy to be of some use, Tom readily agreed and watched as Mrs Gardiner walked upstairs to help the elder Miss Bennet search for any clues. He sat Maggie down on one of the chairs and waited for her to collect herself. He did not have a handkerchief, but it did not matter, as her sleeve seemed to work quite well for the moment. When Maggie finally could speak coherently, the answers she provided were close to useless. He returned with her to the carriage to begin a search. He just noticed that the large bag that Miss Darcy carried was also gone.

He dragged the maid to the carriage. Hurrying the horses as fast as he could manage on the busy streets of Cheapside's commerce district, he soon arrived at the World Goods. He jumped down and retrieved Maggie from the inside of the carriage.

As they walked in, he leaned down to speak to Maggie in a quiet voice, "Where did Miss Elizabeth and Miss Darcy spend their time in here? What were they looking for?"

"Miss Elizabeth was looking for some new ribbon. She bought a green ribbon as a present for Miss Darcy."

"Did Miss Bennet do anything unusual while looking for ribbons? And what was Miss Darcy looking for?"

Maggie confessed that she lost sight of Miss Darcy for several minutes while giving Miss Elizabeth her opinion of which ribbon to buy.

He sighed in exasperation. "That means that Miss Darcy likely bought something and Miss Bennet needed to distract you." He quickly surveyed the bottom floor of the store. "We just have to find out what she bought. Come on."

Grabbing the closest store clerk to him, he began his second inquisition of the day.

"Did a young lady with blonde hair wearing a blue dress buy anything today?"

The clerk shrugged his shoulders and continued to dust the shelves while he answered. "I couldn't rightly say. I do the inventory and a little of cleaning. You better ask Michael over there." He motioned to the store clerk located by the dried goods section.

"Is he likely to remember her?"

The clerk smirked, "Well, I guess that all depends on how attractive the young lady is. The prettier the girl, the better his memory."

Tom took Maggie's arm and led them to the clerk rearranging dried meats and fruits on the shelves.

"Excuse me, Michael?"

"How can I help you?" The man stopped what he was doing to concentrate on helping the customers.

"I need to know if you remember a young lady that was in here earlier today. Blonde hair, the height of my shoulder, and wore an expensive blue dress."

The blonde clerk smiled widely. "Of course I remember her. Any girl that pretty in this store makes an impression. And she had the most incredible pair of dimples when she smiled. But judging by her clothes and yours, you probably aren't related to her, are you?" Tom shook his head in the negative. "I didn't think so. That means you probably work for her though."

"I need to know if she bought anything. Do you remember?"

"I am almost sure that she bought a pack of playing cards."

"Are you sure that is all she bought?"

"I'm not positive, but I am fairly certain."

"Thank you for your help." Tom touched Maggie's arm with his free hand and directed her quickly out of the store.

Maggie spoke for the first time since his inquisition of the clerks began. "Where are we going now? Are we going to the Darcy's or back to the Gardiner's?"

"I think we better go to the Gardiners and tell the mistress what Miss Darcy bought. I never knew Miss Darcy to talk much about playing cards. Maybe it will mean something to Mrs Gardiner though."

***

Jane desperately hoped that Georgiana and her sister had left some kind of note indicating where they went, but after searching their room, she and her aunt found nothing. How could Lizzy do this to her and their aunt? It was so unlike her to run off without leaving word.

The knock on the door interrupted her thoughts. Both women looked up as one of the female servants nervously entered the room. "Mrs Gardiner, ma'am, I know you said you didn't want to be disturbed, but we got a letter for you sent special delivery about ten minutes ago. We have been trying to decide whether to give it to you, but we thought it best to go ahead."

Mrs Gardiner leapt off the couch and grabbed the letter from the tray which the maid carried. "Thank you, Molly. If any more letters or deliveries arrive, please bring them to me immediately."

Mrs Gardiner dismissed the maid and returned to the sofa next to Jane who anxiously waited for her aunt to read the contents of the letter.

Mrs Gardiner ripped open the seal and read aloud.

Dear Aunt,

By now you have likely been informed of our disappearance. Please believe that we are both safe and our departure was due entirely to our own actions. Do not blame Maggie or Mr Darcy's driver as we took great pains to slip away from their care; our determination to succeed made their own efforts to keep us under their care futile.

We have information that we hope will lead us to Lydia's location. We cannot give you any more intelligence at this time as to our plan. If something goes wrong and we have not returned by eleven o'clock tonight, we will send word of our plan and location.

We could not sit idly and wait any longer when we knew of a route to that might lead us to my sister. Please pray for our success.

Yours Faithfully,

Elizabeth

Jane did not know whether to feel more or less worried. What was her sister thinking going after Wickham with only Miss Darcy there to help? Had she lost her senses? The level-headed Elizabeth she knew would never do something so foolish. Certainly, Lizzy could be stubborn and almost impossible to sway once her mind was decided, but it was always well directed. Lizzy never did something without thinking through the consequences.

Jane looked at her aunt and spoke the words that surely her aunt must be thinking as well. "At least they are safe. We may take comfort in that information. But why would they not trust us to say anything?"

Mrs Gardiner brought her hands up to the sides of her neck, trying to calm herself. "They likely knew we would not approve of the plan and try to stop them. You know Lizzy. Once she has an idea, it consumes her until she is able to follow through. Miss Darcy would follow Elizabeth to the end of the Earth. See how they refer to Lydia as 'their sister?' Georgiana feels this as deeply as either of us, possibly even more because of her family's close past with Wickham. I doubt there was anything we could have done to stop them. Where there is such a strong will, there will always be a way."

"I know they said they are safe, but we cannot sit here and wait to find out whether they will return unharmed or not."

"We have to wait for Tom to get back from the World Goods. We could not find anything in their room. If they left any evidence of their plan, we have not yet found it. But the most important thing is that we know they are safe. You know your sister, she and Georgiana will keep each other safe." In a firm tone, her aunt finished, "We will stay here until we know something that will help the situation and not just make it worse."

Mrs Gardiner sat back down, pulling her down too. Jane listened as her aunt, in a composed and controlled voice, asked her, "What if we took turns reading from Shakespeare's sonnets?" Mrs Gardiner stood quickly, took a well-read book from the shelf and sat back down next to her. "This should keep us occupied until Lizzy and Georgiana return."

Jane sat next to Mrs Gardiner on the sofa, each taking a turn reading from the book while waiting for Tom and Maggie, or Georgiana and Elizabeth to return. As the sun set, she looked nervously out the window. The sound of her aunt's voice had quieted, although not silenced, her fears. Now with the onset of the night's darkness, her worst fears began to resurface. What would her family look like once the sun reappeared in the morning? Would her sisters be returned safely or would another be lost? She could not think of that; it made her heart ache with pain.

Hearing the clock chime seven times, Mrs Gardiner closed the book and took her niece's hand. "We only have to wait a few more hours until they walk through the door. What's more, the gentlemen will be returning tonight as well."

"Aunt, you didn't tell me that you knew they were returning! When did you receive word?"

"Dearest Jane, I have not heard anything. But if there is one thing that the last few days taught me, it is that we must put faith in our family to bring us through difficult times. We care very deeply for each other. If one member falls, the others will be there to pick her up. That is why I have faith that the men will return. If we need them, somehow they will know and will be here."

"You seem so sure, aunt."

"Because I have no other choice and neither do you. Now I suggest we wait for the driver to return with any news he discovered. Until then, we should return to the bard."

Jane and her aunt calmly read to one another until they heard a firm knock at the door. Maggie opened the door and appeared with Mr Darcy's servant following closely behind her.

"Mrs Gardiner, we went to the World Goods. Miss Bennet purchased a ribbon that Miss Maggie helped her select. Miss Darcy bought a pack of playing cards."

"Did either one purchase anything else?"

"Not that the clerk knew of, ma'am."

Mrs Gardiner nodded and spoke quickly, "Thank you. Now please go to Darcy House and ask the housekeeper if she can search Miss Darcy's room for anything unusual or out of place. Find out if they went to any other area of the house and ask the housekeeper to check those rooms as well. I am sure that you can trust her to be discreet in her search."

"Yes, ma'am. If you don't mind, I would prefer to travel without the carriage. I should be able to make better time if I ride horseback."

"Of course. Mr Gardiner has a horse you will be able to use. Just ask the groom to prepare it for you."

Tom fled the room with Maggie close behind him. Mrs Gardiner looked at Jane and asked in obvious confusion, "Do you have any idea why they would want a deck of cards? Lizzy does not usually play cards when it is offered after dinner. I have not known Miss Darcy to be a great card player either."

"You are not mistaken. Neither particularly enjoys whist or the normal parlour games. Each is quite talented at Three Card Brag though."

Her aunt asked in confusion, "Three Card Brag? What in the world is that and why would Lizzy and Georgiana be so talented at it?"

"Three Card Brag is a game which young men at taverns often play to gamble money. Lizzy learned the rules from the Lucas boys one summer and taught all of her sisters to play. We often play for ribbons. The winners of the night would pick one that belonged to the losers. Miss Darcy learned how to play from one of her former companions. She knew her brother would never approve, but she enjoyed it, so she continued to play in secret whenever she could. One night at Pemberley, the three of us played several hands. I still don't know why they would need a new deck of cards though."

"Let us go through what we know so far. We know they bought a new deck of cards because the ones they had readily available here would not be acceptable for their purpose, otherwise, they would use the deck we found in their room. We know they bought cheaply made dresses. Again, they could not wear the clothes they dressed in this morning for some reason. We know they left the supervision of the servants sometime after three o'clock. We know they plan to return at eleven o'clock tonight. So whatever they needed to do, they could complete their mission this afternoon and therefore would not need to travel outside of London."

"That is something to be thankful for." Jane thought about what her aunt said. "But if Lydia and Mr Wickham are somewhere in London, where are the gentlemen? As you said earlier, we cannot possibly search all of London."

"We could at least narrow down the areas they might be. We know it isn't in the fashionable area. Otherwise, they would have kept the dresses they wore this morning. Also, Miss Darcy would surely be recognised if in the nicest areas of London where her family usually visits. And we know they must have gone somewhere to play cards."

"That still doesn't narrow down the area they might be in. There must be hundreds of taverns located in the unfashionable areas of London. Unless we find out something more, the information we have is useless." The knot in Jane's stomach tightened, forcing her to bend over and clutch it. "Oh Aunt, this is useless. Why would they not simply tell us what they wanted to do?"

"I don't know, Jane."

Chapter 36

"Look, Lizzy, there it is." Georgiana gestured to the green sign hanging above the unpainted wooden door bearing the words "Returning Rogue. Are we ready to do this?"

Lizzy squinted to see the name of the tavern several feet away; the darkness made it difficult to confirm the tavern name. She looked at the girl squarely in the eye and responded, "Giana, I think it is I who should be asking you this question. Are you ready? All I have to do is stand behind you. We can still back out if you want to." Lizzy secretly hoped Georgiana might lose her nerve. Did she have the courage to even do her part?

Georgiana dropped her head toward the ground before finally looking up again at her. "Probably not, but I do not know when we shall ever be ready if we do not do this now. We will not have another chance."

"You remember everything that we talked about. Do you remember what your tells are? You know we must make sure that the last two players remaining in the game are you and Mr Younge. After that, I have a feeling we will end up doing a lot of improvising." She paused for a few seconds before continuing, fear had knotted her stomach making it painful to stand straight. "I wish I could play for us. I hate the thought of making you do this."

"Lizzy, we both know I am the better player. With you behind me, I know I can win." Georgiana held her head a little higher and curved the edges of her mouth upward a little.

How in the world did Georgiana claim such confidence? This girl could not be the same that ran out of the parlour during their first meeting. That girl could not suffer through a tea with a sympathetic audience. Now, she must force her to face a group of grown men and beat them at their own game. She had to know what caused the change. If nothing else, she hoped to harness the same strength. "And where did you get such confidence from?"

"I learned that whenever someone intimidates me, I must rise to the occasion. My sister taught me that." Carefully manoeuvring her bag, Georgiana threw her arms around Elizabeth and they held each other tightly.

Elizabeth knew that as soon as she dropped her arms, they needed to walk through the unassuming door that might change their lives. As such, she did the only thing she could think to do; she embraced Georgiana even tighter. But they could not stand there forever, no matter how much she wanted to avoid the next few hours. Her friend would walk through that door, and she would not allow her newest sister to walk through it alone. After a final squeeze, she released the younger girl and kissed her on the cheek.

With a deep breath trying to untie the knots in her stomach, Elizabeth took Georgiana's hand as she opened the tavern door with the other. Instantly, she felt surprised at the sight before her. Several candles and a small fire brightly illuminated the room in front of her. Over the course of the day, her imagination produced a much more dreary and dangerous tavern than the one she saw before her. No pictures graced the walls, but the floor was clean and no rats could be seen scampering across the floor. The smell was not terrible, but the window was open letting the outside air circulate. A staircase led to what she assumed were rooms for rent. The barmaid in a dress even cheaper than the ones they wore eyed them curiously as they walked inside, but made no advancement toward them, as they stood in the doorway.

Several couples ate dinners of bread, cold meat, and ale. Although the diners were not of her aunt and uncle's status, their appearance was neat and tidy; none looked overtly threatening. They even might provide a level of safety while they fulfilled their plan. Surely no one would do anything to them with semi-respectable personnel in attendance. Several groups of two or three men sat at tables discussing problems at work, the incompetence of the king, or playing cards. All sat with a glass of ale or whiskey either in their hands or on the table. In all, no more than twenty people frequented the tavern that night. She smiled as she did one last survey of the room; they could not have wanted a more perfect atmosphere for their plan.

They walked past several tables before arriving at an empty one where they had a clear view of most of the tavern. They put their hoods down but left on the cloaks as the fire did not warm the entire room. The barmaid finally walked over to them and asked what they wanted to order. Seeing that Georgiana was still inspecting the room and its occupants, Elizabeth asked for some meat, bread and tea to be brought.

The overly buxom woman eyed her and then answered, "I want the money before I bring the food. Too many people leave without paying." She paused, allowing Elizabeth to understand the importance of her next statement, "The owner makes sure somebody only does that once."

Nodding in understanding, Lizzy took a few shillings out of her purse and gave it to the barmaid. Knowing full well that it should be, Elizabeth still asked, "Will that be enough?"

The server smiled, took the money, and answered. "Yah, it'll be plenty. Do you want a few extra cups of tea?"

"Maybe a little bit later." The barmaid left as soon as Elizabeth answered.

Georgiana grabbed her arm and whispered to her, "Lizzy, see the man who just sat at the table by the bar? That is Mrs Younge's brother. I am sure of it."

Mr Younge! Finally, it all made sense. Georgiana was going to persuade the brother of her former companion to tell them of Wickham's location. Why did she not guess it sooner and save them all the trouble! This must be the same brother that taught Mrs Younge to play Three Card Brag. Of course, he would be friends with Wickham! How easy it would be for Mrs Younge to become acquainted with Wickham through her brother's acquaintance. If only she guessed it earlier and had time to tell her aunt and Jane. It was too late. Now they could only rely on one another.

"Giana, why does she have the same name as her brother if she was married?"

"Fitzwilliam found out later she was never married. She just made herself Mrs Younge to receive the job."

Elizabeth took the time to study their opponent. Mr Younge appeared to be Mr Bingley's height and stature. He possessed neither the muscular definition of Colonel Fitzwilliam nor the height of Mr Darcy. His brown hair fell loosely around his shoulders; Elizabeth wondered when the last time it saw a comb. When she studied his face, she believed the answer was the same as when his face last saw a razor. He didn't have a full beard, but the long stubble was on its way to becoming one. The shirt and pants he wore displayed markings and patches from several tousles but were otherwise clean. If not for the jagged scar on his right cheek, she may not think him to possess a particularly menacing demeanour, but the scar seemed to scream a warning to anyone that might choose to challenge him. But now he would be challenged by a sixteen-year-old girl.

"Let's watch them, learn what we can, and eat some dinner. I wouldn't want hunger to interfere with anything."

After they finished the food that the barmaid eventually served them, Elizabeth raised her eyebrow, silently asking Georgiana if she was ready to continue.

As previously agreed, Elizabeth took the lead on proposing their plan to Younge. They stood, with their purses in hand, and walked over to the table where Younge played cards with four other men. It was a higher stakes game than Elizabeth would have believed. Trying not to stare, she quickly estimated that each man played with fifteen to twenty pounds in front of him.

The men just finished a hand; it was a perfect time. Not knowing how else to refer to them, Elizabeth used the first term that came to her mind. "Gentlemen, excuse me, but my sister and I have a request."

Younge looked up from the conversation at the table and without any pretence, ran his eyes over their figures. When he finished, he smirked and finally answered back for the group. "And what would some pretty things like you want from us? And why would you be here without an escort?" Younge's nasty smirk only served to intimidate her, but she could not let it show. If she did, she would play the game by his rules for the rest of the night and that could not happen.

"My sister wants to join your game. You are playing three-card brag, are you not?"

"If you want to play with the men, I can think of much better things to do than play cards. I am sure that any of us would be up to it."

She managed to keep her composure, expecting from the beginning that this might be the men's counterproposal. She made the mistake of looking over to gage Giana's reaction. The girl's eyes were wide with shock. Had she ever heard that kind of proposition in her life?

"As I said gentlemen, my sister wishes to join your game. That is our only interest. Well, I suppose that is not entirely true; we also have an interest in the chance to increase our money. We have one hundred pounds which we would like to see grow."

Younge eyed Georgiana's purse, which the girl responded to by clasping the bag tighter to her body. Finally, he stared back at Elizabeth and said, "And you think that we are going to lose to you or that mouse who you call your sister? This is a man's game, and it takes a man to win."

"If you think you can easily win, why not let one of us play? It should be easy enough for you to win the money from us."

Eyeing Georgiana's purse once more, Younge answered calmly, "Why can't I just take it from her now? I don't think that anyone here will hold it against me." His friends laughed and confirmed they would not stop him as long as they received their share.

She needed to think of something quickly. "But where is the fun in that? I thought the joy of winning was worth more than just the coin you take home. This way you can tell your customers tomorrow night how you won one hundred pounds from two young ladies that wandered into your tavern. That story, combined with the winnings, is certainly worth your time."

There! She had him. By the way that he sat back in his chair and took a slow drink from the ale the barmaid brought him, Elizabeth knew that Younge was intrigued with her idea.

Unfortunately, she was not the only one that saw the sudden interest on Younge's face. The massive and incredibly hairy man to his left suddenly injected his opinion, "Younge, you may want to play with the chits, but I have no intention of gambling with two whores where the only prize is money."

Elizabeth didn't dare look at Georgiana this time; she already knew the combination of rage and shock that filled her young friend's face. But she would not allow that barbarian to gain the upper hand in this contest! "We are not whores!"

Younge responded again, instead of letting the ogre to his left. "How else would two girls like you get one hundred pounds to gamble with? I agree with Alex. If you wish to play, we'll call you whatever we want. Like I said, it's a man's game and men don't try to sweet talk girls whose only interest and use is to play cards with them."

That was not exactly what she wanted, but it was better than her alternatives. Seeing no other option other than to agree to Younge's terms, Elizabeth set her lips in a tight line, moved an extra seat to the table and gestured for Georgiana to sit at it.

Alex drank the remaining whiskey in front of him in one gulp. "I told you, Younge, I am not playing with no whore!" Alex started to gather his money from the table until Younge put his hand on Alex's forearm to drag him back down to the chair.

"YES YOU ARE unless you are afraid you might lose to her?" He took another large drink of ale before saying anything else. Finally, Younge smiled menacingly at his friend and continued, "Besides, think about what you might win if she runs out of money? You must admit that this little spitfire looks like a fun one to take upstairs with you. I'll even let you have a room for free for an hour. I doubt it will take you longer than that. You may even have enough time for a second helping if you are quick with the first serving."

Settling back in his chair and releasing his money, Alex focused his eyes on Georgiana's fully covered cleavage, licked his lips, and answered, "You're right. This may turn out to be a better night than I planned. But I will go for this little blonde one. If she looks this scared now, imagine what she will look like when I am ripping her dress open and taking her like the whore she is." He spit into the floorboards and wiped the residue hanging from his mouth with the back of his sleeve.

What in the world had she let Georgiana talk her into? This was all her fault! Something was going to happen, she just knew it! They had to get out of there. She stared at Georgiana, sitting in silent shock next to

Alex. Would she still be able to play and win? As if she could hear her, the girl looked up at her and nodded slightly; but Elizabeth saw the fear clearly reflected in her face.

Younge took the cards scattered around the table, ready to deal in Georgiana to the next hand when Elizabeth stopped him. "We won't play if you use those cards. We bought a new deck today that we shall use."

Quickly, Younge thrust his chair backwards and slammed his hands on the table. "What are you saying? Are you calling me a cheat?"

The anger in his eyes bore into her and Elizabeth held his stare, took a deep breath and answered in a confident, but not a cocky voice. "No, I do not think you would cheat on purpose. But you must know which cards are worn and bent and which have a small tear after constant use. It is an advantage that we cannot afford to give you. We will let you open the new card deck and look through them to ensure we aren't cheating either. Agreed?"

Younge pulled the chair back and sat back down with a snarl on his lips. "I wouldn't want anyone to think I cheated two little whores. What kind of man would that make me? I will agree, but I have a requirement of my own. Seeing as you have more money than anyone else at this table, you can't raise the stake beyond what the next player has on the table. There will be no winning by default. I would make you play with less money, but there are an awful lot of things I could do with one hundred pounds that suddenly fell in my lap one night."

"We will agree, but the other players are allowed to counter with something other than money if all players betting agree to its worth."

The fury in his expression has faded slightly, but he still eyed her suspiciously. "And what do you think you are going to get from me?"

Elizabeth raised her eyebrow and responded; she would not allow him to make her feel like this. She would take back her pride and dignity. "Perhaps your pocket watch? Possibly the deed to your tavern?"

"That is rich. You want to own the Returning Rogue. I can see you two now turning it into your very own whorehouse." He chuckled, as though her proposal was ridiculous to even consider. But he did answer, "Anyone has a problem with this?"

Elizabeth looked around at the men at the table; each man remained silent. Apparently, at the Returning Rogue, Younge made the rules.

The man waved his hand in front of the other men, "It appears that all conditions are agreed to. Now give me the deck."

Elizabeth hoped that Georgiana was able to start making small movements, taking control of her faculties again. Fortunately, the girl unclasped the lock on the purse, reached in and took out the deck of cards, situated at the top. She meekly held it out for Younge to take.

He took the deck from Georgiana, lightly fingering the palm of her hand as he did it. The girl just closed her eyes in disgust, but Elizabeth could do nothing about it. They needed to start the game.

Once again addressing Elizabeth, Younge asked, "Does this one talk, or do you keep your mouth moving enough for the both of you?"

"Please just deal the cards," Georgiana answered in a weak voice that could barely be heard.

After smirking once more at her, Younge finally dealt the cards. Following the script of their plan, Georgiana lost the first several hands, making sure to stay in long enough to gain an understanding of each of the players at the table. Elizabeth could do nothing more than watch at this point. Fortunately, Georgiana's silence and timidity served her well. She looked petrified no matter what her hand held. Now, her friend simply needed to keep that look to prevent the other players from guessing whether she was bluffing or not. Once Georgiana felt more comfortable, it would be time to start winning.

Chapter 37

Tom returned from Darcy House to Gardiner's home with no new information for Mrs Gardiner. The lady questioned him first as soon as he walked in. "Did you find anything at Darcy House?"

"Mrs Blaine searched Miss Darcy's rooms and the library. She didn't find anything that would be of use. She said those were the only rooms the ladies were in today."

Mrs Gardiner sat down next to Miss Bennet and stated calmly, "We will wait another two hours until eleven o'clock when the next note will arrive."

"Excuse me, Mrs Gardiner. Did you say something about notes arriving?"

Mrs Gardiner looked up at Mr Darcy's servant. "Yes, a delivery service dropped off a letter from Miss Darcy and Miss Elizabeth at five o'clock. The letter said to expect another letter at eleven o'clock if they have not returned by then."

"Do you know what delivery service delivered the message?"

"No, otherwise we would have gone there to retrieve the eleven o'clock note."

"Oh." He just needed to think of something; he could not sit and wait. He turned to walk out the door, but just before he closed the door behind him, he stopped. "Mrs Gardiner, they might have walked to the delivery service from the bakery. If they had, there could only be a few within walking distance. I could ride there and check right now."

Mrs Gardiner looked at him with obvious sympathy. "They could have also taken a coach to another location. The services are closed by this time of night. I do not see how this will work and I hate to send you on a wild errand in case something happens and we need you."

"Please ma'am. I need to do something. Mr Darcy trusted me to watch over his sister and I failed. If there is any chance I could help find the two ladies, I must do it."

Mrs Gardiner nodded slightly and answered, "I was wrong to dismiss your idea. You are right. We must try everything possible. No matter what, please return by eleven o'clock and let us know if you found anything."

He stood a little bit straighter. "Yes, ma'am. May I take the same horse?"

"Of course, take whatever method will be quickest." Mrs Gardiner stood up and walked with Tom to the hallway. She retrieved her purse and gave him five pounds. "In case you need this, I would rather you return with more information than with the five pounds. Also, change your clothes; my husband's manservant should be able to help you find something to wear. We don't want anyone to associate two lost young ladies with the Darcys."

"Thank you, ma'am."

The last thing he saw as he rode away was Mrs Gardiner, with her arms wrapped around Miss Bennet, intently watching his departure from the window.

He returned to the bakery and looked around. Not knowing where else to start, he asked one of the street urchins begging for coins on the street if they knew the location of any delivery services. For a few shillings, a young boy gave him directions to four delivery services within a ten-minute ride in any direction. He knew it would take close to an hour to cover them all, but he had no other choice.

Tom went to the first three and found the services closed. No matter how much banging on the door he did, he received no answer. No one from the adjacent shops was available either. There was only one more service on his list. For the sake of his own health, he prayed he found information about Miss Darcy at the final one. He couldn't return without something to prove to Mr Darcy that he helped to recover his sister.

***

Jane began to lose her faith as the clock struck one hour from the dreaded eleventh hour. Surely Lizzy or Georgiana would have found a way to come home by now if they could. And still, they had no word of the men who they last saw driving away from Pemberley on Sunday morning.

She did the only thing she could; she kept careful vigil, watching for any signs of life outside the parlour window.

Did she imagine it, or was there a young man walking up and down the opposite side of the street? There he was again. This time he passed in front of a window with some light shining through. What if he was the messenger? She had to find out. Surely her aunt wouldn't mind. She was just leaving the house for a minute. Jane grabbed her shawl and tried to silently open the front door. She slipped out and only partially closed the door behind her.

How was she to approach the young man? Propriety did not matter at this point. Her sister was likely in serious trouble. She crossed the street and walked purposefully toward him. He tipped his hat, and she curtseyed slightly in return.

"Sir, I was hoping you might be able to help me suppress my curiosity. Would you be a messenger by any chance?"

"Yes, Miss, I am tonight."

"Would the message be for the home across the street?" She pointed to Gardiner's home.

"Yes it would, but I cannot deliver it until eleven o'clock tonight."

"I am sure that you do not want to wait that long."

"I am sorry, miss, but I did make a promise."

Jane stuck out her bottom lip, feigning pouting. "I promise I won't open it. I hate to have you wait for a whole hour to deliver it. I promise that I will not open it."

The young man reached into his coat pocket. "If you promise miss, I suppose I could give it to you."

Trying to control her hand from forcibly grabbing the letter, she calmly took it and thanked him profusely for his help. Once safely in her hand, she walked back across the street, slipped back through the front door and into the parlour before tearing open the letter.

Dear Aunt,

If we have still not returned home, something went wrong. We thought we could persuade Mrs Younge's brother to tell us about Wickham's location. Mrs Younge was Georgiana's former companion who had a long-standing relationship with Mr Wickham. Mrs Younge a few times mentioned her brother during her employment with the Darcys. The first time occurred when Mrs Younge once told her that her brother owned a tavern called the Returning Rogue. Mrs Younge learned how to play three-card brag from him, a skill she later passed on to Georgiana. The tavern is located on Roscoe Street. The second occurrence happened when Mr Wickham arrived at Ramsgate last summer; Mrs Younge told Georgiana that her own brother could further vouch for his behaviour and character.

After the incident at Ramsgate, Georgiana never mentioned Mrs Younge or Wickham again. She never told her brother of the recommendation provided by Mrs Younge. She didn't remember the connection until after the gentleman already left Pemberley. We waited to be able to tell them once we arrived in London, but decided we could not wait any longer.

We planned to go to the Returning Rogue, play three-card brag with Mr Younge, and eventually gamble with enough money that Mr Younge could not cover his loss. Upon this event, we would trade him the information of Wickham's location for the money we used to gamble with. We hoped to leave the tavern no later than twenty minutes past ten o'clock tonight to make sure we return home at eleven o'clock tonight.

We fear to have to write this next line, but it must be done. If we do not return by eleven o'clock, please send whatever help is available. Please know that we love you and are terribly sorry for the further pain we caused.

Elizabeth

She had to go to Lizzy and Georgiana. Her aunt Gardiner would never let her leave willingly. She would slip away, just as the girls did. She did not know how, but she knew deep in her heart that her sister needed her. She found her black cloak and reached in the small pocket to make sure it still had the money left from when they last shopped in town; it would be plenty to pay for a coach to the Returning Rogue.

Did she need anything else? She only needed to retrieve something from her uncle's study before she left. Then she could leave. She had to save her sister. Nothing else mattered. How could she let something happen to her dearest sister?

***

Tom returned to the Gardiners thirty minutes before eleven o'clock. Mrs Gardiner walked down the stairs and opened the parlour door for them to enter. She clutched the top of her breast as they search the room and realised that it was empty.

"Where is Miss Bennet? I left her here to wait for--?" Mrs Gardiner did not finish her statement. She noticed an opened letter on the table. The woman proceeded to read aloud.

Tom beseeched the woman who silently sat with her head lying in her hands once she finished reading aloud, "I will get them. Please, Mrs Gardiner, trust me to get them back for you. I will look for them on the way to the tavern and make sure they return here safely. If I don't find them until I get to the tavern, I will be there to help them."

Mrs Gardiner just nodded. Her entire family was missing and likely in danger.

Tom ran out the door without regard to his surroundings. He needed to get to the tavern as fast as he could. Before he could climb back onto his horse, an arm grabbed his shoulder in an attempt to stop him. Tom turned, prepared to fight whatever man tried to keep him from his mission. The face he saw was the one he both feared and praised.

"Mr Darcy! You returned. We have to hurry! Miss Darcy and Miss Elizabeth ran off -"

Mr Darcy grabbed his other arm and immediately interrupted him. "What do you mean my sister and Miss Elizabeth ran off?" Mr Darcy's eyes darkened and narrowed.

"Miss Darcy and Miss Elizabeth went to the Returning Rogue tavern to convince Mrs Younge's brother to tell them where Wickham is. They have been missing for the past several hours. I do not know when, but we think that Miss Bennet already went after them. Mrs Gardiner and I only found out a few minutes ago where they were. I was leaving now to go get them."

Colonel Fitzwilliam, Mr Gardiner and Bingley all listened breathlessly to Darcy's conversation with his servant.

Mr Gardiner asked him, "You said they went to the Returning Rogue?"

"Yes, I know the area, but not exactly where it is. Do you, sir?"

"Yes, is everyone ready?" Mr Gardiner looked around at the other men in his group. By the time Mr Gardiner asked the question, all the men but Tom had already mounted their horses, but he was not far behind. They had to reach the tavern in time.

Chapter 38

Georgiana looked nervously at the small pocket watch in her purse. It was twenty past ten o'clock. They should have left the tavern by now to return to the Gardiners before the letter arrived. She had won two of the last four hands, but Younge had already folded when the last two players remained in. No matter what her next hand contained, she had to try.

Alex already lost his money several rounds before. If not for the looks given by the others at the table, Georgiana wasn't sure he would willingly leave the game. Fortunately for her, he lost the final game to his friend; her stomach tightened when she allowed herself to think what he would have done if he lost to her. Now he sat at a table nearby, watching and waiting until she got up to leave. His eyes hadn't left her since she sat down. But she couldn't think about that now. She would think about that later after she beat Younge.

She glanced once more around the table. Only three others remained in the game, fortunately, Younge was one of them. It was Georgiana's turn to shuffle the cards and deal. Before beginning, Georgiana glanced at

Elizabeth silently sitting off to her side. The intensity of Lizzy's stare almost frightened her. Instead, she used it to draw the strength she needed.

Miss Darcy looked at the pile of bills and coins in front of her. She silently counted the money; she estimated over one hundred and fifty pounds sat in the neat pile in front of her, almost all of it came from her own purse which originally held more than the one hundred pounds that Lizzy claimed. But for her to lose twenty pounds was much less serious than anyone else at the table. For most of the people in that room, it was more money than they would likely see at any one time in their lives. Now, she was planning to give it away for one piece of information. She stared once more at the considerably smaller pile of money in front of Younge. This was her chance.

"It is getting late gentleman. I suggest that we up the ante. How does five pounds sound?" Seeing the other players cast a suspicious glance at her, she continued, "I don't know how much longer my sister and I will be staying tonight. It is a chance for you to win back some money that I won from you."

"So, what do you say?" Georgiana watched each of them reluctantly nod, "Five pounds it is." They each threw five pounds into the centre of the table. The last game of the night began. It was too late to stop.

Georgiana took a deep breath and picked up the deck of cards. Before she had time to deal three to each remaining player, the door opened for the first time in almost an hour. When she instinctively glanced up to see who entered, she felt her eyes widen and her stomach drop to the floor. There she saw one of the few people that could ruin everything.

Quiet, serene Jane Bennet appeared neither calm nor composed as she stood in the doorway. The flash and anger in her blue eyes were enhanced by the black cloak that surrounded her face and body. Georgiana quickly looked around the rest of the tavern; everyone had their gaze focused on the beautiful but enraged face that just entered. She tried to swallow, but a lump in her throat made her unable. This was not a good sign.

Without considering the consequences, she did the only thing she could do; she dealt three cards to each, starting with the player on her right and dealing herself last. Now that the cards were dealt, no one could leave the table. In the same timid voice she used the entire night, she asked if anyone at the table opted to bid blind; all refused, but with their eyes still focused on Jane who had not moved from the doorway.

Finally, in long strides, Jane started to walk across the room, directly to where she and Lizzy sat. Then Elizabeth leapt from her seat, grabbed her sister's arm and dragged her to a corner where no one else sat.

The next few minutes were the most critical of the entire night. Georgiana slowly lifted the edges of the three cards in front of her. In her hand, she found a straight with the 8 of clubs, the 9 of diamonds and the 10 of diamonds staring back at her. The cards in front of her were far from the best hand of the night, but they certainly were not the worst either. But the cards barely mattered; it was now or never. That was why it was called gambling, wasn't it?

Sutton began the betting by putting another five pounds in the table centre. Younge, Barney and she each followed; with forty pounds on the table after only the first round. Of course, no one wanted to be the first to fold and lose their chance to win it. But all she could do was play her own hand and hope that Younge would stay in while the others soon left. After Georgiana, Younge did have the most money remaining on the table, even with a managing to lose the most over the course of the night. The more he had to lose, the better her chances were.

The second round began with Sutton upping the bet to seven pounds. Barney folded; his cards must not have been good enough to risk losing the remainder of the twenty pounds remaining in front of him. Younge checked his cards and examined each person at the table. When his eyes focused on her, it took every ounce of strength she had to hold his piercing stare. She felt her legs begin to shake under the table. She tensed her legs and wrapped them around the chair legs, hoping no one could see her chair shaking. After an eternity, Younge picked up seven pounds from the pile in front of him and slammed the notes in the centre of the table. With a quick glance to Jane and Lizzy who still seemed to be arguing in the corner, Georgiana followed Younge's lead, checked her own cards again, and put seven more pounds in the pot.

Sutton alternated between looking at the other two remaining players. He had a lot less money than either of the other two at the table. If they decided to stay in the game, he would lose the rest of the money in front of him no matter if his cards were better. Georgiana was counting on that. But even though she expected it, she felt her hands begin to shake as he slammed his cards on the table, took a large drink of ale, and threatened, "I'm finished. Younge, you better beat this little whore. She will not be walking out of here with all of our money."

Younge glared at Georgiana and slowly his face changed to one with an ominous smile. "Don't worry, Sutton. I'll get our money back. You can try to win it back from me tomorrow night."

Georgiana felt the goosebumps cause the hair on her arms to stand up on ends while her heart pounded inside her chest. She did not know if she could go through with the last part of the plan. How could she intimidate Younge into confessing Wickham's location? She looked over in desperation to Bennet sisters. She caught Lizzy's eyes and silently pleaded with her.

"Hey! You are on your own little girl. No one here is going to help you!"

Georgiana dropped her eyes' from Elizabeth's and stared at the floor. Eventually, she looked up, back at Younge. She heard the footsteps of her friends' creek on the floorboards as they walked towards her. They were near her even if she could not look at them.

Younge picked up the remainder of the money he had, all thirty-five pounds, and dropped it in the centre of the table. Georgiana silently and carefully counted out thirty-five pounds from the pile in front of her. She mentally did the math and realised that ninety-eight pounds remained.

Younge hissed, "So, are we going to finish this? Show me your cards."

It was now or never. She could do this. She heard Lizzy's heavy breathing by her side. "If you agree, I would like to change the rules. I want to continue with one more round of betting, but you are out of money."

Younge slammed his hands against the table. Georgiana jumped slightly; her legs tightened further around the chair legs, keeping her safely grounded in the seat. The money and cards shifted erratically around the table. "So you really do want my tavern to turn into your own whorehouse. That will happen over my dead body, you little hussy."

Georgiana was surprised she could hear anything over the sound of her own heart beating. She wiped the sweat from her hands on her dress and violently shook her head. That was definitely not what she wanted to happen. If she never saw this tavern again, she could sleep peacefully at night.

Younge calmed down considerably. "In that case, I'm listening. What do you have to offer?"

Elizabeth stood up from where she had sat silently with Jane and walked behind Georgiana. She could see Georgiana beginning to shake and needed to be her strength. In the clearest and most direct voice, she could muster, she said, "We will bet the rest of the money we have. In exchange, you will bet the information that we want and you have. If you have the better hand, you win all the money already betted and the money on the table that belongs to my sister. If my sister has the better hand, you will tell us the information we want and you will tell us immediately following the game. Do you agree?"

Ever so slowly, Younge stood from his chair, cowering over Elizabeth's eye level. She could smell the alcohol reeking from his mouth every time he breathed on her. His dark eyes glared and alternated between looking down on Elizabeth and Georgiana who still sat in the chair. Elizabeth clutched Georgiana's shoulders and somehow managed to stand a little taller; she did not want to give him any feeling of superiority over her.

"So now the true reason for your little escapade to my humble tavern comes out. I must know something that you want. And this is a rather expensive piece of information. You are willing to give me one hundred and fifty pounds for it." He stared at all three of them a long moment and when he was done, plainly stated, "But it doesn't really matter to me what the information is. I don't value anything I know more than one hundred and fifty pounds so, you have yourself a deal."

Elizabeth reached for her seat and moved it so she practically sat in Georgiana's lap. She leaned even closer and whispered in Georgiana's ear, "I hope that you have some good cards under there."

"It is too late now if I don't, isn't it?" Elizabeth heard whispered back in her own ear.

"Well ladies, let's see what your future holds." Younge looked entirely too confident for the ladies' comfort.

Elizabeth took one last glimpse around the room. All sixteen sets of eyes in the tavern watched as Georgiana timidly turned over her straight containing an eight, nine and ten. She could do nothing but stare at the never before used cards. They just staked the entire

Bennet family future on an average hand. She would not want to bet a bonnet she liked with those odds. What were they thinking!

Finally, Elizabeth looked up into Younge's face to see his reaction. With one motion, he grasped the corners of the table and threw it to the side of the tavern. She instinctively pulled Georgiana back to the ground as the table flew across the room.

"You stupid whore! I know you cheated somehow. I ain't telling you shit!"

Clutching Elizabeth's arm while still laying on the floor, Georgiana pleaded loudly without thinking, "But you promised!"

Jane quickly stood up and dragged Elizabeth and Georgiana to their feet.

"We need to leave here. Now. The money doesn't matter."

Elizabeth whispered back, "We can't. We risked too much to leave without finding out what we need."

She would never forget the pain in her sister's eyes as Jane answered, "If you stay, I will be by your side. But Lizzy, please, we need to leave here now before something worse happens."

She smiled sadly at her elder sister and turned to Younge who had remained remarkably quiet while Jane spoke to her.

"You must tell us. We need to know what we came here for. If you don't, every man here will know that you cannot keep your word when playing cards. Is that the reputation that you want for your establishment? Who else will play with a known cheat?"

Younge licked his lips as his eyes raked over each of the three girls' figures. He walked slowly over to the counter, now that the table had been overturned. The man picked up his pint of ale from the long counter and addressed the room. "Isn't that cute gents? This feisty little whore thinks that insulting my honour is going to let her leave with my money and the information she wants."

Four of the men standing rather close to the table laughed wickedly. Changing the focus of his speech from the room-at-large to Elizabeth in particular, he continued. "It is too bad that you forgot two little problems. The first is that I am no gentleman and not under such restraints as the gentlemen you normally service. And the second, if I am blackmailed by two, excuse me, three pretty whores, no one here is going to have one shred of respect for me, anyway. Even less so than if I cheat you out of this information you so desperately want." He took a large drink from the mug he held and laughed when finished.

Clutching Jane and Georgiana's hands, Elizabeth examined the room that seemed smaller by the minute. The crowd that assembled there when the game began was largely gone. She was so intent on the game that the change in clientele had not registered in her mind. How could she be so blind! She only focused on the game, not on what would happen after. No other women remained behind; even the barmaid had left. Several of the men sitting at the side tables carried swords or knives. None of the other fourteen men in the room looked at them with particular concern for their welfare.

They were on their own and it was her fault. She had nothing to protect them. The courage that Elizabeth found earlier completely evaded her. She heard Georgiana quietly crying from behind her. Jane was completely still, but she could still hear her sister's heavy breathing.

Younge started to take a few small steps toward them. "In fact, I don't think I should let you three ladies out of here anytime soon. It was kind of you to bring a third for the party, and she is such an appetising looking piece at that. Who knows, I may even let her watch while I take you so she knows what she is in for. Maybe when we are done with all three of you upstairs, I may even find it in my heart to tell you what you want to know so badly." Younge eyed her ravenously once more. "And I can promise you ladies, no one here will be wondering about what kind of man I am by the end of the night."

This was it. They needed to leave now! Forget the money, forget the information! If they did not leave right then, they might not ever. With equally small steps, she brought her sister and friend backwards, toward the door. The once small room now seemed impossibly large. All the men in the room had their attention focused solely on them.

It was Alex, the creep that focused his attention on Georgiana all night, that proved to be the one that stopped them from their escape attempt. Now that he stood in front of her, she realised how truly massive he was. He tightly gripped Elizabeth's arm with both his hands and wretched it out of Jane's hand. He used the momentum to fling her at Younge who placed both of his arms tightly around her before she could control her flailing body. She watched helplessly as Alex took Georgiana's arm. Sutton came up behind Jane, put an arm around her neck, and whispered something in her ear that Elizabeth could not hear. From Jane's expression, she could only guess at the severity of its disgusting nature. What had she done?

Alex's cruel voice broke her thoughts. "I think that brown-haired one will be far feistier than the others. She has a spirit; breaking it will be a pleasure. We will hold the two blonde ones for you until you are ready for them." He ran his fingers along Georgiana's cheek and down her throat before continuing, "If you don't hurry back, I can't make any promises about what state you will find this one in though."

Elizabeth stared at both Jane and Georgiana, completely unsure of what to do next. She felt one of Younge's hands wrap around her shoulders while the other grabbed and tightly squeezed her breast to the point of pain. Her entire body constructed from the repulsion of his hands groping the most private parts of her body. His hot breath made her skin crawl as whispered in her ear, "Don't you worry, lass. I promise you that I am going to enjoy it plenty. This is a night you will never forget."

Georgiana thought back to the purse she carried all day; only she knew everything that it held. She looked around the tavern and saw all eyes were glued to Elizabeth and Younge. The arm that was lightly holding her let go as the man went to pick up another drink. She had no other choice. She could not allow this to happen to Lizzy. This was all her fault and now her friend would pay the price for her insane idea.

She looked up and caught Jane's eyes and led her to look at the purse close to her feet. Jane barely moved her arm and reached into her cloak. The shine of the blade was momentarily exposed from Jane's cloak. Apparently, the eldest Bennet sister had the same idea that she did. At this point, she could only hope that Jane could subdue Sutton. She had to concentrate on getting

Lizzy away from Younge; that was the most immediate danger. She looked around the room one final time, realising that all eyes were still on Elizabeth. Trying to move as swiftly and quietly as possible, she reached down to the ground, undid the clasp of the purse, and removed the final object she took before leaving her brother's library. When she had the weapon firmly in her grasp, she jumped back from the rest of the room.

"If you don't let go of my sister, I swear I will kill you!" Every eye in the bar turned from Elizabeth to Georgiana. The girl raised the pistol with both hands and aimed it at Younge. "I swear to you. If you hurt her, I will kill you." She was having a difficult time controlling her breathing and keeping the pistol level with each breath she took. She felt the beginnings of another hyperventilation attack coming on.

While she held everyone's attention, Jane did exactly what she hoped she might. While Sutton kept one hand around Jane's shoulders, she covertly moved her arm inside her cloak, getting leverage to hit Sutton squarely in the gut. With one deft move and all the force she could muster, Jane elbowed her captor squarely in the stomach, causing him to yell in pain. But the man managed to tighten his grip around her even further.

But Even with both of Sutton's arms around her, Jane managed to manoeuvre her hand once again inside her cloak. She removed the knife from inside the pocket in the cloak and without time to think about the consequence, reached her arm around her own body and with the knife, quickly stabbed Sutton in the side, under the concealment of her cloak.

The sharp cry from Sutton before could not be compared to the rage he unleashed as he threw Jane against the wall. Somehow, she managed to keep the bloody knife in her hand through the fall. Standing quickly up against the wall and moving towards Georgiana, Jane kept the bloody dagger close to her body, clearly afraid of what Sutton would do if he recovered even slightly from the wound inflicted.

Then with the pistol firmly secured in both hands and aimed toward Younge and Elizabeth, Georgiana shrieked in desperation one final time, "Let my sister go! I swear I will kill you!"

Chapter 39

Elizabeth's eyes swung from Georgiana's pistol to the thundering crack from the tavern's front door. She had to blink thrice in rapid succession to make sure the vision before her was real. Mr Darcy, her uncle, Colonel Fitzwilliam and Mr Bingley stormed the tavern with weapons drawn. What seemed almost impossible only a minute before, now brimmed with hope. The fifteen men that remained in the tavern no longer controlled their fate; those same men now faced five armed men and three women, two of which had weapons of their own.

She was not the only person that immediately felt the power shift. Alex abandoned his purposeful creep toward the gun-wielding Georgiana and ran clumsily to the back side of the room, directly opposite of the ladies' newly arrived heroes. Grabbing his pierced side with one hand and a knife with the other, Sutton lunged toward Jane, hoping to reach her before Jane's protectors could react.

With her heart racing, Elizabeth yelled in sheer panic, "Jane!" She tried to spring forward, out of Younge's grasp, but he held her too tightly to move.

Mr Bingley shared Elizabeth's fear. Entering just after Darcy and with his sword already drawn, the eyes of her sister's fiancé immediately leapt to Jane at the sound of her terrified scream. The bloody dagger in Jane's hand and the blood seeping from Sutton's side made it entirely too obvious what Sutton planned to do in revenge for Jane's attack. Without hesitation, Mr Bingley raced past Mr Darcy and hurled his sword into Sutton's gut, only inches before Sutton managed to come within an arm's length of her sister. Mr Bingley wasted no time yanking his sword from Sutton's frame and kicking the now lifeless man to the floor. Her future brother then moved swiftly, taking his place by Mr Darcy's less protected side.

Mr Darcy had stepped in front of Georgiana, raised his pistol, aimed it at Younge, and used his other hand to lower his sister's pistol. Colonel Fitzwilliam grabbed his young cousin's free arm and ordered Tom to protect Miss Bennet and Miss Darcy by the door. Tom took the pistol from Georgiana's hand, held it tightly in his own, and moved his body so that anyone in the tavern must make it by him to reach the two ladies. While Mr Bingley still dealt with Sutton, the Colonel moved to take his place by Mr Darcy's right. Her uncle who had entered more cautiously than the rest drew his own pistol and moved to stand next to Mr Bingley, seeing the majority of men in the tavern on Mr Darcy's left.

If only she could wrangle herself away from Younge! As she felt one of his hands momentarily drop from pinning her to his chest, she dropped one shoulder to twist away from his grasp, taking advantage of the opportunity. But before she could manoeuvre her body away from his, she felt a cold blade ever so slightly pierce the side of her throat; the sweat dripping down the side of her throat stung where the blood dripped from. The feeling of the cold metal could only be one thing. If she moved again, he would be able to slit her throat before she could wrestle free. Her heart continued to beat wildly in her chest.

Mr Darcy could not shoot Younge without risking her life in the process. And if any of the men tried to reach her with a sword, the villain could kill her before they had a chance. Younge chose that moment to move his arm from the top of her shoulders to wrapping it tightly around her waist, applying pressure that made it difficult to breathe. She closed her eyes, trying to calm herself and keep from collapsing.

At the sound of Mr Darcy's voice, she opened her eyes. Without turning his head to address his driver, Mr Darcy spoke in a voice far too steady for the severity of the circumstances. "Tom, when we have all the ladies, you are to get them out of here immediately. Take them to my house and do not let them leave."

As he spoke, Elizabeth examined him, fearing it may be her last chance. She had never seen a man seething raw, unadulterated rage. Mr Darcy's eyes no longer looked human; they could not be the same that enticed her to lean against his strong chest and calm all of her fears; the eyes staring back at her belonged to the devil. How could she do this to him? He would never forgive her; his eyes betrayed his feelings toward her; that she knew without a doubt.

She felt Younge change his breathing rate to deeper sporadic breaths instead of the calm, calculated ones before Mr Darcy entered the tavern. The man holding her hostage had to know that his options were limited.

"Whatever man here wants a share of the two hundred pounds on that table, he only needs to help me get out of here with this girl." Elizabeth quickly searched the room, trying to see who might agree. Not a single man stirred. Younge quickly continued. "Not like any of you ever turned away from a fight before. It's a lot of money. The money there will keep you for a long time." He turned his head from staring back at Mr Darcy to the three men from the tavern standing in semi-close proximity to Mr Bingley and Mr Gardiner. "Henry, Michael, Jacob. You know what to do." Younge motioned to them with a nod of his head. "Come on! They are gentlemen; the only fighting they do is in a ballroom wearing their pretty stockings. They aren't real men."

Elizabeth watched as the three men each took out knives with blades twice the length of her hand; a blonde picked up a sword from behind the counter. The ruffians took several seconds examining her heroes before they moved. Why one of them chose to go after Mr Bingley when they saw what he did to Sutton only minutes before, she could not understand. Of course, the cool hardness of Colonel Fitzwilliam's countenance might easily dissuade even the most experienced fighters. It was then that she looked at her uncle and understood the men's plan. If only her uncle appeared more dangerous. Even she could tell he was not as comfortable with a weapon in his hand as the others in Mr Darcy's group. It would be three against two, and her uncle did not appear to be a great threat.

Her uncle and future brother-in-law prepared themselves as the three men lunged towards them. The smaller balding thug rushed toward Mr Gardiner, trying to take out what everyone must believe to be the easiest target. Her uncle did not appear to be the type of gentleman that would actually use the gun that he gripped in his hand. He never took his eyes on the approaching foe.

But the ruffian should not have underestimated her uncle. With the hammer already cocked, Mr Gardiner took aim at the man who rushed toward him with a knife in hand and squeezed the trigger. For the first time in his life, her dear uncle was forced to use deadly violence. As she watched him observe the man lying on the ground, she could tell that her uncle felt no regret. Her family would never be the same after tonight.

The second the gun fired and the other two attackers momentarily stopped their advance to look at their dying friend. Elizabeth's attention was diverted to the brute that terrorised Georgiana. Alex grabbed a slightly rusting sword from the table where he previously sat. Instead of going after her uncle, he attacked Colonel Fitzwilliam in a frontal assault while the other two attacked Mr Bingley and Mr Gardiner in a coordinated attack. Thankfully, Mr Darcy's cousin was ready for the attack. He raised his own sword, successfully blocking the brute's first attempt. Afraid to watch, Elizabeth closed her eyes and only listened to the crash of metal on metal. Finally, when she heard the Colonel speak, she opened her eyes to see their swords crossed and their faces on inches from each other.

"And what were your plans for the ladies?"

Alex snapped back, "Nothing you didn't already get from the whores."

Elizabeth knew that was the exact wrong thing to say to a man who spent the last fifteen years in His Majesty's Army and loved his little blonde cousin as a sister. With immense force, he shoved Alex backwards, causing the hairy fiend to lose balance, crashing on the floor. As Alex lay helplessly on the ground with the sword still in hand, the Colonel used his positional advantage to make sure that Georgiana was never threatened by that terrible beast again. Showing no guilt for his actions, he then removed his sword from the man who now lay on the floor and silently challenged anyone else to approach him. No one dared.

Tearing her eyes from the dead man, Elizabeth looked back to Georgiana. Jane now held her tightly, making sure that the girl faced the door instead of the room at large. Tom kept his body firmly between them and the danger.

Then, with a perfectly timed and angled thrust of his sword, she saw Mr Bingley sticking his sword into the stomach of his enemy. But the sharp pain in her throat brought Elizabeth back to the reality of her position. The sudden movement of her head caused the knife to dig in once more to the side of her throat. She could not move as she felt blood begin to trickle down her neck.

With intense anger, Younge roared at her, "Don't move bitch. One more jerk like that and I am not responsible for what you do to yourself."

When Elizabeth returned her eyes to Mr Darcy's, she saw her future. At that moment, she knew the extent of the repercussions from her actions that day. He had given her his heart and his trust only a few days before. She gave him hers in return. And now, with her actions that day, she threw out the most precious gift she ever received. The only emotion she would see from the gentleman again would be his abhorrence for placing his sister in this heinous situation.

Mr Darcy could do nothing more than watch blood drip down Elizabeth's neck and listen to her quiet sobs. How was he supposed to contain himself when only one thought circulated in his mind? He could not allow the monster before him to hurt the woman he loved. He would not survive if she left his life. Four men already lay dead and still, Elizabeth was in as much danger as when he first stormed the tavern. All they managed to do was make Younge even more desperate. One thing he knew, desperate men make stupid decisions. He could not allow this to go on much longer.

He only looked away from Younge when he heard a cry of pain from Gardiner. There he saw the third man further drive a knife into Gardiner's shoulder. He could not move to help him. If he did, Elizabeth would be killed. Fortunately, Bingley also heard Gardiner's cry and retracted his blade from the man on the ground. Without any pretence or long battle, Bingley repeated the same action he performed only thirty seconds before; he killed the man whose hand suddenly dropped from the knife in Gardiner's shoulder.

Darcy heard Gardiner speak as he clutched his shoulder with his good arm. "I'm alright."

Not moving his head from facing Younge, Darcy addressed the room at large. "Men, I have a slightly different deal for you. I will let you take all the money in this room and will make sure you don't face prosecution for your actions tonight if you go to the room in the back and lock yourselves in. I will make sure that someone comes by in a few hours to let you out."

From the side of the tavern, one of the men asked, "And if we don't take the deal?"

"As you can see from your friends lying on the floor, we will fight any of you that attempt to stop us from taking these ladies out of here safely. Even if you manage to kill one of us, I promise that at least one of us will make it out of here alive. He will tell the authorities and you will all be hung for murdering and attacking the gentlemen. It probably will not matter as most of you will be killed in the fight anyway." For the first time since entering the tavern, Darcy looked at each of the men in the tavern that stood either next to or behind Younge. "The choice you have is life with a significant amount of money in your pocket," he paused for effect, "or death. That is the only choice you have left to make tonight."

One of the men in the back yelled at him, "Why the storeroom? Why can't we just leave?"

"Because I do not want you to follow us or attack us as we leave. You have my word that I will ensure your safety. Unlike the man that owns this establishment, I can be trusted to keep my word."

Darcy heard mumblings amongst the men. How could any man truly be worried about being labelled a coward with the proposition before them? With the choice of death or life with money, not many men would even view it as a decision. Fortunately, the majority proved sane and louder than the small minority worried about their reputation. That would certainly make this easier if the men went in the back room without further incident.

When he heard enough to know he won that decision, he spoke in the same voice he used to maintain Pemberley. "Richard, get ready to move them into the back room." Now once again addressing the crowd but keeping his eyes focused on Younge, he asked, "Is there anyone of you that the others trust to keep the money and distribute it?"

He heard several mentions to give it to a man named Jackson.

Without lowering his sword, Richard called the group, "Which one of you is Jackson?"

Out of the side of his eye, he saw a man in his forties dressed in a rumpled brown suit come forward.

Thankfully the Colonel took over for him from this point. With his sword, he motioned to the man that had stepped forward, "Jackson, take the money off the table and get the others into the back room. I will lock the door when all of you are inside."

"Stop! You can't do this! How dare all of you to betray me! How can you take the side of a man like him over one of your own?" Yelled Younge.

Jackson responded angrily to man's rantings. "I thought you said that we didn't have any appreciation for a man's honour. If we have no honour why would we want to give our lives to protect someone else? I did not enter your tavern today with the intent for it to be my last night on Earth. There is no choice Younge."

The man screamed in anger if possible pulling Elizabeth even closer to him. The scoundrel slowly moved toward the wall next to the small storeroom in the back, dragging the woman with him.

Meantime, Jackson collected the money, walked over to the other men, and herded them toward the cramped room. Only a few made any indication they were not inclined to agree with the majority decision, but the others in the group took the decision from them. Darcy watched as any dissenters had a man grab an arm on either side and strongly encourage them to follow the rest into the storeroom. Jackson, who held the money from the table in his hands, was the last one in. The Colonel followed the man to the door and closed it behind the group. He grabbed the wooden bar next to the door, placed it inside the handles, and then shook it several times to ensure it could not be opened.

"Younge, it looks like it is just you and us now. What will you chose to do?"

The man laughed quickly before answering. "So now I have a choice too? What kind of deal will you make with me? You may have left me all alone, but I still have the one thing in my arms that you seem to want. By the look in your eyes, I'd say you want it bad. I think you would give me a pretty good deal to get this whore back. She certainly is tasty - but I am sure you already know that." And then Younge reached down into Elizabeth's dress and touched her breast.

"Here is the deal I am prepared to offer you. I will think about letting you go if you give her back to me now and tell me where Mr Wickham is. If you don't, I will tear you apart, inch by inch and I will make sure it is far more excruciating than anything you have dreamed."

Darcy watched as Younge slowly lifted his filthy hand out of Elizabeth's dress. But the snarl on his lips betrayed that he had no intention of releasing the lady. Instead of letting her go, he watched Elizabeth tremble violently as Younge's filthy appendage slowly moved from her breast down to toward her stomach. He feared that Younge's hand had not finished its travels yet.

He heard him murmur loudly in her ear so everyone left in the tavern's main room could hear, "Doesn't sound like a very good deal to me, does it?"

Elizabeth cringed again as Younge licked her ear; Darcy was helpless to stop the bastard. As long as he held the knife to her throat, he could not risk attacking him. All he could do was wait and hope that Younge made a mistake.

Speaking much louder, Younge continued. "I think that you should give me a better deal than that. I think she is worth it."

He couldn't take it any longer. He took a step towards her, but Younge responded by tightening the knife against Elizabeth's throat. He didn't know how she was still managing to breathe. Blood continued to drip slowly down her neck while her face paled even further. Her eyes; he would never forget their fear. Darcy took a step back and motioned for the others to do the same.

"In fact, if that is the best deal you are going to give me, I think I should take her with me. If I die, I will make sure I have the company of your beautiful whore to pleasure me in my next life."

Darcy watched as Elizabeth closed her eyes tightly. When she opened them again, the tears had stopped, but the emerald centre of her eyes was still encircled by redness. She locked her eyes with his and bit her bottom lip. He knew that look of determination. She was going to try to do something to Younge! He had to stop her! It was too dangerous. This wasn't like fighting the Lucas brothers. Younge would kill her if she failed!

He then watched as her knee pushed out the skirt of her dress. She must have garnered every ounce of energy she had because after she slammed her heel down on Younge's foot, the villain screamed out in pain and surprise. Instinctively, the man reached down to grab his foot and made the fateful error of reaching down with the arm that he previously held against her neck. Elizabeth then jammed her elbow into Younge's side, just below the man's rib cage. She twisted her body to get away, but Younge's other arm still held her tightly.

Darcy raced forward to free Elizabeth from Younge's grasp while the Colonel tackled the bastard. He felt her fall forward into his arms alone. She was safe in his grasp. Without saying anything to her, he sent Elizabeth to Tom and told him to take the ladies to the house immediately.

Chapter 40

Younge didn't have a chance against the Colonel's rage and the damage already inflicted by Elizabeth. Darcy watched from the door as Richard lunged for the knife desperately held onto by Younge and wrestled it out of the monster's hand. He threw the knife across the room, far from Younge's reach. Clearly, in charge of the fight, his cousin delivered blow after blow until Younge's face was little more than a bloody and misshapen mess. When he finally moved from the door to see if his cousin would let him assist, Darcy listened without pity as Younge finally screamed for mercy with promises to cooperate. It was too late for that - the villain had to know he would not leave that tavern alive. During a short pause between Richard's assaults, he grabbed Younge by the shirt, forced the vile scoundrel to stand, and pushed him against the wall.

With his face only inches from Younge's, his cousin spoke to Younge, blurting out the thoughts swirling in his mind. "And what could you possibly have that we want now? I believe the gentleman made it very clear what your options were, and you chose rather poorly."

"I still know something that you want to know. I will tell you if you let me live. I swear it."

Younge managed a small blood-filled smile between his heavy breaths. How dare that vile wretch to think he could walk out of this with all of his limbs intact?! Darcy slammed Younge against the wall and yelled, "There is nothing that will let you live now!"

After receiving Bingley's assistance to stand and gain control of his body, Gardiner grabbed Darcy's shoulder and coerced him to the opposite side of the tavern. Bingley took Darcy's place holding Younge with Richard's assistance.

Gardiner stared intensely at Darcy as he guided them across the room, moving to block his eye line to Younge. He had no choice but to give Gardiner his attention.

"I know how much you want revenge. I want it just as badly as you do, but the blaggard is right. He knows something that we need. Are you prepared to sacrifice getting Lydia back and finding Wickham to have revenge on Younge? I have three nieces that I am trying to look out for. I am not prepared to choose revenge for two simply to damn another to some unspeakable fate."

In a strangely confident voice that carried across the tavern, Younge spoke. "I knew the older gentleman would see it my way." Younge managed one final satisfied smile. "If I have your word I will live, I will tell you whatever it is you want to know."

Richard punched Younge squarely in the gut, forcing Younge to gasp for air.

"Fitzwilliam, I believe we have another option that this miserable creature has not considered. We can always beat the information out of him." Darcy looked at his cousin who smiled fully in return. "I do believe you learned a few skills during your last campaign. I am sure His Majesty wouldn't mind you perfecting your skills for a good cause."

His threat worked. Confident smile now was gone, Younge looked to Gardiner and begged, "It may be too late by then. Besides, how much longer do you think I will be conscious enough to answer your questions?"

Younge tried again to plead with Gardiner, "Killing a man in self-defence is a lot different from killing a defenceless man. You don't want to remember that feeling when you wake up in the morning. Trust me on this."

Gardiner looked back at him with a resigned scowl. "He is right, we can't kill a defenceless man."

"I beg to differ. I have killed enough men that one more voice screaming in my head will not make a difference," said the Colonel.

Gardiner looked at Younge, "I suggest you start talking immediately and give them a reason to keep you alive. There is nothing I can do if you don't cooperate and do it very soon. We want to know where Wickham is."

"Wickham! Are you telling me that this entire night was about finding that bastard?" Richard nodded while Darcy held his breath.

Younge looked to Bingley and asked, "What time is it now?"

"It must be fifteen past eleven o'clock. What difference does that make?"

"He's been coming over here right before closing at half-past eleven. We play a few hands and finish drinking anything that is left. You just have to wait for him for another fifteen minutes. He will be here, I can almost guarantee it." Darcy watched as Younge's eyes widened with fear. "Now you know. You have to let me live!"

If Darcy was capable of feeling pity for the man, the man's pitiful pleading might have done it. Instead, he felt pleasure once he crossed the room in four long strides and punched the wretch once more in the gut. "We don't have to do anything. You gave up your rights to demand anything when you violated and threatened the woman I love!"

This time Bingley stopped Darcy from doing or saying anything further. He forcibly pulled him back from being within reach of Younge. "We need Wickham to come here. In order to do that, we need Younge to be alive for Wickham. I am not going to try to convince you not to kill him. If I saw Jane," Bingley stopped and stared at the ground... "the way that you saw Elizabeth, there is nothing I wouldn't do for revenge. And for what those bastards did to Jane, I will help you do whatever you plan for retaliation. But we need to at least do this the smart way to save Jane and Elizabeth's sister."

Darcy stared back at his friend. If he sacrificed Lydia for his revenge, would Elizabeth forgive him? No matter how foolish her sister was, Elizabeth would never choose her own satisfaction over her sister's safety. He pulled his arm from Bingley's grasp and returned to where his cousin was holding Younge.

He grabbed Younge's shirt from Richard's grasp making sure that Younge could see the unadulterated hatred in his eyes. "I still haven't decided whether to kill you. You certainly improved your chances by telling us about Wickham. Now you have another opportunity to improve your chances of living. Tell us where Wickham is staying."

Younge alternated looking between the Colonel and him. "What guarantee do I have that you won't still kill me?"

Darcy answered with a small smirk, "You don't have any guarantees. I heard you didn't appreciate a gentleman's word."

"I will take that gentleman's word." Younge lifted his hand a few inches in the air and with great effort pointed to Gardiner. "If he tells me that I will live, I will tell you where Wickham is staying."

Gardiner answered too quickly for Darcy's taste. "You have my word. But if you cross us, I cannot vouch for the actions of my friends. Do you understand what I am saying? If Wickham isn't here or at the location, you tell us, I will leave you to whatever fate my friends chose for you."

Younge answered immediately. "Agreed. He is staying at the Crown Inn."

Younge's attention shifted back to Darcy and asked a final question, "Do you mean that all of this happened because of some stupid chit that my friend plucked?" Younge laughed until the Colonel stopped him in the most efficient manner he knew how with another strong left hook to Younge's jaw.

Darcy told Gardiner and Richard to go to the Inn while he stayed behind with Bingley to wait for Wickham.

His cousin immediately spoke. "Darcy, why are you splitting us up? Wouldn't it be better for all four of us to wait for him here?"

"But what if he already came by, saw the situation, and immediately returned to get Lydia? We need someone to go there. I need someone who hates Wickham as much as I do to be there in case you find him. And you need Gardiner with you because he is the girl's relative."

Richard nodded in agreement. "Promise me one thing. Don't do anything foolish until I return. Wickham will rely on you to lose your temper to find a way out of this. I can't believe you have stayed as calm as you have until this point. I am afraid that just seeing his face will put you over the edge. You have to stay calm for Miss Elizabeth's sake."

The Colonel touched Gardiner's good shoulder, asked if he could still ride, and motioned for them to leave. Darcy watched as the gentlemen left the tavern. Only Younge, Bingley, five dead bodies, and he remained. And all he needed was Wickham.

Chapter 41

Georgiana Darcy walked swiftly down the dark and almost empty street, with Tom driver closely wedged between her, Elizabeth and Jane. As they walked, she could not help but glance over her shoulder every few steps. Each time she saw nothing in their wake.

Her brother and cousin were still in danger and she put them there. If not for her foolishness and stubbornness, her family would be safe!

Her walk turned into a slow run as she urged the others to keep up with her. She had to go home where her brother knew they would be safe. Tom pulled back on her arm, forcing her to slow her pace.

"Miss Darcy, you must slow down. I do not want any attention. We look strange enough as a group without running through the streets of Cheapside."

Before she had time to think about it, Tom handed her into a coach. Lizzy and Jane had already stepped in, not making a sound. Instead of sitting on the other bench, she squeezed between Lizzy and the door. The three of them needed to be together, with nothing separating them. She belonged sitting with her sisters, not on the other side, watching them comfort one another.

None of them spoke a word until the carriage finally stopped. What could she possibly say to make the situation better? There was nothing she could do. She had done enough and now her family had paid the price. The danger had not ended when they left the tavern and only the morning would reveal the results of what she foolishly began.

When they reached Darcy House, Tom asked, "Miss Darcy, where do you want to wait for Mr Darcy? I thought the library may be best."

"I know that my brother told you not to let us out of your sight, but I think we need to clean and change clothes. And Miss Elizabeth's neck has to be attended. I would like us to be able to go to my rooms instead."

The servant looked at Elizabeth's dress and the cuts on her neck.

"Miss Darcy, I do not think your brother would mind if the three of you went to your rooms. Will the three of you swear not to go anywhere? I can't do this unless you promise me."

"I promise that the three of us will stay in my rooms tonight until my brother returns. We will only leave when he allows us to do so."

Tom nodded. "Will you mind if I knock on the door every twenty minutes or so to make sure you are fine?"

"We can agree to that," Georgiana said.

"And so you are not surprised, I am going to sit outside your door the entire night with the pistol loaded. If anything happens, you must yell for me right away. Do not take any chances."

Taking Lizzy's other arm in hers, she and Jane guided Elizabeth upstairs and to her chambers. They waited outside the door while Tom searched her room, ensuring no one was hiding, waiting for their return. Under normal circumstances, she might have rolled her eyes at his protectiveness, but after today, his efforts were more than welcome.

They led Lizzy to the sofa in front of the fire and sat down together. Elizabeth laid her head against Jane who wrapped her arms tightly around her younger sister. Georgiana leaned against Lizzy's other side and wrapped her arms around her waist. The younger Darcy sibling could do nothing but wait and listen to the calming sounds of Jane's hum while she stroked her sister's hair. If only Lizzy would say something to show that she might recover if given enough time! But Georgiana was not that fortunate; her friend had not made a sound since they left the tavern and there were no signs of that changing.

All three looked up when they heard a gentle knock at the door and they heard Mrs Blaine's voice on the other side. All three ladies turned their moist, puffy red eyes to the older woman at the door. Even years of training could not stop Mrs Blaine from the shock that momentarily appeared on the housekeeper's face at viewing Miss Darcy with the Bennet sisters. But what else could she expect with their blood covered and ripped clothing, falling hairstyles, crimson cheeks, and the cuts on Miss Elizabeth's neck? Thankfully, the housekeeper's shock quickly turned to compassion. Not saying anything at first, the woman walked over to them and explained that she would be here as long as they needed her.

"I am glad to see that Tom started a fire; that should warm up the room in a few more minutes. And now, the first thing we need to do is to get the three of you into some clean clothing. I am sure that Miss Darcy has some extra nightgowns that the Miss Bennets will be able to use."

Georgiana watched as her brother's servant left the room and walked to her closet. Lizzy's gaze had not moved from the growing fire. The younger Bennet sister had not acknowledged Mrs Blaine's instructions.

The housekeeper returned a few minutes later with three clean nightgowns and placed them on the chair near the sofa. "I am just going to go downstairs and retrieve warm water for you. I will be back in a few minutes if you will excuse me."

Georgiana started to get up to move, but could not feel Lizzy or Jane doing the same. Following the eldest lady's lead once more, she returned to her place on the sofa and listened to the return of Jane's gentle humming.

She had no idea how long they might have sat there if Mrs Blaine had not returned as she promised. The housekeeper looked expectantly at the three of them to see which moved first. Dropping her arms from Lizzy's waist, Georgiana reluctantly rose from the sofa and asked Mrs Blaine to help her take off her dress while Jane continued to hold her sister. Once she removed her dress and all of her underthings, she slipped the clean nightgown over her head. The soft fabric resting against her skin immediately helped to ease the knot in her stomach. It felt as though she shed her skin from the night's events. Mrs Blaine then took the girl over to the porcelain basin which was filled with half a pitcher of water.

Georgiana took time to carefully wash her face, hands, neck and anything else she could immediately access with the warm water while Mrs Blaine helped to hold her hair back. "I wish I could bring up enough water for you to take a proper bath. Unfortunately, to heat and bring up that much water would require waking up additional servants. But I will make sure that in the morning warm baths will be waiting for all three of you. Whenever you wake up, just let the maids know when you are ready."

"Mrs Blaine, this is fine. I do not think that we would feel comfortable seeing anyone else right now."

The elder woman nodded in understanding.

"Jane, would you like to change now?"

Miss Bennet alternated between looking at her and her sister. Finally, she nodded and moved Elizabeth's body weight to Georgiana.

She watched from the sofa as Jane change into a nightgown and then wash the blood from her hands and arms; the same blood from Sutton's stomach as Jane stabbed him. The crimson tinted water in the bowl proved yet another reminder of what Georgiana was responsible for. If only her mistakes could be washed away as easily as the blood on Jane's hands. She was responsible for making the most compassionate woman she ever met stab a man who wanted to violate her. She would never forgive herself; she equally knew that her family would never forgive her either.

Georgiana saw Jane finish at the water basin, but waited for Mrs Blaine to empty the water before softly asking Elizabeth, "Lizzy, are you ready? I am sure it will make you feel better. Would you like for Jane and me to help you?"

Finally, Elizabeth made some form of communication with her. She made a small nod of her head and moved to rise from the sofa. Georgiana held Elizabeth's hand as she stood up next to her. When Jane came over to hold her sister's hands, Miss Darcy let go of Lizzy's hand and pushed the strands of hair falling down her back to the side in order to reach the buttons on the back of her dress.

"Now, let us get you out of this dress and into something clean." Georgiana helped Lizzy with the ruined dress, then the petticoat and chemise. Finally, with Jane's help, she slipped the soft nightgown over Elizabeth's head, trying to avoid staring at the bruises forming on Elizabeth's stomach and breast. Yet another reminder of what her idiocy did to the people she loved. Elizabeth paid the biggest price for her foolishness and the proof was plainly on display for her to see.

Georgiana walked over to the basin now filled with clean water and motioned for Elizabeth to follow her. She made sure to keep Elizabeth's back toward the basin stand; she wanted to prevent her from looking in the mirror until she repaired her friend's appearance as best she could. Thankfully Jane seemed to understand the plan and kept her younger sister facing away from the basin.

Georgiana put the cloth in the water and proceeded to ring out the excess liquid. First, she started with Elizabeth's hands; taking each of her fingers inside her hands, she washed and towelled them off as Lizzy stood silently looking over Jane's shoulder. Not knowing what else to do, she then brought the wet cloth to her neck and carefully wiped off the blood that had dried around the cuts and down her neck. She pushed back the curly and tangled hair, revealing the cuts themselves. She brought the cloth up to the cuts and tried to gently dab at the wounds. For the first time since they left the tavern, Elizabeth showed emotion. The sting of the water against the cut caused her to wince in pain. With that finally done, Georgiana rinsed off the towel in the water basin and then proceeded to wipe off Lizzy's cheeks and forehead. Ensuring she had completely cleaned her friend's exposed areas, she nodded to Jane. Together, they turned her around to face the mirror. Georgiana looked over Elizabeth's shoulder and arranged a few wisps of hair that framed her face. The younger Bennet stared blankly back at her own reflection.

"That looks much better, doesn't it?"

Georgiana's words echoed through Elizabeth's mind as she stared at both of their reflections in the mirror. Finally, she spoke without turning to face her older sister or Mr Darcy's young ward. "I thought I was the older sister? Georgiana, shouldn't I be offering you comfort?" Lizzy turned to face the two girls who loved her most. How could they ever look at her the same? Her life was over! Her eyes stung with the tears she successfully withheld until she finally looked at the pain in reflected in Jane's and Georgiana's eyes, the pain that she caused by not finding some other way to convince Miss Darcy that there must be another option to find Wickham.

When she finally heard the door close behind Mrs Blaine who had gathered each piece of the discarded clothing, the floodgates opened and she could not control her emotions or her body. No longer having the strength to stand, she let her body collapse toward the floor but she felt warm arms wrap around her and stop her descent. How Jane managed the strength to catch her as she fell, she would never know. But was that not the way it always happened? Did Jane not always catch her as she fell ever since they were born? It took a moment before she realised that her sister's hands were not the only ones that stopped her from crashing to the floor. Georgiana's strength also formed the embrace that enabled her to stand.

"Lizzy, certainly no one can doubt that we are sisters now. We will get through this together - all three of us. We will find a way."

If only Georgiana could understand! The same words that were intended to comfort Elizabeth, ripped at the seams of her heart. They would not always be together. Georgiana and Jane would both be taken from her!

Soon Jane used the same gentle voice that comforted her since they were children. "What we have been through tonight made us closer than sisters. We are bound together. Our lives can never be untwined from one another."

Elizabeth felt the girls drag her to the sofa where she tried to find the courage to tell them that Georgiana would never be their sister and soon Jane must leave her too. How could she live without these two and Mr Darcy? Everyone that she loved she must lose because of her actions that day.

She looked up when she heard Georgiana speak in a tone unlike any she heard that evening. "Since I cannot imagine not having you as a permanent fixture in my life, I should warn you of a few things. Contrary to what you have seen, I am not always cheery in the mornings and the only thing that makes me feel better when I am sick is warm chocolate and a novel that Fitzwilliam considers trash reading."

The tears down her cheeks did not stop with her young friend's feeble attempt to lighten her mood. She would gladly supply Georgiana with an entire library of novels if only the girl could remain a permanent fixture in her life. But that could not be. Not knowing what to say, she buried her head in Jane's nightgown until she felt the moist spot grow to cover a large area of the gown.

"Georgiana, if that is the thing we are to fear most when spending time with you, we will be willing to face our fate. As long as Lizzy or I have a steady supply of chocolate and a good book, we shall not fear your wrath."

She could not bear this! Elizabeth did not know how much longer she could listen to them talk of their shared future. Jane and Georgiana would spend many holidays together with Mr Darcy and Mr Bingley. But she would never be invited, nor could she suffer seeing Mr Darcy happy with another woman as his wife.

"Well, I haven't told you yet about Fitzwilliam. He snores terribly on long carriage rides and is an absolute fright if it rains for more than a few days in a row and he isn't able to ride."

Elizabeth could not take it any longer. She sobbed until her breaths came out in haphazard spurts. This night took everything that she loved. Elizabeth would never forget Mr Darcy's face as he stared at her in the tavern. He was repulsed by her. But the more she struggled to be let free to flee the room that turned into a cage, the tighter that Jane and Georgiana held her.

"Lizzy, please talk to us. We almost lost each other tonight. If we distance ourselves from each other, we will never recover. When something bad happens, you must embrace your family. Do not do what I did last year."

When Elizabeth controlled her breathing enough to finally confess what was in her heart, she could only utter, "Georgiana, I lost more than you know. I lost the man I loved forever."

"Fitzwilliam loves you! Tonight would never change that! My brother stands by the people he loves."

She had to make Georgiana understand. It was not fair to Mr Darcy to make him explain. It was her fault; she must bear the burden of making his sister accept the new reality.

"You did not see the way he looked at me. I have never seen such hatred in someone's eyes. He could not even look at me like I was human. Until the moment when Younge grabbed me, I thought your brother would forgive me for what I did. You were right when you told me earlier that family is the most important thing to him. I was the one who promised him to take care of his sister and I was the one who put her in a dangerous situation. I was the one that made you threaten to kill a man. He walked in and saw you holding a pistol at someone while swearing that you would kill the bastard. He saw Jane was crawling on the floor with a bloody dagger in her hand trying to get away from that monster who almost... This is entirely my fault. Our lives will never be the same. Mr Bingley or Mr Darcy will never allow either of you to be near me again."

"NO! YOU did nothing wrong! You are my sister! How dare you think I would give that up? We are family and family never leaves by choice!"

In complete contrast to Georgiana's anger, her sister spoke calmly to her, "Lizzy, we are sisters and bound closer than anyone else could be. No one will keep us apart and no one will dare try, least of all the men who love us. We are all responsible for what happened tonight; Mr Darcy and Mr Bingley know that. And of course Mr Darcy was looking in your direction with hatred in his eyes; but that hatred was focused on Younge, not on the woman he loves. We were all foolish and naïve, but each of us only wanted to save the people we love and there are far worse crimes to commit in life than that."

"Jane you are too good to think ill of anyone. This night was too horrifying to ask for forgiveness from."

Instead of Jane, Georgiana answered her again, this time completely livid. "Why would you think that there is anything for me to forgive? I was the one who came up with the plan. I talked you into it. I refused to tell you where we were going to ensure that Jane or your aunt could not try to stop us. How do you think that makes me feel? I am the reason that a man held a knife at your throat and tried to kill you. I am the reason Jane had to almost kill a man who wanted to violate her. All I could do was watch while I wondered if both of you were going to be killed right in front of me. The only one who should beg for forgiveness is me!"

Elizabeth could think of nothing to do but promise her sisters that they had her eternal love. Until they could forgive themselves for what their actions led to that night, they could not move on with their lives. Without it being said, she knew that forgiveness would only come when they learned the ultimate results of their actions. If one of the men never came home, or if Lydia was never found, forgiveness would never be theirs to claim or give. No matter what happened, this night would be their cross to bear for life.

Chapter 42

Darcy surveyed the wrecked tavern in anticipation of Wickham's arrival. The disgusting sight appeared exactly as it should after the horrendous events of the night. But if they left it in such a state of disarray, Wickham would likely run as soon as he opened the door. The first things he needed to deal with were the pile of dead bodies scattered around the floor. Blood already began to pool around several of the ladies' attackers.

What had they done? Before tonight, neither he nor Bingley did more than hit a man in anger. He could not say for sure about Gardiner but would be willing to bet that Elizabeth's uncle never even hit a man in anger. Now Bingley had killed three men in self-defence, Gardiner shot a man, and he held another at gunpoint trying to save the woman he loved. Richard was an entirely different matter, but even after so many campaigns, he must still feel something after taking a man's life, especially when it was a barroom brawl. But he could not dwell on that. If they failed to capture Wickham tonight, every terrible thing that happened would be for nought. They needed to clean up the mess and Bingley had already done enough.

"Bingley, watch Younge. I need to take care of this before Wickham arrives."

Darcy waited until Bingley took the pistol from him and fixed it on Younge. Then he walked to the body furthest from the bar, lifted the corpse's arms, and dragged it across the room until it was hidden behind the bar. He tried not to think about the trail of blood left behind, but the candlelight reflecting off of the sticky crimson stain continually drew his eyes toward the line. He still had four more bodies to move, and he needed to do it quickly before Wickham arrived.

Darcy spoke to Bingley as he simultaneously threw a cloth kept behind the bar to his friend, "Have Younge clean himself up. We need to make sure Wickham comes all the way inside before he senses something is amiss."

"Put the gaming table farther away from the door. Younge can sit with his back to the door. If Wickham sees his face first, we are done."

Doing as Bingley instructed, Darcy, righted the table back on its four legs and moved it to an obscured angle from the door. Bingley yanked Younge to his feet and dragged him to the chair that Darcy set up at the table.

Being careful not to move his eyes from Younge, Bingley asked Darcy what time it was.

Darcy pulled his pocket watch from inside his jacket. "It is three minutes until eleven thirty. For you, Younge, that means that you have a reprieve for another thirty-three minutes. If Wickham does not walk through that door by midnight, the deal is off. If you do anything to warn Wickham before he enters or once he comes in, you are done. If you try to help him or attack my friend or me, you will join your peers behind the bar. Are we perfectly clear?"

Younge glared at Darcy and reluctantly answered while still trying to wipe the blood from his face, "I hear you."

"Bingley, take the pistol and sit at the table with Younge. Hide it under the table, but keep it aimed at him. Make sure that both of you have your back to the door. Wickham isn't as likely to recognise you as he is me. Besides, it may look strange for Younge to be sitting there alone." Then, Darcy went behind the bar, carefully avoiding the pile of bodies partially covered by a large sheet he found behind the counter. "Here, take a glass of whiskey for each of you." He poured them each a drink and stepped over several bodies to walk and place it on the table. With nothing else to do, Darcy concluded his instructions. "Now, we wait. For your sake Younge, I hope we aren't forced to wait too long."

Darcy took Bingley's sword and positioned himself on the side of the entrance allowing himself to be concealed behind the door. They had nothing to do but wait in total silence. He could not help but wonder if the ladies made it to his home safely.

After ten minutes of rather tense silence, Darcy heard carefree whistling from the street. He immediately recognised the tune; it was the same he heard often in his childhood.

He held his breath as Wickham opened the door to the tavern and stared at Younge's back. In a loud animated voice that Darcy knew all too well, he heard the man declare, "I hope you are ready to drink like real men because tonight we certainly have something to celebrate." Wickham strutted like a peacock into the tavern and closed the door.

Making sure to not make a sound, Darcy moved swiftly behind Wickham. "Yes, Wickham, we certainly do have something to celebrate." He made sure the blade of the sword penetrated the back of Wickham's jacket. He felt strangely satisfied as he heard Wickham sharply intake his next breath. "Perhaps you wouldn't mind some extra company during the festivities."

Bingley took that moment to stand from the table and clearly point the pistol at Younge, who could do nothing but continue to sit there completely impotent to do anything to help Wickham's situation or his own.

"My good friend, you came to wish me good luck on my journey. That is certainly very kind of you. It is only fitting since you will be the one to finance it."

Darcy felt his cheeks flush as his anger grew. "I can assure you, I will not be wishing you well on this night. Now, you will sit at the table." With the sword still firmly in Wickham's back, Darcy prodded the man to the chair at the table, leaving an empty seat between the two scoundrels. He kept the blade ready to plunge into Wickham if given the slightest provocation.

"Come now old friend; watch where you put that sword. I assume you have something for me. I have something of yous, and it seems only fair that we should make an even trade." Wickham sat lazily down in the chair that Darcy indicated and winked at him. "Besides, if you wanted to kill me, I would already be dead."

"I won't be giving you anything tonight, except a rather easy choice, Wickham." Turning to address Younge, Darcy continued. "I am very good about offering choices, aren't I?"

Younge snorted and offered a snarky reply to the rhetorical question. "You're a real angel." He reached down and brought the bloody cloth back up to tend to the cuts on his lips.

Darcy withdrew the blade and moved to face Wickham. "Did you hear my glowing recommendation? Now perhaps I should give you the choice which will decide the rest of your life."

"I'm listening."

"This will be the easiest decision of your life. Your first option is to go to America where I will never hear from you again. You will disappear and never return to England. Your second option is to go to Newgate prison for so long that you will die a miserable old man in the darkest pit that I can find where you will never see sunlight, eat a decent meal or live without the fear that the man next to you will stab you while you sleep." He moved a few steps closer, brandishing the sword and making sure the tip of the blade brushed against Wickham's neck, just to ensure his childhood friend understood that he meant every word.

Wickham reached up and with his forefinger and thumb, casually removed the sword from his neck and directed the blade toward the floor.

"What, no third option? The first two don't seem overly appealing. I am sure you can do better than that."

"Wickham doesn't want to know what the third option is, does he, Younge?" Darcy moved momentarily to look at the man. But Younge did not even make eye contact with him, only shook his head negatively in response. "Only you, Wickham would make light of a situation where you are facing near death."

"Actually, I don't have to choose either of your options. Would you like to hear why?"

"Enlighten me with whatever scheme you concocted after you walked in the door."

"I have no desire to go to America. I have always felt that the Indians were cheated by the settlers who took their land. I wouldn't want to take something from a man which should be rightfully his."

When would Wickham ever realise that the older Mr Darcy owed his steward's son nothing!

Wickham continued before Darcy had a chance to vocalise his response to Wickham's first charge. "As for the second option, I have done nothing that would cause me to go to jail. I have not abducted anyone, stolen anything, or killed anyone." Wickham leaned toward Darcy and crinkled his now before continuing. "Judging by the smell of this room, I have a feeling that you can't say the same."

Wickham turned to look at another gentleman. "Bingley, would you mind getting me a drink from behind the bar?" Bingley only glared back. "I didn't think so. How about you, Darcy? Could I interest you in some whiskey? My friend usually has a few decent bottles hidden away."

Darcy could not bring himself to answer.

"Even if you believe I took the little chit against her will, you would never make your future sister testify at a public trial to ensure my conviction. We both know you certainly would never make dear, sweet Georgiana's plight known to improve your case, so I don't have to worry about that. Lydia's father is too old to duel me and win, so I am safe in that respect as well. If you are to challenge me, I may not win, but you know as well as I that I could get at least one good shot off before you kill me. You value Georgiana too much to leave her all alone in the world." Wickham paused before continuing, "And don't let me forget the delectable Elizabeth. I am sure you would not want to depart this world without tasting a bit of her flavour. I am sure it is exquisite."

Darcy looked over at Younge, just to make sure Elizabeth's attacker had no plans to add to the conversation. He ensured that Younge felt the full extent of his hatred in a single glare. Luckily for him, the bastard just looked to a spot on the ground several feet away from the table and kept his mouth firmly shut.

"So you see Darcy, I hold all the cards. If you don't give me my money, I will make sure that Lydia's indiscretions are known throughout London. I will follow through on my threat to make sure that she is not just known for running away to elope either; it will be something far too terrible for her family to ever recover from. You will never be able to marry her precious sister and then you will die a miserable old man. And since I know you would never kill a defenceless man, I am perfectly safe sitting here as long as I don't pull my own weapon on you." Wickham demonstrated his point by lifting his feet, putting them on the table, and leaning back in his chair with his hands behind his head and the smile still prominently displayed on his face.

How grave of a mistake this was, Wickham had no idea, but Younge certainly must have. Darcy's entire body tensed, just as it had when he saw the knife to Elizabeth's throat. That devil inside that was about to be released had no compunctions about killing an unarmed man or doing anything else to save the people he loved.

"So you think you have me. What do you think I did over the past several days? Do you think I just followed the chase you led us on around Bath and the rest of England? Do you really think I would just play your little game and would not have my own plan?"

For the first time since entering the tavern, Wickham truly looked at him. That was his mistake. Darcy knew that Wickham was finally starting to realise the gravity of the situation. He had never tried to manipulate or fight this Darcy. This Darcy never existed before tonight, even while at Ramsgate. Wickham's smile lessened but still did not disappear.

"Once I received your letter, I had a man go to Hertfordshire and around London to see if he could find you. I must admit that most of your friends kept very quiet about your activities. Unfortunately for you, your enemies were not so kind."

Wickham quickly retorted, "No one who knew where I was hates me enough to give me up."

Darcy smirked first and answered the second. "You're right; those who hate you did not know your current location. But they knew what you were either doing or had already done. You see, there is one constant about you from the time we were children. You can never manage to live within your means and refrain from enjoying the finer things in life. You leave a trail of debts behind that I always take care of. In honour of the old times, I had my man do the same for all the debts you left this time too. Meryton is a small town, so it was not difficult to track down how much you owed. London was slightly more difficult, but not terribly so. Once my man explained that you have a tendency of leaving town with a pile of unpaid debts behind you, the merchants and tavern owners were more than willing to sell them to me."

Darcy gave Wickham a few moments to digest the information. The man finally figured out how Darcy could successfully send him to jail; it was the moment the smile was completely fell from Wickham's face and he dropped his feet back to the floor with a thud.

"I now hold your debts for over one thousand pounds. That is plenty to send you to debtor's prison for the remainder of your life. And if by some miracle you can come up with one thousand pounds, I am sure there are plenty more of your debts I can acquire to put you back in prison. In addition, I must start adding interest to what you owe and you know how that starts to add up. I remember that mathematics was never your strongest subject, so I am willing to help you again for old times' sake. Just let me tell you this, it is far more than you will ever be able to repay, especially while rotting away in prison."

Wickham stared back at him, over the blade of the sword that Darcy kept aimed at his chest. "If you do this, I will tell everyone about Georgiana and Lydia."

Just as calmly as before, Darcy answered. "No, you won't. You know that I can get to you even if you are in prison. If you do anything else to hurt the ones I love, my honour will not hold me back from seeking revenge." Darcy let the threat sink into Wickham before continuing. "Now, perhaps you will take my good wishes for your travels. But where are you going to go? How about it Wickham, is your future in America or in prison?"

"How are you going to ensure that I will not send word once I reach America?"

"You will write and sign a new blackmail letter. It will state that you will make up an outrageous tale about the female members of my family if I don't give you ten thousand pounds. If you tell anyone of what happened, I will offer the letter as proof of the tale's fabrication. It won't be enough to convince everyone, but I have enough influence and money to convince the others. After that, I will send someone after you and there will be no mercy from me then."

As an afterthought, Darcy added, "I think my cousin will be first on my list of people to ask if they want to be the one to go after you. I know how much you liked playing with him when we were younger."

"You managed to package this all up rather neatly didn't you?" Wickham finally gave Darcy the gift he hoped for as Wickham began to lose control. The man quickly stood from the table and took a few steps, pacing next to the table. But Darcy made sure to keep the blade focused on his chest.

"I choose America."

Darcy could not help but smile as he answered. "You leave in the afternoon. I have already purchased your ticket."

"You BASTARD!" In one quick motion, Wickham picked up the chair and slammed it against the table. "Why can you never just give me what is rightfully mine! I just want you to admit it one time, just one time. Admit that your father loved me more than you!"

Darcy just shook his head slightly. "You need to stop mistaking amusement for love. You were a pleasing diversion to him, nothing more."

Every person in the room stared at Wickham as the outraged rogue tore at his own hair in frustration and collapsed, slumping back into the chair. During the commotion and drama, Bingley made a fateful error. He took his eyes off Younge just long enough for Younge to seize the opportunity to lunge at Bingley. Darcy watched as his friend began to fall to the ground with Younge on top of him. He grabbed Bingley's arm still holding the pistol and struggled for the gun, pushing the pistol out of Bingley's grasp and onto the floor.

In one swift motion, Wickham grabbed the seat of his chair and kicked both of his feet out, attacking Darcy's knees and causing him to fall. With his legs outright, Wickham pushed his body from the chair and slid to the ground toward the pistol that lay only inches from his body. Bingley and Younge, both on the ground, punched, jabbed and pulled at each other, both trying to reach for the pistol. But neither Bingley nor Younge could grasp the weapon before Wickham grabbed the gun, sat up, and pointed it straight at Darcy who lay on the floor.

Wickham screamed in anticipation of the event he waited so long for, "See you in HELL!"

The last thing Darcy heard was the sound of a pistol firing.

Chapter 43

Elizabeth had not slept since Georgiana shook her awake at the Gardiners that morning. That morning seemed like an eternity ago. How could anyone keep expecting her to sleep when the men she held dearest were still in danger? And Lydia! She had no idea what her fate would be. Would they recover her sister in much the same state as when Lydia left Longbourn or were they too late? Would all the pain, sacrifice and danger that night prove justified? Or did she sacrifice her own future without providing Lydia the chance to recover hers?

Lizzy sat in silence with the other two ladies, waiting to hear any noises behind the closed door. Even if there were footsteps passing by, she could hear them through the heavy wooden door. She longed to hear that distinct rapping on the door that Tom used to let them know it was him. He was their link to the world and with his silence, they lost that connection.

But then she heard it! Heavy footsteps stopped by the door. She held her breath, waiting to hear if a knock would accompany the footsteps. But instead of Tom's distinctive knock, she heard several soft raps on the door. She looked behind her at Georgiana and Jane and proceeded to grab their hands. She opened her mouth to answer, but no words came out; only the sound of their exhaling could be heard. Once again, Elizabeth turned around in fear, trying to get strength from her sister.

Jane's calm voice answer the knock, "Come in."

How her sister had the strength to speak, she did not know. Of course, Jane simultaneously made her hand throb from the pressure exerted as the words flowed from her lips.

Lizzy's eyes glued to the door, waiting for it to move. She watched as the door handle slowly lowered and Elizabeth finally heard the creak of the door moving in towards them. She closed her eyes, hoping to delay the chance that her world had ended. Then she heard Georgiana's quick squeal. When she had the courage to open her eyes to face her fate, standing before her she saw her angels sent from above.

Mr Darcy stood in silence while Mr Bingley opened his arms for Jane who no longer sat on the sofa beside her. Her sister shot into her fiancé's open arms while the gentleman crossed the room in two long strides to meet her. That was precisely the acceptance that Jane needed; it was exactly what Jane deserved after the hell she went through today; the pain that Elizabeth blamed herself for.

Elizabeth turned from watching her sister's reunion to finally gathering the courage to lock eyes with Mr Darcy. Reflected back, she saw neither love nor hate in his dark eyes. They seemed empty, void of any emotion or life. That confirmed it. As if she needed any more evidence, the gentleman just stood there, without his arms open to her. His arms would never welcome her. But she already knew that would never happen. After the way, he looked at her while at the tavern tonight, there was no hope for a joyful reunion. Suddenly her other hand felt cold too, having lost its companion as Georgiana leapt from the sofa and ran to her brother. Without showing any hesitation, he opened his arms to welcome his younger sister. Of course, he would forgive her; he always acted more as her father than her older brother. And no father could stop loving his child. But many men stopped loving their wives. The bond was different. Was her dear father not proof of that? Georgiana could never be forgotten while Elizabeth feared she may still be disposed of.

Instinctively, she bit the insides of her cheeks, hoping the pain would keep the tears from beginning again. Her hands flew to her face, hiding her anguish. She had to get out of that room. Her heart could not survive watching Jane and Georgiana's blissful reunions while she sat alone on the sofa. When Elizabeth finally gained the strength to look up, hoping to find the easiest way to leave without notice, she saw Mr Darcy and Georgiana standing in front of her. With a quick glance, she realised they were the only ones left in the room. Elizabeth had no idea where Jane or Mr Bingley went, but undoubtedly her sister was ecstatic at this moment.

Elizabeth's eyes locked with Mr Darcy's. Everything else in the world stopped, except the shaking of her hands. Would he throw her out of his home? What would he finally say to her? Would he say anything at all? No amount of self-inflicted pain by biting the insides of her cheeks could stop the tears welling up in her weary eyes. Would this be the last time she would be allowed to explore the depths and clearness of his dark eyes?

Before she could think of anything else, she felt his strong arm wrap around her shoulders and bring her entire body to his warm one.

After only a few seconds in his embrace, Elizabeth's shaking and crying quieted. She wanted to treasure this time in his arms. She needed to remember his minty scent, the feel of the stubble on his cheek against her skin, and the warmth and safety that his embrace offered. This would be the last time she would experience this euphoria. Every detail needed to be internalised and committed to memory.

All too soon, Mr Darcy loosened his grip on her and Georgiana quietly asked, "Fitzwilliam, please, we just need to know..." but her voice trailed off.

Of course, Georgiana could not finish the question. She could not even find the strength to think about asking the question. But they had to know what happened once they left the Returning Rogue. In a quiet and gentle voice, Mr Darcy told both of them that Richard, Bingley and Gardiner were all alive. Lydia was recovered and staying at the Gardiners. He did not know the extent of Gardiner's wound, but it had stopped bleeding by the time Gardiner left the tavern which was promising.

The knot in Elizabeth's stomach instantly released its pressure from her body. Their plan was not a complete disaster. At least some good resulted from the tragedy of the night. They achieved their goal of Lydia's safe return. Her sister had a future still full of promise even if she had to forfeit her own to achieve that result.

As Georgiana grabbed her hand stationed firmly on Mr Darcy's back, embracing him with a sigh of relief, she surrendered to her exhaustion. Elizabeth shared Georgiana's relief that the evening's events had not ended as badly as they feared. They both leapt over a massive hurdle in the path of forgiveness when Mr Darcy told them that everyone they loved lived and was relatively safe. But how could she ever return to Gracechurch Street again?

She felt Mr Darcy's arms drop surrounding her body. When she felt his head move backwards from hers, she knew her time in his protection was over.

She opened her eyes again and saw Mr Darcy dropped leading his sister into her bedroom that adjoined the sitting room. Now she could leave the room but she froze by the door leading to the hallway. She heard behind her back as Mr Darcy closed the door to Georgiana's bedroom, walked across the room, took her cold hand in both of his, and led her back to the sofa. Never letting go of her hand, he sat down on the corner of the sofa and gently pulled Elizabeth down to sit next to him. Putting his hand on her shoulder, he urged her to lean back against him.

But she made a feeble attempt to pull away. "Please, just let me go."

"Ask anything of me except to let you go. I cannot bear it."

"But you hate me. Offering me comfort now makes it so much harder to know I will never feel this again. I have lost you forever."

She buried her head in his shoulder, but he was not about to let her hide from him, not now. He lifted her head between both of his hands and forced her to look at him. Before he could think about them, the words flooded out. "Why would you ever think that I hated you? You are the most important person in my life. If something happened to you, I would not survive. The pain would be unbearable."

"But the way you looked at me earlier tonight. I have never seen such hatred."

"What do you mean? I could never hate you."

"At the..." He waited for her to finish. "When Younge held me, I saw the rage in your eyes. There is no mistaking how much hatred was boiling inside of you."

He moved to put both of his hands around her face. He wanted no misunderstanding for once. "I was looking at Younge. You thought I was looking at you?"

He watched helplessly as the tears welled up in her eyes. "After what I put Georgiana through, how could you not? You trusted me to protect her, and I failed. I could have gotten her..."

"My love! When I arrived at the Gardiners, I was told that you, Georgiana, and Jane disappeared and went to find Wickham. When I arrived at the tavern, I heard my sister scream that she was going to kill someone. When I walked in, I saw her pointing a pistol at a man who then held a knife to your throat. I can never tell you what I felt at that moment. I have never felt such..." Using his thumbs stroke her cheeks as his hands continued to hold her face, he finally continued. "Elizabeth, I love you. I am supposed to be the one to protect you and I could not. The only thing I could do was stand there and watch as he... Because I did not do anything, you further endangered yourself and fought Younge yourself. I could not protect you. I will never forgive myself. As for Georgiana, you did protect her. My sister was not there alone and I cannot, I will not, imagine what might have happened if she had been..." Darcy hung his head in shame and dropped his hands from Elizabeth's face to cover his own. How could the woman he loved ever look at him as a man again?

He could scarcely believe it when he felt two soft hands lift his face. The smoothness of her fingers gently caressing his cheeks produced a euphoric state that he believed he would never feel again. When he finally opened his eyes, he saw none of the accusation or pity he feared he might. Instead, he saw a light and brightness he could not comprehend the cause of.

"But there is nothing to forgive. There was nothing you could do. You and I both know that if you tried to attack Mr Younge from where you stood, he would have done something terrible to me before you reached him. You did the only thing you could do; you scared that monster so that I could distract him long enough for you and Colonel Fitzwilliam to subdue him. If you had rushed forward without regard for my safety, tonight's conclusion would be very different. You are the only reason that I had the courage to do what I did. I knew no matter what happened you would protect me. I never doubted you and your actions proved I placed my faith in a strong, capable man. But how could I live with myself if you were hurt trying to rescue me because I just stood there?"

Too full of emotion and with no idea what to say, Darcy buried his face in Elizabeth's curly locks, but she was not finished. "You are the best man of my acquaintance. How could I have doubted the man that I love and trust so completely?"

Darcy felt all the turmoil, hurt and impotence that plagued him for the last several days dissolve. With a hope he almost feared, he locked eyes with her and asked the question plaguing his heart, "You love me?"

She tilted her head so that her forehead touched his. In a quiet whisper, she confessed, "I hate that you ever doubted it."

"I should have asked you something before I left Pemberley, but I wanted the moment to be perfect. Now I see that my selfishness left both of us without any guarantee of the commitment we so desperately needed."

He moved his hands to hers and intertwined their fingers. He brought her hands up to his lips and tenderly kissed each one of her fingertips. He needed to savour this moment. It would be the one he would remember for the rest of his life. "I believe that I am still allowed one more question, per the rules of our agreement.

Remember, your answer must be truthful. You cannot hold back or lie to save my feelings."

Elizabeth's smile lit up her entire face. "I promise. You will only hear what is in my heart."

He brought their clasped hands to his chest. "My dearest, loveliest Elizabeth, you are my future. I cannot fathom my life without you beside me to share its joys, its blessings and even its pains. Without your laugh, your smile, your challenging wit, my existence will be desolate. I want to be the one you smile at in the morning, laugh with in the afternoon, teasing at dinner, and love at night. I will do everything in my power to be the man you deserve. Would you do me the infinite honour of becoming my wife?"

He had never seen such joy in her face. Her eyes glistened, but he knew the difference between the tears of her past and the ones in her eyes now. And that smile; there was no mistaking her love for him with that pure, emotion-filled smile.

"Oh, my dearest, flawless, formidable Mr Darcy, you are my future. Without you, my life will have no joys, blessings or pains; it will be empty of everything of meaning. Without your quiet strength, your knowledge of the world, and your adorable dimples, my existence will be desolate. I want to be the one you wake in the morning, challenge in the afternoon, laugh with at supper and love at night. I will do everything in my power to be the woman you deserve. I will be honoured to be your wife."

Darcy severed the connection between their hands and moved his own fingertips back to her face. He drew her face slowly to his. Seeing her eyes close in anticipation, he savoured the moment before he finally possessed her lips as his soon-to-be wife. He couldn't wait any longer. He raised his own head to close the slight distance between them and finally felt his lips lightly caress the woman who lay against him and agreed to bond herself to him for life. He revelled in the sweet taste, but he wasn't satisfied, not even close. There was so much more that he needed.

He used his fingers to lightly push down on her jaw while he tentatively pushed his tongue to her lips. It took longer than he wanted, but eventually, Elizabeth cautiously provided him with a slight opening between her lips. He gently sucked on his love's upper lip between his own. As Elizabeth let out a soft sigh that could only be caused by a longing similar to his own, he felt his heart about to burst from elation. Darcy slowly pushed his tongue into her mouth and felt her respond to his quest with equal desire and emotion. This kiss proved to be everything he imagined. His entire body felt alive with emotion; every sense heightened to revel in the experience. And when Elizabeth began to caress the tips of his hair, just as she did at the inn the week before, he couldn't contain his excitement. But he needed to find some control before he lost all chance to do so.

"My love, please tell me you want a short engagement. I need you. I need you as my wife, in every way."

She responded in the musical laugh he could not hear enough of. "How short were you thinking?"

"I just need to procure a special licence which shouldn't take long since Archbishop is my Godfather."

"A short engagement then."

Just before he attacked her mouth with his own again, he said, "I suppose it is."

He responded by kissing her on the forehead. Before he could contemplate where to kiss her next, he heard the clock strike four o'clock. "I think it would be best for both of us to sleep at least a few hours this morning. It was a long day and night and you need your rest."

"Arranging my life already, Mr Darcy?"

"I do believe that I asked you to tease me only at dinner. As it is much closer to breakfast than dinner, I have several more hours of reprieve until your teasing may commence." In response, Darcy heard one of his favourite sounds, Elizabeth's pure and unadulterated laughter. Darcy chastely kissed her one final time on the forehead, quickly stood from the sofa, and bid his fiancée a final goodnight.

Elizabeth immediately felt the void and emptiness of the room when he left. She hugged her knees to her chest, smiled and stared at the fire for several minutes. How quickly the world transformed from a bleak and cheerless world to the one full of happiness and promise that she now saw before her?

Despite Jane's assurances to the contrary, Elizabeth never considered that Mr Darcy would need the same reassurance that he was not responsible for the night's events. In no way did he cause their predicament; he saved them from an unthinkable outcome. She remembered everything she learned about him during their walks at Kent. Of course, he would blame himself. How could she have thought otherwise? She never knew a man to take more responsibility for his loved ones than Mr Darcy. And now, she would never be afraid of being excluded from that group.

Chapter 44

Darcy walked inside Gardiner's home behind Elizabeth and Georgiana. The maid directed them to the parlour where the rest of the family was already seated. As they entered the room, Darcy took careful note of the place. Bingley and Richard stood by the window taking turns looking out the window. Mrs Gardiner sat with her husband on the striped sofa, looking overly concerned at his every movement. The man sat with obvious pain and carefully protected his injured shoulder from any movement. He looked up when they arrived and immediately asked if Tom drove them to the house.

Somewhat curious by the question, but definitely not planning on withholding any information, Darcy quickly answered. "He did. He is outside with the coach."

Gardiner looked him squarely in the eyes and answered, "With your permission, I need him for another task."

This was definitely not a good sign. "What do you need him for?"

"I need him to watch Lydia. I would rather not let anyone else know the details of our predicament. Jane is currently upstairs with her, but we need my niece for this conversation. If you and Elizabeth could bring her back down with you, I would appreciate it. I would do it myself, but much movement hurts my shoulder."

"Of course. I will go outside now to get him." Darcy left the room and retrieved his driver from the carriage. Unaware of any particulars regarding the reason, Darcy told him the only thing he knew, that he needed to watch Miss Lydia and not let her out of his sight. Returning to the house, Darcy met Elizabeth at the bottom of the staircase and the two led Tom upstairs toward the voice he instantly recognised at Miss Lydia's.

"Jane, let me go! I know that George is waiting for me. All of you lied to me!"

Elizabeth opened the door without knocking to find two of the Bennet sisters sitting on the bed. Darcy's eyes immediately focused on Miss Lydia's hands; they were tied to a large chair next to the bed. What in the world happened here last night to cause such a punishment?

He then heard Miss Bennet's ever calming voice answer the youngest sister, "Lydia, please, just lower your voice. No one in our family lied to you. Wickham was the only person who lied to you. We are your family. We love you. We only want what is best for you."

Darcy watched as Elizabeth walked to sit next to her sisters and take one of Jane's hands in hers. When Miss Bennet's attention turned to the door and saw him, her face coloured to a deep red. Should he leave yet?

"Miss Bennet, your uncle and aunt need to see you downstairs in the parlour. Tom will be able to watch Miss Lydia until you are able to return."

Miss Bennet and Elizabeth stood from the bed and walked with Darcy to the top of the stairs. Before they walked down, Miss Bennet confessed to him, "I am so embarrassed. I apologise for having you witness her outburst. She has been trying to escape ever since her uncle brought her back last night. Lydia really is a good girl; she is just confused and scared. She needs her family so desperately right now."

Not knowing what else to say, for he did not think Miss Bennet really wanted to know what he thought, he answered simply, "She is lucky to have such a loving family to support her."

Darcy followed his soon-to-be sister-in-law and fiancée into the parlour. He took his place behind Elizabeth who sat next to Georgiana on a two-person sofa. Miss Bennet walked to the larger couch holding her aunt and uncle and took the space next to them. Mrs

Gardiner asked the maid who served tea and biscuits to the room to leave, close the door, and that they should not be disturbed. Richard moved to stand behind Georgiana and Bingley took his place behind Miss Bennet.

Once the maid closed the door with a definitive thud, each member of the group quickly stopped talking and inspected the others occupying the room or random spots on the floor. Obviously, no one was sure what needed to be said first or who should start the discussion. As it was his house, and he was the one that called the meeting, most of the other eyes in the room rested on Gardiner.

His attention was intent on examining Georgiana and Elizabeth. After several minutes of careful study that made Darcy nervous, finally, the master of the house moved his attention to the others in the room and spoke in a firm voice. "I think that everyone in this room needs to talk about what happened last night. We will have this discussion once and only once to discover the facts of the night. Everyone will have all questions answered before we leave. Nothing will be left out of the conversation. We will not blame each other or feel guilty for actions either taken or not taken. We will not discuss what happened with anyone outside of this room. I know that we will need to discuss this again, likely in smaller groups to work through any emotional problems that might occur as a result of last night. I hope that everyone in this group will feel comfortable going to anyone else in this group, whatever their particular kinship may be with each other. Last night made us family and we should treat one another as such. Georgiana and Elizabeth, I think that you should begin since only the two of you know where this should start."

Elizabeth had felt her uncle's stare intently fixed on her. His speech neither made her feel better nor worse. Somehow, she felt so many emotions about last night that she could not trust anyone of her feelings to stay in check. Not trusting herself to look anyone in the eye, Elizabeth found a worn spot on the carpet several feet away and stared at it. Then she took a deep breath and started from the beginning, continuing to stare at the rug. She described how after the gentlemen left Pemberley, Georgiana remembered the link between Wickham and Mr Younge and how the group might be able to find Wickham. The ladies persuaded Mrs Gardiner to take them back to town so they could tell the gentlemen what they knew, but the men had already left London without a word as to their whereabouts. She and Georgiana waited for two days but decided they could not wait any longer and devised their plan to find Wickham. Elizabeth explained that Georgiana, Jane, and she all shared a common love for three-card brag and it was the perfect way to get the information from Younge. As she mentioned Jane's name, Elizabeth could not help but look up for the first time to observe her sister's reaction.

"Why did you not include me? I would have stood by you and we could have possibly found another way.

And if we could not, at least the three of us could have faced the problem together, from the beginning."

Even though Jane forgave her the night before, the pit in Elizabeth's stomach ignored Jane's precious gift. Last night not only changed her, it also irrevocably changed the people that Elizabeth loved.

"We wanted to include you, but we did not want to leave Aunt Gardiner without someone to comfort her after we disappeared."

Jane looked satisfied with their answer and Elizabeth continued. She told the group how she and Georgiana bought a deck of cards, took the money and the pistol from Darcy's library, changed dresses and cloaks at the store, and slipped away from Tom and Maggie. They sent two letters through a delivery service. The first letter was meant to ease any distress Aunt Gardiner and Jane felt. They hoped to return home before the second letter even arrived. They arrived at the Returning Rogue and persuaded Younge to accept their challenge for a game of Three-Card Brag. After a few hours of playing, Georgiana managed to corner Younge into betting a piece of unknown information against several hundred pounds. That was the same time that Jane found them at the tavern. After Georgiana won the hand, they demanded Younge tell them what they wanted to know, but Younge refused. At that time, Younge grabbed and threatened Elizabeth. Two other men in the tavern took hold of other two ladies.

Georgiana managed to escape from her captor without a problem, but Jane was forced to stab hers to escape. While Younge held a knife at her throat, Jane moved across the floor trying to escape Sutton, Georgiana aimed a pistol at Younge and threatened to kill him. With a deep breath, Elizabeth finished her part of the tale. "That was when the gentlemen found us."

Elizabeth could not continue to speak or even keep her eyes open; it took too much energy. She did not know how she managed to put into words what happened, even with the scarce details she offered. Darcy put his hands on her shoulders, immediately transferring his strength and giving her comfort.

She looked behind her where Darcy stood when his sister spoke for the first time. In the same quiet voice that reminded Elizabeth of the first moments of her acquaintance with her, the girl spoke to her elder brother. "Fitzwilliam, Elizabeth left something out. It was my plan, and I made her come with me. She tried to talk me out of it but I told her I would do it no matter what. Please forgive me." Elizabeth watched as the girl hid her obviously pained face between her hands.

"Giana, you did not force me to do anything. We did this together."

Darcy moved from standing behind Elizabeth to kneeling in front of her and Giana. Darcy spoke to them, in a voice just loud enough for Elizabeth and Georgiana to hear him, "There is nothing for me to forgive. In the end, we are all safe and together. You did what you thought was right to protect your family." But Darcy wasn't finished. "Do I wish you had stayed with Mrs Gardiner and Jane and let us handle the situation? There is no question. It wasn't a wise and I hope that this also taught you a lesson. But what is done is done and for the moment I prefer to remember only that you both are safe. I must demand that neither of you ever do anything like that again. That night could have ended much worse."

"We will never again be that foolish. I am so sorry for everything we caused." Sniffling and with tears running down her face, Georgiana nodded to echo her agreement to Elizabeth's promise.

Mr Gardiner spoke next. "I suppose it is up to me to fill in what happened before we arrived and how we recovered Lydia."

"Wickham sent Darcy a note telling him to meet in Bath, however, Wickham never arrived. Just as we were about to return to town, Darcy received two notes. The first had the information about Wickham's debts and how many of them that Darcy's man Marcus had managed to buy. The second note was from Darcy's housekeeper at Darcy House. She told him that the same young boy that delivered Wickham's first message noticed something unusual; the housekeeper deduced it was Wickham. She also mentioned that Miss Darcy was staying with Elizabeth and Jane at my home. We immediately left for London and when we arrived, we found Tom racing out the door. He told us that the girls disappeared earlier in the day and were at the Returning Rogue trying to find information about Wickham."

Gardiner continued his part of the night's events. "While at the Returning Rogue, Bingley killed the man who attacked Jane. Then three men rushed Bingley and me. I shot one and Bingley used his sword to kill the other two." His wife gasped at his admission. With that reassurance, he spoke again. "Bingley saved my life by killing the one who cut my shoulder. While we were attacked by three, a fourth attacked Colonel Fitzwilliam and he killed him. The other men in the bar realised to further challenge us would result in more of their untimely deaths; they agreed to remove themselves from the situation in exchange for the money betted that night. When only Younge remained as a threat, Elizabeth kicked him and managed to escape from his grasp. Tom immediately left with the ladies. Darcy and the Colonel tackled Younge and convinced him to tell us where Wickham was. It was then that Fitzwilliam and I left to get Lydia from the inn where Wickham stayed."

"We walked to the room Younge said that Wickham rented. Once inside the small room, we found Lydia sleeping in the bed dressed in a nightgown. When I woke her, she recognised me and screamed, knowing I wanted to take her away before she married Wickham. The Colonel put his hand over her mouth in order to quiet her; we didn't want anyone to hear her cries. When I finally convinced her to calm down, she asked where Wickham was. Lydia believed they planned to go to Gretna Green in a few days."

"At a party last week, Sir William Lucas told her and Wickham that Elizabeth and Darcy were soon to be married. Wickham saw it as his chance to blackmail Darcy and knew exactly what would cause him to pay. He convinced Lydia to run away with him to London under the guise he needed to finish some business before she could walk down the aisle."

"Lydia refused to believe that Wickham had no intention of marrying her no matter what we said to convince her of the contrary. Colonel Fitzwilliam told her that Wickham would not be returning to retrieve her, ever. I think his commanding presence finally convinced her. She agreed to go with us if we told her where Wickham was. We waited outside her room while she changed into some more suitable clothing." He stopped speaking, then more to himself than to the others, he mentioned, "I truly thought we had convinced her."

Shaking his head and snapping out of his private thoughts, he returned to the story. "The Colonel went back to the Returning Rogue and took Lydia back to my home, but when we were about to enter the house Lydia realised I did not intend to return her to Wickham, she twisted away from my grip and tried to run down the street. Just then my wife opened the door, seeing us through the window and managed to wrestle Lydia into the house. Lydia threatened to run away as soon as we left her by herself, saying that we could not hold her there alone. I somehow knew she meant it. And I also knew I wouldn't be able to stay awake all night and Lydia would run at the first moment possible. We could not think of anything else to do, so we tied her hands to a chair for the night."

He felt his wife's hands move his head to face her. He heard his wife's voice for the first time in since they started their confessions. "Darling, it was our only choice. We knew it was the only way to save her. If she left the house, who knows what would happen to her late at night with no money and no place to go? If she escaped, would she survive the experience? I will accept the guilt we now feel rather than live with the guilt if we allowed her to leave. We did what we did out of love, not to hurt her. And although she is uncomfortable, she is not hurt, which likely could not be said if we allowed her to leave."

Now they needed to face their next problem, what to do with Lydia. "We need to find a way to make Lydia understand the true nature of Wickham without letting her know the evening's events. She believes that Wickham loves her and still wants to marry her. I didn't know that Wickham died until the Colonel arrived here very early this morning. I honestly do not know what she will do when she finds out. I fear she will be impossible to control."

"In the blackmail note, didn't Wickham threaten her with something terrible if you didn't comply, Darcy?" Asked him his cousin.

"Yes, he did."

"I am willing to bet that you found out what that terrible thing was, didn't you?"

"I did."

"And what was that terrible thing?"

"I do not wish to say. The information will only upset some of the members in this room."

"I think the audience in this room is past the point of being shocked by anything. We promised the truth would come out today. Darcy, you need to tell us or we cannot solve the Miss Lydia problem."

"Wickham sold her to a whorehouse for fifty pounds."

Mr Gardiner spoke before the Colonel had a chance. "That bastard sold my niece to a whorehouse for fifty pounds!" Shaking his head in disgust, he added, "I shouldn't be surprised."

Richard walked to the window, looked out it, and finally turned around. "That was what I feared and hoped for."

"Why would you hope for such a thing?" Bingley looked at him as though he lost his mind.

"As Gardiner said earlier, we need to make her understand. The best thing we can do is take her to see what her life would be if she stayed with Wickham. If Miss Lydia is half as hard-headed as I believe her to be, nothing less will work."

"You expect me to take my niece to a whorehouse and introduce her to women who work there?"

Very plainly, Richard answered, "No, I expect Bingley to do so."

Darcy stared at his cousin. "This isn't Bingley's place. If anyone should take her, it should be me."

"Cousin, I am afraid you can't take responsibility for this and neither can you, Gardiner. Miss Lydia would never believe anything you have to say about Wickham. He had the last several days to completely poison her mind against you. Bingley's good humour is well-known by Miss Lydia and Bingley told me that he even invited Wickham to the ball at Netherfield. I am guessing that Lydia knows this. I would take her, except I honestly worry I might strangle her if left alone with her. Bingley has just the right amount of sympathy for the girl, no known ill-will towards Wickham, and the nerve to make sure she fully understands her fate and cannot escape."

Darcy listened as Bingley answered. "Richard is right. I will take her tonight after sunset." Darcy watched as Bingley took Miss Bennet's hand and told her, "Lydia is soon to be part of my family. There is no burden or danger too great to ensure the safety of the ones we love. This is a rather small sacrifice compared to what we have already done."

Moments later Darcy took over relaying the night's final events. "I suppose it is up to me to finish relaying the outcome of the events at the Returning Rogue. Bingley and I convinced Wickham to leave for America. Once Wickham agreed, Younge took the opportunity to attack Bingley. He managed to wrestle the pistol from his hand and it dropped to the ground. While I helped Bingley, Wickham kicked the sword out of my hand and then managed to get the pistol. Wickham aimed it at me and then I heard a pistol go off... Fitzwilliam entered the tavern the moment before his pistol fired. The bullet hit Wickham in the chest. Younge tried to scramble for the pistol by Wickham's side to ensure his own safety. I grabbed my sword which I had dropped and used it to kill Younge."

"So both Wickham and Younge are now dead?" Elizabeth asked.

"They are."

"I am ashamed to say this, but I am glad. They both caused such pain to our family." That was the last thing that Darcy expected to hear, especially from Georgiana. Of course, they all thought it, but he could not believe that she put it into words. He looked around the room. Each person seemed lost in his or her own thoughts; no one else said anything for some time. If their thoughts echoed his own, each thought of what they almost lost the previous night, what they owed the ones they loved, and how each person's determination to protect the ones they loved allowed every future laugh and moment of happiness. Even with Gardiner's injury to his shoulder, the group escaped the night relatively unscathed compared to what could have been lost.

"I would like everyone to know how proud I am to be a member of this family," said Gardiner. "Some families go through their entire existence without ever knowing if they can truly rely on their loved ones for support and protection; no one in this room need ever fear that. I know that each of us feels some guilt for our actions over the past week; none of us is innocent or acted perfectly. But we can never know what might be today if any one part of the last week changed. I submit that we all thank God for each person in this room; he gave us each other for a reason. Instead of the blame which I am sure each of us places on ourselves, I would ask instead that we each thank God for giving us this family to watch over us in our times of need."

"I believe after what happened over the past few days, we have a duty to ourselves and to each other do whatever is in our power to ensure our happiness," stated Darcy and took Elizabeth hand in his. "End Elizabeth have given me the greatest honour and happiness and accepted my proposal of marriage."

Every member of the room offered Darcy and Elizabeth their profuse congratulations.

"Am I right to guess that you two don't want a long engagement?" Asked hopefully Mr Gardiner after giving the pair his well-wishing.

"You are right, I intend to obtain the special licence within a few days if of course, Mr Bennet will give the consent."

"Good," stated Mr Gardiner. "I believe that your marriage to Elizabeth would justify Lydia's disappearance."

"I do not see how my marriage to Elizabeth can justify Lydia's disappearance."

"As far as we know, no one in Hertfordshire knows that Lydia did not go to Brighton. We can assume that information will eventually leak out from one source or another and create a scandal. We need Lydia to be somewhere safe, any other place than where she was, starting last Sunday." He turned his attention to his wife. "Madeline, is it safe to assume that you and the girls have not left the house much since returning on Monday?"

He watched as his wife looked curiously at him and answered, "That is true. We kept very close to home in case you returned without warning. We wanted to be here to offer our support."

"So none of our neighbours could say with any certainty whether Lydia arrived with you after you returned from Pemberley with the others?" His wife nodded and offered him a gentle smile; she must understand his plan.

"I am going to relate the manner that I remember the events of the last few weeks. I hope by the time I finish, everyone will agree with my recollection." Of all the gentlemen, only the Colonel looked at him without a severe amount of scepticism. Of course, he was the one who wanted Lydia to go to a brothel. His own plan was certainly less stressful for the family than that.

"Darcy proposed to Elizabeth while together at Kent several weeks ago and she accepted. As he had not the time to ask her father for his blessing, they kept their engagement a secret from society as a whole. They did confide the news of their engagement to members of their immediate families. Darcy, being the rather impulsive man that he is, decided to write Mr Bennet before he left for Pemberley and asked permission to marry Elizabeth. And while at Pemberley he received a message that required his immediate attention and because the lovers didn't want to be apart for long, we all decided to return to London earlier."

Gardiner took a sip of tea to relax and quickly examine the other occupants of the room. None seemed to take any offence so far to his slightly altered recollection of the events of the past few weeks. As such, he continued with more ease. "Everyone knows how Lydia loves surprises and planning parties, right? Elizabeth engagement was still a secret but Lydia discovered it somehow and not wanting for her spreading the news around Meryton, Mr Bennet sent her to London and she went with us to Pemberley. People of Maryton don't have to know that she didn't get there and we all know that gossips of all kind going to float anyway. And there were already rumours about Darcy's and Elizabeth's upcoming wedding so the people not going to be very suspicious about it. The most important is the official version of the story that will keep Lydia and her family from ruin. Not to mention the news about Elizabeth's nuptials to the noble Darcy family should hopefully put Lydia's case to rest."

Gardiner finished the rest of his tea in a single gulp and set it on the table. He was almost done when the Colonel asked. "Why the engagement was keep in secret?"

Darcy immediately had an idea. "Our aunt, Lady Catherine. I didn't wish the news about my engagement reach her before the wedding, knowing how passionate and irrational she was about me marrying her daughter."

"It seems to be a good plan and believable story," stated the Colonel.

"I think this whole story is an excellent idea. When did you work all out, Mr Gardiner?" Asked Darcy.

"I admit I thought about this last night and this morning. Of course, there were some details that I still needed to consider, but the general framework was already planned. I had a strong suspicion that you would arrive this morning with the news you brought. I was never wholly convinced that you were not already engaged after you arrived from Kent, despite telling me that you were not."

Now that that was over, he needed to say the last part. "There is one more condition which I must insist upon. We must not officially announce your engagement or marriage in the papers until the day the marriage occurs."

This time Elizabeth asked. "But Uncle, isn't the goal to make sure people know we are marrying?"

Before he could respond to his niece, the Colonel took the chance to answer from him. "Gardiner, if you would permit me, I think I know the answer. Darcy, Miss Elizabeth, we want for your marriage to have a scandal behind it. It will not be a massive scandal, but enough for the gossips to keep focused on that."

Jane gasped, "Hasn't our family endured enough scandal without purposely adding to it?"

Once again the Colonel answered. "Miss Bennet, Darcy marrying secretly your sister will be the subject of considerable gossip regardless of anything we do to try to limit it. Even if they waited six months after their engagement, the marriage would still be the topic of many conversations and unlimited gossip and speculation. If we add a little to it by not mentioning it until the day of the marriage, the scandal will be all relating to Darcy and Miss Elizabeth and even if gossip about Lydia reach London, no one will be really focusing on that. The fact that your youngest sister went to London to be with Miss Elizabeth instead of Brighton will never be mentioned. If it is talked of, it certainly will not be nearly as entertaining as Darcy's impetuousness and the scandal of an engagement that was never announced until the day of the wedding."

Gardiner spoke then to another gentleman in the room, "Bingley, what do you think of the idea?"

The man alternated between looking at Darcy and Jane before he spoke. "I am afraid to mention a large hole in the plan, but I feel it is my duty, nonetheless. The servants in your home know that Lydia did not arrive until last night or that she left for Pemberley and they must have heard her rants throughout the night and throughout the morning. Servants will talk and the truth will become known."

Gardiner had not thought about this particular problem. He leaned his head back against the sofa. He needed a break. Besides, his shoulder was throbbing, and the doctor told him he needed to rest, something that he had not been able to do.

He opened his eyes when he heard his wife answer. "Our servants, which we have few, are well paid and loyal to us. We treat them well and give them the respect that is their due. They do not know the reason for our early return from Pemberley. They know that Lydia is trying to run away and that Lizzy and Georgiana disappeared yesterday, but they don't know exactly why or what transpired to bring her here. Also, our servants do not interact with the ones from Longbourn or Meryton. Maggie knows enough to be a problem, but I trust her discretion. Only Tom knows the entire truth about the events of last night and I am sure that Mr Darcy would not entrust Miss Darcy's care to him if he could not be trusted."

Bingley spoke again before Gardiner was able to. "I hate to keep doing this, but there is another problem. What about Mrs Younge? Won't she be able to guess what happened and then will try to blackmail us?"

Seemingly already prepared for that question, Colonel Fitzwilliam answered it. "Mrs Younge has already been dealt with. Apparently, she was upstairs in one of the rooms at the Returning Rogue last night. On Darcy's behalf, I gave her the boat passage reserved for Wickham and plenty of money to start over in America. She did not seem overly upset at the demise of either her brother or Wickham. In fact, she seemed rather happy at the chance to start her life over again with plenty of money to keep her for the rest of her life."

Once again, Gardiner listened in worry as Bingley spoke up. "And what about the seven dead bodies in a tavern that are bound to create at least some problems for us. At the very least, we will have some questions to answer.

Col Fitzwilliam's voice was the first one that Gardiner heard. "I took care of it. I released the men from the stock room. Most had fallen asleep, but a few stayed awake throughout their time in confinement. I asked if anyone heard what happened and two reluctantly raised their hands; one of them was Jackson. I asked for those two to stay and sent the third man to get the police. I knew we would have to deal with the authorities eventually and preferred to do it before daybreak. The police arrived and saw the five dead bodies behind the counter and the two still lying on the ground where they fell. I explained that the two younger sisters of an acquaintance had run away to find their brother and ran into several problems. I explained the scene I saw when I arrived. I then told them how the five behind the bar attacked my friends and me when we tried to secure the release of the girls. Jackson and the other man verified the veracity of my accounting of the events. I explained how we subdued Younge and that I left in order to assure the safety of the sisters. When I returned to the tavern, I saw Younge attack one of the members of my group and another man grabbed the pistol. The unknown man aimed it at my friend but I shot the unknown man first. Younge then tried to grab the fallen pistol, but my friend killed him with a sword first."

"Jackson and the other customer could not verify the second half of the night's events, but could with certainty say they heard the man they knew as Wickham scream in anticipation of killing someone just before they heard the pistol fire. Their testimony, combined with an accounting from a Colonel in His Majesty's Army, provided enough evidence that we only killed the men in self-defence. I refused to give up the names of the girls or my friends as that would certainly harm their reputations. The policeman reluctantly agreed when I reminded them of my family's standing in Parliament. He even agreed not to use my name when filling in his report."

Darcy eyed him suspiciously. "And you were able to convince him of all this using only your superior oratory skills?"

"The policeman knew that we did not do anything that was not necessary, given the situation we found upon arrival. Because Jackson and the other man corroborated my accounting, the policeman trusted that I had a good reason for withholding the names of the other people involved. And while I am sure this did nothing to factor into his decision, I assured him that an anonymous donation will soon be made to the local police station for the families of the constables who die in the line of duty. I know you already support that charity and hoped you wouldn't mind adding in a little extra this year. Also, I have the names and addresses of Jackson and the other man who learned my identity during their discussion with the police. I think it would behove us to make their lives a little easier. I was very careful to never lie, and I did not bribe anyone to lie for us or to overlook any important information. Any further information gleaned from an investigation would not have changed our innocence; it would have simply damaged our reputations."

"Well, I can live with that. Consider the donation taken care of."

"Does anyone have any other questions or problems with my recollection of the events that occurred?"

Bingley spoke up once again. "If we need any more scandal to help hide Lydia's discretion, I am sure that

Jane and I would also volunteer to a double marriage with Darcy and Elizabeth."

Gardiner looked at his lovelorn future nephew with some pity. "I do not think that will be necessary. In fact, I am counting on your wedding to occupy the people of Meryton and London with plenty a little gossip to quell any future speculation as to Lydia's disappearance."

"Well, I hope Mr Bennet will not plan on us waiting for six months. I believe the longest I can be forced to hold out is about two months. I would prefer four weeks at the most."

Gardiner watched the silent exchange between Bingley and his eldest niece and knew that any longer than a two-month engagement would be met with insurmountable resistance. He pitied his sister only having two months to plan for a wedding and wedding breakfast that needed to be no less than spectacular.

"Now does anyone else have any issues? If not, the plan is set." Gardiner waited for everyone to silently nod in confirmation that the conversation was finished.

Darcy addressed his future uncle, "Gardiner, may I have a few moments to speak to my fiancée in private? We have a number of plans that need to be rearranged due to this morning's conversation."

"Of course, Darcy. You may use my study. If the rest of you are hungry, there is a small meal waiting for us in the dining room." Specifically he addressed Darcy and Lizzy then, "We will expect the two of you shortly."

Darcy led Elizabeth out of the parlour and into the study crowded with books and newspapers. Elizabeth immediately buried her head in his chest.

"My love, what is troubling you? Is the wedding is too soon?" He asked noticing her troubled face when her uncle revealed the whole plan.

Unable to look up, she answered into his shirt. "This must be so difficult for you. I know how much you hate disguise and it seems that is all this last week consisted of. To make it worse, marrying me has cost you so much. How can my father ever repay you? I am supposed to bring a dowry with me to enhance your life. Instead, I bring debts to be paid and a troublesome family."

"Elizabeth, you bring me a life. Without you, I am empty. There is no amount of money in this world that could ever improve my life more than simply having you as a permanent part of it. As far as the disguise, if I did not conceal my relationship and dealings with Wickham, to begin with, none of this would have occurred."

"Come."

Darcy offered her his arm and led the way from the library to the dining room.

Chapter 45

Jane pleaded with her favourite sister, trying to make Elizabeth understand. "Elizabeth, you must know that I have to go with Lydia tonight. I cannot make Mr Bingley or Lydia endure this without me by their side."

"No, Jane, I do not understand. What if someone recognises you? One reason why Mr Bingley is going to take her is so that no one will associate her with our family. You have been out in London society. If you are there, how can they not connect Lydia to our family?"

As calmly as she could, Jane explained, "Our aunt lent me one of her dresses that she wore when she was large with child. I used a pillow to fashion a large belly and our aunt also found a dark-coloured wig from uncle's store. When I put a pair of spectacles on to complete the disguise, no one will recognise me. Mr Bingley is going to wear some sort of disguise as well. We have a servant's dress and cap for Lydia to wear to hide her appearance."

"But Jane..." Elizabeth's voice fell off. The second eldest Bennet sister could not finish her argument.

"Lizzy, you will not dissuade me. Now tell me, what is the real reason you do not want me to go?"

Her younger sister looked up from examining the rug in their bedroom with true sadness reflected in her expressive green eyes. Jane gave her favourite sister a large and warming embrace, hoping to eventually coax the truth from Elizabeth.

"I have already taken so much from you. After what you will see and hear tonight, whatever is left of your innocence will be completely taken. It is bad enough that our youngest sister must endure the knowledge of this information, but I see no reason why you must be traumatised as well."

"Lizzy, it is our duty as sisters to always stand by each other, especially when it is the most difficult. Imagine how hard this will be for Lydia to deal with. I told her a few hours ago about Wickham. At first, she refused to believe me. I am still not sure if she completely does. She still does not know the circumstances of his death. We will find something to tell her tomorrow. Once she finally understands that fate that Wickham sold her into, she will need someone to comfort her. You cannot deny our youngest sister that small luxury this night. Although much of her pain is due to her own foolishness, we cannot abandon her while there is hope. I know that I cannot."

"Jane, you are entirely too good. The rest of us do not deserve you."

"Lizzy, God gave us one another for a reason. He knew we would need to watch out for one another." Changing the conversation, Jane added, "Now finish getting ready for dinner at Mr Darcy's. You are going to finally meet Colonel Fitzwilliam's parents, are you not?" She saw Lizzy nod. "Are you still planning to bring Georgiana back to the Gardiner's after dinner?"

"No, she is going to come tomorrow morning after Mr Darcy leaves for Longbourn."

"Alright then. I will come to your room tonight after Lydia goes to sleep to tell you how Lydia is doing. You will then tell me how much you liked Mr Darcy's aunt and uncle. So you know, I told Maggie to move my things to Lydia's room. And I think it would be best if I stay close by her for the next few weeks, even after we return to Longbourn."

***

Through the darkness of the bedroom, Jane found her way to the warm bed where she could hear her sister's light breathing. "Lizzy, are you still awake?"

Immediately, Jane heard her sister's voice. "Jane, is that you? How is Lydia?"

"I think Lydia understands what her fate almost became. She now knows without a doubt the kind of man Wickham really was. She also believes he is dead. Fortunately, she never wants to hear his name again and has no interest in hearing how he died." She stopped for a minute to think before continuing very slowly. "But she saw and heard things that no young lady should ever have to know about. I think it will be some time before we see her laugh and smile in the carefree manner she once did. But, I do not believe her liveliness is lost forever. We just need to constantly remind her of how much we love her and that we will be by her side." Jane then lay down next to her dearest sister. "I think that I may ask Mr Bingley if Lydia may live with us soon after we wed. I believe that would be best for her, at least until I am sure that our mother will not..." Jane could not finish.

"Jane, since you cannot say it, I will. It would probably be best that Lydia live with you until she is not a threat to or subject of our mother's nerves." Jane felt Elizabeth's arms wrap around her neck and then Lizzy whispered in her ear. "You are a dear, loving sister for asking Mr Bingley to let our sister live with you. I do believe you and Mr Bingley may be the only people that she will listen to now."

"Lizzy, if you saw how much she hurt. Your heart would bleed for her."

"I know Jane. But you are the only Bennet sister with a heart that is both kind and strong enough to ensure that Lydia is Lydia once more. Perhaps a more subdued version would be better, but one with the same spirit. As you said before, God gave us one another for a reason and this week seems to be that reason."

Chapter 46

Georgiana Darcy was on the way to the library, but at the sound of her aunt's booming voice in the foyer, she froze mid-step, not wanting to attract any attention. If her aunt noticed any movement, she would be caught. The girl held her breath, worried even that slight movement would betray her presence.

She grimaced when she heard her aunt's demand resonate through the entire house, "I insist that I see my nephew this instant!"

"Lady Catherine, I regret to inform you that neither Mr Darcy nor Miss Darcy is at home right now," Mrs Blaine explained calmly.

"When will Darcy return? I must speak to him immediately."

"I am unsure of Mr Darcy's plans at this time. He left yesterday and did not inform us of when he planned to return."

"What of his sister? Where is Georgiana? I DEMAND to know."

Mrs Blaine told the Lady that Miss Darcy spent a great deal of her time outside of Darcy House and was not sure of her schedule either.

"What does my nephew pay you for? You are the most incompetent housekeeper I ever had the displeasure of addressing. What will Darcy say when I tell him that you have no knowledge of the whereabouts of your master and mistress? You will get no letters of recommendation from him or your new mistress when you are dismissed."

***

Elizabeth walked in front of Georgiana down the stairs, slightly resigned to her fate of entertaining Lady Catherine for the next few hours. The thought of the Lady's presence in the house when Mr Darcy returned that afternoon was not a circumstance she was looking forward to.

Lizzy glanced behind her, seeing Georgiana walk with seemingly heavy feet. Each step forward seemed to take considerable effort from her soon-to-be sister. After everything they went through, she had no idea how Lady Catherine could intimidate Mr Darcy's sister.

She greeted Mrs Blaine when she saw the housekeeper walking in the hallway toward them.

"Miss Darcy, Miss Bennet, good afternoon. I was on my way to find you."

Elizabeth was the first to answer. "Yes, we heard that Lady Catherine came to visit."

"I asked her to wait in the parlour until Mr Darcy or Miss Darcy returned. Would you like me to announce your return now to Lady Catherine or would you prefer to wait until Mr Darcy returns, Miss?"

Georgiana turned to her, "Lizzy, I suppose we should go see her now. Perhaps Lady Catherine found out somehow about your news and came to congratulate you and Fitzwilliam. I cannot think of any other reason that would bring her here from Rosings."

Elizabeth's raised eyebrow displayed her own doubt about her friend's words. She could think of any number of reasons why Lady Catherine would choose to visit her nephew at this particular time and none of them had to do with wishing her nephew a joy. "Giana, I do not believe even you actually believe that, but it does you credit to hope for the best. And as we do not have any proof to the contrary, I suggest we let your aunt guide the conversation and hope for the best."

Mrs Blaine dismissed herself and walked toward the parlour.

"Lizzy, what do you mean? Why do you really think Lady Catherine and Anne are here? And don't just continue to look at me like you have no idea what I am asking. I know when you are withholding information and lying, remember?"

"Giana, I told you that I stayed with my friend Mrs Collins at Kent. While there, your brother and I spent a lot of time together. You know Lady Catherine's intentions for her daughter and your brother." Georgiana nodded. "Well, she observed that your brother paid a great deal of attention to me and was not pleased with either him or me when last I saw her."

Elizabeth led Georgiana from the hallway and entered the parlour. It only took her one look at Lady Catherine's severely displeased countenance to know that this was not a social visit or one where joy would be wished. It was going to be a very long afternoon indeed. Poor Anne! The young lady appeared utterly defeated.

Before either Elizabeth or Georgiana could greet their guests, Lady Catherine stood and took command of the conversation. "Georgiana, what is Miss Elizabeth Bennet doing with you?"

Georgiana spoke before Elizabeth could decide on the appropriate response. "Good afternoon, Lady

Catherine, Anne." Georgiana curtseyed and Elizabeth followed her younger sister's lead. They both sat on the sofa opposite of Georgiana's aunt and cousin. Once again, Miss Darcy spoke far more calmly than Elizabeth imagined possible after her aunt's rude greeting, "Miss Elizabeth is a dear friend of mine. We came to Darcy House because I wanted to show her a new dress when Mrs Blaine informed me that you brought Anne for a visit." Georgiana smiled at her cousin who made no similar gesture in return. Instead, Anne dropped her eyes to stare at the teacup wobbling slightly in Anne's shaking hand.

Lady Catherine glared at Elizabeth as the older woman spoke to her niece. "Georgiana, I am seriously displeased. Miss Bennet is not a suitable companion for a girl of your social standing. Anne will prove to be a much better friend and guide for you when she marries your brother. Are you not going to wish your new sister joy?"

Georgiana's eyes widened and stared at Elizabeth in utter confusion. With Lady Catherine's statement went any hope of being able to find some pleasant or innocuous conversation topic to pass the time until Mr Darcy returned.

Seeing no reason for Georgiana to be the sole recipient of the attention from intimidating woman sitting across from them, Elizabeth answered for her.

"Lady Catherine, I wasn't aware that Mr Darcy was engaged to your daughter. When did he propose?"

Lady Catherine's eyes focused all of their anger directly on Elizabeth. "Their engagement has always been of a peculiar nature. Anne's obvious improvement in health during Darcy's last visit to Rosings proved the wedding should take place immediately. I am here to inform Darcy of the news he waited so long to hear. Now, Georgiana, it is time to wish your future sister joy."

Elizabeth looked at Anne, who sat there silently in obvious discomfort. Yes, Anne had appeared considerably healthier toward the end of Elizabeth's time at Rosings than she had at the beginning. But now the young lady seated across from her looked barely able to breathe without assistance. Whatever improvement Anne made previously had completely vanished.

"Georgiana, take Anne to the mistress' rooms," said Lady Catherine, never breaking eye contact with Elizabeth. "She will need to supervise their redecorating. I am sure that Miss Bennet and I can entertain one another while you show Anne her new accommodations."

Georgiana grabbed Elizabeth's hand and quietly answered, "Lady Catherine, I know you must be exhausted after your journey and would enjoy a few moments to rest in solitary. Elizabeth, would you like to come with me while I show Anne around the house?"

Before Elizabeth could say or do anything, Lady Catherine stood and spoke in no uncertain terms, "That will not be necessary, Georgiana. Leave Miss Bennet and I. I need to speak with her in private."

"Georgiana, as Lady Catherine said, I am sure we will find some subject on which to converse in pleasure while you have a chance to visit with your cousin." Elizabeth nodded her head in the direction of the door. After facing Younge, she could handle Lady Catherine by herself. Then she stood, not allowing the lady to look down on her as if she was a child in trouble.

Once the door shut behind Anne and Georgiana, Lady Catherine wasted no time. "Miss Bennet, you ought to know that I am not to be trifled with. However, insincere you may choose to be, you shall not find me so. My character has ever been celebrated for its sincerity and frankness; and in a cause of such a moment as this, I shall certainly not depart from it. A report of a most alarming nature reached me two days ago. I was told, that you, Miss Elizabeth Bennet, would, in all likelihood, be soon afterwards united to my nephew, my own nephew, Mr Fitzwilliam Darcy. Though I know it must be a scandalous falsehood, though I would not injure him so much as to suppose the truth of it possible, I instantly resolved on setting off, that I might make my sentiments known to both you and my nephew."

"If you believe it to be impossible," said Elizabeth, colouring with astonishment and disdain, "I wonder you took the trouble of coming so far. What could your Ladyship propose by it?"

"At once to insist upon having such a report universally contradicted."

"Your coming to town to see Mr Darcy, and myself by my proximity to him, will be taken rather as a confirmation of it."

The redness in Lady Catherine's face quickly brightened. "This is not to be born. Miss Bennet, I insist on being satisfied. Has he, has my nephew, made you an offer of marriage?"

Elizabeth felt her heart begin to pound and a small trickle of sweat fall from her brow. But she did everything she could to not allow her fury to show. In as calm and calculated voice as she could muster, Elizabeth notified Lady Catherine, "Your Ladyship has declared it to be impossible."

"It ought to be so; it must be so while he retains the use of his reason. But your arts and allurements may, in a moment of infatuation, have made him forget what he owes to himself and to all his family. You may have drawn him in. I am almost the nearest relation he has in the world and am entitled to know all his dearest concerns."

"But you are not entitled to know mine, nor will such behaviour as this ever induce me to be explicit."

"Let me be rightly understood, Miss Bennet. This match, to which you have the presumption to aspire, can never take place. No, never. Mr Darcy is engaged to my daughter. Now, what have you to say?

Elizabeth held her head a little higher as she answered. "Only this, - that if he is so, you can have no reason to suppose he will make an offer to me."

"The engagement between them is of a peculiar kind. It was the favourite wish of his mother as well as hers. Honour, decorum, prudence, nay, interest, forbid you from coming between them. You will be censured, slighted, and despised by everyone connected with him. Your alliance will be a disgrace; your name will never be mentioned by any of us."

"These are heavy misfortunes indeed, but the wife of Mr Darcy must have such extraordinary sources of happiness attached to her situation, that she could, upon the whole, have no cause to repine."

Elizabeth watched as Lady Catherine clenched her fists and snapped back, "Obstinate, headstrong girl. I am ashamed of you! Is this your gratitude for my attention at Rosings? Is nothing due to me on that score?"

"Your treatment of me whiles at Rosings demands a great many debts to be repaid, but those debts must be satisfied at some point in the distant future and likely will not be paid by me. I feel our future acquaintance will be brief indeed."

Lady Catherine's eyes widened fully as she demanded, "Are you engaged to my nephew? I will not have you ruin my daughter's happiness. Now answer me!"

Right then, Elizabeth made her first decision as the future Mrs Darcy. She had no doubt that Darcy would support her next statement. "You have insulted me in every possible method. I would appreciate it if you would please leave this house immediately."

Elizabeth was so intent on not backing down from her request that she did not even notice Lady Catherine lifting her hand. She had no warning before Lady Catherine slapped her cheek with more hatred than Elizabeth thought possible from the lady. She instantly felt the physical punishment inflicted sharply sting her cheek and heard two gasps at the door. She turned to see Georgiana and Anne standing by the doorway. Whatever they saw, it was more than either Elizabeth or Lady Catherine intended. Both girls rushed to Elizabeth's side to comfort and support her.

"Lizzy! Are you hurt?"

"Mother! How could you!"

Not giving Elizabeth a chance to respond, Lady Catherine snapped, "Anne, stay out of this."

"No, you have taken this too far. It is over. Please just admit it."

With the same force that Lady Catherine just struck Miss Bennet, the lady did the same to her own daughter. Anne fell to the floor in pain, clutching her cheek.

"I will not tolerate any opposition from any of you. I made myself perfectly clear at Rosings, to both of you! Or do I need to convince either one of you further of my serious displeasure?" Lady Catherine tried to drag Anne to her feet, who attempted unsuccessfully to free herself from her mother's clutches.

After this display, Elizabeth could guess what followed Lady Catherine's tirades against Anne at Rosings. She would not allow the girl to suffer through that punishment anymore; certainly not while Anne was at Darcy House. Elizabeth did the first thing that entered her mind, as loud as she could, she yelled, "Tom! Tom!" Elizabeth knew Tom promised Mr Darcy that he would never be out of shouting range while Darcy was away.

Within seconds the servant ran into the room, followed by two of the footmen.

Lady Catherine quickly changed her focus to the muscular young men that entered the room. "Get out of my way! You have no business being here."

Tom answered plainly, "I am sorry, Lady Catherine, but if you hurt Miss Darcy or Miss Bennet, this is exactly where my place is." He turned to Elizabeth, "Miss Bennet, how can I be of service?"

"Miss Darcy, Miss De Bourgh and I will be upstairs in Miss Darcy's room. Please make sure that Lady Catherine stays here and does not leave." With a very pointed look at Tom and the footmen in the room, she added, "Do whatever is necessary to keep her in this room; Mr Darcy will want to see her when he returns." Not saying anything to Lady Catherine, Georgiana and Elizabeth each carefully took Anne by an arm and led her upstairs.

Once safely secured in Georgiana's sitting room Elizabeth turned to her future sister. "We need to ask Lord Matlock and Colonel Fitzwilliam to come here immediately. I do not know exactly when your brother plans to return from Hertfordshire and I think he will want the other members of his family present when he does see Lady Catherine."

Georgiana smiled slightly at her. "We will make such wonderful sisters; it is already done. Anne asked me to send a note asking for them to come here as quickly as they could when we left for a tour of the house."

Both ladies turned their attention to the girl sitting quietly on the sofa. Not sure of the reception Elizabeth would receive, she allowed Georgiana to begin.

"Anne, do you want to talk?"

"Not yet, Georgiana. I just want to ask Miss Elizabeth for her forgiveness."

Elizabeth sat down on Anne's other side and took Anne's hand firmly in her own. "There is nothing to forgive. I have a personal philosophy of never holding the actions of the parent against the child."

"You have no reason to be kind to me, but yet you are."

Elizabeth brushed a few strands of Anne's hair lightly away from the girl's face. "If I am not mistaken, you were very kind to me on two occasions. You helped to match me with your cousin at a great expense to yourself. Both Mr Darcy and I are very grateful for everything you did."

"You must know that I never wanted to marry Fitzwilliam and he never wanted to marry me."

Elizabeth smiled warmly and quickly answered, "I realised that after you convinced my cousin to let me travel with your cousins back to town. When you made the point of telling me that your mother forced Mr Darcy to ride with you later in the week, I felt sure of my belief."

"I want to wish you both every joy in the world. I sincerely hope you are very happy together. Would you call me Anne as we are to be cousins?"

"I would be honoured, but only if you call me Elizabeth."

Smiling at their newfound understanding, Georgiana took a deep breath and cautiously asked, "Anne, would you like to see the new dress I plan to wear to the wedding? It is the most divine colour of blue. It looks just like the ocean on a calm morning."

Once Georgiana brought out the dress, it led to the unveiling of several others which the girl had not found the occasion to wear. Although the latest fashions were not what Elizabeth thought they should be facing, there would likely be plenty of time for that much later. For now, the mindless chatter helped them avoid the large elephant in the room that would have to be faced all too soon. The conversation appeared to ease Anne, and that was what truly mattered. After they made a determined effort to look through a small part of Georgiana's closet and bonnet collection, a maid informed them that Lord Matlock and Colonel Fitzwilliam waited in the library.

Chapter 47

Elizabeth led Georgiana and Anne down the hallway and stairs until the three found themselves at the library doors, left slightly ajar. She knocked lightly, was granted entrance, and found Lord Matlock and Colonel Fitzwilliam each helping themselves to a glass of Mr Darcy's favourite whiskey from Scotland. She had only met Lord Matlock once before, but she could not help but feel considerably calmer now that Lord Matlock arrived to help with Lady Catherine. If his sister might listen to anyone, it should be the head of the Fitzwilliam family.

After the three ladies sat down together in one motion, Lord Matlock questioned them in an overly easy manner, "Georgiana, why did you send for us in such a hurry? No one appears to be missing any limbs or beaten."

Anne spoke first. "Since Miss Elizabeth and Georgiana don't know the real reason I am here, I suppose that I shall begin. I will keep this as short as possible. Darcy began to court Miss Elizabeth while at Rosings. I am not sure how mother learned of it, but

Richard and I each made our discovery based on Darcy's very unusual behaviour, especially whenever Miss Elizabeth appeared. When mother found out, she tried to hurt Miss Bennet to the degree that she would never want to see any member of the Fitzwilliam family again. I confess that I am very pleased that she did not succeed." Anne gave Lizzy a small half-smile before continuing.

"When Miss Elizabeth, Darcy and Richard left Rosings, mother believed she had persuaded Miss Bennet that she would never be welcomed to the family; my mother's plan for Darcy to marry me was safe. But I knew better. I knew Darcy would not give up Miss Elizabeth that easily. Mr Collins called on mother two days ago with a news though it was more a gossip. Sir William told Mrs Collins that he saw Darcy and Elizabeth in town, mentioned that she was invited to Pemberley as Darcy's guess, and so believed their engagement was imminent. You can imagine my mother's reaction. She immediately decided to come to town to force Darcy to marry me. When Miss Elizabeth and Georgiana joined mother and me for tea today, mother immediately began questioning her and asked us to leave. When Georgiana and I left the room, I knew what the mother planned. I used the time to ask Georgiana to send a note to Matlock House asking you to come right away not knowing when Darcy returns." Anne took a deep breath and in what seemed like one long word, Anne blurted out, "When we decided to return to the parlour, we saw Mother slapping Elizabeth across the face and did the same to me when I tried to persuade her to stop." Anne let out the breath and then continued. "That was when we left the room. My mother should be still in the parlour where we left her."

The Colonel looked expectantly at Anne. "Is that everything that we need to know?"

In a small voice that even Elizabeth who sat next to Anne could barely hear, Anne replied, "Richard, please do not ask me that."

Lord Matlock walked over to his weary niece and knelt in front of Anne. He took one of Anne's hands and gently told her, "Anne, I am afraid that we must know everything in order to be able to help you and properly deal with your mother." Lord Matlock then looked at both ladies. "Miss Elizabeth, Georgiana, perhaps you two better leave now and we will call you when we are done."

Anne pleaded with Lord Matlock, "Uncle, please let them stay."

"Father, I do not believe there is much that will shock Georgiana or Miss Elizabeth."

"All right, but I must still insist that you tell me everything," the Earl looked at his niece once more.

Anne looked around the room and met each set of eyes that focused on her. She started speaking in a barely audible voice. "This was not the first time mother struck me."

Richard knelt down in front of Anne and took her hand. Obviously encouraged by her cousin's support, the girl continued. "There are a few marks on my back and other places that aren't visible. Ever since I told her that I did not want to marry Darcy a few years ago, mother used force to persuade me to keep my sentiments from Darcy. When I noticed that he is in love with Elizabeth, I stopped trying."

Anne lifted her head and locked eyes with Richard. "After you left Rosings, the worst began. I could not contact anyone; she would not allow me to write to anyone for fear that I might ask for help. When Mr Collins told her of Darcy's alleged engagement, my mother lost her mind."

"What did she do?" Lord Matlock asked.

"She struck me until I agreed to her plan."

"What plan?"

"Please, don't hate me. I had to."

"There will never be anything to forgive, Anne," said Richard. "I could never blame you for anything your mother forced you to do. My biggest regret is that we did not take you with us when we left Rosings. But you will never have to go back there until your mother remains there."

Anne looked at Elizabeth. "Mother made me promise that I would compromise tonight. I was supposed to slip into his bedroom and make sure that servants, my mother and her friend Lady Charlotte saw me exit late in the morning. She brought a draught intended to make Darcy sleep heavily through the night so he would not notice my presence. Mother knew Darcy's commitment to family and he would save my reputation, even if it meant sacrificing his own happiness."

Elizabeth felt her stomach constrict.

"Elizabeth, please know that I was never a willing participant in mother's plan. I agreed under duress and with the knowledge that I would have to come to town where I knew I could find some way to contact Richard and Lord Matlock. In the worst-case scenario, I planned to confess everything to Darcy so he could take proper measures to protect himself."

Lord Matlock stood from kneeling by Anne and surveyed the room. Colonel Fitzwilliam appeared fully prepared to strangle Lady Catherine and Elizabeth doubted Darcy would look any different when faced with the revelations confessed by his female cousin.

"Anne, what you did was very brave. Telling us the truth took a great deal of fortitude and courage. In return, as your guardian and head of the Fitzwilliam family, I promise you here and now that your mother will have no control over your life or your decisions. She will be immediately removed to the dowager house at Glenmore. After the death of your father, you became the mistress of Rosings and it is the highest time for your mother to acknowledge it."

"To acknowledge what?"

"Mr Darcy!" Elizabeth jumped off the sofa hearing her fiancé's voice.

"Why is Lady Catherine in the parlour with Tom standing outside like a sentry? And why is she there alone while everyone else is here?" Hearing only silence in response, he continued. "Do I want to know?"

"Ignorance is usually bliss, but unfortunately very unhelpful in this case. I think it would be best for Anne, Georgiana and me to excuse ourselves while you talk to the gentlemen," said Elizabeth. Darcy nodded and greeted his fiancée properly kissing her hand. She smiled at him and then followed Georgiana and Anne to the door.

Once he heard the door firmly closed, Darcy stood there, waiting for any kind of information from his family. He watched as his uncle finished the last of the Scottish whisky in his glass "Darcy, I was hoping you wouldn't return for several more hours."

Darcy moved and stood by the chair closest to the window. "I am sorry to be a disappointment."

Richard walked over, handed him a full glass of whiskey and told him to sit down. He eyed his cousin suspiciously and but eventually took the drink and complied. "I do not like the feeling festering in this room. What happened?"

"Darcy, this conversation will not be over quickly," the Earl ran his finger around the edge of the glass before continuing. "You must promise me that no matter what I say, you will not leave this room until we both agree you are calm enough."

"Just tell me."

"Darcy, Lady Catherine is much, much worse than we had any idea. She physically beat Anne into submission for years and now forced her to agree to compromise you by slipping into your bedchamber tonight." Richard walked over to where he stood so their faces were only inches apart. "And Lady Catherine slapped your fiancée after Miss Elizabeth refused to break her engagement to you."

Darcy clutched the glass tighter in his hand and felt the same deep and unadulterated hatred from the Returning Rogue resurfacing. This time there was no one he loved preventing him from taking revenge for the woman he loved. There was only one place he needed to be right now. This was a problem that he could definitely dispose of. With one swing of his foot, Darcy kicked the library door open, completely removing the oak door from its hinges.

Darcy, and Richard after him, stormed into the parlour where Lady Catherine sat fuming after being summarily dismissed. He could hear Lord Matlock hurrying to catch him and Richard. From the corner of his eyes, Darcy watched as Tom closed the parlour door after Lord Matlock had slipped into the room. The cousins took their positions across from their aunt.

But the lady did not wait for Darcy to speak before she attempted to strike the first blow. Without grace, Lady Catherine stood as though she planned to meet a battlefield opponent. "Darcy, how dare you allow your servants to treat me in such an infamous manner! Miss Elizabeth Bennet showed such insolence that I was forced to remind her of her place and she refused. You have allowed your life to fall into complete disarray. If you married Anne when I first told you to, none of this would have happened!"

Darcy moved forward until he stood less than a foot from his aunt. He allowed his presence to tower over her as stared down at her in complete contempt and revulsion. "Lady Catherine, I should have told you this several years ago. I will never marry Anne. I am engaged to Miss Elizabeth Bennet and will marry her next week."

Lady Catherine quickly retorted, "Darcy, you -"

"Do not interrupt me again. You will be immediately removed to the dowager house on Glenmore, something that should happen years ago. And your daughter will be free to live her own life according to her own wishes."

"You cannot -"

"I will neither acknowledge any communication from you nor any other attempts to contact me. If you force yourself on Anne, Georgiana, Elizabeth, or me, I will make it my mission to find what you most fear in life and ensure it comes true. Do you understand?"

Changing tactics, Lady Catherine moved from Darcy to try to bully her older brother. "Hugh, you cannot allow your nephew to speak to me like this."

"Catherine, I would suggest you agree to his terms rather quickly. His offer will expire soon and I do not think you will like mine any better."

Lady Catherine's ire was past anything Darcy ever saw or heard from his aunt during any of her previous tirades. "I am your sister. You cannot do this!"

Lord Matlock swiftly answered, "Catherine, you may be my sister, but you are acting like a child and what is worse, you abused your own daughter. You know as well as I do that I have every right to do this. Lewis left me in charge of administering and managing Anne's inheritance. I have allowed you control of Rosings, but you demonstrated a complete lack of competence and concern for the care of your own child. With this decision, I am merely fulfilling the promise I made to your husband to ensure Anne's safety and well-being, a promise I am ashamed of how poorly I executed until this day."

Moving back to Darcy, Lady Catherine proved her worth as an adversary. In a calm and triumphant tone she told her audience, "Darcy, you say you already have a marriage ceremony planned for next week?" Seeing that her nephew refused to respond, she continued. "That will work out quite well. I shall leave you gentlemen so that I may help my daughter prepare for her wedding."

Darcy grabbed Lady Catherine's shoulder and forced her to turn around and face him. But it was Lord Matlock who looked into the eyes of his sister, eyes that exposed an indisputable craze and questioned, "Catherine, what have you done?"

Lady Catherine turned to Darcy and revealed a wicked grin. "It no longer matters. It is too late. There is nothing you can do. Darcy will marry Anne at the ceremony he planned for his precious Elizabeth Bennet." With that statement, Lady Catherine sat down in a chair, spooned one lump of sugar into her teacup, carefully brought the teacup to her lips, and glared at her male relations in complete triumph.

Chapter 48

"Catherine! Tell me! What have you done?!" Yelled the Earl.

"It is too late for you to do anything about it. Besides, I want to see your face when you accept the inevitability of your marriage to Anne. Now, Darcy, go and check the evening paper. I took the liberty of announcing your engagement and impending wedding. All of London now knows of your engagement. You cannot break it without destroying both Anne's reputation and your own. If you choose to marry Elizabeth Bennet now, society will never accept her, you, and Georgiana will be ruined as a result. And as much as you might try to rationalise the supposed prudence of a marriage to Miss Elizabeth, in your heart you know I am correct. You will never sabotage your own family."

He swore his heart stopped beating for almost a full minute. His future just went black. How could she just sit there and watch him in sheer elation? Darcy felt a hand on each of his shoulders, dragging him away from the lady. If not for Richard's assistance, he feared he may have fallen on the short trek to the other side of the room. After managing several laboured breaths, Darcy did the only thing he could think of and followed Lady Catherine's instructions. He stormed out the door and returned a few minutes later, feeling an even greater degree of agitation than when he left. He returned carrying in his right hand a copy of The Times opened to the society section. Without any discussion, he handed it to Lord Matlock and listened in pain as his uncle read aloud the article prominently displayed on the section's front page.

"As happens with so many young men of society, one of the most sought-after bachelors in England proved he too is subject to a rather severe case of fickleness. Only last week, I thought a certain gentleman from the North finally chose his permanent dinner partner; apparently, she only served as his temporary companion for the soup course. It seems his tastes were not satisfied with the unknown female and he moved on to a more acceptable young lady to share the main course and dessert. A certain very well-to-do young lady from Kent arrived today with her mother for an extended visit with her much sought-after and devastatingly handsome cousin. The lady arrived bringing several items from her trousseau and made an appointment with the best modiste in town to procure the rest of her needs for the upcoming season. Although it is known that the young lady's mother always spoke of the joyous event, most mothers and several fathers in the ton held out hope that the gentleman would choose a bride from outside his family. Not even his unspoken announcement from the gentleman in question at the theatre three weeks ago dissuaded London's society from their hopes; for as long as his intentions were unspoken, the mothers could pretend the gentleman's plans did not exist at all. Alas, to the dismay of several families with high hopes of seeing their daughters settled at an illustrious northern estate, the solicitor of the gentleman in question was seen procuring a special licence only yesterday. The only thing left to assume is that two of the most splendid fortunes in England are about to unite. I can already hear the hearts breaking all across Grosvenor Square."

Darcy sat quietly fuming in his chair, watching the reactions of his uncle, aunt, and cousin. Lady Catherine's smugness grew until Lord Matlock finished reading but suddenly fell at the end.

"Father, Darcy, perhaps we should remove ourselves to Darcy's study for a more private conversation." Richard then looked to Lady Catherine, winked, and with an even wider smile and told her, "Lady Catherine, I must thank you for being extremely helpful."

It was official that Richard had definitely lost his mind. At this time, there was no other explanation for his cousin's happiness. Well, there was only one way to discover the source. With much less anger hanging over him than when he last walked out of the room, Darcy once again left the parlour. Before joining Richard and his uncle, he needed to find several footmen to watch Lady Catherine while he conferred with his uncle and cousin. No good could possibly come from letting his aunt out of that room. Once the footmen arrived and Tom was left to supervise them, Darcy scowled once more at his aunt and then followed his uncle and cousin to the study.

After Richard poured three glasses of Scottish whiskey from Darcy's collection, he told both gentlemen to sit down. But before the Colonel could say anything else or Darcy could take a drink, Lord Matlock demanded, "Richard, why in the devil's name would you thank Catherine?"

"Because Father, Lady Catherine loves to be useful, and she just proved it now."

This time Darcy managed to speak before Lord Matlock. "Go on."

"Anne didn't tell you everything. She was waiting for me to speak to you and now seems to be an ideal time. Anne and I are engaged."

That was not what Darcy to hear. But that did not mean it was unwelcome.

"And when, may I ask, did this happy event occur?"

"Darcy, what did you think I was doing while you spent all your time wooing Miss Elizabeth? I rarely saw you that entire week. In fact, I rarely saw you that entire visit. I had to amuse myself with something and Anne proved to be quite an entertaining companion; there is more to our cousin than you ever saw. When outside the company of her mother, the Anne we knew before her father died reappears. She laughs easily like she did as a child. She is remarkably well-read, although her reading selection at Rosings proved rather limited due to her mother. Apparently, Georgiana smuggled in several books last time she visited and would send her a new one whenever she could. I wish I knew of their arrangement; I would have brought her several myself when we visited. Fortunately, she will have access to all the books she desires when we marry. She delights when sitting in the sunshine and lights up when able to spend the day as she pleases. Lady Catherine wasn't lying when she said that Anne's health improved during our visit; however, it was due to my company, not yours. She is truly an amazing young lady."

Still slightly sceptical of regard which he never heard Richard speak of before, Darcy was dying to know the answer to one more question.

"But why did you not tell us earlier? Why did you not take Anne with us when we left Rosings?"

The smile on Richard's face fell when he answered. "I needed to find out if I could resign my commission first. With the war on the continent, I did not want to discover I had to leave Anne within days of our marriage. She agreed to subtly begin to suggest to her mother that she planned to marry me instead of you. At the time we left, Anne believed she could still change her mother's opinion and receive her blessing. If I knew then what I know now, I would never have allowed her to stay, no matter if I had to carry her out on my shoulder."

"Richard, shouldn't you be as angry as I am about this article? Surely you see that your marriage to Anne will be much more difficult. Everyone will believe you married her because I didn't want to. Or this will keep you from being able to marry her at all."

Richard's grin suddenly reappeared. "I see no such thing. I see an article that speculates on Anne's marriage to her cousin. Granted there are a few items in the article that cannot be explained away, but that will be forgotten in time. Mrs Markham, the author of this article, did us a great service by never mentioning specific names or officially announcing an engagement, which I am sure that Lady Catherine planned on her doing. As Mrs Markham reported, Anne is engaged and will be marrying her cousin. As a woman and mother of the bride, it would not be wholly proper for Lady Catherine to announce the engagement. She was forced to rely on gossip combined with a few facts to make people accept your engagement to Anne as a fact without offering any. The only proof offered of your complicity is the procurement of a marriage licence, but you are indeed getting married. You were not supposed to announce your engagement to Elizabeth before the wedding but now I think this must be considered."

Darcy stared first at Richard, then his uncle, and then back at Richard. He felt the pressure on his heart and stomach immediately decrease. "So all I have to do is marry next week as I planned, and all will be well?"

For the first time since his son started talking, Lord Matlock participated in the conversation. "Almost. We need to find a way to clarify the marital status and intentions of all my son, nephew and niece of marital age. We need to go to The Times now!"

In some perverse way, Richard enjoyed watching his father try to deal with everything revealed in the last few hours. It felt comforting to share the burden of the last few weeks with someone else that he trusted. "Father, don't we need to deal with Lady Catherine first?"

Stopping mid-step and simultaneously sighing in defeat, his usually calm father answered, "I almost forgot about Catherine. Yes, we must deal with her first. But then, we will pay Mrs Markham a much-deserved visit."

They walked through the hallway to find the housekeeper who soon approached her master.

"Mrs Blaine, I need for Lady Catherine's things to be immediately packed and loaded back onto her carriage. She will be going to Glenmore tonight and will be staying there for a significant amount of time. Please inform the footmen there that the dowager house needs to be opened for Lady Catherine's immediate occupation. Also, send Miss De Bourgh's things to Fitzwilliam House. She will be staying with the Earl's family for some time."

Mrs Blaine nodded after hearing the instructions. "Everything will be done exactly as you said. Is there anything else which you require?"

"I am leaving now, please informed the ladies that I should be back in two hours. And we are not home to any visitors today."

***

Mrs Evangeline Markham picked up her small bag and as was her habit, she looked down on the street from her window on the second floor of The London Times before readying to leave for the day.

Were her eyes playing tricks on her? There were three gentlemen who just walked in and she recognised two of them; Lord Matlock and his nephew Mr Darcy just walked into the building. What business could they have at The Times? It seemed an unlikely coincidence that these two gentlemen would happen by on the same day that their family appeared in her column if their business was not with her.

She watched carefully as Lord Matlock, followed closely by his nephew, strutted towards her desk where she stood. The scowl on the Earl's face was unmistakable.

"My Lord, I thought you or your lovely wife might want to pay me a visit. I am honoured, you were able to see me so soon. You must be extremely busy with the upcoming marriage of your nephew and niece."

Lord Matlock forced a reply. "Mrs Markham, as always it is a pleasure. You remember my nephew, Mr Darcy, and it is my younger son, Colonel Richard Fitzwilliam."

"Of course. Colonel Fitzwilliam, will you be standing up with your cousin when he marries?"

"As a matter of fact, I will."

Mrs Markham's smug smile broke into a full grin. Mr Darcy was behaving exactly as she thought! Even if he did not plan to get married to Miss De Bourgh this morning, propriety dictated that he now had to. "That news is wonderful. And Mr Darcy, I wish you a joy. When will the happy occasion occur?"

"Next week, at Darcy House."

Her full grin just morphed into an ecstatic one. "You certainly didn't waste any time." She could not help but add, "I hope my little column did nothing to interfere with your plans. I understood that you were anxious to wed, and I wanted to share the happy news the moment I received it."

"Actually, it did," stated Darcy but allowed his uncle to continued.

"We are here for an entirely different matter, Mrs Markham. We know how carefully you guard your reputation. After all, what good is a society columnist who simply fabricates stories to fill her column? People read your articles because more often than society cares to admit, it relays what society goes to great lengths to keep hidden. Unfortunately for you, this is one of those rare times where you failed to live up to your reputation and I wanted to let you know that you ought to begin working on a retraction for tomorrow evening's paper."

That was not at all what Mrs Markham wanted to hear. It didn't even make sense. If Mr Darcy was to be married next week, what could there be to retract?

"Lord Matlock, as certainly your wife has told you, I am never wrong. I have never needed to write a retraction and certainly do not intend to do so now."

Without being invited to do so, Lord Matlock moved to sit down in the chair by her desk. "Unfortunately it only takes one time, assuming the blunder is as obvious as this one, for everyone to discount your ability to let the world know the private business of the ton. After all, if you could err so completely in your recent column, it stands that you could be wrong about so many other items that you have printed. And you had such a splendid career. It is unfortunate that it had to end like this. I do hope you find somewhere tolerable to live in the country. I fear your invitations to any events in town will be few and far between."

She stood a little straighter and responded without thinking. "Lord Matlock, I don't understand. Mr Darcy just admitted he planned to marry his cousin."

A wicked half-smile appeared on the Earl's face. "My nephew said nothing of the sort. He said that he planned to marry next week. But he never said anything about marrying his cousin."

"If not his cousin, may I inquire as to whom it is that Mr Darcy will marry?"

"Miss Elizabeth Bennet of Longbourn in Hertfordshire will become my wife, Mrs Markham," announced Mr Darcy standing behind his uncle. He pulled a letter out of his jacket pocket and handed it to the lady. "Here is the announcement."

"I don't understand, why is Miss De Bourgh in town shopping for a trousseau if she is not going to marry you?"

"Regarding that piece of information, you were correct. My niece is marrying her cousin," Lord Matlock allowed the information a moment to sink in. "However, it is my son Colonel Fitzwilliam that she is betrothed to."

"What of my source? As a person more closely related to Miss De Bourgh and more knowledgeable of the young lady's personal affairs than yourself, she seemed very certain that Mr Darcy was going to marry Miss De Bourgh. This little announcement of yours seems rather contradictory."

"I thought you might be slow to acknowledge your mistake even with the world of the three gentlemen in your presence and written announcement by Mr Darcy so we shall resort to using hard evidence. Mr Darcy's marriage licence was procured a few days ago with the names Mr Fitzwilliam Darcy and Miss Elizabeth Bennet. My son's licence was procured last week with the names Mr Richard Fitzwilliam and Miss Anne De Bourgh. You may check the names and the dates on the licences issued by the church if you continue to disbelieve me." Lord Matlock paused, stood from the chair, and leaned in closer to her. "Of course, I would not want to be the person questioning the honorability of our clergy and by proxy, the Church of England. I do not see how that would work out well for one's reputation."

Mrs Markham could feel her palms begin to sweat.

"Not that I don't appreciate this information, but why are you telling me this now? What do you want in return?"

"It is what we do not want, Madam. We do not want continued speculation for the next several years regarding the engagements which took place. We want you to print the truth tomorrow and not let these rumours and outright lies floating around for the ton to latch onto. In this case, silence will do us no good."

"You want a column that explains the engagement announcements of your son and nephew. You could simply publish an announcement yourself that would do almost the same. But the spin that I could put on it would put all rumours and gossip to rest instantly. What do I get in return for my service?"

With perfect clarity, Lord Matlock answered, "If you comply, I will not make it my mission to make sure your name is dragged through the mud. Otherwise, by the time I finish with you, your own family will not want to acknowledge you."

"Tsk, tsk, Lord Matlock. Do you think you are the first person of illustrious heritage to threaten me? You are simply the latest to join the long line and will find no more satisfaction implementing such tactics than they have. Somehow, even after such firestorm attacks, I always seem to rise like the Phoenix. I will ask you again, what do I get in return for helping you?

The grimace on Darcy's face was priceless. "What is it you want?"

"I want to attend Mr Darcy's wedding and Col Fitzwilliam's wedding. I think a first-hand account of the weddings will do just the trick to make my article truly believable and entertaining for my substantial audience. And I will provide a clarification of what some readers may have misunderstood in tomorrow's edition." Mrs Markham smiled in triumph as she watched the silent exchange between gentlemen. What other choice did they have?

"NO! Absolutely not!" Cried Darcy when his uncle looked at him sharply.

"Agreed, but I have one condition. I must approve of what is printed," said the Earl.

She nodded in agreement and chose her words carefully. No matter what she claimed, she preferred not to have Lord and Lady Matlock as enemies. "I will only print the truth."

"If you print the truth, you will find no edits from me. You have my word."

Mrs Markham felt her entire face light up. "Lord Matlock, you have yourself a deal."

***

Once the gentlemen were safely ensconced in the carriage and driving away from The Times, Darcy sat on the opposite bench not hiding his displeasure. "You invited the most notorious gossip in England to my very private wedding. How could you?" He felt his blood begin to boil again.

"I am sorry Darcy, but it has to be this way. If she was not invited, she would make your wife's acceptance into respectable society difficult for the next several years."

"I was just thinking that Miss Elizabeth and I need an extended wedding tour. Several years might suffice for my plans. By the time we return, no one will remember Mrs Markham's name."

"Darcy, you cannot do that. She promised to write a favourable piece and clear up any misunderstandings about your and Richard's engagement and that of Richard's."

"Misunderstandings that she created! And you are the Earl for God's sake!"

In no uncertain terms, the Earl explained, "What is done is done. We can only try to control the damage already inflicted. This is the only way, Darcy."

"So you expect me to willingly expose the most intimate occasion of my life to the biggest gossip in London."

Richard finally spoke. "Darcy, I understand. I truly do. She will be a guest at my wedding too. We are both going to sacrifice our privacy for the women we love. If we back out now, there is no limit to the retribution she will inflict. Do you want that for Elizabeth? I certainly don't want it for Anne. And don't forget about Miss Lydia. There are other things you would like to keep in secret."

There was nothing else for him to say. He knew he needed to agree to this plan. For Elizabeth.

Epilogue

Darcy lightly kissed the sensitive skin just below her ear, causing a sharp intake of her breath. Her heart fluttered with anticipation of what was about to come when they go upstairs to her bedchamber.

Elizabeth heard him whisper, "Elizabeth, what was it your mother whispered to you before she left?" Elizabeth's cheeks instantly heated and she could not help but stiffen in his arms when everything in her body went rigid. Instead of the quiet she hoped would follow his question, he continued, "My love, what did she say to you?"

"It was nothing," Elizabeth replied softly. It was all she could manage. She was surprised she managed those three words.

"Elizabeth, we have been married for less than four hours. Please do not push me away. We cannot begin our lives like this, not after everything we conquered to come to this moment. I know she said something to distress you, I saw your face when she whispered to you. What was it?"

"She apologised for not being able to speak to me in private." Elizabeth hoped he would allow her to leave the conversation at that.

But her husband was not to be dissuaded. "What else?"

"She planned on speaking to me yesterday, but with their delayed arriving to London she did not have a proper opportunity."

She did not look up when she heard Darcy clear his throat. When he spoke, she noticed the edge in his tone was gone. Instead, it was replaced by something far worse, fear. "Elizabeth, did she want to speak to you about our wedding night?" Elizabeth knew he could guess exactly what her mother spoke to her about. What else would a mother have to say on the day of her daughter's wedding?

Once he saw the instant flush in Elizabeth's cheeks, he knew he guessed correctly.

"My love, do you know what is going to happen?"

"Not exactly." Elizabeth paused and looked up at him, her eyes full of apprehension, "Do you?"

"I know parts of it."

Elizabeth buried her face in his chest. He could barely discern her words as she spoke, "Then I suppose I should ask you my final question of the five you promised me. How do you already know what tonight will be like?"

"Elizabeth, are you sure you want to discuss this tonight?" Hearing his wife's short deep breaths into his jacket, he knew the answer. She would never calm down until he told her. So talk about it he would. But he wanted to know one thing first.

"Elizabeth, before I tell you, would you first tell me what your mother said?"

He leaned his head down to hear her whisper, "She told me it would be painful, to close my eyes, not make a sound, think only of my pin money, and you would be done with me soon enough."

It was official; it was going to be a very long time before Mrs Bennet would be invited to Pemberley. That could not possibly be what Elizabeth thought he wanted from their marriage. After their time at the inn and when they spend time alone before the wedding, she had to know that he revelled in the thought of being with her and in the knowledge that his actions delighted her in return. Remembering the timidity of her voice as Elizabeth asked her fifth question, he knew she had doubts. No matter what he thought of Mrs Bennet, she was still Elizabeth's mother and Elizabeth must put some credence in her advice. He needed to ensure that she understood perfectly what he planned for their union. And that plan had nothing to do with a quiet, disinterested wife who anticipated his departure each night.

He took a few minutes to consider his exact choice of words; this conversation must be done perfectly or it might take years to recover from. While contemplating his words, Darcy continued stroking the curls that had fallen from Elizabeth's hairstyle with the help of his removal of several hairpins.

"Before I went to university, my father took me to town for a short trip. He told me that I still needed to learn several things before I became a man of the world. We went to a brothel, one of the higher end ones, but a brothel nonetheless. I had never been with a woman before that time. I spent the day and night with one of the women who worked there." Looking down at his new wife who hadn't shown her face since he started talking, he asked her if she wanted him to continue. He saw her head slowly nod in the affirmative. He almost wished she had not.

"She taught me what I needed to do to please a woman and how to have my own pleasure. In the morning, I returned home to my father. I admit that I was anxious to return to see the woman the next time I came to town and I am sure it showed on my face. But as soon as I returned home, my father put me in a carriage and brought me to one of the poorest sections of London. We exited by a filthy run-down building with beggars lining its sidewalks. He took me inside and what I saw scared me unlike anything else I knew. I saw men scratching their privates to the point where blood could be seen dripping from their trousers. I saw others who appeared raving mad. Others lost their hair and their sight and simply sat in a corner, waiting for death to take them from that hell."

He waited a few moments to let Elizabeth take in what he had already said. When he felt that he gave her sufficient time, he began again. "My father did not say anything else in the carriage ride home and left me to think about what happened over the last day. When we returned, we went directly to the library where he gave me three books. The first book was a foreign text that contained information on positions and other things to do with one's marital partner. The second book was a medical journal containing information on diseases that men caught from frequenting brothels. The third book had a much deeper meaning. It was the Darcy family bible which contained his marriage certificate to my mother."

Darcy did not even notice that his wife's face was no longer glued to his jacket. At some point in his confession, she must have lifted her head to his shoulder and began stroking his chest with her free hand. Only when she spoke did he notice the change. "Did he offer any explanation?"

"He intended me to use the first book to study. He believed it was a gentleman's job to please his wife and to ensure that she enjoyed their time together as much as the man. As he intended the second book to scare me away from ever visiting another brothel, I needed something to continue my education. Even without the second book, seeing first-hand how the diseases affects a man's body, I believe I would have stayed away without having a book to remind me why."

Elizabeth inquired, "But why would your father take you to a brothel knowing the harmful effects?"

"I asked the same question. He didn't know how else to teach me the basics of what I needed to know and thought it would be better to learn in an environment that he had some control over. He also said he paid that particular woman to remain chaste for one year prior to my time with her to ensure she was free of disease. He made a point of saying that she began her regular routine as soon as I left to keep me from returning to her."

"Why did he choose that time to give you the Bible?"

"The third book proved more complicated in its implications for my future. My father loved my mother and produced Georgiana and me from that love. He believed that those acts which can produce a child should be treasured and only performed between two people that love each other and commit themselves to their combined and eternal happiness. If I used women to satisfy my desires by performing those same acts, I would dishonour my mother and father's love that brought me into this world. I realize now the slight hypocrisy of it after he just took me to a brothel, but my father was afraid the lure of the forbidden and the unknown would overwhelm my good sense. He thought that some knowledge would be better than none in this circumstance."

"After explaining to me the significance of including my parents' marriage certificate, he showed me the listings of each of the Darcy marriages and births. He knew that a young man has certain urges, and it takes a strong force to overcome those desires. He knew I would be faced with situations where I could compromise a young lady that I did not love and with whom I had no fear of contracting a disease from. If I followed through with that act, I might make her with child, causing shame to all those people who came before me. If I did the honourable thing and married her, I would go against my parents wishes that I marry for love and never feel the same connection which they had. He finally reminded me that Georgiana relied on me for guidance. How could I introduce her with values that I could not follow myself?"

"In the library that day, I promised my father that I would wait for my wife before being with another woman. And then he told me something that made me anticipate tonight from that day on. He told me that when I joined with the woman I loved, I would feel a completion in my soul that no other experience could ever rival." He gently lifted Elizabeth's head from his shoulder and made her look at him. "When I said I know what to do, I know the mechanics. I have no idea what the moment we join will feel like. But if it is anything compared to the feeling when I touch your hand or even look into your eyes, I am sure that God could not have created a more perfect heaven."

Elizabeth gazed up at him, her eyes sparkling with love. She now knew that he waited for her, just as she waited for him. In truth, Darcy felt as nervous as his wife.

She asked him tenderly, "So tonight will be a first time for both of us?"

For the first time that day Darcy leaned down to softly press his wife's lips to his own. When he finally looked into her eyes shining back at his, with every ounce of emotion he felt over the last year, he told her, "Mrs Darcy, it is time we finally begin our life together."

*** THE END ***

Made in the USA
Lexington, KY
08 April 2019